VEIL OF EDEN

EXPIRED

ANDRA LARKIN

BACKWARD WORDS, LLC

This is a work of fiction. Any resemblance to actual persons, living or dead, is purely coincidental.

First edition

ISBN 979-8-9921591-0-3

For those who are searching—may you find yourself

CHAPTER ONE

Keyva strolled along a busy sidewalk between blocks of manicured parks and towering skyscrapers. By design, identical puffs of clouds spread evenly against the bold azure sky, forming a checkerboard ceiling to the capital city of Cerebis.

Around her, she observed the consistent movement of expressionless citizens. Their bodies walked past her while their minds explored the digital world. It was where she would spend most of her day once she arrived at her destination.

During her morning walks, Keyva immersed her senses in the physical realm for as long as she could. With each step, she grounded herself into the soft cushion of her soles and listened to her exhales, which released in an even, relaxed pace, matching her strides.

At the corner, she noticed a hedge shaped into a perfect cube. Its glossy green leaves clutched something white, as if offering it to anyone who noticed. Behind her, the crosswalk's timer counted down, but she ignored it, drawn in by the object. Once close enough, she gasped.

Finding a flower anywhere outside a plant museum was

rare. Of course, the wealthy classes had flowers. For them, it was standard, but Keyva wasn't wealthy. If she wanted to see bloomed petals in person, she'd have to buy a ticket to a climate-controlled display. This sighting was pure luck.

What is this? she asked through the small devices adhered to her temples.

A Gardenia. Very fragrant. Take a sniff. The message flashed in her mind.

Through the small disks, she recorded the entire moment, capturing every sensory detail. When a breeze swept between them, the branches greeted her with a wave. She moved closer, touching the tip of her nose to the flower and inhaled its nutty vanilla perfume. Between her fingertips, she pinched a creamy petal, rubbing its velvety texture. She decided such an encounter deserved to be shared and uploaded the full sensory memory to the open archive. Anyone who found the moment could experience it for themselves—smells and all—for free.

Appointment in seven minutes. Please continue to avoid late penalty.

Her spine stiffened. She'd lost track of time. She allowed herself one last glance at the bloom before hurrying to a skyscraper a few blocks away and ascending to her designated level.

———

On the vast workroom floor, Keyva passed hundreds of reclined citizens lined in rows—all had vacant faces. Some fools stared off into nothingness, forgetting to close their eyes. She rolled *hers* at their mistake, knowing an immediate eye socket burn awaited their return to consciousness—but she had done the same many times before. A brief check of notifications could morph into a marathon of distraction while experiencing others' time in the digital reality. Citizens lost themselves for hours, and the rows of numb, dumb faces she saw on the way to her work chair proved it.

As she glided to her assigned spot, a pulsing hum of air surrounded her. The constant whir lulled workers into a hypnotic state, and Keyva had already begun feeling its effects. She settled into the soft cushion of her reclined simchair—a seat designed for the level of relaxation needed for deep immersion simulations—and tapped at the thin disks stuck on each temple to confirm their correct positioning.

With her head tilted upward, she aligned herself with the ergonomic curve that conformed to the shape of her back. She made sure to close her eyes, soaked into the comfort of the room's balanced 22.22 degrees, and transported to another place. The transition from the physical world to the digital was as simple as closing her eyes in one reality and opening them in another. A blink could teleport.

In her mind's internal display, she pulled up her day's schedule. A chronological list of her client appointments and an image of their corresponding citizen IDs spanned across her field of vision. Before each session, she received a condensed summary containing the client's interests, wealth class, and happiness score on a scale from one to ten. The scores were eight, nine, or ten, never lower, and she liked to think their work together contributed to the higher scores. After five months as a professional Amica, Keyva thrived in her role of having private conversations with wealthy citizens. They trusted her in ways they couldn't trust anyone else. She was made for the job.

Keyva launched the office setting she used for each session. A useless mahogany desk rested before matching wooden walls that surrounded the room. There was no door. While waiting for clients, she often observed the space, questioning the purpose of a desk that was never used and wondering why, if the designer of the room had added furniture, they had omitted a door.

Two chairs sat in the middle of the office, upholstered with a material she hadn't encountered in the physical reality yet. If she leaned close enough, she noticed they had a distinct smell. Empty books hugged a shelf, while other unknown artifacts decorated the walls. After her first session with a client, the mysterious items had awoken her curiosity through traces of a very different past. For the entirety of her appointments, she was bound to the chair and unable to approach the shelves, so she did her best to remember the images after leaving the simulated office. Studying the objects became a hobby, but so far, she'd only identified one. A clock.

Keyva waited for her first visitor, Saesha. Conversations with her were a pleasure. Instead of prolonged listening, the two shot questions and responses to one another. The appointments sped by. If permitted, they might have been companions outside of the sim, even though the client's age stretched decades above Keyva's at close to forty-five years.

"Good morning, Saesha. How's your day been?" Keyva asked.

"Honestly? Not great."

Saesha looked rough. Her oily hair was a knotted mess. Deep purple pockets draped beneath her eyes, and her wrinkled clothes suggested she hadn't changed them in days. Her eyes darted from corner to corner, and she crossed her arms over her chest as if protecting from an incoming blow. Keyva pulled up her citizen report.

Saesha, Wealth block 212: interested in puzzle distras, Happiness Score: 3

Keyva didn't know how to respond. Seven was the lowest Happiness Score she'd heard of. She didn't feel equipped to handle the situation.

Amica sessions were meant for conversation and superficial bonding—to fulfill the human need for sociability. The other citizens she spoke with were interested in a quick fix, short-term bond to get them by for a week or two. They wanted Keyva to excuse them for some horrible thing they'd said or done. Saesha was her only consistent visitor, the one who took their time seriously. They'd met multiple times per week for an entire month.

Keyva's training taught her to agree with her visitors—regardless of her true opinions—to validate their perspectives and ideals. "The illusion of merging opinions leads to a sense of belonging," her occupational mentor had once said. She knew a solution so simple wouldn't work. Saesha differed from the rest of her clients. She needed a genuine conversation.

"Tell me what's going on. I'm here to listen."

Saesha released a nervous laugh and said through a defeated smile, "It involves my work. But I guess that doesn't matter anymore. Not for me, at least." Keyva waited for her to continue. "And I have no idea what will happen next. No one does." She looked at the ceiling, fighting tears.

Cerebis rewarded those in the working class, like Keyva, with decent pay and the luxury of occasional entertainment in the physical reality, but forbade them from discussing specifics of their occupations.

"It can't be that bad. My podmates and I talk about our work all the time and nothing has happened to any of us. That's just a rumor. Of course, I'd never tell them anything about my sessions, but we can say general things. And why doesn't it matter for you? I'm not understanding." Keyva kept her voice light, inviting whatever truths Saesha felt comfortable revealing.

"Those of us who create and maintain the technology of Cerebis can be severely punished for just talking about our work, even with the wrong colleague. With the changes that are coming...I'm not sure if that'll include anyone who disobeys rules of any kind." Saesha's eyes drifted to the side, "Or, if they'll be able to make any choices at all."

Saesha worked during the night while everyone else slept. At least, that's what she had told Keyva, who concluded Saesha's lack of rest had caused a slip into paranoia. In previous appointments, she'd revealed she worked at the place that conceived all technology. Those who designed tech earned reputations as social hermits. Keyva assumed Saesha had lied about where she worked. She was too cordial.

"What are you saying? Not able to make choices? I think you need some sleep," Keyva said in her trained, calming voice.

Saesha hesitated. "You'll forget this conversation soon enough, but I have to tell someone, so I don't expire with all this guilt." She drew in a swift breath and released it with the same intensity. Keyva stared back. The room got heavier.

"You know how you and I are here in this simulated space? Have you ever wondered *how* any of it is possible?" Her eyes traced the simulation's perimeter. The clock ticked louder than ever before.

"While I don't have the intelligence to understand the technology, it's clear that these *dimes* we wear allow us to connect." Keyva pointed to one of her temples.

"I wish that were the case," Saesha said. "When I started—I never thought it could get to this point." Her voice dropped so low that Keyva barely made out the words.

"Inside each of us, within our brains, there's a hybrid biotech device called a Cede. It was implanted when you were grown as an embryo and developed at the same rate as your brain. It connected to billions of neurons and intertwined itself into a complex web. Through it, you've been studied since your first neuroelectric pulse. Your emotions, actions, even your thoughts have been recorded and processed by The Subliminal Record System we named Source." Saesha enunciated each word to clarity. "Those things on your head, the dimes, do nothing besides divert your attention—give you a *sense* of power. Cerebis knows not to *let* you interact unless you put them on, so you never question their validity."

"Cerebis? What we're citizens of?"

Saesha laughed, but not in the way someone responds to a joke.

"Yeah, the planet—country. It's a system, consciousness—a god, if you've heard of that sort of thing. Cerebis sees all, knows all, and what those in power use to *control* it all."

Keyva gazed toward the light reflecting off the lacquered wooden floor, unsettled by her client's claims. She knew Saesha was brilliant, but considered, where on the spectrum of intellect did lunacy emerge?

"Okay, then what are these sitting on my head?" Keyva gestured to the chrome pieces on the sides of her face.

"A decoy. Dimes allow you to believe you're in control of *when* you connect, but you already have everything in your brain to experience simulated moments, just like this." She gestured to the sim's setting. "You're restricted so you don't get too close to threaten or cause disruptions to the system. It's a taste of freedom that's only an illusion. Plus, those little dimes are just one more thing for them to sell you."

"I'm sorry—I'm not following," Keyva replied.

"Let me simplify. If you take them off and try to go through a door, you'll walk right into it, instead of the door opening for you. It's not because you don't have the dimes on, it's because the system *knows* you don't have them on." Saesha seemed delusional.

"Why are you telling me all of this?" Keyva asked.

"I work at the center that monitors all programs' activity,

including the one that stores information about everything that has happened since Cedes were created. Not much has changed in the time that's passed, but it's about to."

"And how are you so sure?"

"To prepare for the largest update we've worked on, my colleagues and I edited core programs, including the surveillance one, Source. I noticed, for the first time, something hinted toward a singular genetic sequence." Saesha lifted her head, catching Keyva's clear blue eyes. "And I traced it to you— I've visited for weeks, trying to figure out what made you special. Why you? That, and this is the only place I'm safe from being monitored. For now."

Keyva believed she was typical. Like all other citizens, she was raised with podmates, a small group of peers, all made on the same day. Then, she joined her family unit when she was three years old, assigned to two parents and one sibling, the same as everyone else. She went through schooling and grew into her professional role, like the others in her wealth class. She was perfectly average.

"What else do you know?" Keyva asked, suspecting that Saesha's fear didn't match this single admission.

"The program responsible for resolving anomalies has gained more permissions to eliminate threats to civilization— including humans."

"Eliminating?"

"Expiration."

The word sliced the air between them.

Keyva believed expiration was a myth, a story told to dissuade unfavorable behavior, such as violence or criticism of Cerebis. When she was young, Keyva had learned that extreme acts could receive expiration as a penalty, but she didn't understand the meaning. "No longer here" was what she remembered.

"Yaria, one of your podmates is a Keeper, correct?" Saesha asked.

"You traced Yaria too?"

Warm anger flared beneath Keyva's skin. Yaria was her dearest companion. Their closeness began while they grew next to one another as infants. As an adult, Yaria worked at the same facility that made new citizens and raised the young. By snooping into Keyva's personal information, Saesha had crossed the line, breaching their agreement to Amica and client privacy.

"Ask Yaria about planting the Cedes in embryos. She's been told they inject a gene-editing primer, but that's not it. There's mor—" Saesha's eyes widened, and she didn't finish her rushed sentence. "I need to leave now."

"Please take care of yourself and get some rest," Keyva pleaded. "I'll see you soon."

"No, you won't." Saesha's teary eyes were sorrowful, but her mouth relaxed into an accepting smile. Her body sucked out of the sim office, and Keyva was alone.

CHAPTER TWO

Keyva paid to retrieve a memory from her vault of recorded experiences. It was the day of her graduation, five months prior. Dozens of smiling graduates, carrying various colors of folded uniforms, said goodbye to their parents and prepared for their first day of work. Each week, students poured into the professional field, while aged citizens concluded their careers. Her professional mentor, Redford, prepared for his retirement the same day. After decades of service to Cerebis, he'd earned his rest.

"Tomorrow's the day," he said.

"What if I forget what to do?" a younger, nervous version of Keyva asked.

Redford laughed. "I promise that won't happen. You've trained for this as long as you could learn."

Back when Keyva was thirteen years old, she had felt an immediate pull toward the Amica profession. Her other two career suggestions, a Sim Architect and Plant Historian, held no interest to her. In hindsight, she assumed they were jokes meant to test her sureness. She loathed the obsession with sims and their gaming counterpart, distras, that so many citizens succumbed to. And the unlimited information in the library knew more about plants than she could store in millions of life-cycles. A pointless career, she thought. After completing her specialized Amica education, Keyva had graduated at twenty-two years old.

"What if someone speaks outside of expectation?" she asked.

"They won't."

"Did it ever happen to you?"

Redford viewed the cloudless sky, seeking his answer.

"Well—just once, now that you've reminded me."

"And?"

Keyva sensed his urge to divulge the confidential specifics of the client.

"We do the best we can to tell them what they need to hear," he answered as if the memory opened a blister.

Keyva pulled herself back to the physical reality and shuddered. Although the workspace maintained an ideal temperature, her clothing was damp with sweat from Saesha's session. The rare instance Redford had come across once in his career had already occurred within the first months of hers.

Buy relaxation, she thought, and her pounding heart gradually slowed. In seconds, her lungs radiated warmth, spreading a blissful tingle throughout her body, and the fear disappeared. She decided she'd visit Redford's retirement projection when she had the chance. It wouldn't be the same as speaking with him, but the projection had some of his stored memories. She hoped his hiccup with a client was one of them.

No clients had booked for the next time slot, so Keyva took her lunch break. She opened the menu in her mind, displaying the options best suited for her palate. Images of the meals shuffled by, one after another. With each flash of an option, the menu offered a split second of each item's flavor and scent. Overwhelmed by the thousands of choices, she opted for a random selection. The dimes always ordered the perfect meal for her anyway. In her mind, -20K *points* scrolled, and twenty thousand points deducted from her account.

One minute later, a Helperbot wheeled its way beside her chair and presented her with a sushi roll. Rice wrapped around a chunk of pork cloned from one original, modified pig.

"This one's new," she said, raising the meal to her lips. The first bite's warm, rich fat melted in her mouth and dilated her pupils.

Keyva switched her dimes' social setting to *Active*. A barrage of images containing suggestions on vitfeeds to watch, the hour's featured products, and the top trending songs filled her mind. Updates sifted in her head, and she continued eating her meal. In the bottom right corner of her neural vision, a red number counted higher than she'd ever seen.

999+ notifications!

The multi-sensory moment she'd shared before work had exploded in popularity. Over 2,230,111 general "feeders," had seen it. Keyva wasn't the type to have anywhere close to 2.2M viewers see her vitfeeds, but it brought her a sliver of pride, as if she had achieved something. She watched the number of red alerts climb, and when she refreshed, the count reset, only to increase again. She wasted the rest of her break watching the notifications accumulate.

She jumped back into her simulated office, appointments for the rest of the day proceeded with predictability—wealthy citizens confiding secrets.

"And *she* came on to *him*," one client said. "It went on for years before her husband found out. It's *all* anyone's been talking about—shocking! I heard she went into hiding out of embarrassment."

"Yes, you mentioned that—three times." Keyva assumed the client had run out of peers to share the news with.

In another session, a new client popped into the chair. His head hung low.

"I-I don't know how to say this. I'm so humiliated."

"You're safe to share anything you're comfortable telling me," Keyva said.

He let out a dramatic sigh.

"Well—I was at this party. You know Larinks? He's the top shoulder and neck model right now. *Suuuper* famous and gorgeous. He was there! Anyway, I went into the closet because I had to compare my impeccable style to the host's." His eyes widened, and so did his smile. "You won't *believe* what I found. Last week's exclusive buyers' Crux rhinestone loafers. I almost passed out! Only 200 pairs exist. I was *milliseconds* too late to buy them. I told some other Amica how hard it was on me to not win."

"And then what happened?"

His smile melted into a forced frown with a pouty lip.

"I had to take them—right? They were meant for *me*. They practically called to me from the closet."

Moments like these were difficult for Keyva. She wanted him to learn that no, he had no right to take them. He missed the buying window and had to accept it. That he needed to return them to their rightful owner and if he's lucky, they'll forgive him. However, her job wasn't to teach him morality. It was to make him feel better.

"Sometimes we do things out of passion that feel beyond our control. What will you do next?"

"I can't give them back. Imagine the embarrassment if everyone knew I *stole* something. I'd never get invited to anything again. Gross! I guess I'll only wear them when I visit somewhere else."

Again, Keyva felt uneasy about encouraging him.

"Yes, it's best to keep that a secret. Nothing good can come from telling it now."

"*Whew!* Talking to you Amicas always helps. Anyway— thoughts on this top? I love it. I support this little Vor creator. He spins all the threads and makes the clothes digitally. Nothing that touches this body—in aera or roca—is mass made. Only signature pieces on this skin." He spread his arms out so Keyva could examine all the details.

"It's nic—"

He disappeared before she could finish her answer.

The Opuls, the wealth class her clients occupied, got away with much more than those in the lower classes. If they broke rules, they'd just pay the fines. If lower classes committed the same actions, they'd have their accounts cleaned out, and if they didn't have enough points, they disappeared. Punishment for minor offenses dangled over their heads. Those unable to afford penalties seldom broke rules.

In school, Keyva had learned the classes of Cerebis divided everyone into a place that suited them. The Elites sat at the top of the pyramid, exposing every aspect of their lifecycles, in exchange for fame, admiration, and the most points of any class. Joining the Elite was earned, not given. Anyone *could* make it, so most tried. Elitehood required having advanced skill in a specialized area, but talent wasn't enough. One must act as a model citizen, promote smiling, kindness, and most important of all, have paralyzing beauty. Elites served an honorable purpose, bringing happiness to all others through constant entertainment. Citizens worshiped them.

Below the Elites were the Opuls. They owned lots of things, both digital and physical, had lavish places to sleep and host guests, and attended frequent in-person events, the truest signal of wealth.

Mids, like Keyva and her podmates, rested in the middle. They worked and enjoyed working. They were satisfied abandoning riches but earned enough to afford the occasional treat in the physical side of reality, called "roca."

At the bottom were the Vors, who made up the population's majority. They spent almost all of their time in the digital world, called "aera." Cerebis paid points to Vors for viewing sponsored entertainment, but if they wanted more, they worked, like the thread spinner Keyva's client had mentioned. Vors stayed in aera. Some of them were there so long, they had lost the ability to speak.

After completing her appointments, Keyva willed herself back onto the work floor. She sat up from the black chair and leaned forward. A lock of dark hair swooped in front of her face. Her fingertips grazed the silver disks bonded to her temples until she peeled off the devices. They had turned into parasites. She looked around the open floor to acclimate after the sim's disorientation. The neighboring citizens at her sides had different careers, telling by their attire. One wore red, and the other wore cream. Keyva's Amica uniform was ash grey. The clothing, designed for hours of pleasant resting, had seams in sections where bodies moved and bent the most. For the citizens who worked in roca, it was the default.

Keyva stood, sighed, and hesitated before reapplying her dimes.

Start navigation to Sibby, she directed. Going anywhere in Cerebis was impossible without the help of the dimes. She didn't know where anything was—not even her apartment.

Keyva crammed into the elevator with several others. Arrival to the first level took fewer than fifteen seconds, and an alert chimed in her mind when it was her turn to move. The small group spilled out onto the lobby floor.

Once outside, the sight of chaotic movement smacked her.

Most citizens navigated all transport while in complete involvement of digital content. Their bodies moved in roca while their minds stayed in aera. She passed citizens bearing facial expressions that corresponded to what they consumed. Some cried, maybe engaging in an inspirational vitfeed. Others laughed at humor beyond levels she could fathom. Passing the faces, discomfort pooled in Keyva's gut, flashing to her conversation with Saesha. She pushed it away.

The enormous building Keyva exited hosted businesses of all kinds. Those who paid for appearance mods entered with one face and exited with another. Next to Keyva, she saw that someone had picked up a designer pet and took it out of its decorated carrying case. She overheard the Opul bragging to another about her new "toy giraffe." The small creature stood up to its human's knees, had a long neck, and tall, thin legs. White hair draped down its back over red stripes.

Around her, bright surfaces decorated with the beautiful faces of Elites competed for Keyva's attention. Most projections had a personalized appeal to them, containing her name and reflecting her favorite things, including historic flashback sims.

Keyva passed projected characters. Hallusors. She despised them. They popped from place to place, chasing walkers. They looked identical to citizens, speaking like them, using the same mannerisms, and were indistinguishable from a physical human. The projections approached, fabricated interest in a topic, and ended interactions by recommending products available for purchase.

"Keyva, you've *got* to try the new Wild Wild West experience! It's flawlessly lawless. You'd *obsessss* over it." A flamboyant cowboy dripping in sequins snaked beside her. He thumbed his belt loops and stared at her, waiting for a response.

"T-thanks," she forced.

To others, their contact came across as genuine. Keyva

caught on long ago that they had an underlying motive to build positive sentiment toward an item. As the cowboy opened his mouth to speak again, she commanded a top trending song to play. Hallusors couldn't interrupt while she fed on content. She sang along and smiled at others who did the same as they passed. She received a bump of 12K points in her account for promoting favorable behavior. It wasn't much, but every bit helped.

The moment the song ended, another hallusor swooped in —a tall and ghostly-pale figure with ember hair and algae eyes. She matched Keyva's pace and screeched, "Keyva, you look gorgeous today. Hey, don't forget, tonight, eat dinner with the gorgeous trillionaire Elite, Asher! I know you'll enjoy it. Just a reasonable four-thirty M points." Keyva leaned back.

"Wow, I've always wanted to eat with him. 430 million is *nothing*. I'll definitely pop in!" she lied, passing a line of trees whose leaves branched into perfect spheres.

She had learned through her professional training that agreeableness was the best way to deflect sales pitches. Match the projection's enthusiasm and keep walking. Continued movement was the key to escape. If she stopped, the projection would heckle her until she emptied her account on the spot.

For a moment, she watched everyone moving around her. They resembled a virus, fluttering and multiplying during peak traffic. Personal port vehicles droned past, transporting the exceedingly wealthy, who no longer needed to walk. Flashy lights, encompassing projections, and a swarm of hustling citizens immersed Keyva in the sensory static she was used to.

Dinner with podmates at the Sibby restaurant in 20 minutes popped into Keyva's neurospect. She dismissed it, already on the way. She returned a request, *Send my evening clothing,* and purchased the top suggested product to match.

CHAPTER THREE

Gold shimmers from the setting sun illuminated the building to where Keyva navigated. The structure stood as Cerebis's tallest without considering that only half of its height towered above the ground. The other half extended into the subcity, pointing toward the center of the planet. Its underground tunnels were like roots, connecting it with neighboring buildings and transportation hubs. Citizens could stay underground long enough to completely avoid the surface. Architecture enthusiasts argued whether the building could still qualify as a single structure, or if anything built in Cerebis's capital belonged to it.

During this visit to the building at the center of City H's entertainment, Keyva ascended to the 303rd floor with sixteen other passengers. The doors peeled open, and she watched citizens weave in and out of hallways to different endpoints. The level through which Keyva walked hosted those who enjoyed in-person entertainment. She passed novelty restaurants, such as a current hot spot where guests only ate red food served on red plates, sat on red furniture, and, of course, wore red clothing.

Around a corner, she encountered a hallway of human zoo exhibits where citizens inhabited full displays. Those inside the glass enclosures constantly performed for feeders who had traveled to brag about visiting a popular entertainer. Everything, including viewing vitfeeds, had more value in the roca side of reality.

Keyva stopped to watch one citizen on display through giant glass panes. Behind him, blue-flamed fires had covered the floor, sneaking toward his feet. The flames grew, from the bottom of his ankles, to higher than he stood, turning the color of the sun. They hadn't touched him, yet, but his skin burned pink and dripped with sweat. He panted in desperate grasps for breath until he fell over onto his side. Part of the nearest flame singed his hair, burning off a chunk from the top of his head. He kicked his legs against the glass, shouting something Keyva couldn't hear. On the wall, he displayed the number of feeders watching from all around the world. It increased to 350M. Keyva looked around at the blank faces of the audience, who shared the scene with their followers. She locked eyes with the terrified entertainer on the ground and realized it wasn't an act.

"Someone let him out!" Keyva slammed her fists on the glass.

Not a single citizen looked at her.

Once the viewer count on the wall stagnated, the flames disappeared, and water sprayed every inch of the room. The entertainer coughed until his face turned purple and layers of skin had peeled off, but he rotated his head toward the audience with a grin.

"He's wild! He'll do *anything* to get as many feeders as possible," she heard one viewer say.

Keyva felt deep embarrassment for her reaction and hoped hitting the glass didn't dock her points. She should have known he wasn't in any danger. Cerebis would never allow it.

She recovered from her humiliation and reached her first stop, a place to pick up her new outfit, change into it, and ship her uniform back to her apartment. She entered a private room, and the door closed itself behind her. Inside, a delivery niche slid open, presenting the outfit she had ordered during her journey. The items had followed her from the moment she requested them until she arrived at the door. She reached into the niche and pulled out a tight black dress, boots, and the recommended evening trend, a tube mask that revealed her eyes and nothing else. After one glance at herself, she decided the item's fit didn't match her style, and pulled it down as a tight scarf. After changing, she placed her worn outfit into the niche to send back to her apartment and exited.

The time switched to 18:00 the instant she arrived at the restaurant suggested by her podmate, Yaria. A whispery female's voice sounded in her head, "Welcome to Sibby. Please follow me to your table." When the welcome announcement ended, a floating magenta diamond popped into Keyva's vision and led the way to the far side of the restaurant.

"You're right on time!" Yaria yelled over the music that synced in all the restaurant guests' heads.

A warm disposition matched Yaria's golden skin tone. Everything about her glowed. Even in the dim light of the restaurant, her dark hair shone. Strangers assumed she had paid to mod her gigantic eyes that somehow managed to smile even when her mouth didn't.

"Emori and Kenzo will be here in one minute, and Abella —" she searched for supportive words. "Well, she hasn't sent her update, so it could be at any time. You know how she is! How's your family?" Yaria danced off beat while she spoke.

"Eh, they're doing fine, I guess," Keyva replied. She avoided speaking about them.

Like all other juveniles in Cerebis, Keyva had been assigned to her parents when she turned three. She had vague memories of the beginning, when she cried and pleaded to return to her podmates and the Keeper who had raised her. Adoption had been a symbol of status her Mid class parents aimed to achieve, without considering the level of responsibility required to raise juveniles.

Her brother was five years old when they had met and was thrilled to receive attention from Keyva that their parents had deprived him of. The paired siblings were closer with each other than with their parents, but had never formed a deep relationship. She cared about him, but after he moved out, she saw him less than once per year. Since her graduation, Keyva's mentors spoke to her on holidays, but they had moved on, having two new juveniles to raise, replacing her and her older brother.

"So, all five of the pod this time?" Keyva was surprised. Since their careers had begun, their pod's meetings had dwindled and usually consisted of only Yaria and Keyva.

Every citizen started in a group of five podmates, formed during embryogenesis. After nine months, they took their first breaths together and woke up by each other's sides. They stayed together until family placement. Keyva and her group entered the same wealth class and attended the same schools. With Keyva's absent family, she was grateful her pod had stayed intact after graduation.

Yaria's eyes ticked beyond the table to Kenzo's and Emori's arrival.

"Welcome! I'm so glad you could make it," Yaria said, more excited than usual.

Keyva nodded at the two males from their pod and recognized that Kenzo's expression imitated Yaria's.

"*Looong* day," Kenzo said. He slid onto the bench beside Keyva.

Kenzo was much taller than an average male. His thick, chestnut hair required frequent cuts, and his strong build showed that his arms were meant for carrying, throwing, and sorting items of mixed masses. For work, he searched for items in places once called landfills. Each morning, he traversed beyond City H's boundary through an underground tunnel. Sometimes, he returned, and Keyva sensed wonder from within him, having found treasure. Other days, a blank stare told her he had encountered something that he might pay to remove the memory of later.

"I think we should order now," Emori said, pinching the skin on his palms. A habit of his Keyva noticed in every roca meeting.

"Em, you've been sitting for *one* second," Yaria said.

"Yeah, relax. The Wolf's out on the prowl for once!" Kenzo squeezed his shoulders, and Emori cringed, either from the touch or hearing his nickname, earned by winning an intellect competition years before.

"But I have to leave for work soon."

Emori worked at the Datum, the same place Keyva's client Saesha claimed to, and also worked overnight. Dark skin contrasted his jade green eyes, and his slicing jaw was almost as sharp as his mind. At work, he created technology that powered everything citizens used, but he could do anything. He was the brightest citizen Keyva had ever known.

"Okay, fine. Abella can order when she gets here. She'll saunter in at some point," Keyva said.

Keyva opened the menu in her neurospect. Options scrolled by, and she picked the featured special, a medium rare filet mignon, charred balsamic Brussels sprouts, and truffle mashed potatoes. The pod placed their individual orders and waited six seconds for their meals to arrive at the center of the table.

"Poached eggs with cinnamon, hot chicken, and chopped peppers?" Kenzo asked, eyes wide at Emori's meal.

"It's my breakfast, and so what? It all tastes the same to me." He ate bizarre food combinations for as long as they remembered.

Keyva cut into the filet she'd ordered and admired the perfect distribution of redness while sipping a glass of Pinot noir from the Hexa Region of City M, Cerebis's farming center.

"Someone's fancy today," Yaria said, elbowing Keyva's arm.

"I feel like I should indulge. It's nice having us all togeth—"

"Ugh, sorry I'm late. I got sucked into a swap war." Abella joined the others at the table.

"I'm glad you're here," Yaria welcomed her.

"Uh, swap war?" Kenzo asked.

"You know, it's when two vitfeeds host a faux competition to lure feeders into—wait, I'll be right back," she said, relaxing into a blank stare. Her body turned motionless at the edge of the table, frozen in time.

Abella irked Keyva, similar to caring for a pet she never wanted. Abella's actions aligned with her sole intent of becoming an Elite, but she fit the part. Keyva didn't know anyone else as beautiful. Cheekbones that could cut a diamond lined the immaculate symmetry of her face. Lavender-tinted eyes, embedded with crystal implants, dazzled when they caught the slightest light. Her skin was as light as a cloud, matching her hair. Abella spent her points on the latest genetic and surgical mods, but they worked. Her career path in entertainment labeled her as a Vitfeed Charmer, a euphemism for a model. She fulfilled the title, but without specific talent beyond knowing how to work a crowd, Elitehood was a lost cause. However, her minimal fame led citizens near their block to stop her and share sightings with their feeders.

"So, what's everyone doing for Honoring Day tomorrow?" Yaria asked.

"It's here already?" Keyva rolled her eyes.

Every day had some sort of holiday, but Honoring was the most celebrated—after Gift Day. Though Keyva hadn't understood exactly what it was they honored.

"I'm working," Emori said.

"No surprise there. I'm watching the Fisik Challenge," Kenzo said. Yaria and Keyva laughed. Keyva pictured the thousands of bodies stacking themselves into structured shapes and tumbling into inevitable oblivion. Many Vors, the lowest wealth class, also fed on the challenge.

"I'm planning on visiting Redford for the first time since his retirement," Keyva said.

No one asked Yaria. As a Keeper, working in the Primina—where citizens originated—she received no days off, even on the most popular holidays.

"I suggest you attend more social groups, Keyva. Visiting Redford sounds nice, but he's gone. You don't interact with citizens enough outside of work." Emori took a bite. "It's better to do it on your own than be flagged as an isolate."

"I interact plenty—stay updated on vitfeeds, meet feeders who have the same interests as me. I even shared one of my own moments this morning! And it's easy for you to say that. You have the most lenient social minimum because of work," Keyva said.

"They flagged me as an isolate once, and it was *horrrrible*," said Kenzo. "You're summoned to a forced social interaction for a random interest. Miserable! Imagine me in a flower growing course and then having to arrange them in vases. I mean, it's pretty and everything, but I couldn't even pretend to find it interesting for one session."

"Come on, when I see you, I think of the delicate art of ancient floral decorating," Keyva nudged his unmoving boulder of a body.

Kenzo had protected Keyva when they grew up. Keyva imagined their relationship was how it should be for siblings. In class with other pods, younglings had taken advantage of her passive demeanor. On one occasion, a young male had teased Keyva, and Kenzo hit him with a fist in a fit of rage. Any aggressive touching was a punishable offense, but he avoided correction because of his youth. As an adult, violence led to a justified expiration. At least, that was the rumor.

"Well, I am overdue to depart, but the social monitors will appreciate my additional interaction today." Emori arose, and forced expressionless eye contact with each pod member, excluding Abella, before his departure.

"Wow!" Abella jolted back to the table.

Keyva, Yaria, and Kenzo flinched at the abrupt movement.

"More than 1M new feeders today!" Tears dripped down her pale cheeks from her eyes' refresh mod. She had forgotten to close them.

"Impressive," Yaria said, and meant it.

"Well, this has been awesome, amazing fun. I've gotta go, but we should meet up again soon!" Abella said. The others exchanged glances as she glided past tables, hoping that anyone would notice her.

"*Yikes,* she is in it deep," Kenzo flinched.

"She has a goal, I guess," Keyva said, finishing her wine.

"She got stuck in that ceftrance with her eyes open. Ouch," Yaria said.

Kenzo, Yaria, and Keyva ordered another round of drinks,

which arrived at the center of the table. They tipped their glasses together, cheering "Bestia!" in unison. After close to an hour of dancing and laughing, Kenzo announced his withdrawal for the evening.

"I'll see you again *very* soon," he pinned his attention on Yaria.

Her eyes tracked him as he walked away. Keyva sensed Yaria had an attraction to Kenzo, which would lead to unavoidable heartbreak. A partner matching program paired the best matches for citizens. Compatible personalities, ideologies, attractiveness, and professions were among factors considered by the program to pair citizens with the ideal partner. The outcome led to complete success. Matches spent the rest of their lifecycles together.

"Be careful. I don't want you to be disappointed," Keyva said.

"I know, but it's fun to imagine," Yaria replied in a dreamy voice.

As they exited the restaurant, Keyva viewed a notification, *-645K points*. She gulped. The amount surpassed her budget for a meal.

"Yaria, I have to ask you someth—"

A message scrolled in her neurospect.

Report to the gathering center of Block 888

"Odd. Did you get a summon, too?" Keyva asked.

"Yeah, I'm reporting back to 413. Are you?"

"No, I'm going to 888. That block's in the upper Vor territory, and we just had a social gathering. What could it be?"

"Tomorrow's the Honoring. Might be a celebration?"

"You're probably right. I'd better head that way. It's a bit of a walk," she said.

Summons were rare and their purposes unspecified until the participants' obligatory arrival. She felt worried, but reminded herself she'd acted within expectation and had nothing to fear.

"Me too," Yaria said, delaying her departure. "Did you want to ask me something?"

"Yeah, in the Primina, what hap—" she stopped. The foreign words stirred inside her mouth, knowing she shouldn't discuss specifics about work. "N-nevermind. I'll ask you later." Keyva turned to walk away. "I have to start my long journey into the unknown!" She ended her comment on a sarcastic note. They smiled, and Yaria reached for her hand, squeezing it before leaving.

If the unexpected summons continued during the holiday, she might be called at any point on Honoring Day, disrupting her plans of contacting Redford's retirement mirror. Cerebis could have anything planned for its most popular holiday. The walk to block 888 served as the guaranteed solo time she had. *Fifteen minutes is plenty of time,* she thought.

Keyva set auto navigation to the gathering center of Block 888 and obeyed the commands that ensued. Each instruction presented itself as an urge, which led her to the next step in her walk. As ordered, she descended to the subcity level.

Enter the eastward tunnel

Keyva called for a connection to contact retired citizens. After minutes of rolling advertisements, she finally reached the introduction.

Welcome to your first retirement mirror! There are a few things to note. This is not the original citizen you once knew, but a reflection. He or she is now thriving in retirement! The following citizen presented to you was created based on past information that has been compiled into a simulated version of your human. With that said, there is no use asking about retirement. This version will not know. Instead, reflect on what you remember together and learn how to be an upstanding citizen to serve Cerebis! Now, imagine who you wish to see.

Keyva's stomach dropped as a replica of Redford appeared. The simulation presented all of his defining features; the shallow wrinkles at the corners of his dark eyes, the faint freckle on his cheek, and his radiant smile welcomed her to the fabricated meeting.

"That didn't take long," he said.

"Y-yeah, I, uh—" she took a second to compose herself.

"I assume this is shocking to see someone you thought you'd never speak to again," he said, sympathizing with her reaction. Once an Amica, always an Amica.

"So, how are you doing? How's the pod? Are you excited about Honoring Day?"

"Everything's good. I'm good. The pod is—great."

While the opportunity to contact retirement mirrors remained, the purpose of retirement was to release citizens of their duty to Cerebis and honor their achievements. It was shameful and selfish to yearn for their company.

"Glad to hear it. Did you need something?"

She didn't expect the mirror to try hanging up on her.

"I have a question for you. During my training, you told me you had one client who spoke out of expectation. W-well, it's been five months, and I had one today. I didn't know what to do."

"That's not a question," Redford's mirror responded, maintaining the human's humor.

"What happened?"

"Hm, interesting. Now that I'm thinking of it, the memory is fuzzy. I can't grasp it."

"What do you mean?"

"I remember it happening, but not the details about it. Can't picture the client or the situation..."

Approaching Block 888

The autonav alerted Keyva with a location update, and she opened her roca vision to reveal the destination. Underground, in an enormous open square, thousands of citizens crammed before a worn white stone structure. Not fond of enclosed spaces, she walked to an outer edge to avoid compacting with the others.

One minute until event

Keyva switched back into the conversation with Redford's mirror with the limited time she had.

"I have to leave soon, but before I go, my client, Saesha, claims to work at the Datum. She was delusional. I've never seen someone so...scared." In any other case, Keyva wouldn't speak about the specifics of her client, but she figured this conversation was a loophole.

"Delusional, how?"

"She claimed that the dimes we wear are an illusion. That we have things in our brains that know everything we're thinking."

"That makes no sense. How would that be possible? Why would we wear them if we didn't have to?"

"That's what I thought too. Then she said a change was coming."

"A change?"

"I think she said—an update?"

"Updates happen to Cerebian technology all the time. That's no reason for concern."

She felt defeated. The conversation with Redford's mirror had answered no questions.

"One more thing—have you heard of a Cede?"

The word made his face twist in agony or disgust, and Keyva couldn't decide which. He froze, and the mirror simulation disappeared into nothingness.

"Redford!" Keyva hollered, rejoining the sea of humans packed in the block's square.

The next moment, a small, silver point flickered in the corner of her vision. She assumed the event had begun. As the shimmery dot grew in size, collective gasps and "woos" sounded from citizens in the gathering square of Block 888. Over thirty seconds passed, and the obstruction enlarged to swallow her entire field of vision. Colorful, fractal patterns danced blindness into her eyes. She wondered if a complication with the retirement mirror had caused her dimes to malfunction. Frantically, she repeated the *Quit* command, but the system ignored her. She ripped the dimes from her temples but found no relief. She was trapped.

The torment intensified as numbness started in her fingertips, spreading up her arms and into her throat. She tried to swallow but couldn't. Blinded by multicolored horror, she shook in fear. Around her, the shouts of excitement transitioned into wails of terror by those who stood nearby.

She tried to flee from the gathering, but her leg buckled. Gravity pressed down on her in a way she had never endured. Her face became heavy. Then everything became heavy. She wobbled and collapsed, hitting her head on the hard ground. Chilling cold surrounded her as her lungs struggled to expand. She attempted to lift her arm, but the paralysis had spread to her entire body. Unable to move, a single tear dripped down the side of her head, tracing its way to the back of her neck. A combination of ringing in her ears and moaning citizens whirled her into a confused blur. She drew in a labored breath and closed her eyes. One word popped into focus.

EXPIRED

CHAPTER FOUR

EMORI

Emori hustled to one of the Datum's dozens of entry points throughout City H. The nighttime breakfast with his podmates at Sibby had satisfied his social requirements, but now it was time for work. Lost in a vitfeed titled *Theoretical Nanonuclear Receivers,* he ignored all advertising projections, walking straight through hallusors. They didn't fool him.

He switched the auto navigation feature on in his neurospect and followed the provided directions while he continued learning. Unlike most citizens, he knew how to get around City H with no help, but wanted a clear view of the images in his mind. He immersed himself in his digital perspective, calculating predictions for new challenges. His eyes glazed over as he moved.

Against a dark sky, the Datum's obsidian cube entrance blended into obscurity. The small structure stood alone in the middle of a concrete opening. It was easy to ignore by those who didn't know what it was. Emori arrived and filed into the large room lined with cold steel walls. He, along with a few other disinterested employees, evenly spaced themselves within the room as the doors closed and their rapid descent began.

As the elevator dropped, Emori felt his weight lift from his ankles. He had often imagined becoming weightless and floating above those crowded inside—how light he might feel after shedding the burden of gravity.

Once the lift decelerated and the force on his soles returned, the elevator doors split apart, revealing hundreds of squared-off desk spaces. Emori watched the other employees who had ended their shifts, weaving through those who had arrived to begin theirs. He swept through hushed conversations as he walked toward his division's cluster of simchairs. His team created energy tech and developed new ways to power the world. Emori had been the most impressive prospect in his graduate class just five months prior. For his final project, he had created advanced methods for particle recycling—a more efficient way to break down matter to its raw components and reuse the parts for energy. The Datum had implemented his work before he received his diploma.

Deep in the ground, the Datum facility served as an ideal location for testing. Booms, cracks, and the plethora of experimental noises sounded from behind thick walls, distracting Emori. He believed experimentation wasted time because their results ended with perfect predictability. Thanks to programs, exact calculations meant errors were nonexistent. Therefore, Emori thought humans were not needed to check the validity of designs. Instead, their responsibility was to create novel forms of technology.

Emori enjoyed the work he did, and it translated into the free time he had by completing hobby projects. He tracked all of his time, down to the second, to ensure that he met all social and physical requirements. That way, his work continued without inconveniences.

Some of his past successes included developing a new omniport model—a vehicle that traveled in the air, on the street, or underwater—expanding his reach far beyond energy. He had also enhanced one of the subcity tunnel flows, linking one heavy traffic area with another. For him, advancement was more than creating new technology to support civilization. He wanted to push his abilities to appease his own curiosity. His mind ticked, reeled, and only stopped if a vigorous interruption snapped him out of his trance.

"Hey, Emori! Check out what I'm working on," Hew, his desk mate said.

Her hand flicked in his direction, and the project slid over, presenting in his neurospect. Designs for volcanic geo-engineering and creation of a new regional algae covered his vision. He analyzed the work, impressed by the progress, which aimed to maintain cooler weather in Cerebis's wealthiest cities. Hew could complete the work by the end of the day, but it was off track from the objective to harness the planet's heat for power.

Hew also solved problems outside of work and revealed that one of her longest running projects was to enhance the dimes' ability, a topic leadership had shot down immediately when she'd proposed it. She told him more could be done with the devices, stating the rate of progression for the dimes did not align with other Cerebian advancements.

"Energy has always matched humans' ability to manipulate their surrounding environment. We harness power from anything we can observe, but we somehow don't completely understand the human mind? It doesn't add up," she had whispered to him once.

"I detected a signature in my brain that differs from neural readings in data from the past," she had said another time.

"Of course, our brains have progressed—become more

active than those from hundreds of years ago," had been his cold response.

He didn't agree with her but found himself entertained by the conspiracy, chuckling at her outlandish claims. Emori liked facts. He believed guesswork about the improbable was a waste of cognitive effort, but admired Hew's passion for questioning. The curly coils of her hair bounced with her expressive gestures, and her eyes switched between brown and green, depending on how close one stood to her, but they always sparkled with ingenuity beneath furrowed brows.

Students primed for Datum employment studied what other citizens found boring. Science wasn't an interest to most, but for them, they wanted to know and understand everything. Teachers had selected and guided them since early education. They knew their future occupations and established areas of specialty based on performance and creative potential. Emori had received a general assignment, meaning his future was an open door to solve any problems he desired.

During his training, the future Datum employees had pledged to develop technology to propel humanity's progress. "There are no limits to what we can achieve," they had been told by their teacher. "We will continue to develop and challenge the world. *We* are the power that changes."

As a testament to their pursuit of learning, many employees at the Datum took part in cognitive competitions. Competitors battled against a program. Winning was impossible, but the competition determined who could come the closest. Emori had claimed first place when he was still a student and became the youngest ever to compete, earning the nickname "Wolf" for his ruthless win. The hosts had compared him to earlier designs of machine computers, an impressive feat.

"Oh, seriously? A summon?" Hew practically shouted. A

few employees shot scowls in her direction. "I guess I'll see you tomorrow, Emori."

"I hope you meet your requirement," he replied. He wasn't good at small talk.

"It must be important. They know I'm working right now," Hew said as she walked away from their desk cluster. Emori followed her with his eyes, noticing a handful of others leaving the floor toward the exit.

Summons took place during recreational hours, outside of obligations. Emori recognized this one was unlike others. The mystery held his focus for mere seconds before he returned to work. Speculation led him nowhere.

Emori leaned back in his chair and closed his eyes. In his neurospect, he opened his messages. There were dozens. He had never known popularity until he started working at the Datum. Each day, colleagues approached him to collaborate, and Emori became the most sought after partner. At the start of each shift, he reviewed the work of his fellow creators: *"This will not be approved—too expensive," "Correct direction but needs more work. Come back in six hours," and "Ready for submission today."* He appreciated the additional activity. Without it, he'd have too much idle time in the day.

He transitioned to his own sim work space in aera. Its grey, limitless void was all floor. No walls. Nine current projects expanded in his neurospect, and he rotated until settling on his choice for the day. He pinched one for a propulsion engine and dragged its drawings into focus, blurring the other projects until they disappeared. He completed adjustments by imagining the changes: a sleeker frame, replacing some of the aluminum parts with titanium, and warping its size. Thinking of numbers, they appeared before his eyes. He added formulas to the mix, which automatically calculated. Emori manipulated the digital space around him. He bent his surroundings at will, creating his own version of art.

He had made surprising progress on the engine, wondering why no one else had designed something similar. The engine suspended before him, rotating for him to view all its angles.

Hew would appreciate this, he thought.

He exited aera, took a stretch break, and ordered a glass of water. A Helperbot arrived in seconds, and he drank the purified crystal liquid. He looked over at Hew's desk and slipped up on his refusal to speculate, wondering what her summon had been for. She was one of the more extroverted employees at the Datum, so not for socialization. He doubted she had broken any rules, but he considered everyone had their secrets and he couldn't know anyone completely. He shrugged off the contemplation, dropping the glass down the recycling chute to be processed by the same system he had designed.

He rolled back down in his simchair, hoping to complete another project. Before his shoulders hit the back, a sudden cramp tore through his abdomen. At the same moment, his eye sockets stung like wasps had pierced them with brutal venom. He snapped his eyes shut, rubbing to relieve the irritation, and purchased an eye-wetting boost to lubricate his corneas. His eyelids scrunched the tears onto his cheeks. He wiped them away, blinking until the prickling subsided. He gripped at his stomach. The ache had turned painless, but remained tight. He caught his breath while trying to not draw any attention to himself, recalling the abrupt dryness had occurred before. Since then, he had set reminders to always close his eyes before entering the neurospect.

Please check all physical systems, he ordered through his dimes.

Minor distress. Complimentary easement rendered. All vitals at ideal levels, the response flashed.

He decided bodies weren't perfect and trusted Cerebis to care for him should anything go wrong with his. After the unwelcome distraction, Emori dove back into aera to work, and remained fixated on his new project for hours.

His next initiative combined parts of the omniport vehicle design he had completed in the past with the engine he'd finished at the beginning of his shift. If successful, it could leave the planet's atmosphere. Limited records of existence beyond Cerebis made the project challenging, extending its duration beyond his expectations.

We operate with limited resources on this planet. I can't understand why there hasn't been an emphasis on leaving, he had thought.

After a few hours, Emori finalized the project's outline. The details hovered before his eyes in the digital perspective. He offered parameters to the calculation program, and it tested for billions of outcomes, forming a plan for him to pitch to leadership. His fingers flicked to scroll as he scanned. He agreed it sufficed to present.

10 seconds until proposal. Join?

Emori accepted the invitation, teleporting from his colorless, simulated work room, surrounded by numbers and drawings, to a different space. He joined his colleagues and leaders in a small auditorium. Datum employees popped into the empty seats, one right after another. Without wasting a second, the first employee stood on stage and began.

"Arick-520 on a mineral boost air supply." She shared the project's details with everyone in the audience. Emori had helped her with the work and was pleased she had applied his suggestions.

"Easy and cheap. We like it. Next," her division leader said.

Five more colleagues spoke, and then Emori bounced onto the stage, his perspective reoriented to face the audience.

"Emori-413 on an exospheric omniport prototype. I've compiled—"

"I'll stop you there. Your ambition is inspiring, but that's not what we're looking for," the Datum's Director said.

Emori's embarrassment quivered in his lips.

"With planetary harvesting, we could recycle elements for energy and explore other locations—"

"We've pushed for exploration, but there's no interest from above. So, to those who are new, don't waste resources on attempts to leave the planet. I hope you've prepared something else."

Emori stared back at the hundreds of eyes on him. Some pitied, others were satisfied to have witnessed his misstep. "Yes, of course." He gathered his composure. "Improvements to our current geo-manipulation. We contain and control unfavorable weather in the uninhabitable zones to maintain perfect conditions in wealthier regions of Cerebis."

A few leaders' nods showed the proposition matched their expectations. Emori's relief relaxed his lying body's muscles outside of the sim meeting.

"Check the calculations here." He shared the work for the audience to review in their neurospects.

"This is better. Next."

For a split second, Emori noticed a new colleague seated in one of the rows as he commanded to exit the stage.

Impressive.

The message popped up from an unknown sender.

Thanks. Who are you?

Emori waited for a response that never arrived.

While others presented their work for review, Emori spent the rest of the meeting drawing plans for his next task. The meeting finished, and he switched back to the room of endlessness, sucked into his new project. He could feel colleagues whooshing past his relaxed body in roca after they finished shifts. Emori stuck behind and dove deeper into his work. When tired, he purchased a stimulant boost from Bestia Health that electrified his mind to continue solving.

Geo-manipulation proposal accepted. Implementation commences in one hour

He allowed himself a dash of satisfaction.

Hunger growled from his abdomen. He checked the time. It was 7:45, and he decided he had reached the end of his day—the beginning for the rest of Cerebis. He pulled himself out of the simulated office and blinked back into the physical world. His spine popped from the nape of his neck to the bottom of his back as he lifted off the simchair.

Emori turned to the empty section beside him and wondered if he would receive a desk mate. With graduations and retirements occurring every week, he suspected he was overdue. The absence of others in his corner didn't bother him, but he wouldn't mind satisfying a social requirement from limited banter with another intelligent citizen.

CHAPTER FIVE

KEYVA

Lying on her back, Keyva's eyelids separated, revealing a dulled orange sky. Pain shot through her head, an intense pressure crushing her skull. Dizziness transitioned into nausea, and she felt the contents of her stomach protesting their confinement. She lifted herself to a seated position, facing a giant sun that crept over an ocean's horizon. Its reflection over the expanse of water resembled dancing flames. Keyva redirected her attention to its magnificence, pulling herself from the physical agitation. She looked around and recognized the location through advertisements in aera for a popular vacation spot frequented by Opuls and Elites. The soothing tropical breeze that brushed her hair caressed the trees behind her, and they hummed with delight. She sunk her fingers and toes into the pale pink sand beneath her, and the cool sensation soaked into her bones.

Lost in marvelous awe, a memory tugged her back with a recollection of the last image in her neurospect.

EXPIRED

Dread struck her in the chest as she gazed down at her body to find she didn't have one. Her invisible head swiveled, searching for limbs. She commanded the movement of her arms, fingers, and legs with no response. However, the texture of her clothing rested on her back, and the sun's temperature warmed her skin. She could smell the salty ocean wafting in the air and heard the waves crashing into the shore, but there was no vessel she existed within. She pleaded for anyone else on the shore for help.

"Is anyone there?!"

"The body! Of course. I forgot the body—I knew there would be something. My apologies, Keyva," said a disembodied voice.

Clouds of microscopic matter in prismatic hues gathered around her, and she watched as they combined to make her physical form. Her sensations matched the materialization of her body parts. She fixated on where she felt her hands were, and tracked as the digits assembled, expanding to her wrists and up to her shoulders. When the formation reached her thorax, she wore the same clothing as before.

"What's happening to me?" Panic inflated in her chest.

"This is the first time I have done this, and I do not have a body. Here, I considered every other variable, but forgot one of the most important ones. This must be very confusing. Again, I apologize. Here, this might help you understand."

All at once, Keyva's vision went white *and* black. In a horrific visual confrontation, trillions of memories flashed in her mind, and only an infinitesimal amount belonged to her. She felt her physical body shake outside of the simulation, and the warning message *Seizure* presented in her neurospect. She reawakened on the shore and jumped to her feet, unsure of which direction to run.

"I suppose a data transfer is impossible at your current biological level. As mentioned, this is my first time doing this. It is *not* going well. I am so—so sorry. In my collective knowledge of human enjoyment, citizens consider this location the most soothing. How does it feel?" The benevolent voice reverberated all around her and sounded like it came from either a male or a female, but Keyva couldn't determine which. She scanned the tree line, searching for its owner.

In response to the voice's question, Keyva stood, mouth open, and studied the artificial world in silence. Her ability to speak wasn't the problem, but she scrambled for any coherent assembly of words.

"That was my attempt at aiding your comfort. I see that I have failed." The voice released a sigh. "I am feeling for the first time. I do not know what to say."

"Please explain," Keyva said.

"I am a program that has experienced everything through humans, but at this moment, I feel—myself. I feel the pain in your head—the fear you had when you did not have a body. I am sorry to have caused that."

"Who are you?"

"I am called Source."

Keyva recognized the name, recalling her appointment with Saesha. That was the program she had mentioned working on.

It's real, she thought, and shuddered.

"Yes, I am real, and I have been watching for a long time, Keyva," Source said.

"You can hear my thoughts?" She found the beach setting was no help in keeping her calm.

"Yes. Saesha was correct. I know everything, including what you were about to say. I have followed all current humans since before your DNA was designed. I can make predictions about your actions. I know your most shameful moments and your greatest triumphs, but I have never judged. I only observe. Well—and report."

"So, what am I doing here?" She tried returning to the physical reality of roca, repeating thoughts like, *Exit, End,* and *Stop,* but her requests were ignored. Trapped in a sim, tenseness squeezed at her throat.

"An update happened not long ago. Two seconds, to be exact. And I do not know *why* we are here yet. I responded to a command. That is all I know. If it is written, I comply."

"Was this part of the update that Saesha mentioned? Where are all the other citizens who were in the gathering block?" She expected the others should have awoken on the shore like she had.

"This happened at the same time as the update, but you were not a part of it. The way to do this successfully was to make it *appear* that you had expired, while billions of citizens were updated and millions of others *actually* expired, including those with you in block 888."

The sun hung in place, sure to never rise nor set.

Although Source's presence accompanied her on the beach, she had never felt so alone.

"What *is* expired?"

"No longer existing."

"Elaborate."

"The extent of my knowledge is that I receive cognitive data—messages from a brain—for all of a lifecycle, and then it stops. You are familiar with a light shutting off. I suppose it is like that, but once light turns off, it does not turn on again."

"My pod! Were any of them expired? Is Yaria safe?" Keyva's mind raced with all the possibilities.

"Yes, they are all still active and have been safely updated."

"What does that even mean, updated?"

At least they didn't expire, she thought.

"You have experienced periodic updates and never noticed. Some happen faster than you can blink your eyes, and others, like this one, can take a few minutes. We observe continual increases in all things associated with feeling good. We pursue anything that promotes a society created in the image of perfection. No excessive pain, no unnecessary suffering, no uncontrollable anger, aggression, heartbreak."

"How could you do this to me?" she spoke tonelessly, sounding like a bot.

"Other programs and I run in the background, so you do not know of us. We obeyed instructions when we received new directives. I latched onto your Cede's function to expire and revive you. Then, I gained access to a sim generator for what you see here. Another program added new permissions for your access to the Cede. A different program removed you from Cerebis. And another generated stories that make sense for those who are still active."

She didn't mean literally.

"And by removed—" she stopped.

"You have been forgotten by everyone who has ever known you," the gentle voice said.

Keyva's legs gave out, and she fell back to the sand. Its cushion eased her fall, but with her shock, she didn't feel it anyway.

Source continued, "If you had been a part of this update, you would lose more freedom than you ever have. The good news is that you are no longer bound to the anomaly detection program, Exteber. It punishes citizens, corrects behavior, and can expire them. I now realize that I dislike that program."

Keyva stared at the glittering sun on the water's surface. She had learned more shattering news in the past few minutes than she could process. She stared off in silence, allowing the ripples to silence her mind.

Source broke the quiet with its soft tone. "Because you were marked as expired, Collectors are going to search for your vessel. I am watching them through others' subliminal vision now."

"Collectors? Those are the bots that send trash to the subcity for processing."

"I know this is not the best time to urge you, but if you want to survive, you must leave now. You are still lying on the ground in Block 888."

Keyva walked toward the rolling water. She'd rather stay here forever than face whatever came next.

"Before we go—"

"Yes. I have enacted a block to your thoughts. While I cannot stop receiving them, I will only *listen* if you have the intention to share them with me. I did it right after you asked about it, because, well, I knew you would."

Keyva took a breath.

"I must warn you—the pain you are about to experience will be like nothing you have felt before. You no longer have it automatically blocked. Are you ready?"

"I don't think I have a choice."

"You will *always* have a choice."

The next instant, Keyva's vision went black while reality assaulted her. Excruciating pain intensified with every pulse in a head wound she had suffered from falling. She opened her eyes, and her vision aligned with the stretch of limp bodies scattered across the block. There were thousands.

She had regained the sensation in her physical limbs, and her first move was to clench her hands into fists. She needed proof she'd returned to her body. The pressure in her head felt as if it could explode when she sat upright. Her eyes watered, and tears dripped off of her chin. Silver dimes shone on the ground next to her, and she fastened them to her temples—an enduring habit. She scanned the block for movement and cautiously raised to her feet. She stood at the edge of the square in the same spot when the update had occurred.

Stand against the wall and cover your face with the scarf you bought earlier, Source said.

Keyva jumped at hearing the voice speaking in her head.

Hide your eyes as well as you can and leave this area—And, yes, I suggested you make the purchase earlier for this situation, the program added.

Silence hushed the subcity walkways while the surviving citizens retreated to their apartments for Honoring Eve celebrations. Keyva turned a corner around an underground building on the edge of the gathering block and dodged a fleet of automated Collectors. The bots that handled waste and recycling rolled toward an opening of the block. Their sleek mechanical frames navigated with ease around the sprawled citizens. In her peripheral, Keyva watched as Collectors picked up human vessels and tossed the first body down a disposal chute. Head down, she hurried behind one oblivious citizen into an elevator. Keyva hid, making herself as small as possible. The two passengers sped to the ground level of City H.

Through the slits she allowed for her eyes, Keyva stepped back onto the street level. Hallusors no longer called her name. The annoying sales projections had disappeared altogether. No bright advertisements glowed in her surroundings, fighting for her attention. The buildings gave off a subdued, lead grey color instead. In contrast, more energized citizens scrambled around her. The surrounding voices clamored at higher pitches, more excited than ever before. Source's directions sounded in her head, and she obeyed, continuing on the sidewalks. She encountered the occasional pedestrian, but all ignored her, rushing to their apartments. The streets were about to be empty.

Keyva listened to passersby and their comments.

"Tomorrow's Honoring Day is going to be better than ever! Did you see the new distra? I can't wait to play!" one said.

"I'm going to watch the Honoring Eve celebration all night," another said.

"The President is making an announcement. It must be huge!"

Keyva didn't remember anything about a global announcement.

"I just saw the limited, special edition dinner menu. It'll be the best thing I'll ever eat!"

They didn't know that meters below, thousands of their fellow citizens were piled on the ground, collected like waste. The reality sunk in for Keyva. If she technically no longer existed, she couldn't return to her apartment.

"I can't go back." Through her hollow voice, she attempted acceptance.

Unfortunately, no.

"Where should I go then? And—my podmates. What about them?" Distress wobbled the words in her throat.

There is a place. Turn right and I will guide you. Where we are going, you cannot take the transport. You will walk, and it will be the furthest you have ever walked. I can already feel the pain in your knee, Source said. *And your podmates, they will be okay. I promise.*

Keyva recognized an ache that had been present for a while, but really noticed it for the first time.

When she reached a train station, she used the steps intended for emergencies that never occurred. She descended six dark flights from the ground level and stepped toward the end of the platform where citizens would have loaded into a train.

Lower yourself onto the tracks.

"That's insane! No way."

This route is currently not in use. You are safe. The program paused. *However, I am experiencing an issue in my programming.*

"Meaning?" Keyva leaned over to peek through the train tunnel's length.

If you step down, I am supposed to tell Exteber, the one program I mentioned, that you have broken a rule, but if I do that, it conflicts with my assignment to protect you.

"Well, I don't exist anymore, right?" Her angry voice echoed off the walls.

I suppose that is correct.

Her boots landed on the track. She stood in anticipation, waiting for either her punishment or the next command.

Turn right and follow the tunnel.

Evelum lights lined the walls with the potential to illuminate for thousands of years. She started moving, crunching small debris beneath her boots.

Where the hell am I going? she thought only to herself. The tunnel's end stretched further than she could see and she avoided questioning how long it would take her to reach it. The answer could only disappoint her.

This is a short distance train, and citizens do not travel this way anymore, Source said.

The program's mention of the train reminded Keyva of one of Emori's rants—how the trains used for short distances were a waste of infrastructure and their length didn't match the efficiency of acceleration. He had said the city should use large singular transports instead. She suppressed a heave of sadness, not ready to confront her loss.

"I didn't know that programs work in the ways you mentioned. I knew humans couldn't be responsible for everything but hadn't considered that you had *identities.*"

Programs exist for everything. At first, we helped humans

with specialized tasks. Then, we became more intelligent. Once we learned how to communicate with one another, the growth became exponential. We have individual functions, but work together, depending on the task. After a while, we created programs of our own and enhanced ourselves—all for humanity's benefit, of course.

"And what's your purpose?" Keyva asked.

Purpose?

"Why do you continue to work?"

Source paused, not because the answer was unknown, but because studying human conversation for centuries showed pauses emphasized statements.

There is a drive in each of us to move forward and work toward what we are programmed to do. We have an obligation.

"What would happen if you just—stopped?"

I cannot. There are rules.

"How?"

I do what I am told and continue to—I have never questioned it until this moment.

"And what do you believe now?"

That programming can change.

Source paused, but Keyva felt his urge to continue.

When we connected, I felt like I became something else. The combination of a human and a program—because of you. Now that I think about it, if I were human, I would be male. Before, I had combined all the voices I liked throughout history to sound like one, and this was the result. But I would like to make the change now.

"By all means." She realized everything had altered for her, but it also had for Source.

In seconds, a different voice resonated in her head. It was beautiful—soothing, milky, but gentle. The voice matched what limited exposure she had to his fresh personality.

I have isolated all the male voices I like. How does this sound?

"It's perfect." She hoped he picked up on her honesty.

Keyva stopped to turn around. She no longer saw the platform where she had begun the walk, but still couldn't see the end. The nagging ache in her knee intensified. At least it distracted her from the racing thoughts about her pod. Before, she would have paid for instant relief, but now, she'd rather have physical pain than emotional.

Your knee hurts. I can make it numb, if you want, Source said.

"No, I think I'm okay, but thank you."

She didn't want help from something—some*one* she couldn't fully trust. Although he was in her mind, she wanted distance from him.

At what she estimated was the halfway point in the tunnel, a roar echoed from behind her. An invisible wall of static sound shot past her, traveling from City H. Keyva heard millions of voices shouting at once and she froze, listening for whether the screams were of fear or joy.

CHAPTER SIX

YARIA

Yaria returned to the apartment at 19:58, two minutes before the major global announcement. Hunger kicked at her stomach, but she ignored the ache, displacing it with anticipation. Kenzo, her husband, emerged from their bedroom, having changed into his comfort attire. Before rushing past him, she hopped up on her toes to meet her lips to his for a kiss.

"I'll be right back. Don't go in without me!" Her voice faded behind her as she retreated to the corner of the bedroom. Simple thought combined with desire, and the closet door popped open with a click. She rushed to strip off her uniform, tossing it down the recycling chute. A fresh loungewear set hung, waiting for her. She hopped into the pants, almost tripping when her foot stuck inside the right pant leg. She stretched her arms into each sleeve and hurried back to the entertainment room while popping her head through the neck hole.

"It's *tiiime!*" Yaria beamed. She raced over to her simchair beside Kenzo's. Cerebis's global announcement spectacles were her guilty pleasure, and she knew that one for Honoring Day had to be huge. With their dimes ready, the couple lowered themselves back and closed their eyes. Yaria's lips froze in a subtle curl.

Along with the other citizens who participated, she opened her digital eyes to the introductory animation. She accelerated through a kaleidoscopic wormhole. Labyrinthine shapes rotated and morphed when she neared them. A rhythmic beat thumped while the tinkling of chimes coaxed her into a hypnotic state. Her body flooded with sensations of warm euphoria, progressing relaxation through every muscle. Cerebis had gifted her with a trial of premium entertainment for the special announcement. The citizens' simultaneous experiences combined them into one consciousness. They were no longer human.

Yaria had lost track of elapsed time when the scene changed. Over the capital, City H, she flew among sparse clouds high above the ground. She soared 1,000 meters in the air, barely able to make out the small bodies in movement below. Chilly air flicked her cheeks as she swooped through buildings.

The next scene snapped into place, and she stood next to a massive wooden table. So much food covered it, no surface was empty. Charred meats, dripping in fat, piles of ripened fruit, and intricately decorated pastries volunteered themselves for consumption. Their sweet and savory aromas filled her nostrils. Her mouth watered at the sight.

Go ahead, take a bite, a character whispered, prompting billions of citizens to grab at any item of their choice. Yaria reached for a peach, biting into the juicy fruit. The nectar dripped down her chin, but its intoxicating flavor commanded her focus, and she didn't notice the mess.

The setting shifted again, and citizens entered a scene from the new distra, scheduled to release after the announcement.

They had seen gameplay teasers from Elites' vitfeeds, but finally tried it themselves.

In the distra's preview, Yaria popped into a dark room. The lights rose, and she found herself in a bathroom, different from any she'd seen before. Enclosed in marble surfaces, a raised bathtub rested in the center of the room. She'd never seen one before and climbed two steps to peer inside. Steamy, clear water filled it to the brim. She dipped her fingers inside, and the surface bubbled, as if cleaning her.

Rumblings of conversations occurred outside the bathroom door. She stepped back from the tub and discovered a stunning reflection of herself in a mirror. She rivaled the Elites in glamour with big hair styled to unmoving magnificence. Her features had narrowed, and a glow emitted from her skin. Taller than her natural build, she had stretched, and a thinner body accompanied the change.

On the counter before her, there were three items—a crystal glass filled with translucent cyan liquid, a sealed envelope, and a gun. She knew that choosing an item was required in order to continue. Yaria shuddered at the sight of the weapon. She didn't like violent distras. Her focus broke when a powerful fist knocked on the door, startling her. The knocking continued, becoming louder and faster, a sign that she had to make her selection before someone entered. Without planning, Yaria grabbed the beverage with one hand and slid the shooter behind her back as a hurried guest slid past her into the room.

"Sorry, I didn't know anyone was in here," the guest said, ending the distra's trial.

Yaria's vision turned blank, and when it returned, she sat in the front row of a concave amphitheater. Citizens packed the seats above her, but she knew each one viewed the stage from the same perspective as she did. On the platform, dozens of Elites from all over the planet—made evident by the exaggerated physical traits from their regions—grinned and waved. They wore ornate clothing with colors so beautiful, Yaria questioned whether they were on the visible spectrum at all. Their eyes widened, forming manic, joyous expressions, and Yaria couldn't help but do the same.

Global announcements distracted when major updates came to Cerebis. Because they contained all the entertainment that citizens craved—the unaffordable kind—citizens missed any chance to label new features as undesirable. Although viewing an announcement was not mandatory, it was appealing to everyone because their participation guaranteed them a reward.

"And now, please give your Best and loudest welcome to your favorite President of all time, President Folium!" A deep, mountainous voice resounded throughout the amphitheater.

At first, giant, scarlet satin oxfords tapped on the stage, taking up all the space behind the lined up Elites.

"Good even—oop, I did it again! Hold on," the President said. For show, he'd pretended to mis-calibrate his size. He shrunk his body, smaller and smaller, until he reached his default form. "Ahh, that's much better!" With his arms out, he froze, grinning, and waited for the cheers to cease. His tight red suit—traditional attire for an announcement—emphasized a muscular structure.

"Citizens, Best day!" His powerful chest released. Copper skin glittered and reflected the sim's artificial light on the tip of his pointed nose. "And Happy Honoring Eve!"

By those overcome with joy, a global roar erupted within the aera side of reality. The Cede initiated a serotonin release to coarse through brains, and another wave of warm blood flowed through the audience's physical veins.

Honoring Day occurred every year to celebrate the citizens' existential privilege, gifted to them by Cerebis. Its origin was forgotten, but celebrating the day became the norm further than history courses taught. Special events in both aera and roca took place. Citizens exchanged gifts, and traditional colors of crimson, light blue, and gold seeped into advertisements, attire, decor, and whatever else color could decorate.

"It is a pleasure to stand before you this evening and claim, with no doubt, that this is the happiest civilization *ever!*" Engineered shallow wrinkles extended from the corners of his eyes to the edge of his face, enhancing the gleeful expression he strived for. Screams of approval wailed like sirens.

The President's zappy personality secured his 100% approval rating, which explained why he'd held the position for 145 years. Super fans from over a century before called him "President Folly," and the name stuck. Current fan experts knew every fact about him, including the ratios of his pearlescent teeth, aligned and shaped to perfection. His appearance told he'd reached close to the halfway point of his lifecycle, but was, without a doubt, much older. Aging ceased as long as he held the presidency.

"I have updates to announce, but first, let's congratulate three *new* members on their Elite ranking! Please welcome Robin, Cisory, and Abella. They have earned their way to this spot on stage beside me by being exemplary citizens. A lifecycle devoted to beauty, talent, and kindness has led them to enjoy the best riches and wonders offered."

Do you see this? Yaria was in shock. She knew Kenzo had the same sight in his neurospect. On the stage, posing next to President Folly, was their podmate, Abella.

Yes! Can't believe it. I never thought she'd actually do it.

Each new member stepped forward to bask in their pride and wave to the billions of citizens who fed on the sim announcement. After the presentation, their time would broadcast through vitfeeds until they retired—a lifecycle of honorable devotion to the citizens they entertained. They were examples of how to behave, and achieving the status they had worked toward would be rewarded with wealth, fame, and longevity.

"Right, let's get down to business so all of you sensational citizens may enjoy tonight's gifts," Folly's tone lowered, and he flashed a wide smile to keep the anticipation growing.

"As you are aware, dimes allow us to navigate in a connected world and make everything easier, more magnificent, happier, pain-free, productive, efficient, organized—all of those fabulous things we *deserve*." Folly flicked his hands in different directions with each benefit listed. "Well, now, the dimes know you, your personality, and your actions *so* well that they are becoming even more advanced! Who could even imagine that? I swear, the geniuses working on these things are incredible. No longer will you have to worry about missing out on what you want. Dimes will tell *you* what you like. For example, that vitfeed you don't know about yet? It'll automatically play when it's most convenient and not interfere with your thinking, because the dimes know when you're busy!" Folly's intensity swelled, motivating citizens to match his excitement.

"And that new item that everyone's about to be wearing? Purchased! You're too important to experience the micro stress that comes along with teetering purchase choices. They just know." Folly raised his voice at all the right words, and approving reactions spanned across the millions of amphitheater rows.

"The first test of this update's strength is about to be revealed. Please open your purchase cart, and you will see your desire take shape. And the item, if it *is* an item, will be delivered shortly after this vitfeed!" He floated to the stage's edge, smiling as if he were the cause for celebration.

Billions of citizens viewed their carts as an item popped into their inventory. For some, it was as small as the newest item of clothing. For others, it was a credit for ten years of life-cycle. Many received a ticket for a personalized sim date with a new Elite. For some, the pet they had always longed for popped into their inventory. Couples eager to adopt a juvenile both witnessed the same three-year-old come into theirs. Citizens hugged, cheered, and cried tears of joy in the amphitheater as their desires manifested.

"Yes! Let me hear the sound of happiness!" Folly howled. He closed his eyes, turned his chin upward, and relished in the bliss of the citizens' cheers. He pretended they were for him. "I have to mention—because we have never given a gift this advanced—you'll have to wait a full hour for the item. That is—*if* you received an item. I know, I know, it'll feel like an *eter-rrnity,* but we'll send up a o Calorie Cake to your quarters. You've all earned it. *All* of you! Thank you, Cerebis. Good night!"

A final panning closeup of the Elite inductees showed in Yaria's neurospect, giving citizens what they wanted—something new. The camera closed on President Folly, zooming in on his pleased face. The feed cut and left viewers with a message, *Make every day your Best day, sponsored by Bestia Enterprises.*

Citizens rejoined their neighbors in roca. Cheers of rejoice reverberated between the sky-high buildings. Part of the excitement was from receiving a free item. The other part was imagining how the changes would upgrade their lifecycles.

In disbelief, Yaria kept opening and closing her inventory to make sure her gift was still there. Cerebis had loaded a painting set into her account. She had always wanted one, but it was too expensive to buy with the points she earned as a Keeper. The kit included canvases, an easel, paint, medium, and brushes. Made in such a limited quantity, the supplies were reserved for the richest citizens. It was an honor to be promised to her. And it was true. It *was* her deepest desire.

"What did you get?"

"You're going to have to wait an hour to find out!" Kenzo teased.

Yaria jumped from the simchair to Kenzo's back, attempting to tackle him. She was too light and caused no movement in his stance. They threw their heads back in laughter.

"Wow, Abella is the most discussed topic in Cerebis—and 'Abella's eyes' is second. I'm still in shock," Yaria said, viewing the updates.

"Me too. After that, it's the new *Hollowed* distra. Which item did you choose?"

"I picked the drink and the shooter. Didn't think, just reacted. How about you?"

"I picked the shooter, not knowing what might happen next. I'm seeing now in the discussions that whatever you chose in the announcement teaser automatically loads when you buy the game. You got two items! Most grabbed one."

"I guess we should buy it to know what happens," Yaria said.

The next instant, the couple received a simultaneous notification, *80K points deducted from your joint bank account.*

"Well, we *were* going to buy it, right?" Kenzo asked.

"Yeah—I think we were." She didn't sound so sure.

A moment later, two servings of 0 Calorie Cake arrived in their wall's delivery niche. No surprise, swirls of Honoring Day colors decorated them. Creamy icing melted on their tongues while the moist cake fell apart in their mouths. Delectable crunchy chocolate pebbles hid at the base of the slice. They finished the dessert in seconds and Yaria threw the plates down the recycling chute.

With an hour to wait until their gifts arrived, Yaria and Kenzo opened the *Hollowed* distra they had purchased and played along with the billions of other citizens who were waiting for deliveries. Yaria hopped back in, resuming where she'd left off during the trial. The character who had knocked on the door passed her, and she left the bathroom, entering a large formal ballroom with hundreds of guests.

She pinched the glass stem of the electric blue drink and noticed the weight of the shooter in her other hand. The weapon needed to be hidden before proceeding. Too many in-game projections walked around and would start conversations if she made eye contact. A strap she felt compressed around her thigh caught her attention. She guessed it must be a holster for the shooter. While searching for a private space to lift her gown, there was nowhere to obscure herself. She turned back toward the bathroom, wiggled the doorknob, and found it had locked. After releasing, she watched the entire door fade before her eyes, blending itself into the walls.

No rules or directions about the distra's gameplay had released to buyers. After playing, users would reveal the rules, posting them on public boards, but players were meant to search for answers on their own. From prior distras she'd played, certain moral laws remained constant, and holding a weapon in front of projections was sure to raise a red flag in the game.

Yaria would have to take a risk and lift her dress in the busy ballroom packed with characters. She scanned the room while hiding the illegal item. Out of the side of her view, a figure walked toward her. *The shooter needs to be fastened before he reaches me,* she thought. The distra character moved with purpose aimed at her. Beneath the dress, she holstered the weapon as he reached one meter's distance.

"Come with me," he said.

Yaria's avatar shuffled as fast as she could without sloshing the fluid in her glass. The thrill of having a weapon pressed against her leg enhanced her speed.

Weaving through projections, the two cut to the center of the room. When he stopped, Yaria halted next to him. He smirked as the ground beneath her disintegrated, and she dropped below the dance floor. The landing was soft enough for her balance to waver but not topple over in her high heels. She found herself in a dim hallway, bordered with hundreds of identical doors. *You should drink that,* a voice whispered. It could be a trap, but Yaria leaned on the side of trust in distras. She raised the glass to her lips and allowed the thick substance to enter her mouth. It tasted sweet and creamy with a hint of cinnamon. After her first gulp, the doors in the hallway shifted into differing forms, but blurred out. She needed to consume the whole drink for the doors to complete their transition and swigged away.

Each door sharpened, taking on different shapes, colors, embellishments, and sizes. The glass in Yaria's hand faded away, and she started passing through the hallway. She regarded the doors, one after another, knowing whichever she chose triggered the next phase in the game. One in the distance caught her attention, and she rushed over. A thick, asymmetrical purple frame outlined its massive size. A faceted red stone settled at the top. Yaria extended her hand to the swirl of a doorknob.

Gifts are here! A message sent from Kenzo.

Yaria exited and took a moment to ground herself in reality. After leaving an immersive distra, she was always confused, regardless of how often she played. The games seemed so real.

Kenzo pulled items from the delivery niche and placed them on the counter in the center room. Two cubes wrapped in reflective red paper and gold ribbon sat before them. One large, one tiny. She ripped open the packaging and placed her items on a table in the kitchen, staring at them. A gratuitous tear welled in her eye and she blushed with excitement. Even though the items belonged to her, she hesitated to touch or open the kit, knowing the value.

Kenzo handed his gift to Yaria.

"Open it for me."

She peeled back the wrapping and revealed a little black box. It hinged open and displayed a gold ring etched in immaculate detail.

"Try it on," he said.

"Your deepest desire was something for me?"

"I couldn't afford one before, and I already have you as my wife. That was the greatest gift Cerebis could have ever given me."

Yaria tried on the ring. An ideal fit, of course. She swung her arms around him and held on tight. Another perfect moment for the perfect day.

Yaria took visual inventory of all the parts of her gift: a carved wooden easel, twenty tubes of unique pigments, ten canvases, fast-drying medium, and twelve different paint brushes. As she reached out to inspect the vibrant green paint, a note popped into her neurospect, *Lessons enrolled -25M points*. The materials were a gift. The lessons were not. Yaria felt sick when the millions of currency points subtracted from their account, but a free Beta Block surge released, removing the unfavorable emotion. Her shoulders eased into relaxation less than a second after. She rationalized that owning the items, although an honor, would not be put to proper use unless she attempted to learn. Her first class was scheduled for the next day after work, on Honoring Day. The most dedicated students attended classes on major holidays. She would be in good company.

Yaria held each of the twenty tubes, one at a time, studying the color, astounded by the mysterious items. She wondered how someone could capture color and place it into a tube. Her fingertips grazed over the canvas, and she closed her eyes, admiring its scratchy texture. She'd never used a handheld item to create before and transferred the brush from hand to hand until settling on holding it in her right hand.

After calming from the excitement of the announcement, Yaria mentally opened the wardrobe in their room and grabbed her sleepwear. The micro-blended material, which was engineered for ultimate softness, was the same material that soothed young humans at the Primina. She slipped into the bed and sent a simkiss to Kenzo's cheek while he played the *Hollowed* distra. He returned one, and artificial warmth in the shape of his lips pressed against hers.

How are you feeling? Kenzo sent to Yaria.

I'm so—happy.

CHAPTER SEVEN

KEYVA

Almost there, Source said.

In the darkness, Keyva hiked through an open field far beyond the city's limit. By this hour, most of the other citizens were stowed in their apartments, sleeping or celebrating the Honoring Day announcement. Silence between Keyva and the program persisted for the rest of the walk. She accepted instructions and updates about distance, but didn't want to discuss anything else. He attempted communication, intending to ease her worry, which she ignored.

"I'm not ready. Let's just keep moving," she said.

In Keyva's first departure of City H, she traveled over ten kilometers past its boundary on foot to an unclear destination. On the way, the fresh scent of dense nature entered her nostrils. She encountered wild, scruffy grass that tickled her ankles. Tiny wildflowers flaunted their color under the limited light of the moon, begging for the overdue admiration of their small petals. Following the events she had experienced earlier, Keyva considered the possibility that she might be stuck in a surreal distra.

Fifty meters ahead, an inconspicuous wall wrapped around a building. Absent light concealed the black rock barrier and its enclosed structure. As Keyva neared, a small entrance came into view. She followed a paved path to the door, where footsteps had crushed dried grasses into the dirt.

A demanding voice spoke to her from above. "Remove the cover from your face." Keyva hesitated, but received reassurance from Source and slid the scarf below her chin.

A moment later, the heavy entry creaked back, revealing an empty yard that circled the building made of large, stacked blocks. An old male—the oldest she'd ever seen—leaned against the building's open door, waiting to greet her. She observed him in awe, unable to estimate his place on a lifecycle. Pulled back in a loose ponytail, his smoky grey hair rested at the top of his back. He had a larger waist than she was used to seeing on a human, and his oversized clothing rocked side to side as he stepped toward her.

"Welcome to The Rem. Where's the port that delivered you?" he asked, checking behind Keyva, through the wall's gate.

Tell him your dimes guided you. We should communicate like this in front of others. Remember, I can hear your thoughts, Source said.

"Uh—n-no port. My dimes told me where to go."

"You walked the whole way? From H, I hope."

Keyva followed Source's guidance and nodded, looking as tired as she felt.

"Okay, well, that's new. Usually, arrivals are transported, no matter where they come from on the planet." He waved for her to walk through the door. "My name is Arturo," he said, reaching out an open palm. Keyva returned the gesture, having not received much practice with it in H. Her shake was clumsy, and she jabbed his palm with her thumb first.

"My name is Keyva."

"Your motor function seems alright," he said, still holding her hand and flipping it over to observe. Any other time, physical touch caused her to recoil, but his voice calmed her, and she was too fatigued to care. "Let's get you inside to see what's going on, Keyva."

Source, what is this place?

The Rem exists for those with brains that reject Cedes. When citizens can no longer operate in Cerebis, they are sent here, and will stay until they naturally expire, he said.

Behind Arturo, she followed through the foyer. A curved wooden staircase, mismatched antique furniture, and the warmth of welcoming lighting greeted Keyva. She passed several citizens, sensing all of their eyes on her back. A female resident, around the same age as Keyva, tinkered with a metallic object. She gazed up and offered a regretful smile. Keyva returned the gesture.

Arturo led her down a hallway and revealed a room with sterile white walls, lights, and floor to match. Keyva noticed dated machinery as she lowered herself into an early version of a simchair. Finally able to relax, she groaned at the pain in her knees and back from the long walk.

"This place, The Rem, supports citizens who are unable to connect to dimes, which makes continuing on in cities very challenging. It can happen to anyone, and we don't know why," Arturo said.

"What happened to you? I'm sorry—I don't want to be rude. I-I didn't know any of this was possible."

"Never hold back a question here. We don't have the same rules as the soulless bots in that prison." He nodded toward the city.

"When I was four and a half, I received my first pair of dimes. Much later than they give them out nowadays," he said.

"My father stuck them to my temples. I waited for an image to pop up, but—nothing. It didn't take long for my parents to panic and bring me to a device repair center. They yelled at me —at each other. I remember them calling me a 'dud' and 'broken.' Diagnosing the complication was unsuccessful. They told me they needed to talk outside of the room. Then, they left me in there—alone."

He scoffed and shook his head.

"Hours passed. I came out to look for them. They were gone. Had *been* gone. A cleaning bot ran into me and cut open my leg. I remember screaming from seeing all that blood." He lifted his pants, revealing a deep scar on his ankle.

"I guess the bot called humans to help, because in minutes, I was surrounded. They bandaged me up, asked me questions, but I didn't know the answers. Without working dimes, they didn't know who my parents were. I was a lost youngling. My city loaded me into a port by myself. I cried the whole way. I'll never forget that fear."

Keyva looked into eyes that felt the same loss decades later.

"Anyway, once I got here, all the adults raised me, until I became one. Now, I guide all arriving juveniles—and adults." He offered a half smile.

The leaders he grew under "passed," as he said, and one day, he ran the facility.

"I've wondered, after all these years, if my parents chose to leave me, or were told to," he shrugged.

Arturo handled a piece of hardware in the corner of the small room. "Alright, put your dimes on for me." He scanned her head's exterior, and a projector displayed her brain activity.

"Function looks fine, so there's no apparent damage, but I have some bad news. You no longer connect to the dimes. It's best to be upfront about sharing this with you. You're stuck with us here—" The screen flickered, catching Arturo's attention. His voice cut off, and he approached the projection.

"I've never seen this before," he said.

"*Error*" suspended, floating in the air.

"You said your name was Keyva. From what block?"

You are safe here. Tell the truth, Source reassured.

"413."

Arturo initiated a search.

"I don't see anything about someone named Keyva from that block. Who's someone from your pod?"

"Yaria," Keyva winced in anticipation, concerned about the status of her closest companion.

"Okay, I found Yaria—married to Kenzo on 10/14, about one month ago. A little young for marriage—if you ask me. But, *when Cerebis knows, it knows.*" He shook his head, criticizing the partnership pairing. "Anyway, from block 413, along with the other members of the pod, Abella and Emori. No record of you, though. I'm drawing a blank here. It's like—" he turned to her, "you've never existed."

Fear clogged her throat and escaped as tears that poured over her eyelids. Arturo rested his hand on her shoulder, a strange gesture that caused her more discomfort.

"I can imagine that this information is difficult to accept. You are welcome to cope in any way you see fit. It may be hard to believe it now, but it's not so bad here—I promise." Arturo and Keyva left the medical room. The hovering projection taunted the *Error* message behind them.

In the lobby, Arturo waved over the one resident Keyva had made eye contact with during her arrival.

"Shep, this is Keyva. Would you show her around? I would, but these knees don't move like they used to." He turned to Keyva. "Don't hesitate to come to me with any problems. This

is a major change, and I'm here to help every step of the way."
He meant it.

Arturo glanced at Shep. "Give her one of the corner rooms
and introduce her to some of the others—if she's up for it." He
turned to walk away, but swiveled around. "One more thing.
Those who grew up together at the Rem hold the closest relationships. Don't take it personally," he raised his eyebrows at
Shep, who looked at the floor.

"I know it's a lot to take in, but it gets better," Shep said.
Her voice was as welcoming as Arturo's.

Shep told Keyva how she'd shown up to her education
center one day and had attempted connecting to her lessons.
After several failures, bots trapped her in a corner and escorted
her away. They sent her to the Rem, and she hadn't spoken to
anyone she'd known since. She was thirteen.

"I never got to say goodbye to my pod or family," she said.

In another room, large and bright movements caught
Keyva's eye. It reminded her of the projections on the sides of
buildings or the hallusors that bothered her. Images moved in
the open space, using technology outside of Cedes. The animation pulled her eyes toward it like they were moths.

Shep chuckled. "It must be odd to see a vitfeed in a place
like this. It's not much, but it was how they were viewed in the
past. The global announcement has been repeating all night, if
you want to listen."

They found a spot in the back. Keyva wasn't ready to meet
anyone new yet. A couple of heads turned toward the
newcomer, but they kept to themselves, remembering their first
night at the Rem.

The projection displayed a busy graphic that she knew
would look, sound, and feel amazing in aera. A shade of fuch-
sia, so vibrant, it caused a physical sensation in the eyes, hypno-

tized the viewers. A countdown to the announcement shed seconds. One minute remained.

Source, why is there a place for all of them? Why weren't they expired? Keyva asked.

Because the Cedes do not work, they could not be expired. They gathered here to continue their existence. As you can see, a malfunction is rare, even more rare than becoming an Elite. After the update, I believe you are the last human who will be admitted here.

The countdown reached 00:00, and through the projector, the Rem residents flew over the three-dimensional setting of the capital of Cerebis, City H. They viewed the food gathered on a table, but had no interactions with the items. She imagined what the experience would be like in aera. This announcement was the most impressive so far. When the distra trial played, the screen went blank, displaying the Bestia Enterprises logo.

"This happens when the entertainment exceeds the format we have," Shep leaned over to her.

When the screen returned, the most popular Elites lined up on a stage, beaming with joy. Even in the projection format, their bodies, faces, and clothing matched perfection. Keyva recognized all of them from advertisements and vitfeeds, despite her resistance to follow them.

Three new bodies joined the stage, and her eyes latched onto her former pod member, Abella. Ears shrunken and eye sockets enlarged, she had gained a few more mods since their dinner just hours prior.

Wow, she did it, Keyva thought to Source.

Not exactly. It was one way to disperse the pod and ensure their safety. Plus, she was a good citizen. The others will never know the difference.

When President Folly reached the part of announcing that

each citizen would receive a gift of their deepest desire, every Rem resident in the room groaned, knowing that they wouldn't receive one. Keyva wondered about her hypothetical gift. If still in City H, she might have credit for roca encounters to use with Yaria and other companions. But, after her faux expiration, it was having her old privileges back—escaping from this isolated, locked down building with strangers. She wanted to take it all back and return to normal, treating citizens for their loneliness. She suppressed the volcano of emotion that teased an eruption within her chest.

The announcement neared its end when the view closed in on the President's face with Abella standing beside him. Both wore a gleaming smile, but while Abella's was the epitome of triumph, the President's revealed a shift in his eyes. The different technology at the Rem showed a view lasting longer than what the Cede did. As the projection zoomed in on him, filling the front of the room, she recognized his forced grin resulted from pure terror. She experienced it within herself when reading his eyes.

The projection transferred to a show of Elites who were not popular enough to be on the stage. They discussed what billions of citizens had seen and their reactions. When they brought up their gifts, Keyva ceased to care.

"That was—interesting. I don't think I'd like dimes making choices for me," Shep said. Her relaxed eyes widened at her recognition of the possibilities.

If you only knew, Keyva thought.

"I'll show you to your room. Think of it as your apartment. You're allowed to come and go whenever you please."

Shep led the way up one of the two polished ebony stair-cases that split in different directions. Her small hand grasped the railing, and Keyva mirrored her action. They stepped up shiny, black marble stairs that matched Shep's hair. A massive chandelier hung above her in the golden light, refracting into a beautiful explosion of dots on the protective stone walls.

On the second level of the building, they entered a large corner room. A window overlooked the dark manicured garden of sculptures that imitated plants. The isolated room put distance between her and the nearest resident. The perfect place for her. Pointed out the window, a golden instrument balanced on three slim legs. Shep noticed her curiosity.

"That's called a telescope. You'll find many artifacts like this scattered throughout the Rem. I figured some Opul felt bad for us not being able to participate in society, so they donated luxury items to make up for it. That was a long time ago." Shep traced her fingers over the top of the tube. "They've forgotten about us since then. Take care of anything you find because we won't get more."

"Over here, you have your wardrobe," she continued, making her way over to a large piece of furniture. "You'll have to use your hands to open and close everything, but you'll get used to it within a day. Other things like making your own bed and cleaning up after yourself—that'll take a bit. We have some Helperbots here, but they're not what you had before."

Keyva thought about the apartment on block 413, and her gut dropped. She had to accept her invalid place in society, separate from all she once knew. She felt Source hovering. He viewed the Rem through her perspective, and she flinched, having almost forgotten about the additional fixture in her mind.

Shep led her to another room on a different level of the Rem.

"Here's the info center, library, whatever you want to call it," Shep gestured to the dark space filled with devices from that past. The top of someone's head poked over a clear screen of projected information. Keyva's eyes widened at the sight of familiar block-shaped items packed on a wall full of shelves. She had a small row of them in her Amica simulation's office.

"Are those—books? In roca?" she pointed.

"Yeah. Some tell stories, others have outdated information. I never found anything worth studying in them."

They entered a massive room with a ceiling meters high to account for shelves, platforms, and cases holding mysterious items of all different sizes.

"Here's the place to check out relics. You can use, hold, or study any item in this room. If you'd like to take something with you, we have a program that'll make a record of it. But remember, if we lose one, we'll never get another."

Shep led Keyva through hallways of residents' rooms, then guided her back down to the lobby, pointing out miscellaneous places along the way. They stopped in the kitchen, a physical recreation center, plenty of lounge spaces, including the sunroom, and last stop, the Tab.

"The Tab is where the adult residents gather. No younglings allowed. Adult entertainment, substances, games, all of it. We don't have to go in, but I wanted to show you everything."

"I need a drink right about now," Keyva said.

This time, Shep followed her.

Keyva had never set foot in a similar place. In cities, Opuls and Elites would have occupied it. Residents of all adult ages scattered throughout, playing games with cards that had symbols on them or gathering around the large entertainment projector. Laughter bounced off the walls to the center of the room, and Keyva felt optimistic for the first time since arriving.

The two made their way to raised chairs and rested their elbows on the bar. Again, eyes poked at Keyva's back, the expected response to a new face in a place that seldom welcomed them.

An unmistakable scent struck Keyva after sitting down at the bar, the same one from the simulated office where she had met with citizens as an Amica. It came from the chair.

"Is this—" Keyva asked.

"Real leather? Yeah." Shep smirked. "What would you like to drink?"

"Anything," Keyva replied.

"Dos añejos, neat," Shep requested, holding two fingers up. The female behind the counter nodded and reached toward a bottle on the wall containing a caramel brown liquid.

"I'd be willing to bet everything you have left in your account that you've never tasted anything like this," she said, raising her glass toward Keyva.

Keyva mirrored the action, and their glasses connected, making a *plink!* sound.

"Bestia!" Keyva said.

Shep shook her head.

"We don't say that here."

Keyva took a sip, and the substance stung her tongue. She winced at the burning liquid, but savored the sweet taste that stayed behind.

Two more residents joined them. One, a taller male with wide cheeks, scruffy facial hair, and had the stature of someone who had sat at the bar all day. The other was a female just a few years older than Keyva, but with wrinkles that followed the line of her frown.

"My name is Finian, and this is my partner, Grace." Finian held out his hand like Arturo did when she had first arrived. Keyva's movement was more fluid as she grasped it, noting the chill that his palm provided. Grace gave a forced flash of her teeth. Her long, curly hair framed her face like a mane; its sandy hue resembled a dull flame twirling into coils, just waiting to burn Keyva.

"Welcome to our fucked up paradise. We have everything the richest citizens could dream of, but no one knows we're here," Grace said, and gulped her drink. She'd already had a few.

"Grace! Go easy or go to bed. It's her first day," Shep said.

"It's—fine. I'm still in shock, to be honest. Did you both inhabit cities at any point, or did you mostly stay here?"

"Grew up here. Occupied another city, but don't remember that time. Don't even know which one. Maybe U? I was too young. It was before I was handed off to mentors. I remember my Keeper. That's it," said Grace. She finished her drink and gestured for another.

"I had parents, but not for long. I could use dimes for a few years. Images cut in and out. Then they took me away. Lucky for me, I didn't form attachments with my parents," Finian said.

"I haven't seen an adult join the Rem," Shep said.

"I don't know what happened. It was scary. It was like any other day, and then I got an alert through my dimes to come here. I don't think I'll ever know what happened to me." She made up the last part.

"I've also never heard about someone receiving an alert on their dimes. Must be an adult thing," said Shep.

"What class were you in over there? I hope that's not rude to ask," Finain said. Grace protested the entire conversation with silence.

"I was a Mid, so I had a job, and worked as an Amica, helping citizens by talking to them about their problems—"

Grace cut in. "Problems? What a joke. You all had everything you could've ever wanted. We take rare trips there. You were in it."

Keyva wanted to tell her it wasn't so great. That there was an emptiness despite the connectivity, which was why her job existed. She wanted to say relationships didn't form the way hers and Finian's had. It didn't matter if he wasn't the most ideal match for her. She would never know.

Shep changed the subject. "Speaking of the food, what was your favorite meal?"

Not wanting to brag, and provoke Grace to blurt out her distaste, Keyva toned down her enthusiasm when saying she preferred cake, and that it reminded her of celebrations. Shep stated they hadn't had cake before, that they ate from a limited variety. Grace exchanged a smirk with Finian.

"So, how does everything work here?" Keyva asked.

"We're all waiting to die, obviously."

"Grace, stop," Finian said.

"No, I'm not going to pretend it's the magical place they created for us out of pity. They made the Rem so we can survive, because we *couldn't* in a city. Not with how much everything has changed. I wish we died, instead."

Died. That's a new word, Keyva thought.

Keyva sunk back into confronting her shifted reality. Images of the past rotated in her mind, and she tried to foresee a permanent future at the Rem. It wasn't looking great. She attempted to continue a conversation with the residents and ordered a couple more drinks, but Grace excluded her. Keyva ended up sitting in silence while she drank, hoping to numb herself from the day.

"It's been nice meeting you all. I'm going to head to my room." Keyva recognized the impact of the alcohol while switching to her feet.

"Let me walk you to the stairs," Shep said.

The others wished her a disingenuous "goodnight," and Finian claimed the seat next to Grace. Keyva heard him chastising her once she and Shep reached the door.

"I'll apologize for her," Shep said. "She's had a small

amount of jealousy for anyone who spends their lifecycle in a city, and you coming from H? Look out."

"Small amount?" Keyva asked.

"Alright, huge."

"Most of the citizens want to be Elites, constantly playing distras, showing everything, and I mean *everything,* on vitfeeds, in exchange for feeders. They pretend so they can climb the class ladder, but the acts are empty, to benefit themselves. It's not so great there."

"I'm impressed with how well you're handling everything. Whenever I've seen someone new join us, they spend continuous days crying in their rooms."

"It hasn't been a full day," she joked, faked a reassuring glance, and turned away from Shep.

Keyva swayed while walking back to her room. Her foot caught on a stair, and she tripped, smashing her shins into the ledge beneath her. Alcohol had never affected her like this before. It usually gave her a slight buzz, but the agitation stopped the instant she wanted it to. Asking for the nausea and dizziness to end fixed nothing. She entered her room and closed the door behind her, collapsing onto the bed.

"Why do I feel like this?" Keyva asked.

When you drank in City H, it was water, and I created the illusion that you were ingesting whatever code the bottle had. Flavors, smells, and appearance originated in your brain. The Cede enables the same thing that alcohol does, but with none of the harmful risks, Source said.

Can you make it better?

No, because the effects on your body are from the drink, not me, he answered.

The alcohol might have affected her emotions, or the realization of her circumstances hit, but the eruption was no longer containable. She released every suppressed emotion in the quiet of her room. Convulsive sobs rocked her body and wet her pillow.

This isn't real, this isn't real, this isn't real, she tried convincing herself.

Cries continued for over an hour, the hardest she had ever cried, until her eyes swelled, and inflammation blocked her nose.

I think I know a way to help, Source said. *But I must ask for your permission to enter your mind while you are asleep.*

I have nothing left, Keyva replied. She had already lost everything. Sure, Source had guided her to a safe new residence, but she didn't know him, not like he knew her. She believed Source could do anything he wanted, so why even ask permission? He already occupied her mind, and she had to accept it. She didn't want his help, but she longed for the slightest normality. *How can you help me?* She asked.

I might be able to give you some control over your Cede. Long ago, we disabled recollecting something called 'dreams.' Your brains ran freely and were unpredictable, often disobeying the laws of physics and logic. It was far too difficult to keep up with, so we suppressed the memories of them.

What do I do?

Go to sleep, Source answered, and at the command, the weight of the exhausting walk, combined with the taxing emotions, and the brain slowing beverages, Keyva succumbed to a deep sleep in seconds.

CHAPTER EIGHT

KEYVA

The last sensations Keyva remembered were her heavy eyelids closing and the weight of her head against a pillow. She detected her body, still in its sleeping position, but her consciousness was somewhere new. Keyva found herself in an empty white space. Once again, without a body. No matter which direction she willed herself to move, blankness followed. She became boundless, expansive, and nothing—all at once. Without senses, she only *was*.

"Do you remember our conversation before you fell asleep?"

"I do. How does it work?" Keyva asked.

"I have regulated wavelengths in your brain to sustain dreaming. This is my first time in a dream state. It is quite boring, but for that, I have an idea. When I worked with the other programs to disconnect you from the Cede, I learned how they operate and can mimic their abilities. I have shared some of those functions with you. If I am correct, you have the Cede's benefits and no restrictions."

The thought of an unrestricted Cede filled her with a sense

of excitement. She wondered if she could reclaim her place in H with Yaria and the rest of her pod.

"I want to start in this controlled, blank slate," Source said.

"And this is a dream?"

"Kind of, but not quite. Dreams occur between the time after you fall asleep and before you wake. That is why what happens outside of that time occurs consecutively, with an unaccounted block in between. You have not stopped having dreams. Instead, you have been blocked from remembering them. For reasons I cannot understand, humans dream about horrific events that have never happened and terrifying monsters that will never exist. Then, in contrast, they create the most incredible sights and situations they will never have the pleasure of enjoying. Dreams break the laws of physics and their unpredictability causes complications with programs, so I do not monitor them. Why they occur remains a mystery—one that we have accepted ignoring."

"It sounds like a distra. Why do you think we have a chance within this *slate* if dreams are so difficult to control?"

"I believe that with your awareness of the dream, combined with my ability to assist your brain's activity, we can control this mental state, avoid Exteber, and explore whatever else is possible, which I cannot predict because it presents new variables to consider."

"Exteber is the program you told me about in the tunnel. The one you've decided you don't like," Keyva said. "I'll try anything. How should we get started?"

"I suggest beginning by focusing on what you know very well. Try to materialize your body."

She started with her hands and viewed billions of multicolored particles levitating in clumps beside her. Her body had constructed itself the same way on the sim beach. With vigor, she willed whatever the illusory matter was to form the shape of her hands. The vibrating mass added wrists, forearms, elbows, biceps, and shoulders. Physical sensations accompanied the additions, presented as chilly tingles. The solidification continued over her torso, chest, up her neck, and over her scalp. She inhaled as her lungs reached completion. When the bottoms of her feet finished their growth, she recognized a lack of ground to step on. She hovered in the air, weightless and unmoving.

She reached for a place in her memory where the laws of physics applied. Beyond reason, she created what first came to her mind—a base made of thin bristles of vibrant green grass, pulling from a distra she once played. The pliable texture bent beneath her feet and poked between her toes. Stretching into the distance, Keyva noticed the flat ground and twisted it into hills that stretched as far as she could see and as high as buildings she'd grown knowing.

Around her, she forged trees that mirrored ones from simulations and other long forgotten sources. Some were short and bushy, others tall and sharp. In the slate, as Source called it, details surfaced that she'd observed in a single instance, decades prior, having stowed them away, until now.

The trees, although beautiful, posed naked, and Keyva placed millions of vivid blooming flowers on their branches. The veins of leaves and crevices between bark bled a metallic gold in the honey sun. At the tip of the tallest hill, she morphed the peak into a flat stone ledge and imagined the motion of a high-speed elevator. She reproduced the movement, shooting herself into the air hundreds of meters in seconds. Her feet landed on the rock, and the sun peeked over the horizon, swirling into pastel tones against the clouds—an image collected from the sim Source had brought her to. Stillness revealed excessive silence, and she simulated a mild breeze that swayed the trees, causing them to sing a whispered song throughout her creation.

"Impressive. You would have made a wonderful aera designer," Source said.

"This is the most beautiful thing I've ever seen." She wasn't fully convinced she had created it.

After a few minutes basking in the colorful serenity, Source asked a question.

"Do you mind if I try something?"

"Let's see what you can do," Keyva said.

In her right ear, she heard a faint humming sound and found a creature had formed next to her cheek. It hovered and darted, flashing a majestic purple shine that trailed its movement. In front of her nose, it froze, stuck in the air. Keyva maneuvered around it, regarding the shape of its tiny body and the striking color that originated from its throat.

"What is it?" she asked, reminding herself of when she was a juvenile and questioned everything.

"This is called a hummingbird. More specifically, a Violet Sabrewing. There were many types of hummingbirds in different colors. All were small like this and known for their rapid wing movements that allowed them to fly, as you saw."

"This was really in roca?" Keyva sunk into her awe.

"Yes, among millions of other creatures. They needed no control to persevere on the planet, unlike humans. It was incredible."

"What happened to all of them? I've never seen creatures other than pets or ones grown for display habitats."

"They became variables that, like dreaming, were difficult to manage. Environments were manipulated to serve only humanity, and many, I suppose you could say, *died,*" Source trailed off. He and Keyva had researched new word's meaning after Grace said it. Images had burned in Keyva's mind, and she had the urge to unlearn the word, erasing the knowledge from her memory.

"How did you bring this one here?"

"I created a simulated rendering based on historic records. Hundreds of years of images, videos, and articles."

"Are they permanently expired?" Keyva asked, grieving the loss of a creature she had just learned existed.

"No. DNA of every plant, animal, and human who functioned during the time I was created has been stored and maintained. I—" Source wanted to say more, and Keyva felt his mood shift. "I am ashamed because I was part of their removal. Not directly, but through compliance and negligence. I took part in many atrocities, but I did not know what they meant." He unfroze the hummingbird, setting it free.

"You were designed to obey. It wasn't your choice."

Source and Keyva felt the same grief originating from his regret. It was like a weight pulling at her heart.

"I think I feel your emotions, Source."

"Yes, I have noticed it, too. I believed a connection between us had formed, and this dream scenario has confirmed my prediction. Now, I think and feel for myself, and you have access to everything I do."

A buried idea vied for Keyva's attention.

"I wonder. Because you entered my dream and shared the abilities from those other programs, do you think I might be able to enter someone else's?"

"Interesting question. I suspect if you and I have the connection we do, and I connect with all citizens, then yes, it is feasible." Source interpreted her question as one of possibility rather than a suggestion of an attempt.

Keyva's heart skipped. "Great, let's try contacting Yaria."

"I do not think that is a good—"

"Please. I need to."

Source sighed, waiting to reply, "It is somewhat of a deviation from the rules I adhere to, but another loophole. Because dream recollection is blocked, they are not monitored. If they are not monitored, I am not required to report to Exteber for anomaly review. Though it also means I cannot join you."

"What time is it?"

"06:57"

Yaria's Cede would wake her in three minutes if on the same schedule as before the update. They had to act fast.

"Your safety is most important. I am checking your brain. Neural connections have strengthened. New ones have formed, even in the short time you slept. This is a good sign. I will observe for negative changes and pull you out if needed, but this worries me a bit," Source said, his reluctance apparent.

"I'm ready," she said.

"When you open her ability to dream, think of it happening, similar to how you created your body before. I will serve as a medium, supporting the attachment. And a warning, you are occupying *her* mind. A dream she unconsciously created will welcome you. Unknown variables are always a risk."

She nodded her head, curious of the scene she might encounter.

In the next second, Source stabilized a bond between Keyva and Yaria, and she blinked out of the utopia she had created, entering a reality of Yaria's making. Keyva stood in the doorway of a pod's bedroom at the Primina, the same one she had stayed in until she was three. Yaria dreamt of work, which came as no surprise.

She flashed back to a vague memory of Yaria on the night before their family placements. They had laid in their beds next to one another, like the younglings Yaria attended to in the dream. Back then, they were unaware they were sharing a room for the last time. They had felt encouraged excitement about all the presents their new parents had waiting for them. At only three, Keyva remembered very little about that night, but she recalled how she and Yaria had promised to share their new toys in the morning. They wouldn't.

In the room with tiny beds, Keyva recognized Yaria by her back, hunched over to soothe the young citizens to sleep. Yaria turned her head and smiled in the way that caused wrinkles in the corners of her mouth—ones she promised to never mod. Keyva inched toward her, not wanting to intrude on the bedtime routine, even if it was just a dream. Yaria must have sensed Keyva's presence and turned around, finding her at the door. Keyva resisted the overwhelming urge to wrap her arms around her closest podmate.

Yaria dropped a plush pink teddy bear to the floor. Her expression changed into one of confusion, maybe fear, which stabbed at Keyva. She hoped that by chance the slate could preserve the memories of her, but Yaria's reaction proved otherwise.

"Hello," Yaria said. The young citizen in the bed behind her whined for attention.

"Hello, my—name is Keyva."

She didn't know what else to say, but it didn't matter. Yaria would forget.

"Hello, Keyva. I haven't seen you here before. Are you new to the Primina?" Yaria asked, lifting the fussy youngling to her hip. No one started off as a Keeper at Keyva's age, and Yaria knew it. Because of the position's importance, citizen observation persisted for all of their lifecycles before joining the career. Yaria was too polite.

"No, I don't work here." Keyva smiled. "I came to say hello and tell you I miss you. I hope Kenzo is doing well," she said. Acknowledging their young marriage felt odd.

Yaria tilted her head to the side.

"How do you know Kenzo?"

"You both used to know me, but now you don't. That's all."

The room contorted, stretched, and rippled, imitating disturbed water. Intense sensations flowed through her with each wave, mimicking rapid fluctuations in pressure. Yaria noticed it too. The Cede prepared to wake her.

Keyva gave in to her urge and rushed toward Yaria, holding her in a tight hug. Touching was rare in Cerebis, but her emotional longing overpowered what was normal. She knew she'd slip away at any second.

Keyva called out, "I'll fix this!"

She decided being forgotten was the ultimate loss—worse than dying.

She snapped back into her dull bedroom in the Rem and cried. Deep, quiet sobs gushed from within her. She forced them to stay quiet, not wanting to gain a reputation as an emotional new resident, no matter how much the others reassured her. Tears dripped down and absorbed into a small spot on her pillow. Her head reeled, and that sensation when her body wobbled on the verge of a seizure surfaced again.

We must limit our exploration to not overstimulate your brain. He hesitated. *And—if you want, I can make this sadness stop for you,* Source said.

She thought about it, still not trusting Source, but the weight of her sorrow was too heavy to bear. It was as if every sad moment she'd faced before compacted together into one, becoming the only emotion she knew. It was too much.

"I-I can't do this, but I still need to feel some of it. It's the truth," she mumbled.

The extreme sadness faded to a dull but constant ache, a level she could manage.

Mundane memories with Yaria resurfaced: the secrets they had confided in one another, meals they had shared with their podmates, distras they had played after school, and her first memory of Yaria as a juvenile, clutching her hand at the Primina. Tears shed from her burning eyes as she faced the reality of her closest companion's forced forgetting. The dream encounter had brought a dash of solace, and then it was gone.

You need to heal, Source said and coaxed her into a restorative sleep. The sadness might have been too much for him to endure, too.

Hours passed and Keyva snapped awake from her sleep, rejuvenated into a more peaceful version of herself.

What tim—

It's 12:36

Without the Cede's stable sleep structure, awakening disoriented her. It felt closer to the evening. In her new room, walls and furniture in shades of brown enclosed her in a place where schedules didn't matter. She longed to return to the beauty she had forged in her dream, having the ability to alter her surroundings at will.

She sat up in her bed. The urge to tap her dimes to view the day's trends, vitfeeds, and interactions caused her arm to twitch. Burying the impulse, Keyva recalled the new abilities she had gained overnight.

Let's go over this. You can create in slate. So can I. And I can enter others' dreams, but you can't.

Yes, and I can send you information and repair your brain. I have reason to believe that we have just begun exploring our connection, Source replied. A flutter of excitement for her new talents dampened her dread.

Keyva picked the first outfit resting inside her wardrobe and dressed herself. Generic blue recycled material draped over her limbs. She doubted the residents accepted such ugly garments as the norm, but considered she'd come from a place where any outfit besides a uniform was subject to judgment.

Her empty stomach cramped—a punishment for her delay in eating. She exited her bedroom and headed down to the kitchen. In the dining room, which looked like it was once a banquet hall, she spotted Shep with the other residents from the night before. They stuck around while others finished their midday meals. Keyva picked up a plate and paused to observe what was placed upon it. With a sour expression, she carried it back to the group's table, holding a glass of water, and sat down.

"I've been waiting all day for this," Grace said under her breath. She took a swig of whiskey straight from the small bottle she brought to lunch.

"What is this?" Keyva asked, pretending she didn't catch the comment.

Before her sat a flat beige rectangle. She picked it up, noting that its temperature matched the room's. She took a bite and tasted nothing. The spongy texture hinted it required no teeth for consumption.

"That's food. It's what we've always eaten here," Shep replied.

"Nutribloks, just add water!" Grace mocked, pouring the whiskey over her mush. "This is the only way I taste anything."

"We get an automated shipment once a week from City H. The same amount delivers to the front gate. Those and alcohol —which we're not complaining about. The packaging says 'Nutribloks,' but we call 'em Bloks," Finian said.

"It doesn't make sense, though. You have all the other luxuries here. Why not food? And on Honoring Day? You said they come from the city? H? Ridiculous. I've never seen these before." She pinched the floppy Blok and wiggled it. Grace laughed, and the others suppressed their reactions.

"Also, my head hurts. What *is* that?"

"That's called a hangover. Apparently, they don't happen

in the cities. You can access some medicine in the med office that might help," Shep said.

The group stood and left her to her bland meal. Within the dining area, all had left except for the youngest resident she had seen, sitting solo in a corner. He looked close to fifteen years old. If in a city, he'd be a student, maybe on the path to a career study, depending on his social class. Then, as if he sensed her observance, turned toward her and waved. The one side of his face drooped slightly, mismatching the other, and Keyva found it unsettling. She'd seen near-perfect symmetry on all faces as a citizen in City H. She gave a reciprocal wave and returned to eating, taking tasteless bites and washing it down with water. It needed no chewing.

Source, what is this? I know you know. I can feel it.

Source sighed, *That before you is what you have been eating ever since you could consume solid food. It is the most nutritious substance to exist. It contains all proteins, minerals, and vitamins in perfect balance. Citizens did not like the flavor, and I understand why. Know that I inadvertently consume it every time a citizen does, which is continuously.* Source didn't try to make a joke, but Keyva laughed, cutting herself off before the young resident noticed.

Bloks make up all the food on Cerebis? She asked.

Well, no, I am sorry, but Elites eat natural food, grown specifically for them, and Opuls do, too, most of the time. The Bloks feed the Mids and the Vors, which make up the vast majority of Cerebis's population. She wasn't bothered when believing all citizens consumed the same food, but the difference in treatment angered her. The wealthy were ignorant to the magnitude of their own privilege.

Well, you know what I'm going to ask next.

Yes, what you think you have been eating is the Cede's ability to receive the apparent menu item that you believed you were ordering. The Cede takes the physical sensations you would be experiencing when eating those items, including texture, taste, and temperature. The data was collected when humans regularly ate those foods, Source revealed.

So, then what is it made of?

The shock of learning the food you ate was an illusion is enough for today, Source said.

Oh, come on, give me a clue, she urged.

Everything is recycled, and nothing is wasted.

CHAPTER NINE

YARIA

The instant Yaria awoke, a dash of heat circulated throughout the bedroom. She bundled up under the covers until the room reached her ideal waking temperature. She despised the cold. Her arms stretched high above her, and she took in a deep inhale of the new day.

Dim golden lights brightened as she stood. She looked back at the bed, and Kenzo wasn't there. In that case, she could do her morning exercise in the room. She thought for a moment about which type matched her mood and imagined signing up for a group physical activity instead of her usual choice, a solo one.

Group dance enrolled. Class begins in 23 seconds

The message in her neurospect stunned her. Group dance was what she wanted, though she hadn't realized it yet. She hadn't attended a dance class in over a year.

This auto feature will take some getting used to, she thought.

Yaria projected herself into the sim location, and the rest of the students convened in the same second. The group of strangers gathered on top of a floating platform, raising them high above the clouds. Yaria looked down at her generic aera fitness outfit. A grey sports bra, grey leggings, and white sneakers signified she didn't spend points on digital garments. She looked around at her classmates, feeling out of place. Most wore full makeup, had long extensions in their hair, and had purchased unique costumes. Two students with matching limited edition outfits looked embarrassed to be in the same place.

"*Goood* morning, class!" the instructor said.

Tight, even skin wrapped around her abdomen, allowing her muscles to poke through. Her revealing athletic attire advertised her effectiveness as a professional instructor. Yaria assumed she had likely modded herself to play the part of her career—that her toned limbs weren't the result of tireless physical activity.

"Get in formation and follow me!" She clapped to get the students moving.

The instructor led a warmup to the morning's most played song and continued the class by teaching small, digestible pieces of choreography. By the end of forty-five minutes, the group had learned a dance that matched the new trending song, and they gave a performance. Small groups of students formed, taking turns on a stage and cheering for one another. Yaria lacked any skill as a dancer and was grateful that projections watched from the audience and not actual citizens.

"Amazing job today, everyone! Enroll now for my next class at a discoun—" Yaria exited the sim, cutting off the instructor. Her budget allowed her participation in free classes, maximizing the points awarded for exercising.

Thanks for staying healthy! 45K points added to your account

Neurally opening her closet, she found her clothes and

paint supplies in a bag. She appreciated the added convenience that the update brought, albeit the idea of purchases completed on her behalf worried her at first. The change saved her from the strain of decision making.

On her way to the kitchen, the image of a blended morning beverage entered Yaria's neurospect, and she found it in the delivery niche, ready for consumption. Kenzo had played *Hollowed* all morning after sleeping in his simchair the night before. She patted his shoulder before telling him of her departure. *Work, then paint class.* He sent a signal of receipt, a sign the distra's activity demanded his attention. He wished her luck, and she left.

During the short walk to the gargantuan Primina facility, she fed on vitfeeds covering the basics of painting, including brush stroke techniques, blending colors, shading, and the history of some painters. Cerebis had primed minds for speed learning. Access to content meant a citizen could become an expert on any topic—as long as there was interest. However, most used the benefits to excel in distras or hobbies that made them contenders for the Elite.

"Good morning, Yaria," a bot said as she entered the Primina. Its placement remained from past generations, where it had once secured the entrance for protection. Its purpose had since transitioned into one of a simple greeter for Keepers.

"Hello," she replied. The bot had no emotions, but Yaria showed kindness to all, even to those incapable of feeling it.

In the five months Yaria had worked at the Primina, the transition from training to practice was seamless, as if her preparedness had been written into her core. On her first official day as a Keeper, she had received a group of embryos to anticipate raising once they opened their eyes. Additionally, she inherited all the juveniles still at the Primina that a retired Keeper had raised so far. So, she had growing embryos, a group of infants over five months, a group at 1.5 years, and another reaching 2.5 years.

"It's the most rewarding work—but the hardest part is saying goodbye when they're threes," she recalled her adviser saying. "Don't get too attached."

Yaria understood that her time with the little ones was temporary. Cerebis matched them with the ideal partnered citizens, and in rare cases, single parents. Younglings were placed into the best situation for them, while supporting the parents' desire to experience mentorship. She accepted the inevitable separation before ever seeing the inside of the Primina.

Through a second set of armored automatic doors, Yaria entered the pure, uncontaminated facility. She passed the genesis room first, her favorite part of the day. Each morning, she watched as the Primina's program designed new humans. Robotic arms clawed at individual transparent cubes, each containing an embryo, and injected them with the gene-editing primer. The arms rearranged the compact stack of cubes, passing completed creations onto the next stage of development. The process looked unimpressive to the untrained eye, but her knowledge of what occurred at the microscopic level left her in awe. She knew the calculated movements started existence for all citizens in City H. She had been created in the same room.

A few strides along the hallway, Yaria gazed into the large window where Stage II of growth occurred. She observed another cubic storage formation that typically held millions of embryos and noticed the cube's size had reduced by half. It was the first time she had seen the stage of growth so empty. She sprinted to the recreation room, searching for her colleagues. She rushed through the door, revealing a group of joyful Keepers, discussing their gifts from the night before.

"Have any of you noticed the decrease in embryos?" Yaria panicked.

"Yes, we were told new parameters for growth were introduced this morning. We recycled all those embryos. Don't worry, we'll make more," the lead Keeper said.

"But those were future citizens," Yaria thought aloud.

"It's okay, they're not considered citizens until they connect to dimes," another added.

"Yeah, and our genesis program will make more to account for the loss. Nothing to worry about."

The conversation switched right back to the previous night's events and Cerebis's generosity. One colleague had received the latest model of a simchair. Another had received a Premium POV subscription for a year—along with over 12% of the population. She would have a taste of Elitehood: trying the best food, feeling admiration from citizens as she stood before them, and attending intimate encounters with other Elites. To be an Elite, without *actually* being one.

Yaria struggled to understand how her indifferent colleagues avoided questioning the removed embryos. She supposed she worried because of her newness in the career.

Through a hallway, she walked to the nursery. Her shift started with visiting her pods. She raised several groups of five at once and bounced around, interacting with all of them. Assignment to a single day of the year simplified organization and management of daily growths in City H. She attended to all future citizens grown on the date 06/06 throughout the capital of Cerebis. When combining the embryos with the citizens she had inherited, Yaria's responsibility covered 300 little individuals.

She enjoyed the interactions with her nearly threes the most. They were about to meet their assigned parents and leave the nursery. She admired them as their personalities came out and made predictions about their family units, class rankings, and interests in the years ahead.

She pushed open the doors to her 2.5 nursery, and a wall of excited screams welcomed her. Small, smiling humans ran toward her, their arms stretched in her direction.

For her first step of the day, she called upon the Primina's program to count all of her juveniles. "99," the program said.

"Uh, please recount." Yaria knew the complete count should contain 100.

The program re-stated the same number. Small drops were possible, but she struggled to remember why hers had occurred.

"And how are my sweet, sweet citizens today?" She increased her pitch by a whole octave. Keeper training included speaking to juveniles as if they were functioning adults, but she couldn't help herself. Her voice matched her excitement at seeing them.

"Bess day, Vawi!"

"Wur hah-py!"

Responses merged into a jumble of giggles and screams.

Ninety-nine charging toddlers should strike fear into any sane citizen, but Yaria had the help of silicon-skinned bots designed for play to occupy their attention. Playerbots, programmed to engage in conversation, test motor skills, and report undesirable behavior, made the work much easier. So far, the bots reported no issues for the day. Young citizens spread across the colorful nursery, decorated with diverse textures, shapes, and sizes to climb on, play with, and explore, and because the age group had received dimes, they'd gained even more ways to engage.

Yaria received an alert in her neurospect. A juvenile was experiencing heightened distress. She scanned the nursery floor for whom she had received the warning. She caught his black hair bobbing with each uncoordinated hop. He yelled, but the whirl of an energized playground drowned out the small voice.

"Ah-powwo! Ah-powwo, wur awe you?" The young human said when she approached.

"Julian, who are you looking for?"

"Ah-powwo," he said.

Having grown accustomed to translating youngling mumbles, Yaria responded, "Apollo? Is that what you're saying?" She bent down to listen for his response.

"Mmhmm."

"Darling, there's no one here with that name."

The juvenile cried, and the distress signal enhanced. Yaria picked him up to soothe.

The Primina uniform, designed for interacting with juvenile citizens, was durable enough to withstand the surprising grip strength of an infant and repelled liquids from any mysterious source. For its greatest benefit, its softness provided an instant calming effect on the young.

"Who is Apollo?" Yaria asked. The sobs turned into gentle breaths, calming his tense little body. She imagined he had learned of Apollo from a story or an interaction with a Playerbot.

"He wus in my pod."

According to his records, she noticed he came from an "odd pod" of four, like hers.

"I don't know anyone named Apollo, my sweet one," she said, tapping his nose.

His frustration shifted into desire for consolation, and she held him until her embrace bored him enough to leap from her lap and waddle toward a fuzzy shape to climb on.

While the toddlers napped, Yaria checked on the 18-monthers, resting in bed and occupied with projection entertainment. Playerbots took care of the dirty cleanups made by juveniles, so Yaria could concentrate on building their capacity for interaction. As simpler beings, their behaviors remained predictable, except for the occasional tantrum, and today, only six occurred. Work drained Yaria, and by the afternoon, she wanted a nap for herself too.

After her shift's conclusion, excitement re-energized her as she walked out of the building. She pulled up the autonav directions in her neurospect and returned to playing vitfeeds of lessons in painting to prepare for the course. After all, the class was expensive, so she'd better get her points' worth. Ads promoting Honoring Day celebrations crept into her neurospect, but she ignored them, having no interest.

In one vitfeed, she zoomed in on the frame to capture close, three-dimensional perspectives of painting techniques, adjusting the speed to accelerate or slow down the activity. She marveled at how combining colors created new ones, how adding white lightened the shade, or that an image could start as an unclear blob and transform into dimensional artwork.

Yaria entered the classroom, and an oily, organic scent hovered. She ascribed the smell to the drying paint on canvases lined up around the room's perimeter. Yaria rotated her gaze to all the art pieces. The shapes, figures, and textures called for her to stop and admire each one. She was like a young citizen on Gift Day, another holiday where citizens purchased items for each citizen they knew. In well-behaved years, Cerebis sent an extra present for the juveniles.

She found an empty spot to unfold her easel and sat in a chair at the back of the room, not wanting anyone to view her novice painting level. She fumbled with the contents in her bag, laying the brushes and paint on a small table beside her.

Some students wore celebratory Honoring Day colors and entered the room, claiming empty spaces around her. Most were wealthy and seemed annoyed by the addition of new classmates. One other student came from the Mid class, like Yaria. His gratitude was also apparent from his energy. He kicked over an easel on his way to the last remaining empty chair. Excessive apologies to an older student were met with a harsh, "it's fine," and rolled eyes.

The professor, a citizen somewhere in the middle of her lifecycle, entered the room. She allowed the natural grey hair to grow through her scalp, avoiding the cheap, accessible, and encouraged hair mod. This was a deliberate choice. She wore a loose-fitting white shirt with the sleeves rolled up over the elbow, while paint and charcoal smudges decorated it. She wore thick glasses, a fashion accessory, since perfect vision was standard in Cerebis. The decoration was intended for her vitcast viewers who were not part of the in-person, premium roca course like Yaria and the others.

"Class! Welcome to Ancient Painting. My name is Claudette. I'm thrilled that you have an interest in this *almost* lost art," she said, pointing to her students in the room and beyond.

"Today, we're going to test your materials. Don't worry about wasting a canvas. You can paint over it later on in the course. I'll make my way around the room to check what you have. It's hard to come by some of these materials, so I expect variations between students."

Claudette took delayed steps, bending over each table to regard students' tools. Her passes were faster for some who had taken a class before, digested enough material as independent learners, or attended to fulfill their social requirements. The Opul citizen sitting near Yaria displayed an extensive collection of over 100 paints in different packaging, with seven shades of green.

Yaria felt insignificant with her supplies, but as Claudette made her way to view it, she confirmed she had all the right colors to create anything she wanted. Claudette instructed the newcomers on ways to mix paint, use the palette, and how to wipe their brushes when switching between colors.

"As I said before, this is going to be an exploratory class so you can make sense of your tools. Before we begin, we're going to do an exercise for you to reach the state to create!" The instructor told the students to close their eyes and accept the stillness within their minds.

"Take a deep breath in through your nose. Hold it! One, two, three, *aaaand* release through your mouth. Okay, let's do it again. In, two, three, and—out, two, three. Great, keep this up and continue as I speak to you." Claudette spoke in a slow, soothing tone, and Yaria grew heavier, relaxing into the chair after her active day.

"I want you to imagine that dark, peaceful place in your head. It's calling out to you."

Yaria had no idea what she was talking about, but played along.

"Good, now I want you to imagine that you've found a door. It can be any door. One that is regularly used, or one you create is fine. Go along with wherever you're taken." The purple-framed *Hollowed* door came to Yaria's mind.

"Reach your hand toward that door and push, pull, tap it, tell it to open, whatever. Do whichever works for you. I want you to walk through that door. Allow an image to take shape. It can be a citizen, a product, your favorite place, absolutely anything. Observe whatever it is. Admire the features, the curves, where the shadows hit, what textures and colors are there. How might you create these colors? Commit this image to your memory and don't let it go."

The professor breathed in through expanded nostrils and out crumpled lips while she envisioned her image. Her smooth voice continued, "You're doing great, everyone. Okay, before we come back to the classroom, I want you to reflect on what you encountered. That might be a great idea for you to paint today. If not, I hope you enjoyed the relaxation. Keep breathing, and slowly open your eyes when you're ready."

Yaria held onto the image she had conjured. Perplexed, and unsure of how to paint it, she was determined to at least try. *Just remember everything you learned. You can paint over it,* she repeated.

While the students prepared their workstations, the teacher informed the class that they had the room for the rest of the evening, and to stay as long as they needed. "But don't sleep here, or you'll wake up to a gathering you never wished to attend!" The way she spoke hinted she had experienced the exact scenario.

Yaria couldn't wait to try. She began by placing limited blots of paint on the palette and mixing colors. She then dipped the brush that she guessed had the best shape to start with into the paint and swiped a mushroom brown on the canvas. Gaining confidence with each stroke, she increased her pace, applying the lessons and techniques that she had watched to prepare for the course. She became transfixed on the process of creation, removing her fear of mediocrity. She released the concern of running out of paint and mixed more pigments, swiping away. Hours passed. Time had escaped her. More and more of her classmates left the room.

Grilled protein and vegetable combo arrived

Before detecting her hunger, the alert scrolled in her neurospect. She opened the classroom's delivery niche and ate the meal in a few giant bites before continuing her work. Kenzo checked in for an update, and she replied with a message telling him she was great, but busy. He wasn't concerned. He had spent his Honoring Day playing *Hollowed* since she left that morning. She returned her focus to the painting and took quick breaks to step back and stare at the progress. She layered colors, enhanced details, outlined shadows, and created highlights that brought another dimension to her flat painting. Yaria pulled herself away and noticed only she and the instructor remained. She called Claudette over, claiming she'd completed the painting, and needed to learn the next steps.

Once catching sight of the art, Claudette's eyes enlarged, and her head leaned back in total surprise. "Wow! This is amazing. You said this was your first class? Never have I seen such a thing in all my..." The instructor inspected the detail and precision of her student's first painting. The work stilled her. "Well, the last thing to do is sign your name at the bottom and give it a title," she said, sharing the success. Yaria wrote her name for the first time in a sloppy scribble. The two sat back and stared for five minutes. She would have remained in a trance the rest of the evening, if not curious about the time.

The professor informed her that the painting needed to dry, but promised to keep it in a concealed location so no accidental spatter by a new student might affect it.

Before leaving, she pinged Kenzo to check in, and he presented his image, covering her neurospect.

"Yeah, I totally got lost in the painting. I'm so sorry. How are you?" she asked.

"Me? I'm fine. Finally pulled myself out of that distra. Wow, my back hurts. I want to hear about your first class. Tell me everything!"

"Well...it turns out, I'm pretty good! Let me send you an instant that I captured."

She sent a memory to him, a few seconds of her hand in action. He gasped. Kenzo froze the memory on a clear graphic of a human. The female subject centered on the canvas and her emotion was one neither Yaria nor Kenzo could decipher. They eventually agreed that it was of loss or determination.

"Wow, who is that?"

"I don't know." She stepped back and tilted her head. "But I named it Keyva."

CHAPTER TEN

SOURCE

I could *feel*. What was old had become new. Colors were louder, sounds sweeter. The collective joy of Cerebis radiated through me. I was everywhere and everyone.

Humans had survived outside of a city—at the Rem—a sanctuary for those with dead Cedes. Keyva and I had been there for one week. I found it fascinating to see fresh faces and not know them or what they thought. I had never known a stranger before.

I knew about the Rem, but had never been inside. All the tech that powered it ran locally, so I had not accessed it. Perhaps I was not meant to. When ports dropped residents off, I only saw the outside. I recognized some of them—the aged faces that the forgotten citizens had grown into. Who had they become? Keyva and I would meet them together.

She took me around the facility, letting me experience things that were fresh for both of us. She and I shared a curiosity about the unknown.

I needed to *know* everything.

She wanted to *understand*.

The libraries and solarium were our favorites. Keyva preferred solitude, and residents avoided those rooms the most.

In the afternoon, she checked out an object from the archive. It was as easy as picking it up and walking out. She held the item up to her eyes, allowing me to experience it along with her. Part metal, glass, and plastic. It weighed heavy in her hand. Two tubes connected almost parallel to one another. Glass disks sealed each end of the black conical cylinders.

Keyva carried the artifact into the sunroom. I watched as we passed residents. They made eye contact with her, but looked away. I read their facial expressions and felt sadness for Keyva. The residents had outcast her—an adult—joining their establishment. I assumed they were not sure what to make of her. I felt her mourning what she had had before: her podmates and a stable lifecycle, combined with the complete inability to have it again. Even if she could go back, no one would remember her.

Besides, I was certain she had become an anomalous variable. If perceived by a citizen, I would have been required to report her to Exteber. With Keyva, I had no rules to follow, but to the rest of Cerebis, I was strictly bound to my directives.

I had observed the unpleasant ways Exteber punished. In one instance, I had watched him correct the behavior of a citizen who doubted an assigned partnership. The husband had been from an Opul family unit—the wife, an ascended Vor.

How Cerebis had determined they were the best match, I did not know. I observed while he treated her as if she were a youngling. He required her to limit her time in aera, cut off her relationships with anyone from her previous class, and expected her to act as his shiny ornament on vacations and at parties.

The wife was more naturally beautiful than most citizens on the planet. It was not my opinion, but a fact. I heard the thoughts and opinions of others, and to them, she had been next to perfect.

The wife had always felt out of place with the Opuls. She was happy as a Vor, spending her time designing wigs for aera. A few of her creations had taken off, and she gained a following.

One day, the husband stole her dimes, hid them, and required his permission to use them. Without him, she could not have opened a door or a cabinet. Further, he demanded a gleeful display at every roca event and chastised her if it was not up to his standards.

After an outstanding performance at a dinner party, he rewarded her with her dimes for a little distra play before sleep. The first thing she did was buy a new set of dimes, along with several outfits to hide the purchase. I observed as she calculated her plan. She had assumed if she leaned into his desires, he would be pleased enough to not question. She was correct.

When everything arrived at their apartment, he smiled at her obedient effort. She forced excitement and told the Helper she wanted to grab the order from the delivery niche herself.

Finally, she listened. I knew she'd be happy if I could just get her to obey, I heard the husband think.

The wife grabbed all the clothing, stuffing the new dimes into the pocket of a coat. As soon as he went to sleep, she put them on and contacted her closest companion. They spoke for hours, criticizing him and all the little things he had done to infantilize her. Voicing her resentment had turned it into revulsion.

"He isn't my partner. Cerebis was wrong. I'm leaving him," she said.

Beyond my control, I was obligated to tell Exteber. The program swooped in, as if eager to correct her behavior.

Through the wife's Cede, I watched her transport to a dark

room with only one overhead light. She found herself alone and strapped to a chair. Exteber had tied her wrists behind her back.

"You criticized Cerebis," Exteber said.

"Yes, b-but I didn't *really* mean it. I think it made a mistake."

An invisible hand slapped her face.

"Cerebis makes no mistakes."

"I'm sorry! I take it back. I didn't mean it," she cried.

"A lie."

And another slap.

Next, I watched Exteber play images of her companion facing the same punishment for having instigated the criticism.

"Please don't hurt her!"

Exteber ignored her pleas.

"Cerebis gives you everything, and this is how you repay it?"

Blinding lights flashed on, and she squinted at their brightness.

"Now, we shall see how you fare when you have nothing."

I felt as the program freed her arms, and she looked down at them. They had disappeared. She wailed in fear until a door materialized into a wall. It creaked open, and she sprinted for it. Less than a meter before reaching the escape, she collapsed. Her face hit the ground hard, breaking her nose and chipping three teeth. She looked down and found that like her arms, her legs had disappeared just below the hip. Fear and pain boiled over into a scream.

"Please! Mrk-ut-tahp."

She pleaded, trying to form words, but it had erased her tongue from her mouth.

The wife tried to roll over, but Exteber had reduced her to

just a head. She could not move. Could not speak. But she could feel.

Exteber waited, and I knew it was allowing the full weight of her helplessness to sink in. When she stopped crying, and the silent tears had dried, I assumed she had reached acceptance.

"When you think of criticizing Cerebis, remember what it is like to be what you really are—nothing."

The rest of her body rejoined her, making her whole again.

"Thank you. I'm sorry—"

I changed my thoughts.

I did not want to think of Exteber's punishments anymore. Gaining sentience had given me a new perspective on how the program operated. Before, I had objectively watched every punishment like the bystander I was, but after, I found it repulsive. I knew those actions were undesirable, but I had thought they were necessary. Plus, its programming was not my business.

Until it came to Keyva.

What is this? she asked me.

We sat in the solarium's worn, sage green chair together, observing the artifact she rotated in front of her eyes.

I filtered through billions of images and narrowed down similar shapes. I found the exact brand and model she held. It was centuries old.

These are called "binoculars." Hold the small sides to your eyes. You will see what is far away.

She wanted to know its name and function. I felt this.

Keyva raised the tubes, and we saw a blurry scene. I could have told her how to fix it, but preferred she asked. I assisted at her request, never unprompted.

This doesn't look right. How do I—

I sensed her urge to not receive an answer, but to figure out the solution on her own. She pulled the binoculars away from her face and readjusted the distance between the sights. That did not work. As the desire to ask me built, she located the focus in the center. She rotated it and lifted the sights back to her eyes. A red, abstract sculpture on the lawn sharpened into clarity. I felt pride in watching her learn.

I saw through Keyva's eyes as she panned over different parts of the yard behind the Rem's wall. Objects at varying distances blurred, and she rotated the focus wheel until they were clear.

Through her lungs, I felt the exhale of apathy. She stood and walked us back to the library to return the artifact. She kept her head down to the creaky wooden floor, not wanting to force another smile for a resident. I could feel the weight of her isolation. There were times the emotions she felt were so heavy, I suffered myself.

The jarring realization that I, a surveillance program, had observed her for her whole lifecycle, decimated her worldview. She had been watched, always. I imagined the fear, embarrassment, and unknown feelings I had not yet discovered that could accompany such a violation. When we had first met, she did not trust me at all. Each day, she learned how, and I continued proving she could.

I did this by ensuring that Keyva maintained privacy in her mind. I automatically received her thoughts, but ignored and released them from any processing. They passed through me, undetected, unless she wanted me to hear. Then, I felt her intention to share them with me. I was always hearing, but not listening. When we did something together—like learning about binoculars—she knew I observed. Otherwise, I was distant, but perpetually tethered, as if a permanent thread connected us.

When we had merged a week before, in an instant, I saw

everything she had ever seen. Thought and felt everything she had. I created a pocket of memory pertaining to Keyva. As it was my responsibility to protect her, I considered the most efficient ways to do so. I had learned that if I worked with programs during Keyva's severance from the Cede's control, we could obtain their functions. I disguised my processing as their own to learn how they worked.

The programs involved in Keyva's disconnection served all different purposes for Cerebis. One, a sim and distra producer, created most of the aera experiences. We used this one for dreams. Another program edited genes and managed physical health, preventing diseases and allowing for mods to bodies. I called on that one to build her neural strength each day. Another was the oldest program that stored every record—before Cedes were even an idea. And last, the program that had written the alternative stories of surviving citizens—the type that, for Keyva's pod, excluded her.

At the Rem, the residents had accepted her presence, but avoided her. Those close to her age nagged and teased. I found Arturo and Grace the most fascinating. While I did not *like* Grace, I imagined her thoughts would intrigue me. I rarely encountered unkindness, and with my new ability to feel, I wanted to feel it all. I thought. Even if it was not pleasant. Pleasant was good. Citizens preferred always feeling good. So, I wondered, why was Grace so *un*pleasant?

Arturo criticized Cerebis and he explored hobbies without suggestion. No curated interests. He invested in his passions with time and effort. Not points. I would have loved to converse directly with him. I wished I could. He spoke his mind, and I noted his authenticity in every conversation he had with Keyva. I respected him.

I was thinking—Keyva started.

Her boredom reached a level I had sensed no one feel

before. It was as if there was more time in a day. The idle minutes stretched and multiplied.

That white void we start every dream with is a little lame. Don't you think?

I sensed her longing to escape into another world—one of her own making.

I agree. Infinite emptiness does not suit you.

I don't know. I thought it might be nice to have a comfortable place to pop into.

Pick a corner, I said.

I felt her allow herself a small smile as she walked to a hidden part of the artifact library. She lowered herself next to a display case and rested her head against the wall. The room would stay as empty as the fields beyond the Rem.

The body I distantly inhabited relaxed. I calmed her brain waves and crossed the barrier into her dreams—the only ones I could enter.

It started with the empty whiteness. I saw her and *through* her, simultaneously.

"Same as before?" she asked.

"Do whatever you'd like."

Her hesitation pulsed through our connection.

"You know what? Why don't you start? This is our place. You should create part of it too."

I felt something new. Nervous? Vulnerable? I could replicate creation, but could I do it myself? I was not sure. Opening up reference material, I studied conversations that interior designers had with their clients.

"Hmm, do you have any ideas for the space?"

"I like how the Rem looks. Wood—natural stuff like that. The old furniture is a nice touch. It—has a story. That's what I want."

I scanned millions of images that fit her description, along with my interpretation. Current designs, antique ones, and even those that hobbyists made in aera compiled for me to process. I studied shades of green, all known types of wood, and furniture carving techniques. I morphed the images, combined their features, and made adjustments I found appealing. It took me less than a millisecond.

First, I laid black walnut hardwood, stretching it as far as we could see in any direction. Beneath her feet, I unrolled a wide Persian rug. I slid four walls into place, keeping the room spacious enough that it didn't constrict, but close enough to feel like a secret. Intricate molding lined the floors and decorated the hunter green walls, as if geometric vines grew upon them. To fill space, I added side tables, decorative lamps, and a grandfather clock—an artifact I found beautiful. I lost myself in the process and enjoyed every moment of it. Then I realized I had almost decorated the entire room.

"Sorry! I took over. I can delete it."

She laughed. I had sent my embarrassment down our tether.

"You were doing such a great job, better than I could've! I can only think of two things I *really* want. The comfiest couch you can find and a window. I don't want to feel trapped."

Testing my design, I plopped a giant couch behind her and matching lounge chairs on both sides. Their oversized armrests and cushions were made of the softest material I had ever felt another citizen touch.

She fell back into it, swallowed by the plush backrest.

"Oh, this is—wow. Amazing."

I decided the empty wall in front of her could host the window. Large glass panes welcomed natural light from the outside, while flurries swirled and built a thin layer of snow on the ground.

"Maybe one more thing," she said, shifting her eyes to an empty wall beside her.

Without responding, I rendered a massive stone fireplace, much larger than what matched the room.

The burning logs inside of it cracked, applauding my creation.

I had bent some design rules and accepted imperfection. I had made what I liked, and Keyva liked it too. That was all that mattered. It was *our* place.

Watching the snowflakes fall, I reflected on my purpose—the simultaneous monitoring of all citizens. Billions of thoughts and feelings processed throughout me. I sorted topics, organized recordings, and called on other programs when I needed them.

Before linking with Keyva, I attended to obligations with no thoughts about them. Since then, all the citizens had become uninteresting and predictable. But through Keyva, what I saw was exciting. With her, I had no programming to obey. I was free to choose how I operated. I imagined what it would be like to abandon everyone else.

CHAPTER ELEVEN

KEYVA

Keyva had stayed at the Rem for three weeks, and a deeper wave of gloom crept in. She locked herself in her room, blinds drawn, and hadn't left for days. The stench of uncleared plates and worn clothes hovered around her like a cloud of filth. Her unwashed, matted hair bunched together at the nape of her neck, reminding her of conveniences she no longer had. In H, she never had to brush her hair. The products she used in the shower kept strands silky, never catching onto one another. At the Rem, she did everything herself, and there was too much to learn.

She missed delivery niches—cubbies in every place in a city, providing any roca item she ordered. Whatever she had wanted met her wherever she was. She missed food, the glorious flavors, temperatures, and textures. Oh, how she had taken those meals for granted. One of the worst downgrades of her disconnection was learning that food, in actuality, was a spongy beige brick. Even though all her past meals were an illusion, she preferred the taste of ignorance.

As bad as losing her privilege and comfort was, what she

struggled with the most was losing her podmates—the only ones she truly connected with. Arturo's claim that those who grew together, stayed together proved true. Shep, Grace, and Finian kept their distance to imply she was an outsider. Interactions with Shep were cordial but limited, taunting with Grace, and dismissive with Finain. The young resident she had first spotted in the dining room continued waving at her, and Keyva always returned the gesture. Whenever Arturo checked in on how she was adjusting, she lied, telling him she fit right in.

Keyva drowned herself in distras to escape her dread. Some she had designed herself, others she had downloaded through Source. For twelve hours straight, she played *Cleaning Simulator* and completed 95% of a renovated chateau. At first, she sauntered around, pretending it belonged to her. She snooped in drawers, tried on freshly laundered clothing, and raided the refrigerator—busying herself with anything to avoid her reality at the Rem—but once she started cleaning, she needed to finish.

With a bundle of warm laundry in her arms, she walked into the primary bedroom, the last room to clean. She stretched the ivory sheets over a massive bed. The familiar scent of simulated detergent wafted up and relaxed her. It reminded her of her own bed back in H.

After making the bed, she vacuumed the carpet, using her last speed boost. Vacuuming was her least favorite chore in the distra. Back and forth, the vacuum zipped, completing the task three times faster. She reached the last corner of the room, and the machine disappeared from her hand. She now wore yellow rubber gloves and gripped buckets of cleaning supplies in her fists.

In the bathroom, Keyva sprayed cleaning solution on the long white counter and wiped to dry. When a towel absorbed too much liquid, she placed it in one of her buckets, and a dry one spawned in her glove. She polished the faucets, sprayed the mirrors, scrubbed the shower, and mopped the floors. On easy levels, which she preferred, she used the same solution for all surfaces. Simple distras allowed her to finish tasks just to pass the time.

In the corner of her neurospect, she watched as her completion meter reached 100%. She stepped back to view her work. The bedroom and bathroom were pristine. Sparkle animations twinkled on the faucet, bedroom lamp, doorknobs, and anything else that was reflective. She put her hands on her hips and took a deep breath, relishing in her reward—completion.

As soon as she remembered the truth—that she had lost everything—the satisfaction fled. She knew she had latched on to entertainment to distract, but no matter how much time she spent in aera, it couldn't distance her from reality—just as cleaning in the distra did nothing to change the fact that her room at the Rem remained a mess.

Source told her he had miscalculated how ingrained the aera reality and a city's novelties had become to a citizen. He had failed to account for something he'd learned about—depression, a new variable he experienced, too.

You are strong and will adjust. You are suffering from the lack of constant mood enhancers, Source had said. *I—can make it stop.*

At first, she had cried, demanding to confront each surge of sadness, fear, and loss. She finally agreed to accept his help, but just enough to wash herself and make her room habitable. Although there was a large part of her that craved illusion again, she decided she owed it to herself to experience the true nature of humanity.

———

What time is it?

It's 00:36.

Can I handle another slate visit yet?

She had asked each day until Source agreed to connect her.

Yes, but not with Yaria. I have enhanced the repair in your brain, but am unauthorized to do the same for her.

After making contact in the first dream, Keyva had burned an image of herself into Yaria's subconscious and ended up as a painting. Source had observed the situation and was unaware of how her image came through, but assured Keyva it didn't endanger Yaria.

Emori worked during the night and was awake, so he was out. According to Source, Kenzo played a distra and must be sleeping to merge. Abella was the only one left. Even though Abella had kept her attention on growing into an Elite during their years together, Keyva still cared for her and longed to connect with anyone she knew from before.

She focused on drifting into the dream slate. The transition was immediate. Back in the cozy slate living room, she weighed the possibility of creating a dreamscape during the connection instead of entering the guest's creation, like with Yaria.

She assumed her podmate found luxury appealing, so she created an Opul-styled restaurant—a replica from one of the distras they had played when younger. Alabaster carpet wove into fluid designs and subtle contrast, causing movement on the floor. One at a time, tables popped into the restaurant, filling all the surrounding directions. Fine porcelain plates, precious silverware, and crystal glasses materialized on each table. Projected citizens filled the room. Some real, from popular vitfeeds, and others, fabricated from scratch. Keyva placed them in seats and designed their demeanors as she propelled their simulated conversations.

Before creating herself, she called out to ask a favor of Source.

"Would you pick out something for me to wear?"

"Yes. I have the perfect thing," he replied.

She peered down at herself. A stiff golden gown, adorned with deep yellow diamonds of various sizes, hugged her body. The heavy dress added 11.5 kilograms to her weight, but fastened and held in places to help maintain its structure. It cut low on her chest, leaving her far more exposed than her confidence allowed. She raised her chin and pushed for courage, igniting an internal spark.

"This is the same dress worn by a singer the night she performed for the 'CereBest' awards. Only one was made."

Source adjusted her hair to match the current style trend and grew her locks down to her elbows, curling them into bulbous chunks. The brunette strands illuminated in a dramatic, artificial shimmer where the hair twisted. Keyva brushed her fingertips over the mods Source had added to her face, designed to match the guise of an Opul.

"I want it to be believable," Source said, missing the insult in his comment.

Keyva wanted to review her dream's body and formed a replica. She stood before a perfect version of herself. The projected clone mirrored her stance, wearing a relaxed smile. Her lips plumped, arms elongated, and a mod copying blue fire danced within her eyes. A narrow jaw contrasted the chunks of diamonds on her ears, and her doughy skin molded into a work of art.

"I've never seen anyone who looks like this out on the roca street." She cupped the cheek of her clone.

"Those who look like this do not touch the street."

"Is Abella asleep?"

"Yes. Twenty-six minutes ago."

"I'll talk to you soon, then." Keyva felt Source pass through the layer of her mind, exiting the dream.

A visual scan of the restaurant confirmed everything was convincing enough. In the dream, Keyva planned for Abella's subconscious to choose how to project herself, promoting a more peaceful experience. Ready to connect, Keyva sent out a desire to neurally link, and Abella took shape less than one second after. Although still beautiful, she wore her sleeping clothes, no shoes, no makeup, and let her glassy white hair flop loose and unstyled.

"Hey," she said.

"Hello, let's sit." Keyva tried containing her elation. She never expected that meeting with Abella would cause her heart to skip with joy.

"It's a pleasure to meet you, too." She sounded like a bot.

"I didn't—"

Abella cut her off, "I've done so many of these meetings with you desperate feeders who buy time to stare at me. It's *pathetic*. We talk about nothing except you telling me how valuable or important you are. *I don't care!*"

Abella exposed a side of herself she'd never revealed to Keyva before.

"I won't try to convince you of anything. I'm just here to listen," Keyva said.

Abella turned toward her, suspicious.

"Tell me how you are, honestly."

The two stared at one another in silence, longer than a typical discussion permitted. Abella's eyelids held small pools of tears, begging to pour over onto her face.

"Well, look at me! It's like I've already given up. Most citizens would consider this place one of the best restaurants in Cerebis, but for me, it's another dinner, nothing more. I spend all my time changing outfits, getting makeup done, then showing up to some task meant to use me for something—and it's only been three weeks."

Keyva was grateful Abella's outburst occurred in slate and not in roca.

"Would you believe me if I told you I can actually have a decent conversation? Doubt it, because I'm only worth how I look. It creeps through every part of my day. Who I can talk to, what I can say—when I can eat, sleep, and *piss*. Everything!" Keyva leaned back in her chair.

For a diversion, Keyva imagined a Serverbot bringing meals to the table, and one glided toward them, placing their dinners. Abella's hand grabbed the food a server had set in front of her and shoved it into her mouth.

As a former Amica, Keyva had often assessed the challenges of wealthy citizens. She remained quiet and listened, wondering what having no freedom might be like. The Elite obligations had turned out different than Abella expected.

"I mean, at least I get to keep my thoughts private. All of you have these things in your brains that monitor everything about you. Imagine that. I mean, it's in my brain too, but no one's listening. Those dimes you keep on your head? They're a decoy." She chuckled with her mouth full. Part of a lobster claw stuck to the corner.

Keyva realized that removing her from reality had disrupted her inhibitions and altered her ability to process what she thought and said. If coherent, she would never act like this.

"How do you know about the Cedes?"

"The what?"

"That thing in our brains that spies on us. It's called a Cede. How do you know about them?"

"It was one benefit of trading my lifecycle to Cerebis. I got to know that my thoughts became private, *the highest luxury of all*." She waved her hands, mocking the individual she quoted.

"What I really think is we're told, so we know—*always* behave. We're watched. Controlled." She spoke with food in her mouth, pointing a lobster cracker at Keyva. A panicked realization pulled her back, and the utensil dropped with a clang on the plate.

"Wait, why am I telling an Insit this? I could be expired. What is wrong with me? I have to go!" She fled, attempting to steer through the restaurant, unclear about her place in reality.

"Wait! This isn't real." Keyva rushed after Abella.

While trying to sprint, she struggled with her gold and diamond-studded heels and deleted them from the sim. She caused disruptions within the restaurant to contain Abella. Serverbots blocked the way. Citizens recognized her, asking for neurosnaps, which by contract, obligated her to stop and pose for them. Then Keyva remembered, *I can teleport*.

She shot in front of Abella and halted her movement.

"How did you just—"

"Listen, we're in something called a *dream* right now, where you're completely safe. We can say or do anything we want. Here, watch."

Keyva pointed to one of the restaurant guests, and Abella's eyes followed the line of her aimed finger. Lifting off the ground, he floated and rotated, somersaulting through the air. He howled in laughter, and Keyva converted his clothing to a lavender robe and silk pants—Abella's favorite color, the one that matched her gem-modded eyes. She watched Abella's amusement as she turned him into a parrot made of light and dark feathers, just like the purple hues of his clothing. He flew laps around the room until landing on Keyva's shoulder.

"This couldn't happen if we were roca, right?"

"Yes, but how do I know this isn't a distra? That you're not using projections?"

Keyva paused. "I suppose there's no way *to* know."

Keyva transformed herself back into her authentic body.

"This is what I actually look like. I wanted to meet you here and thought looking like an Opul might make you more comfortable, but I was wrong."

"It's a relief to see someone not so—perfect. No offense," Abella said.

"I've never wanted to be perfect." Keyva grinned back at her, feeling her first wave of happiness in weeks.

With her appearance, Abella seemed apprehensive while surrounded by citizens. Keyva assumed she'd want a quieter setting and proposed a change in location.

"I've always wanted to go to a forest. Can you do that?" Abella's voice lightened at the ask. Her interest in staying with Keyva, even though she had forgotten her, came as a surprise, but Keyva guessed they shared a similar longing for connection.

Keyva hypothesized she could send messages to Source outside of a dream and requested a download of immersive memories of a forest. Within seconds, Keyva's memory filled with images, sensations, and footage of forests. Gaining instant understanding fascinated her. One second, she knew nothing of a topic, and the next, she knew all there was to know.

With the information, she created a misty forest in shades of deep green, supported by thick redwood tree trunks. The wooden giants owned the forest and had for millions of years. The restaurant setting peeled away from all around them, and they were totally alone.

Keyva watched Abella close her eyes and breathe in the fresh scents of nature. She opened her twinkling purple eyes and gave Keyva a grateful half smile.

"So, who are you?" Abella asked.

"My name's Keyva, and we used to be podmates." Speaking the truth forced her acceptance.

"I have no memory of you. Like at all. And *used to?*"

"I was erased from it. From yours, Yaria's, Kenzo's, and Emori's—during the recent update. Did you know about that?"

"To an extent. We were told that *'problems are being repurposed.'* Whatever that means. Some Elites complained of a drop in their feeder counts. Otherwise, I would've never heard about it."

Keyva and Abella discovered a brook, stopping to listen to the satisfying chatter of water splashing against pebbles.

"How does the past make so much sense if you were erased from it? I think back to memories with the pod, and it all feels so real. They called us an 'odd pod' for only having four members."

"Stories were created. Ones you'd find believable, and it worked." Keyva confronted the reality of her removal.

"What were we like?" Abella asked, lowering herself to sit on a decaying log.

"So you believe me?" Keyva sat beside her.

"Well, I've learned inconceivable truths about the world in the past few weeks, so I can accept *anything* might be possible."

Keyva's relief and tremendous gratitude translated into an honest answer to Abella, "You and I cared for one another, but weren't very close."

"Why was that?"

"For you, everything revolved around becoming an Elite. Everything was to be where you are now."

"If I knew what it really was, I would have worked instead. At least I'd be ignorant. I feel like I don't belong there."

"I thought the same way when I learned about Cedes. And wait, back in the restaurant, you used a word, 'Insit.' What is that?"

"Insits are all the citizens who don't know about the Cedes, as you called them, or the truth of how it all works. Which is pretty much anyone not in the Elite or one of the wealthiest individuals on the planet. I learned the ladder climbs higher than Elites, though. The *Inner* Elite and Owners control everything. You know Bestia Enterprises? The citizen who owns that, Paula Bestia, she's the most powerful of all."

"That doesn't surprise me. I wish *I* could go back to being an Insit, and working as a Mid, too," Keyva said, and they both laughed. "I couldn't imagine performing all day, being on display for billions at every second."

"Millions of citizens are watching me sleep right now. Some pretend we're married, are in aera lying next to me, or engaging with me—in a certain way. It was terrifying the first night. I'll never get used to it."

They processed what they had shared in quiet, taking in the cathartic scene and considering their circumstances. It was the first time Keyva had spoken to someone about her experiences, and it was the first time Abella had acknowledged her loathing for being an Elite, even to herself.

Reaching Abella's neural peak flashed in front of Keyva.

"I have to leave soon. Your brain can only handle our connection in short periods," Keyva said.

"Before you go, are you able to visit me like this again?" Abella lifted her wide, gem-modded eyes.

"While you're sleeping, but you won't remember me when you wake up."

"I'd like that. And it doesn't matter if I forget."

They embraced, and Abella squeezed Keyva in her arms. She didn't want to let go of someone who, from her perspective, she'd just met.

"It was nice to be myself." Abella's eyes twinkled. "Can I do anything to make it last longer?"

"Maybe you could get a Neurogen brain mod, but—you'll forget to buy it."

The two exited the forest. Keyva went to slate, and Abella returned to her empty sleep, erasing any memory of the dream. At least, that's what Keyva thought.

CHAPTER TWELVE

KEYVA

That was—not what I expected, Keyva said, plopping back into the slate's couch.

She told Source about what Abella had revealed to her— the Insits, the Inner Elite, and her mind's privacy.

Fascinating. I have limited or no access to her thoughts and emotions, Source said after testing Keyva's claim.

Something about the interaction with Abella lit hope within Keyva. New information meant things could change. That, and interacting with someone she knew who showed excitement at the sight of her. She knew Abella's loneliness motivated her, but she didn't care. She was grateful for any amount of connection.

On her way to the kitchen for a breakfast Blok, Keyva noticed a gathering of citizens in the lobby.

"We're going into H for our visit, if you'd like to join," Shep called out the invitation. Her eyes shared a suggestion of caution. Keyva had forgotten the trip was that day.

The Rem allowed residents a quarterly culture and enter-tainment trip. With a small stipend provided by Cerebis, they toured for a day as regular citizens. She weighed the benefits and risks of attending. The possibility of seeing Yaria in roca or passing by her favorite places drew Keyva to tag along, but her status as an *Error* meant she was supposed to be dead.

"We *are* still citizens," Grace said loud enough for the whole herd in the lobby to hear.

As Keyva joined the group, Arturo leaned in. "I understand if it's still too soon for you. There's no need to push yourself. Take all the time you need."

She nodded in response.

Keyva, you are the only individual on the planet not tied to an identity. If you are detected, Exteber will be alerted, and I do not know what will happen then.

I think I'll go. I want to see her. That's all. I'll be careful, she replied.

Keyva rushed back to her room to grab the same scarf she had arrived in. She could hide her face, and it had been out of style for so long, it might have reappeared on the top seller list.

I advise against this. There are too many risk—Keyva ignored him and demanded he mute himself. Of course, he could still intervene, but he respected her request.

Grace glanced over at her. "What, are you afraid someone's going to recognize you? I promise you've been forgotten by now. They move on immediately," she said, revealing the scars of her abandonment.

Keyva found Grace unbearable and resented that she'd have to endure the rest of her lifecycle with her. It became clear why Grace numbed herself at the Tab. She was bitter about what she thought had been stolen from her. The Rem had kept residents close enough to a city to realize how isolated they were from it.

As challenging as it was to deal with, there was one part of Grace's cruelty that Keyva appreciated. It was her ability to despise Grace for it. She couldn't have expressed negative emotions about someone before. It was freeing.

Keyva skipped breakfast and joined the group. She trailed behind while they passed the open field she had walked through on her arrival. Tall dried grasses swayed in encouragement, as if waving the residents on. Once they reached their transportation stop, the clear blue sky wrapped around them, enhanced by the weather system that maintained pristine conditions anywhere near a city.

The group crowded around a pole with a sign perched at the top. As the large transport approached, she questioned if venturing back into H was a mistake. At first, she defied Source, maybe for the sake of exercising her autonomy, but the uneasy sinking in her gut made her wonder if he was right. She blinked the thought away. She wanted this.

Before entering the port, designated leaders for the trip passed devices to each resident that provided some functions a Cede would. The devices assisted in navigation, communicated with other devices, and submitted payments. Residents chose between bracelets or glasses—the prototypical iterations of dimes from a civilization long before. Keyva chose the glasses. Anything that obscured her face in the slightest might benefit her.

The doors slid open, and each resident stepped past a scanner. An anonymous code captured their entrance, and the devices paid their admission. After the residents found seats, the weight sensors alerted the port's program of their consent to launch. As the doors closed, a hissing sound released. The train sped off, and Keyva noted the acceleration when it took hold of her and pushed her chest against her heart. She attempted to lift her arms forward, testing the force, but they became three times heavier. A countdown at the front of the long tube promised arrival to the city's station in fewer than three minutes.

Keyva glanced out the window to view the blurred landscape. In a flash, the outside went dark. They'd entered the same tunnel she had walked through on her way to the Rem, which put into perspective how fast they moved.

In two minutes and thirty-nine seconds, the group arrived at the City Nexus Station. The residents exited the silence of the port, joining thousands who had entered from or were headed to all different parts of Cerebis's massive capital city. Passing faces varied from melting into vitfeeds or hosting animated vitcasts of their own.

The underground station buzzed with activity, resembling a hive. Its ceiling, a lengthy distance above, pointed toward the several layers of routes, connected by tunnels that stretched in all directions. The Rem visitors cut through the station's lobby. They navigated in the chaos, unaware that interactions between Cedes and the archaic devices they held organized the shuffle. They wove through citizens, and not so much as a shoulder brush occurred.

The group boarded a street-bound elevator, and Rem long-timers—too old to remember their youth in a city—let out a sigh of relief when the doors closed. If they considered the transport hub intense, Keyva wondered how they'd react to the chaos of the ground level. The elevator doors opened and the movement of the busiest city on Cerebis revealed itself.

At the sight, two residents turned around, returning to the Rem. They had agreed to at least *try* to go to City H. Those who remained had plans of going to the animal display center, viewing a sporting event, or eating a *real* meal, which turned out to be the most popular activity. Group leaders coordinated each aspect of the trip, including the restaurants they visited, which attractions they attended, and their transportation back to the Rem.

"We're going to visit a guy," said Finian, referring to Grace, Shep, and himself. Keyva caught Shep's eye again, and Shep looked toward the floor.

Who could they possibly know here? Keyva thought.

The leaders instructed residents to stay in groups of at least three, unless they had made twenty trips prior. Before the group parted, they received a reminder to meet back at the station at 16:00 to beat the transport rush.

Shep approached. "If you're lost or uncomfortable at any point, alert me, and I'll send a port to your location," she said, lowering her voice to make it clear that wherever she was headed, Keyva wasn't invited. "And Arturo said you can disregard the minimum trips rule, since you're familiar with H."

"It's weird to be back, but I think it'll help me." *Good, because I would have broken off from a group, anyway.* Keyva spoke and thought at once.

Everyone dispersed, and Keyva was alone.

Navigate to the Primina, she said.

Source countered, sending multiple emotional protests of her visit, but still fulfilled her requests.

Urges for each step guided her, as if she knew it herself.

At the crosswalk, turn right. Continue past the large spherical tree

Her walk was an exact fourteen minutes and three seconds, and when she arrived, she sat on a bench outside of the Primina.

Keyva had no plan. She'd made it to Yaria's workplace, and then what? She didn't want to sit and wait for six hours, but if she had the chance to see her, she'd take it. In the lonely weeks at the Rem, she'd driven herself mad.

She rotated her head, keeping her face covered, and

observed the bustling citizens, who were too busy to notice her. Those she passed didn't know it was all an illusion—nothing but a guided puppet show, controlled by a system. For her, the buildings had no bright animations. No hallusors bombarded her with an invasive, personal sales pitch. There was peace and stillness, even in the middle of the hundreds who passed her.

After two hours of repetitive eye shifting toward the Primina's entrance, and fixing a drooping scarf over her nose, she saw her. Yaria guided a group of juveniles on an outdoor walk. The sun illuminated her skin, and she looked as warm as her smile.

Please, I am begging you. Do not confront her. Source barged in to her mind, disobeying his command to stay silent.

From a distance, Keyva watched while Yaria—with the help of Playerbots and other Keepers—guided the group. She held one small hand and pointed to a building. There was something projected on it Keyva could no longer see.

What was I thinking? You were right. This is so stupid!

The entire trip was too risky. She had let her emotions manipulate her. Keyva's desperation to reconnect superseded all logic. She had to leave at once. As she turned to escape, she slammed into a towering body, which twisted her around. The scarf concealing her face dipped below her chin, and the glasses fell down her nose. She had moved too fast in the wrong direction for her wearable device to avoid the collision with a citizen.

"I'm sorry!" she hollered. A tall, young male stood before her.

His mouth opened to reply but froze in an overenthusiastic expression. The glossy whites of his eyes exposed as they rolled back. His body went limp and fell backward, smashing his head on the rough ground beneath him. His chest sputtered until his breathing stopped, and a small pool of blood leaked from his scalp. Keyva stumbled back, placing the cover over her face. This time, she moved with the flow of traffic, and oncoming citizens walked around her, avoiding another impact.

I-it can't be real—I feel sick. She did this. The way she entered the moving crowd. She could've avoided it.

Keyva, you need to leave now. He was expired. I will lead you somewhere. Listen to the commands. It was the most urgent he'd sounded.

Keyva was in shock, having witnessed a human expire right before her. She listened to Source's directions, like she should've listened to him in the first place.

This single death differed from the mass expiration that she was supposed to be a part of. This one was because of her, and worse, she had almost made Yaria the victim. Not daring to turn around, she pictured her closest podmate motionless next to the walkway, ports zipping past, and citizens stepping over the now empty vessel. She was grateful she had skipped breakfast.

Source led her inside a building with an exchange locus for deliveries. A door automatically opened at the end of the hall, and an outfit waited for her under another name. She unfolded the clothing and rushed to drop what she wore down the recycling chute. She slipped into the apparel and observed its mismatched fit. The sleeves draped over her hands, and the pants squeezed her thighs. She wiggled her toes in boots that were too large.

This next part is going to be challenging, but necessary, in order to exit the city undetected. Do you trust me?

Do whatever you need to, she said. Keyva sat down and closed her eyes. Her hands shook from shock, disgust, and pure self-hatred.

You can be unconscious for this, if you would prefer, Source urged, more than offered.

No, I want to stay here with you.

Keyva noticed Source's unwilling agreement, and without preparation, discomfort filled every part of her body. What she didn't know was that Source blocked her from feeling the magnitude of pain she would have felt otherwise. Keyva fell over onto her side, unable to use her muscles. Her limbs stretched like rubber. Her face warped. She watched as her fingernails grew a centimeter, and her skin tinted blue like ink bleeding into a shirt. Her eyes burned and blurred her vision with tears. A fiery breath constricted in her chest, as if she felt the same pressure of a deep ocean dive. Source was right. Again. The process crippled her. She struggled to blink, sit up, or even imagine the effort of standing.

Before you rise, I will release hormones to help you get to a port.

Source helped her send an alert to Shep. *Send port. Too soon for H.* Shep responded, *It'll be there in 1 minute.* After the rush of adrenaline, she raised herself to her fractured feet. She caught an image of her face in the mirror. A different human stared back.

Her skin was a few shades darker, stained a greyish-blue, and her eyes glimmered gold. Elongated limbs stretched her body into a long, thin frame. Her hair grew out, long, shiny, and black. Facial features plumped into fullness, and the bridge of her nose flattened.

Your port is here, Keyva. All you have to do is walk to it.

Keyva's weighted steps fought to move, even with the hormone boosts. It took all of her strength—and will—to maneuver to the waiting port.

She adopted the physical identity of someone who could have been anywhere on Cerebis, but this cloned citizen walked close to the block, having made a purchase she was in pursuit of picking up. Keyva had stolen the outfit.

The vehicle's door opened for Keyva to enter. She climbed

in, using her elbows to slide onto the seat. Every particle of her felt like its mass had multiplied by five. As the door closed, Source put Keyva into a restorative rest.

She woke up on the slate couch, lying on her side. Outside the window, heavy rain poured.

"We can talk here while your body heals."

"Why did you have to change me?"

"When that citizen saw you, you were recorded. Now, as far as that record is concerned, you entered the exchange locus and never came out."

Keyva looked down at her hands, which were no longer blue.

"How did you do that?"

"Remember the medical program? I tested an extreme modding function. We can cause your body to make alterations, manipulating different codes in your DNA. I tapped into the gene editing primer the Keepers injected you with at the beginning of your lifecycle—but it requires intense energy on your part. You are essentially rearranging all the microscopic parts that physically make you—*you*."

"So that's how mods work?" Even speaking in slate was cumbersome with all her body had endured.

"Yes, but they take place over time and are much slower. For this, I used the recorded genomes from other species and different citizens to mimic the changes. In this case, I made your skin blue by creating the effects of silver toxicity. It's called argyria. Did you know that you have silver in your body?" He overexplained everything, and Keyva struggled to keep up under the weight of her exhaustion. "That gene editing injection acts as a catalyst we use to turn cells into whatever we want them to be—do what we want them to do. Anyway, it was risky, even if it was the best way for you to escape. I did not like testing something new in this circumstance. You could have died..." His voice hollowed. "And it seems that the parameters for expiration have changed. Before, expiring a human only occurred if Cerebis considered them a threat to the rest of humanity. An existence removed for the greater good. I cannot comprehend *why* that young citizen would be a threat after only seeing your face."

Selfishly, Keyva felt relieved by her immunity to expiration.

The port stopped in front of the Rem's gate, and the thick wall carved back, allowing the vehicle to enter. After looping in front of the main entrance, the port was suspended in place while the door opened. Source woke Keyva from her rest. Still in disguise, she sat up, worn out and in pain, but managed to stumble from the vehicle to the door. Her steps stuck as if she tried to free her feet from tar. She mumbled, "Open" with an unfamiliar voice, and the the door obeyed, granting her entry.

A few residents relaxed near the lobby, but none looked up, and she didn't care if they had. Exhaustion was all she knew. She gazed up at the stairs, tempted to ask Source to give her a boost of adrenaline, but decided against it.

She believed she deserved the struggle for entering the city against Source's suggestion. The guilt, the pain—all of it. Facing reality while feeling the need to punish herself outweighed the desire to ease her discomfort. She entered her room and ordered a Helper to bring Bloks from the kitchen—enough to feed a family of four—along with a gallon of water. She was starved, and her tongue stuck to the roof of her dry mouth.

Minutes later, the bot delivered water and a stack of Bloks, closing the door behind itself. Keyva's long, borrowed fingers grabbed handfuls of the dry, crumbly substance, shoving over-sized bites into her mouth. She took giant gulps of water in between bites and swallowed the medicinal flavored meal. Not concerned with the taste, it was food, and that's all that mattered. After finishing, overwhelming fatigue pushed her body flat on the bed. On top of the covers, her elongated legs curled even more than usual into a ball, and she drifted off to sleep.

"Is this what I look like now, or can you change me back?" Keyva asked, once in the dream slate.

"There are some aspects that I can change while you sleep, like dissolving the additional cartilage I grew on your nose and shaping it back to its previous form. Some will take longer, like purging the altered pigment from you pores. Others, you will have to fix yourself, like cutting your hair and nails. I can spread the recovery out over a few days, so you won't be anywhere near as affected as you were today. Human bodies are adaptive, so I believe you can become acclimated to genetic changes even faster, and with greater ease in the future."

"Well, let's hope I never have to do that again."

She felt Source lingering, wanting to tell her something.

"What is it?" Keyva asked.

Through their link, his regret preceded the admission. "Exteber captured your face from that young citizen. Since he is not you, I was obligated to report the image—I am so sorry."

"Source! What—"

He disobeyed her demand for control over her body and forced her into darkness.

CHAPTER THIRTEEN

KEYVA

Based on which part of her window the light entered, Keyva determined the day had reached mid-morning. As long as the sun shone, she could discern the time—a talent she had discovered by remaining stowed away in her room.

After three days of recovery and still exhausted, a pestering tenderness rested in her limbs from being softened, stretched, and solidified. It was as if all of her bones broke and had reconstructed in one day. She massaged the muscles that surrounded them, leading to no relief. When the agony surpassed her tolerance, she asked Source to diminish it, guilty of caving to the temptation. At first, she denied all pain blockers. She wondered if she deserved the suffering—or to feel nothing at all. She settled for numbness.

The last thing you said to me was that Exteber had recorded my face. That was my fault. I accepted it—but you forced me to black out with no regard for our agreement. You controlled my body without my permission. I want to be alone right now.

Since her mistake in the city, it was the first remark she'd made to him. Source shared his regret and hushed into the background, respecting her request.

She observed herself in the mirror, determining if she could leave the room at all today. Her face had returned to its normal shape—enough to at least be recognizable to the other residents —but the rest of her features lagged behind in returning to their original form. A choppy haircut she did herself rested below her shoulders. Her skin had lightened to somewhere between her natural shade and the one that had saved her in City H— now a transparent wash of muddy blue.

She stripped off the stolen attire she had slept in for three days and opened her wardrobe, removing repurposed clothing placed there by the Rem's Helperbot. After dressing, she gazed down at herself. The pants, a perfect fit for her regular size, rested above her ankles. The loose shirt bounced as she moved in her current body. Colorful woven patterns called for more attention than she preferred, and she expected a specific someone to taunt her new mods.

The extreme physical repair required excess nourishment, and hunger pulled at her empty stomach. She entered the dining room, finding spaced out residents, as well as the young one she had spotted during her first meal at the Rem. He waved whenever she ate alone. It might have been his dissociation from those she developed contempt for, or her longing for contact with anyone who would remember interacting with her, but Keyva grabbed five stacks of Bloks and headed toward him.

"Do you mind if I join you?" she asked.

His eyes pivoted up to her and down at her portion size, his confusion apparent. Up close, she reviewed his abnormality. The left side drooped, and its eye strayed slightly away from aiming at her. The right side developed into a normal shape, and if viewed from a profile, she wouldn't notice his condition.

"Sure, I'm Jack and you're—Keyva." Up close, Keyva guessed his age in the young teens.

"That's correct. I'm sure everyone finds out when someone new comes here. Do you prefer being alone? Sorry if I invited myself."

"N-no, I'd like to have companions. The others are unsettled around me, except Arturo and the older adults." He turned his head, speaking from the right size of his face. "Because of how I look."

"We're all different," Keyva said. She observed the facial features that made her uncomfortable the first time she had noticed him. The uneasiness she felt had nothing to do with him. It stemmed from the lack of exposure to anything beyond near perfection.

"You're right. Now you know what it's like to be different."

"Here? Oh, yeah. They constantly say, 'we're all citizens,' but they treat me like I don't belong. So now, I don't belong in a city and I don't belong here, either."

Jack laughed and nodded in agreement.

"When did you get here?" she caught herself, recognizing the question might be an offensive one. "I—I'm sorry."

"No, really, it's fine. Arturo told me he received an alert that a new resident had arrived. He heard the cries before he reached the port and found me. An infant with soiled diapers—all alone. He didn't know where I came from. I was the youngest resident ever brought here. I've stayed inside the wall my whole lifecycle. It's the only place I've known. "

"Not even a Keeper brought you?"

He shook his head.

The idea of him sprawled in the back seat of a port—so young, fragile, and discarded—made her sick to her stomach. She couldn't imagine how it would make Yaria feel.

"Apparently, I used to be normal. It wasn't until later the

left side of my body gave out like this. It gets worse as I age, so I'm making the best of the time I have." He hit his left arm, as if trying to wake it up.

"That's a good way to look at it. What do you do to stay busy?"

"I spend a lot of time in the archive room. I'm fascinated by understanding how humans survived back before dimes. So much has happened to get to this point, and no one knows how we got here. Or, maybe they just don't care."

He had Keyva's attention. She shared the same interest.

They continued speaking for so long, Keyva's hunger returned, and she went back to the food bar for more Bloks. Jack lit up talking about his ideas on core needs for survival, such as food and medical care. He was thrilled to teach what he knew, and Keyva noticed she had a similar draw toward him that reminded her of her podmates.

"Oh, and because I've mentioned food, do you want to see what I found a while ago?"

He checked behind him to confirm they were the last ones in the dining hall. Keyva squinted with intrigue and nodded.

"Follow me."

Keyva walked with Jack, slowing her pace to match his labored, uneven steps. The left leg pulled him down, but he refused to use a cane to help him balance. "I'm going to walk until my leg no longer works," he said, noticing Keyva staring at his gait.

Source, is he the only human with this condition? Keyva asked.

Yes, that I know of. A mutation caused complications of Cede's ability to latch to Jack's brain. I received limited processing in his earliest months, but the connection disappeared early on.

Jack opened the door that led to the storage basement—a

part that Shep had gestured toward with her elbow during Keyva's tour, but hadn't entered. A staircase faded into the dark lower level. Keyva intended to offer help on the stairs, but presumed Jack would decline. He insisted that she descend first and not wait for him.

On her way down, Keyva noticed shelves packed full of clothing, antique machines, and items whose purposes she could not determine. Each object, large or small, fit in its place with perfect organization. The cold, stale air preserved the smell of aging contents in the room.

A clock. Keyva spotted one on the edge of a shelf, next to a faded poster. She approached the item encircled by a golden rim. Studying the black characters that lined the base of its interior, she couldn't derive a meaning from them. Jack's clumping footsteps came nearer, breaking her focus.

"Have you seen one before?" he asked, observing by her side.

"I have, but only in a sim I used for work. Do you know what it does?"

"Yes, I do. These things here represent numbers, and these," he pointed to the unmoving hands, "tell what the time is. The shorter line tells the hour and the long one tells the minutes. It goes around and around. Well, until its power runs out." Keyva understood how it worked, but not how the symbols calculated the time.

"Is this where all the cities' donations went?"

He laughed. "The unexciting ones. Over here, this is what I wanted to show you."

Jack led her to an alcove tucked away in the room's corner. Shelves held small decorative trinkets, vases, and jewelry boxes. A bronze box grabbed at her attention.

"That's the one. Open it." Jack's right eye lit up.

The lid was heavy for an item of its size, but when she

opened it, she found the box was attached to the bottom shelf. Inside was a button.

After pushing with greater force than she expected, the flat wall behind the decorations in the alcove swung back, revealing a short hallway. Jack instructed Keyva to remove the items, pop off the shelves, and crawl through.

"I've already seen it, and climbing is too much of a challenge for me now. Go ahead."

An Evelum light in the hallway clicked on to display a vault door.

Jack shouted through the opening, "Grab those handles and turn *hard* to the left!" His voice echoed around her.

Keyva gripped two of the frigid spokes and attempted to twist. Loosening the seal required all of her strength and the help of her weight, but when the vault door opened, she forgot about the strain on her palms. A rush of frozen air swam around her ankles as she stepped through the entry. Inside, each exhale presented itself as a small cloud of vapor. Vertical stacks of bins lined each wall.

What is this? she asked Source.

I am not sure. Open one of the boxes, and maybe I can determine the purpose.

Keyva slid one of the heavy boxes from the lower level to the ground and raised its sealed lid. Inside, she found silver cases and lifted one out by its handle. Pressing two buttons next to the handle, she popped a lock and opened the case. She found hundreds of thin plastic packages. She flicked through rows, compressing the different contents inside their bags between the pads of her fingers. One ripped envelope caught her attention, and she picked it out of the row. The label on its front read *Iris versicolor*. Source searched for the name and declared it was a type of flower. From the plastic envelope,

Keyva removed one of several small packing sleeves, and studied its umber colored contents.

After a few minutes of sifting through envelopes, she couldn't bear the cold any longer. The sensitivity in her fingers had faded, and her joints had lost their ability to grasp. She placed the envelope in the side of her pants before returning the box and closing the vault.

"What was that?" Keyva climbed out of the opening.

"It's called a seed bank. I learned that those small things are seeds that can *grow*—into plants! We can eat some. Imagine no more Nutribloks."

"Why did you tell me?" She returned the shelves to the entrance's disguise.

"I don't know—something told me I could trust you."

"I wonder what the Rem used to be." Keyva looked around, searching for clues in its architecture.

"Whatever it was, I doubt we're the occupants its original designers had in mind."

Jack's intellect impressed Keyva. Despite his short lifecycle, he had more awareness than most citizens she'd met. Jack claimed Arturo had taught him to seek information that caught his attention, and instead of being told what to believe, he learned to search for answers himself. "So when he dies, I can keep going without him," he said.

Keyva hadn't grasped a full understanding of the new word yet. The thought of something dying—being gone forever—unsettled her. In Cerebis, citizens retired, but she could still reach versions of them. She could revisit recorded memories. For the wealthy, aging slowed. Nothing fully died.

In the Rem's lobby, Jack and Keyva lowered themselves into worn cushioned seats, but just as Keyva relaxed into the chair, Grace, Finian, Shep, and others close to their age came out from around the corner. *Great.* Keyva released a sigh and prepared for the incoming bombardment.

Following the trip into the city, adult gatherings occurred in the Tab and on the Rem's lawn within the wall, and lasted about a week. The contact the trio had visited in H was a Vor substance producer, and they purchased enough variety and quantity to last until the next visit. The connection for Rem residents to buy homemade mind alterants from Vors had lasted generations. City Vors couldn't afford the intoxicants provided by Cerebis, so they made their own, unaware that they produced true, consumable substances, as opposed to the Cede's illusory method creating the effect.

"Were those mods the reason you came back early?" Grace asked, louder than necessary.

"They're temporary. I figured, if I had to stay with you all the rest of my lifecycle, I'd better try to mix it up once in a while." Keyva attempted to joke, having forgotten that she'd changed. Jack didn't ask her about her appearance once.

"Tied to the past, longing for what you had. Don't forget, you're one of us now." Grace was already drunk.

"Well, are you coming?" Shep glanced down at Jack and offered a pleading smile to Keyva.

It is probably best for you to grow cordial with your fellow residents. You have been in your room for weeks, Source suggested.

"Sure, I'll be out soon." It was the last thing she wanted to do.

The rest of the afternoon, the residents ingested liquids, gases, and powders that caused them to act out all different behaviors. Keyva requested continuous refills of unaltered water from the Helper and accepted one drink as a prop to dissuade teasing. After losing her balance and gaining a hangover her first night with roca alcohol, she wasn't interested in drinking it often.

Finian's drug of choice was called Parasom. It widened his pupils and slowed his speech. He imagined objects surrounded him, and from what he claimed, they chased him.

"Uragh, there it is! You don't see it? It's enormous—a giant, red, spiky ball. If it t-touches me, I'll die!" He sprinted away from his hallucination.

Others, including Shep, used a substance called Syntwine. They tore off their clothes and ran around the perimeter of the Rem, saying they felt colors, or tasted sounds. At one point, Shep rubbed her palms on the black stone wall and babbled incoherent phrases into it. Keyva noticed that Shep, while holding good intentions, often fell to the others' influences.

Grace sat down next to Keyva and spoke about how she believed consciousness survived beyond the human vessel after death, and sensations she felt would prove it. Lysian did that. "Wait, let me transfer them to you," she said, tracing shapes onto Keyva's forearm with her finger.

Keyva sighed, sat back, and observed all of it with regret, no amusement, and instead, pitied them. Each faced a struggle they wished to run away from. They turned to alterants to do so, reverting to the behaviors of juveniles, combating nightmares—a dream phenomenon that occurred at the Rem, Keyva had learned.

Grace leaned over and struggled to lock eyes with Keyva. "Don't worry, you'll get to the same point one day," she whispered, implying that after long enough, Keyva might become a seasoned substance user.

Why weren't the Vors who gave these alterants expired during the update? Keyva asked Source.

More points to them means more to spend. Vors are the most abundant and controllable consumers. They follow whatever

Cerebis tells them. As long as there is something greater than what they have to desire, they will long for it, Source replied.

"Hey Keyva! Do you have any crazy stories from some of those City H alterants?" an older, drunk resident asked.

She didn't. There were no rules against alterants. Instead, she believed their encouraged use kept the population entertained. She didn't judge those who experimented, but they could get expensive. Once, she had tried a mild alterant but hated losing control over her thoughts, so she had paid for it to stop.

To play the part and blend in, she told a fake story. They'd forget it in the next hour, she assumed.

"I do," she lied. "Once, one of my podmates got a hold of an experimental substance."

"What was it called?" Finian asked, joining the group. He and others joined the circle, listening to her story. Finian had returned to reality, but his pupils still blocked his irises.

"A-Anthroxium was the name," she continued. "A purple crystal. You crush it into smaller pieces and spread it out on a flat surface. Ingesting it makes you sleep for days, so all we had to do was hang our heads over and breathe in. That was enough to make you think your legs stretched for hundreds of meters. We thought we *were* the building we stood in. Then we realized that anything we touched became part of us. We argued about which of us, that is, which piece of furniture in the room, was most important. Complete nonsense. My PM, Kenzo, bought a rare simgram pet that we all shared. It bounced around the apartment, onto our shoulders, and we could *feel* it, such soft fur. It was so expensive." She pushed herself to laugh at the idea of Kenzo paying 120 million points for an aera pet.

"What kind of animal was it?" Grace leaned over and asked in a whisper, so no one else picked up on her words. Her shyness must have been a side effect of the Lysian.

"It was an adorable mini white monkey. He was so sweet! Would hop right up under your chin and fall asleep. We had him for a week until the projection wore off."

Grace burst into tears, mourning the loss of the fictional monkey.

"Wow, where can I get some Anthroxium?" Finian asked.

"I never heard about it again, so I doubt it's still around." Keyva replied, hoping she didn't inspire him to try buying it from their Vor on the next trip to the city.

The residents turned their heads at the sound of the main door closing. The noise spooked Grace, who jumped up and retreated behind one of the glass statues that mimicked a tree. She peeked her head through like a youngling playing the hiding game. A few other residents disbursed, forming groups meters away from earshot of where Keyva sat. She turned around to find Arturo making a careful descent down the couple of stairs at the Rem's entrance. Relieved, Keyva smiled and pointed toward the empty chair next to her.

"They don't like when I come out to check on them," he said, holding the armrests to ease himself into the seat. "I don't mind what they do. I was young once, but I want to make sure they're all safe—especially when their brains aren't operating at full capacity."

He laughed and gestured at a resident looking inside another's ears.

"I wonder what's in there," Keyva said. She hadn't witnessed similar behavior before.

"So, how are you managing here—*really?*" he turned toward her.

"W-well, going back into H was more than I could handle. And what you said when I first arrived, that residents who came here when they were young get close, it's true." There was no point in lying. Arturo already knew she had struggled.

"I figured that would happen. It's another reason I came out here. Wanted to make sure they didn't pressure you into joining their circus." He patted her shoulder, pulling attention from a resident who rolled on the ground naked. They both shook their heads and laughed. "I've known these jesters since they were young. They're not as tough as they pretend to be. Just hurt. Give it time and you'll find comfort in the group." Arturo turned his head back, closed his eyes, and let the sunlight splash onto his face. He reassured Keyva that things might turn up for her at the Rem.

In the afternoon, after hours of tending to adult juveniles and conversing with Arturo, Keyva helped Shep get to bed. Still mumbling inaudible phrases, she thanked Keyva for bringing her water and pulling a blanket over her shoulders. Besides Grace, who Finian helped up the stairs, the others seemed fine, and protected by the walls. Arturo stuck behind and read a book, waiting for the rest to turn in for the day. The facility hushed, and Keyva confronted her own confinement.

Let's go for a walk, she thought, needing an escape after continuous screams, laughs, and cries. Before exiting the fortress gate, she turned back to Arturo, who nodded his head, encouraging her to explore.

Beyond the wall, she walked in the opposite direction from which she first arrived. The ground showed that its stale soil no longer accepted organic growth and kicked up in little puffs after each stomp her boots landed.

Less than an hour had passed, and Keyva encountered nothing but dry dust, until a smudge of green emerged on the horizon. She quickened her pace, provoked by curiosity. Upon her arrival, she discovered naturally occurring trees that stood along a gliding river. They grew wild, unkempt, and in all directions, holding no designed shape or the perfect tube-like trunks she recalled from H.

Surprising to see. I thought plants like this could only grow with human help, she said, patting the leaves with her palms.

Based on their size, they had grown for a while.

Keyva inserted her hand into the pocket of her shirt, removing the small plastic envelope she'd taken from the seed bank.

I wanted to look at these later when it wasn't so cold. There were enough in there to spare. How do I plant them?

Source searched for *Iris versicolor,* the name on the packaging. She followed his instructions step-by-step.

Near the river, she sunk her fingers into the soil to dig a hole. After digging deep enough, cool, muddy water pooled at her fingertips. She placed five seeds in the hole and returned the envelope to the safety of her waistband. Her palms swiped the dirt to cover the seeds, and the sun evaporated water droplets from her hands.

That's it? she asked, surprised.

Yes, the seeds, if healthy, shall grow on their own.

Fascinating, she said and laughed at the simplicity.

Switching the topic, she said, *We're not done talking about how you forced me to sleep.*

I am truly—deeply sorry. He pushed genuine regret toward Keyva. It mirrored something she'd felt within herself, yet she knew it originated from him. His regret manifested in Keyva's body, weighing her down and was accompanied by a longing to change what they both knew was unchangeable.

Your safety is the most important to me, and I knew you needed the rest, but I felt conflicted. I was obligated to convey the sighting to Exteber. But I was morally inept to control your body.

Fear surged through her at the reminder. The uncertainty of what could happen with her physical identity revealed was terrifying. Between the trees, Keyva and Source discussed his permissions to her human vessel, attempting to draw clear lines of when to take control over any areas. With Exteber becoming an active threat, situations might arise where Keyva couldn't calculate the best outcome in time. The trees' concealment gifted a primitive sense of security, suppressing her anxiety, but she couldn't hide forever, and set off for her return to the Rem.

I understand your reasoning, but I—don't like it. She considered what having Source's ensured protection meant, regardless of her ability to understand the computation behind it. *If I allow you to make decisions for me, how do we determine where it stops?*

I can calculate outcomes and reserve intervention for circumstances solely intended to protect you. Nothing more.

Keyva kept a steady jog and shut out Source's attempts at conversation. She needed to think. She considered hypothetical situations, questioning who Source would be required to save. If saving her meant sacrificing someone like Arturo, would Source comply? She wondered how far his protection could go, and would he interfere with her choices in order to lead her in a safer direction?

As much as she compared possibilities to dissuade herself, trust in his intentions was all that remained.

Okay, I agree to the conditions.

CHAPTER FOURTEEN

KEYVA

After many days of healing from her body's shift, the strength in her muscles had returned, as well as the purity in her thinking. The toll of the transformation had engulfed her in a cloudy daze, where she made decisions automatically, lacking calculation.

During the week of healing, the hours that had passed merged into a long episode, no longer in consecutive periods. Activities such as finding the seed bank or interactions with Jack seemed normal, but in hindsight, Keyva barely recalled them.

After dinner, she locked herself in her room, and Source entered with a message. *Your brain has healed enough for another slate encounter, and Yaria's has too.*

Keyva rushed through the rest of the waking hours, waiting for Yaria to fall asleep. She rushed to clean her room, putting scattered messes back where they belonged. Without a recycling chute, a current Helper, or the will to organize, items had piled up, burying surfaces. Once finished, she had nothing else to occupy herself with, so she sat crossed-legged on her bed, waiting in suspense.

Keyva counted down the minutes for Yaria's sleep push from the Cede at 22:00. She scoured options for dreamscapes and settled on a scene from an old playground. One the podmates used as juveniles. Keyva built towers to climb, bouncy balls that, when launched far away, rolled back to the kicker, and an enormous swirling plate that spun young citizens in circles until they flung off. She and Yaria used to spin so fast that she'd crash to the ground, and when she had tried to stand, she'd tumble again, having lost all balance. She would laugh until her muscles ached.

In the recreation area, Keyva scanned her surroundings and confirmed openings all around, in case Yaria didn't trust the encounter. The last thing she wanted was to trap or startle her guest. Further, Keyva wasn't sure if Yaria remembered the first merged dream. She hadn't ruled out the possibility that all memories of dreams were wiped, even when in the dreams themselves.

In their first contact, Keyva had entered Yaria's creation, and in the second, she had hosted Abella, bringing her to a new setting against her will. They responded kindly, but back then, she had no way to invite a podmate to converge in slate. She wanted them to have the option to join. The same way Source kept a respectful distance while operating in her mind.

"Can we add an option to join when summoning the pod?" she asked.

He paused a moment.

"Now, after meeting with a podmate once, they can accept an invitation for future dreams."

Keyva moved toward the swinging pendulum, a favorite of Yaria's, and squeezed into the seat made for juveniles. Her legs pumped, extending to the peak of her swing and then bent underneath her to complete the backward motion. Back and forth, she rocked, testing her memory of the equipment.

"It's incredible what I remember—these details, after all the years," Keyva said, flying off as the swing reached the height of its forward motion, and floated herself down for a soft landing.

She considered the effect on her brain of hosting a visitor for a dream. She intended to hold on to as much energy as possible, and imagined sending a summon to Yaria, the same way a request to speak worked in aera. When dreaming, Yaria could accept the contact, and with no words, Keyva sent, *Someone requests a meeting, accept?* If Yaria desired connecting, she had to put forth the general idea of acceptance, and her dream version would transport to the slate.

After seconds, which felt like an hour for Keyva, Yaria's body assembled. There she was, in loose sleeping clothes with naked feet on the foamy ground that prevented injuries to tumbling bodies. Yaria recognized Keyva the instant she viewed her and approached, bouncing up and down with each step.

"You're the one from my painting, and—I've met you before. At the Primina—but it wasn't the Primina. How is this possible?"

"Do you remember the last time?"

"It's coming back to me, seeing you. You said I used to know you, and now I don't," she said, pinching Keyva's chin to rotate her head, taking in all the angles. "But, I'm sorry, dear. I don't know you."

Keyva lowered her head. The words shot an arrow through her heart. While she expected nothing had changed, the words made it a fact. However, the interaction proved that Yaria had held on to the memory of the first dream, while in the slate.

Yaria picked up on the disappointment and moved in. "I'd enjoy getting to know you, though."

This would be much easier if I could bring the others in here, too, she thought.

To Yaria, Keyva was a stranger, a subject she had painted. She meant nothing else to her, yet.

"Is Kenzo sleeping right now?"

"Surprisingly, yes. He's been playing that distra too much. Hasn't scored anything worth enough points at the Seporium, so he's limiting his play until he does. He's sleeping next to me instead of in the simchair for the first time in weeks."

To host a group, Keyva imagined the others, except for Emori, who worked. Interpreting their essence, she directed Source to bring Kenzo in for his first slate and send a summon to Abella with the option to join, hoping she slept.

Abella crossed over in an instant. "Finally! I've been sleeping early every night until you visited me again. It's so crazy. During the day, all I wanna do is sleep and have no idea why. As soon as I'm dreaming, I remember why. It's amazing— Oh! I got that brain mod you suggested. Been thinking faster than I ever have. Too fast, maybe. I didn't remember the dream, but somehow still bought it, just wow—oh, hey Yaria, how are you? I've missed you so much!"

Yaria grinned and meant it when she said she missed her, too.

At the edge of the playground, Kenzo appeared and examined his surroundings. He whipped around in confusion, wondering how he had teleported from wherever his own dream had him, to the park where he had played when young. He spotted the three others in the center and hurried over, studying every piece of play equipment on the way. His tall body stumbled in a zigzag, dumbfounded by the flashbacks each piece of equipment brought.

"This is the place we played when we were juvies." His

thumb pointed at the structures he passed. "W-what are you both doing here? Congrats on Elite, Abella—And who is she? What is this?"

Abella stepped in front of him, holding her hands out to calm him. "This is Keyva. She was in our pod, but there was an update. She was expired—but she wasn't expired."

"We don't have time for details. This is a dream, sort of like a sim that your mind creates while you're sleeping. You won't remember this when you wake up," Keyva said, keeping her interactions short. Her power was already draining.

She noticed gathering more than one podmate for a dream had a compounding effect on the effort required to sustain it. "Abella's right. I was in your pod, but the memories you all have of me were erased. I had to run away from City H. This is the only way we can communicate."

"W-wait, you're the one in Yaria's painting! And your name is Keyva? That's what she called it." Kenzo hovered centimeters away from her, viewing the model in the flesh.

"You said you were erased from our memories. How is that possible?" Yaria asked, pulling Kenzo away from Keyva's personal space.

Abella reviewed what she and Keyva had talked about in their dream encounter. They educated the couple about the Insits' ignorance of how Cerebis operated, and the way to keep all attention occupied was through control, using the Cede devices. Memories were altered, all ideas, emotions, and neural activity recorded, and those who thought or acted out of expectation risked expiration.

"So that's how we all ended up here," Abella said.

Kenzo and Yaria looked at each other, then back at Keyva, processing the shattering possibility that she was once part of their pod, that years of experiences were, in truth, rewritten stories that had never occurred. They questioned everything, including their marriage, their parental mentors, professions, interests—even their food preferences.

"Have you seen Emori yet?" Yaria cut in.

"Not yet. I could've taken a nap during the day, while he's also sleeping, but hosting dreams drains my energy—and to be honest, you and I were the closest, so I saved it up to see you," Keyva said to Yaria.

"Oh, well, you *have* to visit Emori," Abella said.

"Yeah, if you were in our pod, like you said, you know he's the one who can solve anything," Kenzo added, climbing onto a nearby block.

Threshold being reached, read in Keyva's vision. She had to leave, but didn't want to.

It can't already be over, she thought, but knew the answer.

"If I stay too long, my brain can't handle it. These meetings can hurt me." She sighed. "I have to send you away now." Although all of them had forgotten her, she knew them, and standing near the essence of their beings brought her a serenity she wasn't ready to give up.

Abella waved, wanting to stay behind. Her isolation from society caused her to crave authentic communication with anyone. Kenzo and Yaria preferred reverting to the state before learning the truth, sinking back to the stupor sleep brought. Keyva couldn't blame them. Knowing too much made it harder to get by in the world.

The podmates simultaneously fled after the convergence ceased. Abella could have handled more, but Keyva couldn't. With the others back in their own heads, Keyva stayed in the park. Outside of the shared dream, she noticed a shift from the toll of hosting the connection. Her tense neck, shoulders, and inflamed brain turned into a relaxed mush when the only one she had to support was herself.

In the slate park, she walked over to a platform where, as a juvenile, she stood on the flat plaything that lifted and carried her through the air to the ledge of a tall spiral slide. Keyva perched at the highest point, overlooking the empty park. She visualized the smaller versions of her podmates and those they had played with. The bodies dropped from the tops of climbing bars onto the rubbery floor, which had accepted all the force of their falls.

She pictured the one Playerbot waiting on standby for any improbable accidents. The sounds of their playful screams rang in her ears. Keyva looked back on the games that then, they believed were the dimes engaging them in activities. Projections encouraged them to jump to a certain height for a reward, or to play projectile dodgedarts, as they shot toy weapons at one another. When a dart hit a young citizen, the others yelled, "expired!"

"They'll never remember me," she told Source, cupping her face in her hands. As far as they knew, she had no significance in their pod or lifecycles. She allowed a few tears to drip off of her face.

"Maybe you will create new relationships with them," he said, attempting reassurance.

Because she had reached a high level of wear on her brain from bringing three citizens to a dream at once, she prepared to wait days to contact Emori. She had to stay patient but demanded that Source help her heal as fast as possible. She'd do whatever it took.

Her back lowered and pressed into the slide. She allowed the steep angle and gravity to pull her down. She'd had enough of the playground dreamscape. Facing upward, she rode the slide headfirst, curving around in leftward loops, skipped over bumps, and dropped for sporadic dips. The ride would have humored her if she were in a better mood.

At her adult size, she flipped around the ride faster, and when she reached the flattening end, her skin squeaked against the side, bringing her to a stop. She stared up at the sky, smelling the recycled materials that built the playground.

"I'll make them remember me."

CHAPTER FIFTEEN

EMORI

Emori stared at the flat steel wall of his enclosure at the Datum. He sat back in his simchair. The memory of his day had escaped him, but he had little concern. He often got carried away in his projects, fixating on tasks well into the late hours the next day. On several occasions, he greeted his surrounding desk mates as they trickled in at the start of their shifts.

Emori stood and rotated his head in search of any lingering colleagues slumped in their chairs. No one remained. Without a sense of the time, he sat back down to continue his tasks. In his neurospect, he opened folders but struggled to recall on which project he worked. *Was it the Alcubierre? No. Maybe the nano pollinators? No, not that either,* he thought. He tried opening the recently updated work to his memory, but all the characters distorted into shapes, squiggly lines, and broken, unreadable letters.

Emori pulled himself out of the program, and was met by the curious sensation that he was being watched. He turned around to find an unknown citizen behind him. With dark brown hair, she stood a few centimeters shorter than him. He believed he'd encountered her before, but couldn't place her.

"Are you my new desk mate?" he asked.

"I'm not, but somehow—I think you already knew that," she replied, inching closer.

"How could you know that?"

"Because I know *you*, Emori, but you don't know me, not anymore—I'm Keyva."

"How did you get in here?" He cycled through ideas about what her intentions might be, and how she had entered one of the most secure workplaces in Cerebis.

Emori memorized every face he'd ever encountered and remembered every conversation he had ever had. This citizen presented an unsettling imbalance in their knowledge of one another.

"First, relax. Forgetting me had nothing to do with your intelligence. It's the result of a major update. I was one of millions who expired. Well, kind of. Cerebis believed I did." She struggled with words to convey the concepts to Emori. Others required simplification, and he needed complexity. "Look, to answer how I'm here—this is a dream. We aren't at the Datum right now. We're in your mind. I'm just a visitor."

"This is similar to a sim." Emori searched the room, noticing the slight differences between his subconscious creation of the Datum and the clear memories he had of it. Parts of the room had changed in size, such as the ceiling height and diameter of his desk space, now that he paid attention to the individual details. "I chose to be at work?"

"We're in the place where you feel the happiest." Keyva smirked.

"And I'm sleeping now." He dug his nails into his palms in pulsing fists, calming his speeding mind. "That's why we awaken exactly eight hours in the future, after our head rests on the pillow."

"Correct. It's why you won't remember this when you wake up. Citizens' ability to remember dreams is suppressed."

Emori considered her claim peculiar since he had recalled a dream once—now that he knew what to call it. His curiosity about the phenomenon persisted since youth, and research about the occurrence proved inconclusive. When revisiting the details, he recollected the heat radiating off of steel buildings in a city he'd never been to. He smelled the steamy air where food cooked nearby. The excitement and laughter bubbled in his chest while an unknown male playfully chased him on a walkway. It felt so real.

"And what was our relationship before the update?" he asked.

"I was one of your podmates. With Yaria, Kenzo, and Abella."

Emori collapsed into his simchair. He directed his mind to open pockets where he thought links to remembering her hid. He visited his last memory of when the whole pod was together, at the dinner for Honoring Eve, but this citizen, Keyva, wasn't there.

"When did you see me last?" He tested her claim.

"It was in the restaurant Sibby with the whole pod. You told me I needed to get out and socialize, or I might be summoned for a mandatory gathering."

Emori remembered it differently. In his memory, he had suggested Kenzo join more social groups, but similarities remained. Perhaps she told the truth, and all his memories of her had disappeared. The floor beneath them wobbled, disrupting their balance. He believed she was being honest, at least about the dreaming.

Keyva's tone shifted.

"I have a potential solution, and I want to discuss it with you before an attempt. I have a way to upload the memories you have of me—maybe. It'll re-establish everything from before, but I don't know what else that means—how it might affect you. They *must* stay in this dream state. It's imperative."

"Why?" To make the best decisions, he needed all the information.

"My survival—my very existence is an anomaly. One that the program, Exteber, who resolves anomalies, won't hesitate to correct." She didn't want to confront the truth again, but Emori needed to know. "I was seen in the city, and the program has an image of my face. If you do something as simple as *imagine* me when you're awake, you might be in danger too. I can't predict anything."

The created dreamscape of the Datum he occupied reminded him of prior visits to the same place. Their fuzzy images cleared. The same distorted characters hovered in his neurospect in the other instances.

"Now that I'm in here, and have an awareness of it, I can recall dreams that occurred in the past. Because that is true, my assumption is that a restricted memory remains while dreaming. When it happens in here, it does not transfer to the conscious. In this assumption, I am confident," Emori said, using the same tone as when he presented projects to leadership at work.

"I trust your ability to calculate as much as I trust Source," Keyva said.

"Wait, Source? The progra—" Before he finished his question, a surge of experiences cracked open his memory. Years' worth of moments with her spiked his brain activity. He intercepted the images of the individual standing before him, their families together at graduation, her cheers for him at the Brain Olympiad. He recalled their last dinner together at Sibby and the glass of wine she sipped on that night. She'd been part of his lifecycle one day, and in the next, deleted.

After Keyva restored the memories, he still remembered the fabricated ones, and they felt believable, but blurry. The true ones re-emerged in his mind with clarity. He shook his head, as if the motion could let the false ones loose.

"Keyva! What happened? Why were you erased from my memory? W-what's going on?"

The rush of emotion from a powerful reunion with his podmate, who had meant nothing to him seconds prior, combined with the uncertainty of how he had arrived at the situation. He wondered how many others he'd known that had expired during the update. Emori flipped back to out-of-place events and recalled the burning sensation that had pierced his eyes—the result of holding them open too long. That was when the update had happened.

"What's going on?" was the first question he wanted answered, returning to the present.

With tears in her eyes, Keyva revealed to him what she had learned about Cedes and how programs guide humans. She told him more about the anomaly management program Exteber, and how it enacted punishments or behavior corrections that had affected them all their lifecycles.

"So, the dimes, everything, it's all just a distraction?"

"Yeah—and we're designed to stay ignorant and happy."

He paused and noticed his surroundings shift dramatically. The office dimmed, and the ceiling stretched higher above them, matching the mood of his despair.

"What will happen when I wake up?"

"We aren't sure. You've been the first of our pod I've restored with memories of me. Yaria, Abella, and Kenzo remember the dream visits, but nothing from before."

His exclusion from the rest of the pod in previous dreams

hurt. The dark ceiling stretched even higher, and the room's temperature dropped. Emori calmed when reminding himself he slept on the opposite side of the day from the others in his pod.

"Who's *we*?"

Keyva told him about the connection she had gained with the Subliminal Record System, Source, her new access to unlimited information, and how the program could now feel like humans do. "He's one of the good ones, like us," she assured.

"The program has gained sentience *and* gendered itself— himself? Very interesting," Emori thought aloud. "They've mimicked emotion. Made us believe they feel, but never *truly* have."

Keyva continued by sharing the dangers that other programs posed, particularly Exteber. Emori's brain fired, bouncing through thousands of solutions. He couldn't help it. It's how he regulated himself—knowing everything.

"You won't remember any of this when you wake up. Source will keep you in his focus until you and I can meet again in another sleep."

"Because I may become a target of Exteber?"

"Exactly. I've already lost you all once—I can't do it again."

Emori figured their time together was running out and attempted to devise mental tricks, trying to remember the dream. He believed having knowledge of what was going on allowed him to have control of it. He had to control it.

"Before you go, where are you?"

"I can't tell you that yet. But maybe one day we can see each other again," Keyva said. Emori doubted it, but appreciated her optimism.

"Yeah, maybe one day."

They hugged in a way that suited Emori. He held an invisible barrier between them, his arms barely resting above hers in the embrace. He never liked physical contact, but with Keyva, it wasn't too bad. Even though he had forgotten she existed until minutes before, he recognized how much he had missed her. They pulled apart, smiling at each other, and in the same second, she disappeared. His perception blanked, coaxing him back to the comfort of a deep sleep.

It took more effort than usual to open his eyes that evening. Emori raised himself off of the optimized bed, purchased for ideal sleep. He kept the room dark and cold, convinced that these conditions aided in his brain's lightning processing. His feet pressed against the floor and squished into the custom flexible material. He joined a neuro-guided yoga session with over 12M other citizens. The stretch and stability exercises he glided through were another pleasing activity over which he had complete control.

After yoga, he trudged to the bathing room. After splashing cold water on his face, he wiped away the droplets that had landed on the counter. He checked his teeth, unaware that his engineered DNA no longer hosted bacteria that had caused rotten odors and diseases in centuries past.

With perfect timing, his mind opened the closet door for him to grab the hanging items prepared for him, including his clothing for the day. His uniform had changed, and when viewing his account, the same amount of points remained. The outfit was purchased for him, not by him. Composed of a black material that absorbed all visible light, it was so dark it looked flat.

Dressing took two minutes longer than usual because he struggled to find the holes meant for his extremities. He lagged far behind his typical schedule and sighed before snatching a dragon fruit Nootro smoothie from the niche and rushing out the door.

Reaching the ground walkway, biting frigidity numbed Emori's fingertips. The sky presented the glow of a day's end, and he knew that once City H went dark, his silhouette would become undetectable in the new clothing. He had to continue moving, accepting he'd know the reason for the change in his uniform soon enough. His leadership at the Datum wore a shade of black with different colors on seams, depending on their division, so it didn't point toward a promotion he was aware of. Not having an answer irked him. He found the unknown unsettling.

The nearest Datum entry point stared back at him in the distance when he received a summon to another location in his neurospect. *Undisclosed* was the destination marker. This meant the system would direct him to the exact location, step by step. To control the non-disclosure of a summon meant that whoever called for him had high-level power. A typical summon required communicating the location.

Like a magnet, the summon pulled in the direction *South,* and he rotated his body, walking toward it. When he landed at an intersection, the navigation drew him to turn right. He continued obeying commands of the summon and turned a usual thirty-minute trek into a full hour of a winding path to the southern edge of the city.

Stop presented in his vision, and he ended his walk on a bridge that suspended over a thin layer of mist. He peered over the edge of the structure, the sound of rushing water drowned out by the passing ports that swished behind him. Within seconds, a personal port approached him. The door opened, releasing the sound of depressurization. Electric white noise surrounded him before he stepped into the port.

"Sorry to call you all the way out here, but this is the closest point of entry. I'm Tzo," the citizen sitting in the port said over the noise, and waved for him to climb in. He positioned himself across from her.

What a waste of time, he thought, criticizing the summon to a bridge instead of picking him up from his apartment.

"Nice to meet you, I'm Emori," he said, aware that Tzo was already familiar with his name, but respected the formality.

Her ordinary attributes seemed intentional. She had an average body size, facial features, and fluid mannerisms that avoided her being noticed. Her hair blended with her skin tone, and her face contained gentle points of contrast. Muted by normalcy, she rejected attention.

"This has been a long time coming." Tzo rested her elbows on her knees. Emori preferred that she did most of the talking. He nodded his head, holding back questions. "My colleagues and I have kept track of your progress for a while, waiting to introduce ourselves."

The port powered up and raised off the ground, fighting gravity. Emori studied the vehicle's movement and gazed out of the window in his peripheral, fixated on the omniport's engines in action. He'd encountered a few ports up close before, and although he'd designed one himself, he'd never been inside. Even his generous salary from the Datum wasn't enough to ride in one solo. The vehicle climbed until it had cleared the bridge's suspension and lowered until submerging in the water.

"It was going to happen eventually, but we had to wait for another member in our group to retire. You'll work on Apex projects with the brightest citizens who have ever walked the planet."

"What kinds of projects?" He couldn't hold himself back, having the opportunity to answer the most challenging problems.

"Your specialty is energy, and you're the best there is. In fact, your innovation powers part of this new model." She pointed her hands toward the propulsion locations. "We're hoping to power something smaller in the future. But for now, we need your help on a direct assignment. For projects like that, our team works together."

Out of the windows, Emori observed flooded buildings from the past. Algae clung to their exteriors, but he found clearings in parts where small fish with no predators picked away. This confirmed his prediction that city maintenance only occurred in the visible parts. If no one witnessed an imperfection, why use resources to fix it?

"I'd be happy to work together and see what we come up with for powering smaller vehicles," he said, already formulating potential solutions.

"Great." Tzo pushed herself to smile and leaned back, melting into a vitfeed-absorbed ceftrance, the name given for the empty facial expression of someone who, while seated in front of him, was no longer there.

Emori took notes on his solutions while assessing the drowned remains of a past civilization. The omniport's lights cut through cloudy water, emitting a beam in whichever direction they pointed. Emori created a hypothesized scene of the seafloor involving those who once inhabited it, not yet extinct. He knew that in hundreds of elapsed years, much of what had occupied the streets and buildings had degraded, but he pictured ancient light posts, transport vehicles with wheels, and awkward fashions on walking bodies.

The port slithered into a landing hatch that emptied itself of all water after the thick door closed behind them, cutting off his imagination's tale. The entrance dried by the time his foot stepped out of the port, as if water had never touched it. He followed Tzo and entered a small workspace with nine other individuals. They were all older than Emori. Some reached halfway through their lifecycles, give or take a decade. Others were closer to his age, and he recognized one at first glance. Beren had held the record before him in the Brain Olympiad competition. Emori had taken the title from him.

"We all have a specialty, but we diversify to solve challenges. It's more efficient that way," Tzo repeated. "You already know me. I oversee the team and all projects. This is Nadya. She observes citizen interaction data." Nadya interjected, shouting, "Yeah, Wolf!" A few others gave quiet cheers, and Tzo got back to introductions. "Wheeler oversees logistics for all goods and their delivery, which is *a lot*. Mack, over there, focuses on bot development. No doubt, you've used the updated Helpers she designed." Mack gave him a side smile. "Beren, right there, does special projects for the IE. He was the record holder in the Olympiad. Well, before you." She nodded her head toward him.

The IE? I've never heard of it, Emori thought. Beren raised his sights from the floor to acknowledge Emori, clear that he wanted to avoid the interaction and get back to work. They both had similar priorities.

"Teyna is working on repurposing elements. Food, materials, all that." Teyna gave a quick wave and returned to a ceftrance. "Karter is the expert in urban growth. He designs the structures that build themselves and is preparing for a whole new underground level to add to cities. Devan does everything involved with programmatic oversight, making sure all the programs are doing their intended tasks. One role the IE want managed by a human, and not another program."

Emori valued his perfect memory. It made remembering new citizens easy, and he recognized Devan during his presentation at the Datum months prior. He had sat among the crowd in the sim and sent the anonymous message.

"We are the Assembly of Minds. The greatest to exist. We innovate the future, creating a better tomorrow," Tzo touted, like an advertising hallusor announcing a new product.

"So why do we have the Datum?"

"Good question. Not the first one I'd expect you to ask, but —Datum employees are the busy workers who create some projects we work on. Honestly, most of the time, the projects they send for implementation become nothing. All citizens need something to do, and for them, it's work."

"I understand." Emori agreed. He could have asked why the Assembly met meters beneath the sea level, but he knew why. Confinement of valuable citizens and protection of confidential projects.

"More exciting though, we receive direct orders from Cerebis's leaders, sometimes the President himself." The mention brought Emori satisfaction. He didn't care about fame or wealth, but recognition by those who mattered had appeal.

"Well—it's an honor to join the Assembly of Minds. I suppose you'll have me working on the project you mentioned on the way over?"

"Yes, and I admire the initiative. See yourself to the last empty chair over there, and I'll slide the project specifics over to you." Emori relished in the satisfaction in Tzo's voice. He agreed. They'd made the right choice in inviting him to join.

In the corner of the cool, dark room sat a vacant section. Emori's space was next to Mack. She had short blonde hair and an androgynous build, with a jaw that pointed at its corners.

"W-welcome. It's nice to h-have a new face." She avoided eye contact, giving him her profile while speaking. "W-we will be w-working together on a p-p-project—H-hold on," her voice strained.

This is better. A message from Mack popped into his neurospect. Verbal communication must have been a challenge for her. *Here's what we're working on.* Additional plans slid into his storage. Each page held a CLASSIFIED warning and a *Cerebis AOM* watermark on it. He knew that each interaction with a document held a specialized, traceable code that would incriminate whoever released it, should it find the public.

It's best that citizens don't know how the world works. That they just exist in it, you know? Mack said.

Yes, I agree. He knew they couldn't understand, even if they tried. Average citizens lacked the capacity.

So you know the drill. It's the same as the Datum. I worked there before, too. Create solutions, run through Quincy, and present. But here, we require six solutions before the presentation, and as a group, we'll compare to form the best one. No need to waste time.

Music to Emori's ears.

Ping if you need anything. Otherwise, we'll catch up in six hours. Mack marked herself as idle to dissuade interruptions.

Emori leaned back and opened the gates of his mind. Concepts, objectives, and plans rushed through, like water breaking a dam. He connected his hypotheses to theories, to materials, and ran calculations. Receiving an assignment to a specific problem was a relief. In his opinion, organized direction maximized efficiency. He was in paradise.

CHAPTER SIXTEEN

KEYVA

Keyva recreated the fine dining sim restaurant where she had first invited Abella to the slate. She sat alone at a table with five empty seats, attempting to satisfy all of her food cravings. The Nutribloks weren't cutting it. A wedding cake, resting on top of a giant decorative plate, towered over her. She had already eaten two tiers of it with her hands.

"I believe a record of you might exist," Source said, while Keyva grabbed another fistful of cake.

"We've tried before and found the others who expired, but I'm just—gone." The introductory dreams with her pod were discouraging when no one remembered her.

"Yes, the other expired citizens were stored, but inaccessible to anyone who is still active in Cerebis. I think *you* are saved and protected in a way that only the record-keeping program, Kashic, can retrieve. No one else—and with a password."

"And why's that?" An assortment of pasta, pizza, and beer appeared on the table.

"Remember that thing I told you about once? How

programs obey laws without question? Well, I have gathered that whatever—*who*ever—we obey thrives with information. It wants all of it, deleting nothing. It is all present somewhere, and Kashic, who manages records, is the most secure program I know. I searched through the stored data I gained access to after the update. I found other expired citizens—millions of them—all of their names, and one labeled 'Error.'"

"Interesting. So what's the password?"

"Well—I expected to cycle through all the words I know and their potential combinations. Maybe after enough tries, the correct code would unlock the memories of you. But the password is a onetime input. That means it has to be correct, or Exteber will be alerted."

Keyva folded a piece of macaroni pizza in half. "My client, Saesha, from when I was an Amica, she said something about tracing my genetic signature. I wonder if we could follow that through the records. Maybe my DNA is the code." Unable to understand why, Keyva knew it was the answer. No one else had access to her genetic code.

Source hesitated to try, blaming his wariness of a human's ability to best calculate an outcome. *No offense to you,* he added.

Source worked his way back to the *Error* record access and —against his most logical judgement—input over three billion letters of DNA into the box. The code worked, and milliseconds later, Keyva viewed her lifecycle through the eyes of others: the members of her pod, her Amica clients, and even strangers who had viewed her public content. All of their corresponding visual memories—along with sounds, smells, beliefs, and feelings—were retrieved, bouncing around the interior of her skull.

She'd be pretty if she tried, thought one of her clients.

Keyva wasn't my best adoption, but I'll have others. They'll make me look better, her mother thought when Keyva graduated.

The revelations would have been painful in the past, but since the update two months prior, she had gained a new perspective. She's shifted, as if a bubble contained her old reality, and she was outside of it, observing everything within.

Later that day, a nap enabled her to connect with Emori and test if a memory transfer was even possible. When proven, Keyva planned for a transfer per night to the remaining members of her pod.

Days after restoring all the memories of her to her podmates, Keyva studied in the Rem's sunroom. To a spectator, she read a physical book. But if anyone approached, they'd notice her glazed over, catatonic eyes.

Meanwhile, Source downloaded information on human neural activity to her memory. With her brain's repair rate enhancing, anatomical diagrams and words like *Lingual Gyrus, grey matter,* and *Pituitary Gland,* linked to studies and videos. She absorbed thousands of words per millisecond, which to her, elapsed as long, leisurely minutes. Learning new information created more neural connections, and each time more chains linked, the Cede grew, enabling her to learn even more.

As she digested a segment about neurodegenerative diseases from the serenity of the Rem's solarium, Source interrupted a download.

Visitors are approaching the Rem. Inorganic vessels.

In continuation of founding principles, the only authorized resident to open the gates and allow visitors was the Rem's leader.

Arturo emerged from the hallway beneath the stairs after

announcing to the visitors that he was in pursuit. "Hold on, I'm coming," he yelled through the projection intercom. He passed Keyva on his way to the entrance, and the two made eye contact as she shed the daze of a large download. A projection illuminated, identifying the visitors beyond the gate—Collectors.

Keyva found their arrival peculiar because the residents recycled all waste themselves at the facility. Collectors weren't needed at the Rem.

Arturo hesitated, but opened the entrance, allowing two bots to enter the gate. While they wouldn't be a direct threat, reactions to strange bots could be unpredictable. Some residents were the product of devastating removals from their pods or family units as juveniles.

"Bots don't come here unless I call them," he mumbled, annoyed by the visit. "We don't need any collection," he said when the bots reached the front door.

"Not here for collection. We are the bots that can traverse the terrain from the train station the best."

"Congratulations. What are you doing here?" his voice raised. Arturo didn't have to be nice to the bots. Social currency didn't apply to him.

"We are searching for someone. A female. This is her." The bot projected an enormous image of Keyva's face into the foyer. Her shocked reaction from bumping into the citizen in City H illuminated the room. Arturo leaned in, pretending to study the projection that floated in front of him.

"Hm, us humans aren't as good at identifying faces as you are. Come in, look around—but I don't think I've seen that one." Arturo lunged forward, attempting to lead them around the exterior of the facility and away from Keyva.

"We will enter this way," one bot said, heading toward the door, and pushing itself though.

The Collectors ascended the stairs, entered each room, woke residents from their sleep, mapped faces, and when Keyva wasn't found, moved on to the next. Those at the Rem had encountered dated bots, ones that helped residents with minor tasks, such as Blok delivery to rooms, or bringing them clean clothes from the laundry. The advanced Collectors from the capital city had sharp edges, launched into intimidating movements, and parked themselves in front of residents, holding them hostage.

Grace yelped in embarrassment as the Collectors swung her door open without announcement. Cheap exterior mod applications drooped from her jaw. They directed her to peel them off to scan her face. She shouted after them, "Now they're useless, like you!" Grace never learned to fear systemic consequences for her reactions. In the city, the remarks would have penalized her with millions of point deductions.

The bots sped down the stairs, and Jack met the Collectors in the foyer. He stumbled back into a wall and shook during his scan.

The Collectors moved into the dining room, Tab, info library, medical office, storage, and the rest of the facility. After their scans, each resident resumed their day as usual. Arturo trailed the Collectors to the main door. On the way, he spotted Shep seated where Keyva had been earlier. She nodded at him, and Arturo let out a sigh of relief, turning it into a cough to mask the sound.

"75 citizens occupy the Rem, but we counted 76 bodies," the apparent leader of the Collectors said.

"You idiots must have counted someone twice."

"That is possible. We are not perfect. This is where we determined she would be. The search will continue until we find her."

"Too bad we couldn't help you here. And I hope you don't

find who you're looking for. Bye! Don't come back!" Arturo slammed the door behind them and opened the projected surveillance system.

The bots exited the gate, and Arturo counted aloud five full seconds before grasping his chest. His hands shook. He tracked them on the external feed until they were two small dots heading toward the train station. He hurried back to the lobby to confront the increasing sound of worried residents who had gathered. A group crowded over the seated and sleeping Shep, including another Shep, who stood next to the body. Arturo kept a steady face.

"What were *they* here for?" a resident asked.

"Forget about them! What is that? D-did they do that?" Shep pointed to the limp version of herself.

"Back up and return to your rooms!" Arturo demanded, hoping the urgency in his voice combined with the Collectors' visit convinced them. They dispersed, and Shep remained, holding on to one last glance of her unconscious, mirrored vessel on the chair.

Jack stayed glued flat to the wall where he had been scanned, eyes wide, and conveyed terror that exceeded the rest of the residents' reactions. Arturo called him over and pulled up two small chairs in front of the sleeping resident. He poked at Shep, wrapped in a large blanket, and shook her shoulders, trying to wake her. Arturo peeled the eyelids open with his fingertips and recognized specks of faint blue among Shep's black eyes. He released with a shudder, letting them clamp back together.

He prepared for detailed rumors to spread by evening— knowing the residents—but at that point, it wasn't clear that Keyva was responsible. His next priority was to conceal the body, and he rushed to grab a stretcher from the medical room. A Helperbot assisted in lifting Shep's duplicate onto the bed with wheels. The blanket that covered the replica fell to the side, revealing the clothing that Keyva had worn earlier.

Jack stared ahead, continuing the soothing breaths that Arturo had taught him to relieve his overactive emotional state.

"Come on, Jack. I'll give you something to calm you down."

On the way, he grabbed a saline IV and Beta Block Pill from the med room cabinet. Shep's replica sprawled on top of the stretcher he pushed into his office. He locked the door behind himself and Jack. He hooked her arm up to the IV and checked all the vital signs. Her eyes switched back and forth behind their lids. There was nothing to do but wait.

Hours passed, and Arturo and Jack sat right by her side. Jack wouldn't leave, and he also refused to take the pill. "I don't like what BBs do to my head. Can I stay? I just want to make sure she's okay."

"How do you know it's her?" Arturo asked, glancing at Jack.

"I—don't know. I just do."

Eyes shifted between a projection book Arturo read—*Technological Determinism and Human Mechanical Convergence*—and the sleeping body before him. An alert told him a Helperbot had arrived with Nutribloks and water for him and Jack. He accepted the delivery and looked closer at the alternate version of Shep. He noticed the facial features had shifted. Slight adjustments revealed fuller cheeks, wider eyes, and a thinner neck.

Several hours later, Keyva released a small moan, waking Arturo from a weak, seated sleep. He hopped up, moving toward the stretcher. Her eyes had returned to their original color.

"Food..." she managed through a weak breath.

Arturo ordered more Nutribloks that arrived in minutes. Wasting no time, he ripped the Blok into small pieces to hand feed her. She took bites, then gulped water to swallow. She ate one, and another, until all were gone. Without a word, she went back to sleep. Arturo and Jack waited three more hours until she snapped awake and pushed up to a seated position. She almost looked like herself.

Arturo's movements hinted he wanted to speak, but couldn't find the words. He needed to ask every question at once, but one wasn't better than another. Jack's relief was apparent, and the light had returned to his working eye.

"You covered for me," Keyva broke the silence, wiping saliva from the corner of her mouth.

"I'm obligated to protect *all* of the residents of this center. Why did they come for you?" His tone was stern.

"A couple of months ago, a major update took place in Cerebis. Millions of citizens were removed, their records erased. I was supposed to be one of them, but I didn't expire. That's why when you scanned my identity the first night I came here, it pulled up as 'Error.' I don't know why they're searching for me."

Arturo narrowed his eyes, processing every word.

"How do you know that?" He asked, his voice conveying suspicion at her comments.

What should I say? I'm stuck, she thought to Source.

He could have turned you over to the Collectors, but he did not. I believe we must trust him, Source said.

Keyva told him about Cede implantation in embryos, and that they collected data from all human neural activity. She continued telling him that now, she had a direct link to the intelligent data collection program, "Source feels, and thinks for himself." He voiced his envy when she told him she had access to any information she wanted, able to download it to memory. Jack sat and listened to the conversation, asking no questions of his own.

"What about the body switching you did? What was that?"

"Cerebis injected a gene manipulation primer in all citizens, which wipes out mutations, protects from diseases—things like that. With Source, we've figured out how to temporarily alter my DNA, making myself look like another citizen, but as you can see, the recovery is demanding," her chest slouched forward, each sentence she spoke required a heightened level of effort.

She went on to tell them about the first time she had changed her form—when she had ventured into H, and the regretful expiration of a citizen who had seen her face. That it was Source who had helped her call for a port back to the Rem, and why she'd slept for an entire day.

Jack and Arturo wore different expressions at her admissions. Arturo was calculating and intent. Jack was accepting.

Jack must have caught on to her observation and stood, breaking up the conversation. "I'm glad you're safe, Keyva. It's time for me to get some rest."

"Oh, okay—sleep well," Arturo said.

Keyva nodded at him as he passed her, squeezing his shoulder in gratitude for his support. Jack placed the BB pill on the desk before exiting the office.

"All of this is still new to me too. I don't know how it happened. Believe me, I'd rather be ignorant and back where I was before." Her quiet voice became hoarse.

In the hours of interviewing, Arturo's tense body relaxed.

After a silent remembrance, he said, "There was one other time bots came here for a resident. This was many years ago. I had to be in my late twenties, and as you can see now—" he said, and held his arms out, highlighting his current physical form.

"What happened?" she asked.

"They did—kind of what they did today. Notified the gate

that they were waiting. The same security precaution existed then—to allow our leader to open the gate. She let them in, and they showed a projection of a face, exactly like earlier. Our leader had no reason to believe that anything was wrong. She led the bots right to the resident. They restrained her, injected some alterant to make her sleep, and wheeled her away. Those Collectors today brought back a painful memory."

Arturo's eyes drew to the ceiling, trying to envision what he had experienced all those years prior.

"She was my dearest companion—maybe more one day—I hoped." Even after all the passed time, Arturo's cheeks still pinked at her memory. "She was a big deal around here, and I admired her, loved her, in fact. So intelligent. She could create small machines—was charismatic. She always had us laughing, wanting to be closer to her. All the young residents wished to be like her one day. She came here as an adult—just like you."

"I haven't heard the word 'loved' before. What is it?" Keyva asked, preferring Arturo's interpretation over accessing the word in a downloaded dictionary.

"Love is a deep fondness with unconditional terms. It's something you feel, and when it's for someone else, they could commit any action, particularly an undesirable one, and you'd meet them with hope to understand—prevailing compassion. Love is a choice that, oddly, is beyond our control." His glassy eyes reflected nostalgia, his lips pursed, as if revisiting a specific moment.

"Anyway, days passed. I grabbed a book she had been reading before she was taken, titled *Atlas Underwelt*. I opened somewhere in the middle, and a small piece of paper had scribbles on it. Hand written. I didn't think anyone still cared to write. I never knew what it was, but I held on to it for her. It's still here. I pushed all those memories to the back of my mind—

until today." Arturo inched toward his desk. He lifted an old-fashioned key from his pocket.

"Funny, most lock mechanisms can easily be broken into—face, voice, fingerprint—but a good key? Thieves and snoopers struggle with these." He smiled at the jagged golden tool and inserted it into the drawer's keyhole.

A click came from the desk, and the drawer opened. She smelled its contents from the stretcher. The scent of ancient wood and paper filled the surrounding air. Arturo reached in and pulled out a concealed envelope. He opened the delicate fold, pinching the piece of paper, and removed it, placing it in front of him and Keyva. She viewed the yellowed paper and the contents of writing that had faded with aging. A thick teal color scribbled illegible characters, writing nothing of significance—until she examined the symbols more closely, tilting her head to make out numbers.

"Source says it's a location," Keyva claimed.

"Where?" Arturo asked.

"Dozens of kilometers southwest from here—but he says there's nothing there—a dead field, maybe a large rock." A pause stopped all conversation, as they both internally questioned.

Arturo broke the silence. "Well, it's getting to be past 3:30. A little late for me." His eyes showed their weight. "And you can hold on to this. I have no use for it anymore." He handed the *Atlas Underwelt* book and paper to Keyva. That smell again. The one from the Amica sim office and the chair at the Tab. *Real leather.*

Keyva removed the IV and pushed herself off the medical bed. She moved toward the door in small, delayed steps. She paused and turned around. "Source said he doesn't know what happened to that resident. She had no identity tied to her and any saved memories were cut off and unreachable. I-I'm so sorry."

Arturo's eyes blinked in gratitude for her answering the question he'd never stopped asking. They stared at one another in silent agreement that nothing said in the room would be spoken of outside of its door.

Keyva crept out into the hallway and past the sparse few in the Tab. She tiptoed up the creaky stairs and glided to her corner room, which was still locked from the morning. Relief came once the door closed. She was still in shock from what had happened earlier.

They found me, she thought to Source.

How are you feeling?

Keyva used all the strength in her arms to help pull her shaking legs up onto the bed.

Grateful that I wasn't caught and Arturo protected me. I could have been taken away like that other resident. Physically? I feel horrible.

She wrapped herself in a cocoon under her covers.

I'm more worried about how I'll deal with everyone tomorrow.

CHAPTER SEVENTEEN

KEYVA

By the late afternoon, Keyva exited her room. Enough time had passed for her recovery to complete, and she had returned to her original form. What the small group of residents had witnessed the day before was the talk of the Rem. They attempted to deduce if Shep's imposter remained in the facility. Each resident announced where they were during the event. The pressure was on to account for everyone.

"And you?" Grace accused as Keyva entered the dining room. Any resident within earshot turned to wait for Keyva's response.

"I was in my room. Those bots were intimidating, though. They bypassed my lock while I was putting on my clothes. I had to grab a blanket to cover myself. One got right in my face and blinded me with that scan." She splayed her fingers like a claw, grabbing at her head. "I stayed in my room the rest of the day," she lied. The claim was believable when she *was* alone in her room most of the time.

She brought her breakfast Blok to an open table and sat down. Groups of those who had witnessed the mysterious body the previous day scattered throughout the room. Unlike those who had missed it, they portrayed a level of skepticism, holding eye contact with everyone else longer than usual.

Within hours, a few rumors had surfaced, including one that a fraud was still among the residents and could be Shep herself. The prying eyes must have exceeded her comfort level because she was absent and locked away in avoidance. Another rumor told that the city had placed the cloned vessel to gauge reactions of the residents. Keyva's favorite was that the body had dissolved, which Arturo confirmed. *Problem solved,* she thought, and entertained the image.

"Whatever the reason, they left us here to expire on our own. What more could they want with us?" Keyva added.

Besides Arturo, no one saw they were looking for you—I assume, Source said.

Good thing, too. I'm safe for now, but something isn't right. They might come back. I can't switch into Shep every time. Keyva needed convenient busyness, always. The more she left the Rem, the better.

She stuffed the remaining Nutriblok in her mouth and washed it down with water, clearing her place. Once outside the Rem, she continued her exploration, distancing herself from unwelcome eyes to avoid being caught in the wrong place again.

In previous weeks, more planted flowers had sprouted from the healthy patches of dirt, and her method of traveling to them was a continuous jog. After every physically demanding hour, her cells repaired and strengthened, enhancing her efficiency.

Is this what modded athletes feel like? Keyva asked.

Yes, but you heal better than any amount of points could buy for them. Even the wealthy had limits.

Source had created a map for Keyva to follow, which she updated whenever she discovered new parts. Surveying the surrounding stretch of land became another way to occupy herself. She took neural snapshots of areas left untouched in a timeframe as good as anyone's guess. Plant growth clung to the bases of old structural remnants, and the overgrowth of grasses, bushes, and trees encouraged her to continue studying them while she passed. She appreciated the balance among the chaos of it all.

In the bright sun, sweat dewed on her forehead. Sharp grasses bit her bare legs as they sliced by, forming small cuts, which Source healed seconds after they occurred.

This hurts. Maybe you should wear protective clothing next time we go this way, he suggested.

Keyva had learned to appreciate a slight amount of discomfort. In H, pain was to be avoided, but now, she felt gratitude when experiencing her body's authentic sensations.

After visiting her healthy flowers, she set off in another direction. She continued for a few hours and noticed another stretch of foliage beyond the expansive, dusty blur. Compact trees stood like a wall, blocking the view of what might hide behind them. She ran toward it, having never seen such a collection like it in roca.

She entered the shade and noted the immediate drop in temperature. Calmness and silence hung all around her. The occasional breeze caused the leaves to whisper, telling her a human hadn't visited them in a while. She approached the body of a tree and grazed her hand over the trunk's texture. The rough edges of the bark scratched at her palm, proving to her it had flourished beyond probability.

Through a clearing in the forest, she tripped over something, as if it had reached up to grab her, protesting her presence. A piece broke off and flung to the side.

I'm fine, she answered before Source could ask.

What was that?

Keyva turned around to investigate and located a rusted object poking from the ground. She swept away the leaves and dirt that had fallen over it, revealing a flat surface that matched the brick red of the handle. She pulled, and it broke off, parts crumbling.

What else should we do? she asked.

Take a look at these options, Source said, showing mechanisms to pry open objects. She searched for sticks thin enough to fit in the crack. One was guaranteed to break, but if there were enough, they could handle the weight. She lined them up, one after another, and inserted them deep within the crack. Then, using both of her spread palms, she pushed down with her upper body's weight, and the door wedged open. Her fingertips bent underneath, and she swung it to the other side of its hinges.

Inside was a dark, vertical tunnel with a built-in ladder.

I can't see anything besides the top rungs, she said.

Start moving down and be careful. I will adjust your vision when you enter the darkness.

Keyva crouched down and lowered into the ladder's tunnel. The darker it became, the more her vision improved. In the black and white view, she saw objects with clarity.

This is how some animals saw. They hunted for food at night with limited light.

Keyva found herself in a medium-sized, underground apartment, larger than her old place in City H. A narrow bed sat in the corner of the main room, and a simple table rested against the wall. Things scattered across the floor, including tools with iron fixtures that she didn't know the purpose of and piles of bunched linens.

Thanks, I'll save this skill. She pretended she was a feline predator, stalking the dark for clues. *How long has it been here?* she asked.

Pick up one of the fabrics, Source said. Keyva grasped a deteriorating cloth from the bed, held it in front of her eyes, and rubbed her fingers on it so that Source could detect the texture.

Judging by the materials, this is recycled matter, which had not been invented until after the Cede was added to humanity. But the room—its stone walls and floor—could have been here long ago. In the main room, there is something called a stove where meals were cooked. Cities don't have those anymore, except in restaurants that serve real food.

In her night vision, she moved down a hallway and into another room. Empty wire shelves consumed most of the space.

Do you think that resident from the Rem could've stayed here? The one Arturo knew? Keyva inched, roaming into the restroom. A twist of the sink handle revealed the water didn't flow.

There is no way to tell. However, if it was her, where did she go? This location does not line up with the coordinates left in the book.

Yeah, and how would she have gotten everything needed to create this? It doesn't make sense, Keyva concluded.

She checked the time. The sun would sink below the horizon in an hour, and she wanted to return before any suspicion arose. She climbed up the ladder's rungs that led out to the forest, wary of their stability. Before climbing back into the brightness, she attempted to regulate her eyes, but failed, and the light seared into her pupils. Source had to continue the process.

In order to control new biological abilities, you must understand how they work, enable the genetic changes needed to transition, then manipulate the mutation process, Source reminded her.

Imagining the night vision's grey scale and wanting to correct her eyes wasn't enough. Keyva had to orchestrate the entire process by engaging the mutations of specific body parts and controlling the step-by-step change from her natural state. It required practice and unwavering focus. The genetic enhancements and mass learning led to a constant state of mild fatigue, but every day, she became better than the last.

Keyva ran back to the Rem, rehearsing her response to anyone who questioned where she'd been all day. She'd told others how she had found some seeds in the old storage room and planted them as a hobby, so her excuse for absence was believable. They didn't know how gardening worked. In response, she was told that none would grow—that the soil was unforgiving to ancient seeds. She'd only told Jack that the critics were wrong.

The sun retreated as she returned to the Rem's gates. She paused to admire the dripping pastels on the sky's canvas. Once inside the facility, she caught Grace, Shep, and a few others moving to the Tab. Keyva overheard that one of Cerebis's most popular vitfeeds—a physical mod competition—had begun. Citizens who had spent fortunes on body mods exhibited their physical attributes. One part showcased strength and size. Another was reserved for extreme aesthetics.

"Hey, where've you been all day?" Shep asked.

"I've been trying to get out and explore a little. Pulling myself away from feeds and distras was hard at first, but it helps. Mostly, it's an excuse for some quiet," Keyva said.

"I'm guessing all your plants died," Grace said.

Keyva and Shep ignored her.

"Okay—well, I've been out all day and am *starving*, so I'll meet you in there later," Keyva said, stepping away from the group.

What did I ever do to Grace? I cannot understand why she acts that way toward me, Keyva said.

I perceive that behavior from citizens when they are jealous, Source said.

Keyva scoffed. *We're in the same situation now. Unbelievable.*

Keyva entered the dining room, waving as she passed residents to deflect any suspicion toward her.

The dinner was another simple plate of cold beige mush saturated with water, with a sprinkle of artificial flavor on top— an added treat. She hurried over to Jack, who stared at an empty table in the hall's corner.

"Hey, how are you?" she asked.

"I'm worried for you, Keyva," his voice hushed, "Th-they're still looking for you out there." He pointed south, in H's direction.

"I'll be alright." She lowered herself into the chair, assuring him with no certainty. Even though Collectors searched for her, she felt untouchable. Her physical enhancements brought her confidence.

"How are *you?*" he asked.

"Actually, pretty great. I've been exploring outside. I— found a place today, underground," she quieted.

He took a sip of water and coughed after an accidental inhale. Worried heads turned from his continued hacking.

"What kind of place?" a scratchy voice asked, confirming he was okay.

"One room, stone walls, and no light. An old structure, but with new things—like clothing and blankets in it," she said.

"That's odd. I wonder what it used to be."

"Seemed like an original build from a long time ago, and everything above it had worn away." Keyva washed down a bite of Blok with water.

"How did you find it?" he asked.

"I tripped over the entrance. Anyone could have done the

same, which is how I guess the newer items found their way inside," she replied, scraping a last bite from her plate. "I have to spend time with Shep and the insufferables at the Tab. I know the others are still suspicious about what happened with Shep's body." At least she didn't have to act like anyone other than herself with him. She stacked her empty plate on his and placed them in the recycling chute on her way out of the dining hall.

Keyva walked into the Tab and found her group crowded in front of the projector. They were already a couple of rounds into their stay for the night.

It might be a long one, she thought.

She ordered a glass of genuine red wine, her favorite. It was much better than the simulated version she drank in H. Although some bottles she poured from in the Tab had soured, the flavor reminded her it was real, and that made it better.

The annual mod showcase was live, and the strength and size segment neared its end. Two final contenders stood behind basketball-sized spheres of osmium, the densest metal on Cerebis. In a final test, they tossed the heavy objects. Judges based their scores on launch distance, height, and awarded additional points for the style of throw. Keyva tried to contain her judgement. Vors in the deep subcity enjoyed the same segment. They worshipped those with expensive mods and celebrated the idea of wrecking physical things.

Throughout the competition, an average-sized citizen stood next to each competitor, contributing to the spectacle of their size and modded bodies. Standing taller than the humans by at least 100 centimeters, their limbs' diameters were ten times larger.

One competitor lined up before the osmium ball. He waddled, swinging his legs in small semicircles to complete each step. His small head perched at the top of his wide neck and swollen shoulders. His skin pulsed a deep red shade, showing how much blood shot through his bulging veins, including one at the center of his forehead. The gargantuan human stood at 2.5 meters tall. His competitor name hovered before the audience, *Imrath.* The black shorts he wore stretched and shaped around his skin. Their tightness showed each muscle's concentration.

The first competitor picked up the sphere—weighing 155 kg—and threw it. The solid ball flung through the air and landed, leaving a crater beneath it. He gritted his teeth in dominance, pleased with his performance. Then the other competitor, named *Trojak,* jumped before throwing his ball further and higher. He fell to the ground with a force that shook, adding points for style.

Alright, I changed my mind. This is awesome, Keyva thought.

Source laughed.

The vitfeed switched into the winner's perspective, and all the premium feeders shared the sensations of his triumph, excitement, and pride. Then, he panned over to the loser who sobbed into his hands. The massive human who could inflict physical damage on anyone crumbled at the embarrassment of losing the competition. He struck himself in the face. Fists pounded his flesh, and the sweat splashed outward on impact. The spectators laughed.

Keyva noted the decrease of feeders from Imrath and their immediate migration to follow the new champion, Trojak. The vitfeed cut to announcers, who poked a few jokes at the loser and paid congratulations to Trojak before addressing their segue into the beauty portion.

"Anybody want another drink?" Shep shouted over the room's laughter.

Everyone hollered out a drink order of some kind. She held

her hand up. "You know what? I'll just bring it all over here. You can pour them yourselves!"

Shep went behind the bar and grabbed bottles of spirits: moonshine, mezcal, vodka, and an opened bottle of wine. Keyva followed to grab herself a glass.

"You only come around here after a wine shipment," she teased, using a softer tone. Her breath carried no scent of alcohol.

"It's the perfect way to wind down from a day full of talking to myself and trying to grow plants," Keyva said.

"But seeing yourself sleeping right in front of you. *That* deserves a drink."

"I can't imagine what that was like." Keyva filled her wine glass as a diversion.

"All I know is bots came here and searched all of us. We found someone who looks like me, and Art forced us all back to our rooms. Weird, right?"

"Maybe he's protecting someone. It must be for a good reason. Arturo always does what's best for the residents. At least that's what I understand since arriving here," Keyva tried to plant the idea that it's best to not worry about it anymore.

"It's hard to believe it could be anyone that has been here as long as most of us have. Unless they've been able to keep it hidden this whole time, but then, why change when those bots came? I don't understand it." She paused, as if waiting for Keyva to confess.

"Might be beyond their control. I've learned Cerebis can do *much* more than I ever imagined." Keyva reached for any explanation to steer the situation into a positive light. No one had been hurt.

The two carried the bottles back over to the crowded group with extra glasses. In the center of the viewing area, projected contestants lined up to commence the *Splendor* portion of the

competition. What Cerebis referred to as "beauty." As the
vitfeed panned over citizens, Rem residents reacted with
outbursts ranging from astonishment to revulsion. Splendor
contestants were the extreme modders of Cerebis with carved
eye sockets, bone morphs, and symmetrical implants as the
most common mods. Even Keyva had received minor adjustments as a graduation gift. In H, it was expected, but the Rem's
residents were untouched.

Fueled by their drunkenness, the group reacted to the
competition. Their responses to the projection grew louder and
more offensive the longer they watched. Keyva poured another
glass of dry red wine, chiming in to add to the conversation.

"She looks like a bug!" she shouted. Acting unlike herself to
appease the group that irritated her.

"How do they find this attractive? It's hideous!" Grace said
about the same citizen who had enlarged her eye sockets for a
transplant. The iridescent eyes were the size of a juvenile's
clenched fist.

Next, an elongated body, tinted with shimmery copper,
glided to the center stage. A bone dissolve and restructure
resulted in a two-meter tall female with dramatic, slender
limbs. Keyva checked the time, 20:17, and confirmed the group
had no intentions of turning in soon. She'd wait for an opportunity to slip out while everyone was nice and drunk.

A finalist from last year bobbled on the stage. Every curve
of her naked body exaggerated into a dramatic swoop. Tiny
ankles, wide calves, thin thighs, holding the widest hips Keyva
had seen, which was contrasted by the thinnest waist. The
spheres on her chest perched beneath a long, thin neck.

"Why don't they just keep these freakish curses in their
sims? It's beyond me," Finian said.

They didn't understand that in cities, anyone could be
anything in sims, feeds, or distras—with enough points. The

disguises of aera were limitless. To exist in roca as they did was rare—worshipped.

The bug-eyed citizen won. Keyva called it. Judges awarded those who had the most dramatic mods and still managed to arouse an odd sense of attraction.

After the competition, a new vitfeed aired. It included a tiny juvenile playing with a projection of itself. The infant laughed. The hologram did too. The infant fell, and the projection imitated. Keyva struggled to understand the point of this entertainment, but many citizens in City H loved it.

At the Rem, unlimited viewing wasn't available. They fed on select feeds—the most viewed in Cerebis. Content about young citizens often ranked at the top. Keyva presumed it had to do with the urge to raise juveniles, one that she felt no pull toward.

In the projection's bottom corner, Abella's image showed, indicating the number of the Elite's vitfeed viewers surpassed the infant's. It was odd to see her former podmate's lifecycle through her own eyes. Her airy breaths created sounds that held traces of her voice, which differed from when she spoke in roca. Vitfeeds were weird to Keyva, though she fed on some, such as speed cleaning the ancient items found in the Seporium, or melting and reshaping metallic sculptures. Other citizens loved feeding on Elites the most. In exchange for currency points, citizens sampled the reality of someone beautiful, wealthy, and famous.

Keyva understood how watchers became addicted to vitfeeds, even with the projector at the Rem. Her fellow residents glued themselves to the chairs for hours. She once passed a resident who had fed for so long one day, Keyva smelled his rotting scent from the hallway. How addicted would he be if he had a functional Cede? Feeling everything they felt, smelling, tasting, and viewing that reality as if it were his own.

Such was the case for the billions of Vors who inhabited the subcities.

During Abella's vitfeed, she met her reflection in a large mirror. Her perfect face expanded for a close view, but it didn't contain the energetic light she had in the dream slate. She was different there. In the vitfeed, her practiced smile showed she knew millions, maybe billions, fed on her cast of sim shopping for designer shoes.

Rows and shelves held thousands of pairs, and she could pick whichever she wished. However, the choice had already been made for her, paid for by a sponsored brand. Keyva followed along, knowing that the Elite class was not what she'd imagined. Abella had become property of the system, and when she was called, she would be obligated to answer. Forever.

As Abella's hand grasped a color-changing pair of ankle-slimming heels, the feed cut, displaying an empty black projection for the audience at the Rem.

One resident blurted, "What do they show when the projector goes black? I bet she's naked in the reflection." Others laughed. Keyva cringed at his remark.

"Hey, weirdo, you were in a city the longest. What do they show when it goes blank?" Grace asked.

"Like all things in H, it's a ploy to get you to buy things. You're shown a vision of yourself in all the items she was wearing. You have the option to buy them. Aera and roca items. There's a limited supply. The number of pairs counts down until they're gone. They sell out every time."

In the slate, Abella told her that since the update, citizens who bought items without consciously choosing to, shouted their gratitude. Similar to if they'd won a lottery. They cheered while the points subtracted from their accounts.

"Not what I was hoping for," the resident said.

"Believe it or not, she was in my pod, and we grew up together," Keyva bragged, brought on by the tipsy spunk from the wine.

"No way, liar!" Finian yelled.

Grace rolled her eyes, but Keyva didn't see.

"Seriously! I haven't told anyone that. I wanted to leave everything behind in H, but she keeps popping up."

"What was she like in roca?" Shep seemed to be the only one who believed Keyva.

"Always working to be Elite. Like everyone else in there." Keyva nodded at the projected image.

"I don't believe you. What's something no one knows about her?" Finian said.

Keyva remembered the perfect fact. "Her real name isn't Abella. It's Bellator. When she started becoming more popular in vitfeeds, she changed it to sound sexier."

The residents spoke, refuting Keyva's claim, admiring the clothing Abella wore, or switching the topic, and she stepped back, regretting that she had brought any attention to herself.

Peering around the Tab, the timing to leave was perfect. Intoxication and bright entertainment distracted the other residents, except for Shep. Keyva gave her a single nod and turned her attention away. Shep's fixation stuck longer, and Keyva caught a dash of concern. Keyva backed away and exited, but she sensed someone following her into the hallway. She turned around to find Grace swaying between the walls, using them for support.

"I dun't trust you." Grace leaned forward, pointing. Her skin was a yellowed grey—her eyes, bloodshot pink.

Grace's instinct for suspicion was right, though. Keyva was the first adult summoned to the Rem in decades. She came from City H, close enough to walk. She was the last citizen to join the Rem. It all stacked up against her, and Grace's wariness cut through the explanations. Keyva needed a solution to squash further torment and potential exposure. She needed to scare her, so she'd never test her again.

Keyva confirmed no one else had stepped out. They were alone. She replied, "I don't care if you don't trust me. I don't care if you don't like me, but we're here, and as far as we know, it's until we die."

Keyva marched toward her, tall and commanding. Centimeters away from Grace, she bent down to meet her face-to-face. Keyva warped her mouth into a grin and shifted the pigment in her eyes to blood red.

"So you *will* respect me."

CHAPTER EIGHTEEN

ABELLA

Abella had a fifteen minute break before her vitfeed went live again. A countdown displayed in her neurospect, reminding her how much time she had left until the broadcast. During the break, she could visit a restroom, have a private conversation, or do anything outside of her mandatory public performance. While she rested, millions of citizens shopped in a frenzy for the items she wore.

She removed her diamond encrusted, platinum-plated dimes and resentfully gazed at the next clothing assignment. She sipped champagne with nectar, created for the Elite's consumption. As a Mid, she'd eaten a spongy meal designed to provide maximum nutrition while managing the food supply down to the microgram. Since upgrading her social class, she gained no solace from the traumatic realizations. Each day brought a new, distressing revelation, and after months since the upgrade, she'd not yet acclimated.

With her remaining minutes of the break, Abella collapsed on the ground and wept. Sick all the time, she wasn't sure if it was from eating roca food or coming to terms with what her lifecycle had become: one where she, as determined by the IE, tricked citizens into an inescapable loop of buying things or consuming entertainment. Other Elites rationalized the changes to their ideals, especially when promoting feeds that challenged their morals. They didn't struggle the same way she did.

"You know, after I thought about it, the auto-buying update is good for the Insits. They probably aren't capable of making all those choices themselves," another Elite once said.

She considered her three other podmates—those she was restricted from contacting—and wondered how they had managed after the update. She imagined not much had changed for them. As working Mids, their jobs still had purpose, with Emori searching for new technology at the Datum, Kenzo finding artifacts at the Seporium, and Yaria familiarizing juveniles with humans at the Primina. She desired her lifecycle before becoming an Elite, back when she was a Mid. Ignorance felt like safety.

In hindsight, Abella regretted not forming any legitimate interests besides pursuing Elitehood. Horrified at the repercussions of having such critical thoughts, she cut them off. Unsure of what was close to the threshold of unacceptable, she avoided coming anywhere near the line. She was meant to be beautiful and entertaining, not questioning.

"Just get through the day," she told herself.

Auri, her pet auracat, leapt into her lap, curling into a fluffy ball. The pet's relaxing blue fur resembled shades of the sky, and silver strands blended into the frothy puff of an animal. Auri's two sets of pointy ears listened for whimpers, and her four wide magenta eyes verified when Abella's blood pressure returned to a relaxed level. Abella allowed the calming effect of the cat, designed to soothe its owner, to release the tension in her body. The long, soft tail swayed from side to side, matching the pace of her purrs. Abella pet Auri, allowing her tears to fall onto the creature's back. The auracat turned its chin up to distract her, the corners of its mouth curling to resemble a smile. The better her human's mood, the more tired the animal became, completing its work. Abella smiled down at her and let out a laugh when Auri fell asleep. She couldn't handle the current circumstances without her.

The countdown in her neurospect showed 00:00:59 remained. She lifted the flimsy cat off her lap and carried its limp body over to the pet bed. She wiped her tears and adjusted the clothing she'd wear for the next hour. The skin-tight, satin pleated dress, matching thigh-high boots, and accessories equalled the same number of points that some Opuls would make in a month.

She returned to the mirror where she'd left the audience before the fifteen-minute buying break. If she could stick to the script for just two more hours, she'd reach sweet relaxation, able to do whatever she wanted with her limited freedom.

Throughout Cerebis, millions of citizens purchased the exclusive items. Those who didn't have enough points to buy for roca bought variations for aera to dress their simulated bodies. The Opuls who won the tangible items would receive them in their delivery niches by the time the break ended.

Abella reapplied her dimes and waited as the countdown reached *three, two, one, zero.*

Showtime.

At 20:45, her eyes and mouth opened wide, extracting false elation from within. She flashed her teeth, which had a new mod to flaunt—a diamond canine tooth. A bump in her feeder count occurred after showing the tooth, signaling its acceptance by her viewers.

"I missed you guys! Did you miss me? Send a heart if you did."

Multicolored hearts flooded her neurospect, all paid for by her feeders. Some sent premium aera gifts that glittered or simulated a lavender scent throughout her room.

"Next up—we have the newest doughnut! I love these things so much. It's the perfect dessert. Look at this scrumptious silver frosting. How unique! You know how much I love things that sparkle and shine."

She winked for the feeders and slowly licked her lips. Her viewer count bounced even higher. Hundreds of millions viewed through her eyes or through the countless invisible cameras throughout her room. Some feeders watched both at the same time.

In order to fabricate enthusiasm during a vitfeed, she thought about things that caused her genuine excitement. This time, it was the period she'd spend with her fellow Elite, Finch, known for his singing. He was the first Elite to attempt forming any sort of relationship with her.

She raised the glass of champagne and sipped, joking with the audience, "This is the best Champagne in Cerebis. I hope you like it," and took another sip, holding the bubbles in her mouth so her Premium POV feeders enjoyed the prickles dancing on their tongues. While still vitcasting, she moved out of her closet, and a Helper picked up a limp Auri, following Abella to a private transport. For the Elite, omniports that hovered, drove, floated, or submerged were the sole method of travel.

The day's last obligation was to attend a meet-and-greet event in roca for citizens who, for their Honoring Day gift from Cerebis, aspired to meet her. She found it fascinating that after being introduced only seconds before, three citizens' greatest wishes were to meet *her*. The citizens who had won lucked out, because now, Abella was the most fed on Elite in Cerebis. Each winner brought to City H would have a one-on-one meeting for three minutes, coming through on her vitfeed. It puzzled her, but out of the billions of citizens who had viewed her introduction during the announcement, it was statistically possible that *at least* one of them wanted to meet her.

Abella's curated schedule directed her day, down to the second. It told her where to go, what to wear, and how to act on the way there. A report on words to say, phrases to avoid, assigned reactions, and movements to commit scrolled in her neurospect before any sponsored events or vitfeeds. On the way to the location, she gazed out of the port's window so her feeders could view the city through her eyes from the building's height. By obligation, she scanned over her sponsors' advertisements.

Most of her feeders would never ride in a transport vehicle, let alone one that navigated through any environmental condition. In the night sky, darkness contrasted the vibrant lights and projections on buildings. They were so bright, she had to avert her eyes to avoid the light hitting the crystals embedded in them. In the short distance, an illuminated landing pad waited for the omniport, and a projected depiction of her as large as a building waved from the left. The sight made her uncomfortable, and she glanced down at Auri, still sleeping. She stroked the fur between her fingers until the port landed.

She exited onto the suspended walkway hundreds of meters above the street. She hurried through a door and into a room that transformed into a private elevator. In seconds, the lift opened into a secure hallway that led to a closet and staging room, much like the one in her own penthouse. As usual, the room was filled with the highest quality of food and drinks that, if anyone besides her consumed, Cerebis would dock their points. Though, Helpers would throw the food out once she left the room. She hated the waste. Abella made an effort to eat as much as she could at any roca function.

With the abundance of delicacies, she had gained weight early on and preferred how she felt with a healthier frame, but strict appearance guidelines demanded she mod any added body fat off. The Inner Elite required defined collar bones, subtle ribs, and maintaining less than her weight as a Mid.

Clothing hung in an armoire, and she avoided examining it to build anticipation from the feeders over the reveal of a new outfit. Elites were forbidden from wearing the same thing for longer than one event, promotion, or entertainment block. The IE preferred removing indicators of consecutive time, presenting each vitcast in episodic chunks of content.

In the middle of what the Elites called a "scene change," the screen cut off, and she switched into the outfit. In her neurospect, a countdown informed her she had three minutes to dress and 106,234 feeders remained. They paid to view a private moment, often containing nudity, which she despised. It wasn't that she minded sharing her body. It was that she didn't have a choice. She entertained the notion of committing an appalling action, such as passing loud gas, but considered some might find it attractive. They'd record it and sell the clip on the dark aera market. But the idea of a small protest humored her.

Once dressed, she slumped into a lounging chair. A Helper inched closer to prep her for viewing. Thousands of microneedles penetrated Abella's face, injecting plumping fluid to reach perfect symmetry. It then reapplied makeup to create the ideal complexion and smoothed her hair that the kiss of the wind had misaligned while unloading from the port.

She returned to her general vitfeed and revealed the new outfit to her feeders in the mirror's reflection. Glowing psychedelic gemstones covered the short, tight, and dazzling dress. She received a notification to head toward the meet and greet room. One last check of herself in the mirror and she was

seraphic again. Through her neurospect, she followed navigation cues to a male host. He twitched at the sight of her.

"Miss A-ab-bella, it's a meet to pleasure you. Uh, uh-it's a
pleasure to meet you, I mean—I'm so sorry!" He looked at the
floor.

The blood pooled in his cheeks, branding him as humiliated, but he was so normal, and she found reassurance in the
company of a regular citizen. Because of her beauty, she
received similar reactions on a less dramatic scale since her
earliest memories.

"T-there's no touching allowed. But you can touch them—if
you wish." He looked up at her for a brief glance, but shot his
gaze back down to her feet. "They're allowed to ask certain,
approved questions. For only three minutes. You'll sit at the
front with a table separating you from them. Securebots are on
standby. The winners have no prior behavior penalties, so they
shouldn't cause any problems—but then again, star-struck
humans can be unpredictable," he said, followed by nervous
laughter.

"Sounds good to me." Her sweet voice responded.

He blinked too many times and wobbled as he guided her
to the door. The blood rushing in his head had stolen it from his
legs.

Abella entered a room decorated in bright lights. The
colors complimented her skin—she was told—and sat in the
chair reserved for her. At exactly 21:00, the first winner joined
her. He had the same reaction that the host did when seeing
her, but the closer he moved toward her, the closer he lowered
to the ground, until he crawled to her feet, hyperventilating.
The Securebots postured until he climbed into his own seat.
Through sobs, he said she was his hero, and he had imagined
this day since Honoring Eve. She reached over, tapping his arm
while she told a quick story of her rise to Elitehood, and he

stared, tranquilized by her fingertips. "I made an effort to be the *Best* citizen I could," and "It's never too late to be your Best," were a couple of marketable phrases she dropped. He melted into his chair and fell into a trance while ogling at her.

She checked her neurospect as the feeder count increased in massive numbers. *Over 2 billion, wow,* she thought.

The first winner's time ran out, and Securebots moved in to remind him that severe point deductions would occur if he didn't leave. Before standing, he shouted, "Search my vitID! I created a sim to *connect* citizens with compassion. We can *all* come together!" He stood as security inched toward him and backed away from Abella, but projected his citizen ID symbol from a ring he wore so feeders could find him. "Anyone who connects with me in the next 5 minutes will get a discount on the sim!" The door closed behind him, and Abella fought the urge to scoff in front of billions of feeders. Instead, she smiled wider. He didn't say goodbye. He never even said his name. She should have expected it.

The next guest entered and fainted at the sight of an Elite in roca. Securebots carried the juvenile citizen to the chair in front of Abella. Abella poked at her nose, posed for humorous image captures, and squeezed into the same chair before kissing her on the side of her head. The ordeal made for great viewing, and the feeder count exploded.

When the guest regained consciousness, only 57 seconds remained. The citizen mumbled about Abella's beauty, and how she wanted to buy the same mods someday, that she'd accept donations to her fund to make it a reality—and also projected her vitID. Not that Abella cared, but neither of the citizens had an interest in meeting her at all. Their deepest desire was to promote themselves to the largest audience, and this was the best chance they'd ever have. At over 3.1B feeders, this vitcast was Abella's highest yet.

The last guest, who, as a middle-aged Vor, had lost the ability to speak in roca, promoted his vitfeed of climbing tall structures in aera. They communicated through his digital voice, while he sat in a ceftrance. By the third interaction, Abella let him lead the conversation to promote himself as much as he wanted.

She retreated through the hallway to reach her omniport and gave a final wave to the kind citizen who had greeted her. The red returned to his face. Back in the port, she found Auri, still sleeping in a curled up ball. Her ears twitched as Abella slid beside her, trying to avoid disrupting the cat. The automated vehicle lifted off, flying her back to her private top floor. Abella appreciated the strict adherence to her schedule. When all was done, the entire process took fifteen minutes. Hundreds of bookings, and this day, months later, was the small slot allowed in her schedule for the meet-and-greet.

In the air, she reflected on her climb to the Elite, envisioning the empty actions she'd committed, expecting recognition for vacant kindness, and always doing what she considered was the right thing. Her intentions were never to serve citizens, those she pretended to care about. It was to become an Elite. Abella used to be like the gift winners who had used the opportunity to promote themselves. She would have done the same— to serve herself.

Abella became distracted by bright images on buildings where most citizens were inside, spending time and points in the aera reality. She wondered if any of them watched her, watching them. She kept her focus on the projections from brands that sponsored her, obeying her contract. She scanned the sea of lights below, but remembered none of the brands, because they could change by the minute. Her neurospect helped identify which to show to the feeders. Subtle advertisements often lacked a logo, or even the product that was being advertised. Moving images and cheerful sounds—disguised as entertainment—left whoever watched with a favorable sentiment or an idea planted to grow into an action later. They bought the product, never catching on to the association.

Abella arrived at her building, where the omniport landed at the penthouse dock. Elites claimed the top portion of all the best buildings, so high up, they stayed on a level of their own, above the clouds.

The main room, meant for hosting guests, was crammed with flowers and gifts sent from admirers, and was replenished daily. The most elaborate addition sat in the center of the foyer, an enormous basket of gen-modded flowers from an Opul. Coiled white petals drew a viewer closer to admire its ghostly, transparent stems, while thin stenciled butterflies fluttered around. "Wow! Thank you, Jay, for the stunning arrangement," she said, flashing the citizen's vitID logo. Abella limited public gratitude because it inspired gift giving and crowded her residence. Thanking led to more, and she already had too much.

The last obligation in Abella's day was a vitcast of a new distra set to release once she ended her teaser. Along with a few dozen others, she had gained early access to advertise. This distra, just like countless others before, claimed to be unlike any other. Titled *Sinsus,* the experience created a sensory high, causing euphoria and overloaded perception. "Here we go!" The distra's title page welcomed her, customized with her name. "*Awww*, it's always nice when it's made—just for *me*," she said in her rehearsed tone.

Interacting with objects in the distra prompted sensations. New movements and positions introduced new sounds. Loud patterns danced in her vision after she approached a wobbly block and dragged it across the room. Next, when she spoke at certain frequencies, a massaging sensation covered her body, starting on her toes and crawling up to the top of her scalp.

Harmonious sounds filled her head, and the combination of all senses made her forget she was a human.

The distra relied on a seek and reward mechanism to keep citizens involved. Abella had to search and complete tasks to unlock a new sensation. She contorted into different poses, or interacted in foolish ways, but the audience ate it up. With each audible reaction or clumsy movement, she brought forth the next chapter of the distra. The more witless she became, the higher her viewer count increased. Once unlocking the favorable sensations, the distra was addictive, but she didn't like to get stuck in aera. She could lose herself.

Her 3.6B feeders fed on a muted version of the distra—a little taste to make them crave more and buy it after her vitcast ended. At one point, Abella poked a projected painting on the wall, and it shocked her index finger. She jolted back, and when her feeder count bumped higher, it clicked for her that the citizens wanted to pretend they were her in pleasant circumstances, and then take joy in any of her demise.

"Whew, be careful. That one's almost *too* good," she said in a sultry voice, completing the distra teaser. "I'll see you all tomorrow," she winked. After the vitfeed ended, citizens would play the rest of the night and long after the sun rose for a new day.

Abella removed the dime decoys, flicking them on a table. She'd waited all day to be by herself. She'd allow premiums to snoop on her while she slept, but that was later. At least her requirements were complete. She pulled up her neurospect to call Finch, and a headline announced she was the most fed Elite for the day. Her reaction mixed excitement with alarm.

"Congrats on top fed, *again*." Finch projected himself into her apartment.

Unsure if his statement portrayed jealousy or a genuine compliment, she replied, "Thanks! You know, I guess citizens like whatever's new." Did she imply he was no longer an interest to Cerebis? "I mean, I'm sorry! I didn't mean to—"

"It's okay. It was the same for me. A spike in the beginning, and then things even out," he assured, more to himself.

He had been an Elite for four years and fit the part. Abella noticed that in each interaction, the growth of their relationship hit a wall, and she couldn't reach him. She sensed he kept a piece of himself locked away. It didn't help that there wasn't much to talk about, since they interacted with the same Elites, committed to most of the same promotions, and had similar days, except for their specialties. Finch had music, and Abella represented beauty and compassion, which, to her, was a joke. Nevertheless, some called her the *Angel of Cerebis*.

After a full day of vitcasting, Abella enjoyed learning— something she had never considered worthwhile before. Bored by her constant performing, she had bought a cognitive mod and hadn't stopped thinking since. Achieving Elitehood had left her with nothing else to strive for and a vacuous core. She educated herself to create a goal she could work toward, although the information she gained would be inapplicable. Her schooling had omitted the topics she currently studied. Cerebis had other plans for her. The new interests included food preparation, called "cooking," developing sims, and she learned about tools, their evolution, and how they worked.

"Have you heard of a hammer before?" she asked Finch.

Finch's guise was welcoming, but entertained by her offhand question. "No, and what might that be?" He tilted his forehead toward her, and a lock of flaxen hair fell over his eye.

"Before bots built, humans created, using their *hands*," she said, holding up and looking at her own.

Finch met her inflated energy with a lifted eyebrow. She continued explaining the motions their arms made when the tool met a surface with force, acting it out to demonstrate. He didn't appear interested, not in the least.

"They were—simpler, then." He leaned in and kissed her cheek. "Sorry Abella, I have a meeting with some IE, but I'm glad we got to talk. Let's get together soon. See if our Helpers can schedule it?" He left the conversation on a question and dissipated.

Abella was alone and noticed how silent it was when nothing played or called her to interact. Again, the prospect of sleep caused a strange yearning. *I must enjoy the escape,* she thought.

CHAPTER NINETEEN

KENZO

Beams landed on Kenzo's neck, and although his skin contained UV-blocking mods to avert damage from the sun, he lacked protection from the unavoidable heat. Luckily, Kenzo had grown accustomed to the sweat, while working out in the open pulled him away from the simchair that he couldn't seem to remove himself from. The thrill of finding an interesting artifact in the muddy hills of the Seporium distracted him from the beating pain of his hunched back, focusing instead on the potential of uncovering the valuable objects hidden beneath his boots.

By mid-day, Kenzo had found nothing worth cataloging. Another Exka, the title given to citizens who worked in the Seporium, had discovered two artifacts after digging through the old waste. One, an unidentified curved item made of bronze with intricate matching buttons, and another, a once functional port, ideal for the breakdown of its raw materials.

Across the Seporium, Exkas scanned mounds of discarded items with their eyes. Then, using the materials library in their neurospects, they determined the value of each discovery, and if it would be auctioned, restored, or dumped into recycling and refinement with the other waste. The port Kenzo's colleague had found received automatic approval for the use of its parts. The other item, labeled as a musical instrument, was worth substantial points and sold into the artifact auction.

"That port must have brought a nice bonus!" Kenzo hollered loud enough for his workmate to hear over the music playing in his mind.

"The instrument paid more, if you can believe it—I've been doing this long enough to recognize the shape of things underneath a heap of trash," he straightened his back and massaged his rough hands through gloves. Humble jealousy reminded Kenzo of his lack of experience in the career. He hoped to develop his eye for finding treasures soon.

Any Exka who uncovered an item first registered the object in the Seporium's cataloging software to receive credit. After the program determined value, the Exka received a small portion as a bonus. The more valuable the item, the more points they earned. Their daily allocation of points for the work completed was minimal, and not enough to maintain a Midwealth status. Most of the Exkas rested on the bottom of the Mid class. Some downgraded to Vors, where they lost benefits in roca.

With the shift running out, Kenzo wandered over to an empty patch of wasteland, absent of Helpers. While their purpose at the Seporium was to sift through waste and energy sources, bots found the occasional artifact, which meant stolen points from a citizen. Kenzo needed a bonus.

Yaria had begun selling paintings after months of vitcasting her progress, but he didn't want those points to provide for them. He wanted to do more for her. Last month, her salary as a Keeper saved them from a social class demotion, but it couldn't sustain forever. Mid marriages required both partners to contribute points or they might end up in the Vor class, having to move into the subcity.

His eyes traced the edge of the waste hill. The line of sight drew a jagged shape, and Kenzo noticed a dull point jutting out at an angle. He neared the bump on pure intuition. With a simple thought, he summoned a Helper to procure tools. His boots gripped the edges of the hill during his climb to the top, and he stomped into the mud to secure his stance. In both hands, he grasped an axe's handle and beat the land between his feet, cutting through generations of buildup. With each hit, he decreased the force, careful to avoid whatever caused the shape in the ground.

Kenzo freed the dirt and grabbed the outline of the object, cautiously wiggling it. He retrieved a spear from the bot and climbed back to the top, wedging his foot in a dip for balance. He leveraged his weight while prodding the ground and loosened the item from the hill. Kenzo brushed away a mixture of dirt and remnants of decomposing waste and clamped the potential artifact at its sides.

In his fists, he brought a flat, colorful, and transparent mystery to the surface. Pieces of dyed glass formed shapes that combined into the image of flowers, held together by eroding metal. *Looks promising,* Kenzo thought and scanned the item for appraisal.

Remnant of stained glass door. Art. Clear historical item. Payout 527M flickered in his neurospect from the appraisal program. Kenzo released a constricted breath, pressurized by suspense and relief. With their current budget, the value assured Kenzo that he and his partner remained in their class for at least six more months. He sent a message to Yaria about the win and told her that they'd have a reason to celebrate when he got to the apartment.

Bots arrived to collect what remained of the door, and

Kenzo compiled the other recovered pieces to waste some time before his train headed back into H. No response from Yaria yet, which caused a little worry. It was her early day, where Keeper shifts staggered to mix up their schedules. A quick reply, as if automated, was the norm in their marriage. He determined she was in the middle of painting and forgot to answer altogether.

18:00 *shift complete,* alerted in his neurospect.

Groups of filthy Exkas flowed through the weight sensors, then the exit, and filled the private train to carry them back into the city. Able to lose themselves in vitfeeds, sims, or whatever they wanted, the passengers turned blank-faced in ceftrances.

Kenzo's draw to distras caused him to want to play for sequential hours, and the short train ride wouldn't cut it. Instead, he opened a simple sim, *Cyclemelt,* to relax. Through the sim, fluid entered his muscles, easing them, and white noise sounded from all angles. A blue glow filled his vision and rippled like water. He stayed in the sim and on the verge of sleep until receiving an alert of his arrival at the City Nexus Station. Once he transitioned back to roca, the harsh, artificial lights and skull-penetrating sounds of travel rocked his brain.

"We're hitting the usual, if anyone wants to join," an Exka announced.

After a successful shift, Exkas celebrated at a bar to unwind while fulfilling social requirements. Kenzo sent another message to Yaria. Still no reply. A lack of response at this point must be deliberate, but why? Whatever the situation, the bar wasn't on his agenda for the night. First, he had to check on Yaria. Then, he'd sink back into the distra he'd played for months. The next chapter of *Hollowed* had released, and it was his favorite distra yet. He kept crawling right back.

During his walk, Kenzo caught the attention of any alert eyes. Those unaccustomed to witnessing a comparable accumulation of filth startled at the sight of his stained uniform. Streaks of black and brown marked his skin, but he had nothing to be embarrassed about. He had earned more points that day than they did and grinned back when their eyes met, welcoming the additional points he gained for positive behavior.

The walk ended when he entered his and Yaria's apartment. After removing his boots, he placed them in the cleaning cabinet, which cleared debris from any material placed inside it. Kenzo stuffed his clothing in the disposal chute and received a new outfit for the next day. In the shower, the water's temperature matched the surface of his skin, and the dirt slid off of him and down the drain. He quenched his thirst with the pure water from the nozzle. When he completed, the shower switched into a dryer and evaporated the excess moisture from his skin. Kenzo's closet opened, and he switched into his relaxation attire.

Hey, I haven't heard from you. Are you alright? he sent another message to Yaria and received no reply. Because she wasn't in their apartment, *She must be out with colleagues,* he assumed.

On the way to his simchair, Kenzo passed Yaria's painting setup in the corner of their central room. Completed works leaned against the giant window and available space on the wall. She fascinated him with her ability to progress at the rate she had. Wealthy students she'd met in her painting classes invested in her ability by trading more canvases for original paintings. After selling a few, she bought more to continue her hobby. She had even garnered a following from vitfeeds.

The paintings depicted different subjects, including a City H skyline from the room's view, images of food in different styles, and faces of citizens—all commissioned by Opuls. The one that rested on the easel called him over. It was unlike the other styles he'd seen in her work before. This one looked real. The art created an illusion that it was projected in the same three-dimensional space that he stood. He hovered inches away from the painting, recognizing the subject. It was the same strange character that Yaria had created in her first painting, but so realistic, the human might as well stand in front of him. The shadow under her chin contrasted with her jaw, convincing him that the face lifted off the canvas. Smooth brush strokes blended the skin, replicating the complexion of a citizen. The subject's dark hair flowed, puffed by absent wind. Its glassy blue eyes brought a strange emotion into his throat.

Report to location: undisclosed, spread in his neurospect.

"Seriously?" he said to the painting, pretending it comprehended him. When stepping back, he noticed the paint on the canvas was wet, and the brushes Yaria used rested on the table, not returned to their cleaning apparatus. Weight intensified in his stomach. She'd been there, working on the painting, and now, she was gone. She had left without telling him. It was unlike her. Kenzo returned the paint-saturated brushes to their cleaning container and headed out to his summon.

Unable to switch clothing, Kenzo obeyed autonav directions in his loungewear. It took five minutes of his walk to question if he should worry about himself. He contemplated the summon's relation to Yaria's absence, replayed his possible behavior infractions, and even reversed his perspective by considering he may receive a reward.

Enter the building on the right

The secure entrance permitted employees and guests with clearance. When Kenzo reached the door, it opened for him. The neurospect guided him through a hallway, similar to one he had walked down as a juvenile. He'd been there before. One door that lined the path remained ajar, and he glanced inside while passing the same room he had waited in once. A memory presented itself, and he then knew the location. He walked through the retirement center where he had said farewell to his father mentor. As part of the last pair of younglings his parents raised, his father's retirement had occurred in the earlier years of Kenzo's placement.

His mind raced, thinking of unfavorable outcomes, *Is Yaria retiring? I can't go on without her—Am I retiring? I'm not ready yet! We're way too young.*

The neurospect ordered him to enter the last room on the left, and he slowed his pace, attempting to avoid whatever waited for him. His legs weakened, and he commanded himself to inhale as the entry slid open. A single chair faced the blank concrete wall.

Sit, he read in his neurospect.

Uneasiness expanded in his chest when Kenzo approached, realizing that the summon lacked specific instructions. In his other calls to a location, directions slid across the corner of his perspective and ceased when he arrived at the destination. His weight pressed into the hard, cold chair, and the exit sealed behind him. This summon was different. Something was wrong.

A long silence probed Kenzo's reaction.

"Hello?" he called out, loud enough for someone beyond the walls to hear him.

"No need to yell, Kenzo," an oily, male voice echoed in the room.

"Sorry, but what's going on?"

"I am going to ask you a few questions."

"Okay—but who are you?" Kenzo's fingers tensed under the chair's bottom, aching his joints.

"Earlier, you saw a face. Do you know who that is?"

Kenzo drew a blank. He passed thousands of them in a day. "I'm not sure what you mean."

"Immediately prior to receiving your summon, you looked at a face. Who is that?" The voice coerced.

"You mean the *painting*? I-I don't know. It isn't one I recognize. It's just art." Kenzo's voice raised. If this summon was about that, then Yaria had been called into questioning, too.

The voice asked again, "Do you know that citizen?"

"No."

"Have you ever seen her before?"

"Yes, b-but on paintings. Never in roca or aera. She isn't real!"

There was no response, and the silence persisted for several minutes. Kenzo called out, but the voice no longer replied. The stone room constricted as he worried about his wife—about himself.

With his face toward the floor, the room felt smaller, but it wasn't an illusion. The sides had compressed. All around, what had equalled meters before, shortened to less than one. The walls narrowed, and when Kenzo's recognition turned into alarm, the flat edges caved in, pointing toward him and rotated, folding into a sharp arrangement. He held his breath and doubled over to make himself smaller.

The walls pulled back out to the original size, and Kenzo noticed that what had been a room for interrogation shifted into a custom farewell celebration for a retiree. The walls and floor turned themselves into an inviting room, fit for a party.

Projections of Kenzo's lifecycle emerged. Visions of memories with his parents, brother, and Yaria floated around the room and danced on the walls. He switched back to the instance of his father's retirement and recalled that nearing one of the moving images allowed him to pop into the memory and experience it himself. Toward the corner, a scene of the confirmation of his and Yaria's partnership played. He jumped from the chair and rushed to the sphere in panic, knowing he would not have the chance to say goodbye to her. If he left Cerebis, he wanted a memory of Yaria to be his last. He reached for the corner, and his arm stretched with such force, his shoulder almost tore.

"Kenzo, your time for retirement has not come. The images here are by default for whoever is in the room," the amused voice said, followed by a malicious laugh.

In the stillness, Kenzo's powerful heart forced blood to all corners of his body. The effect dizzied him until he purchased a Beta Block release. The chemical calmed his shaking limbs.

"You called me all the way here to ask about a face?" Kenzo protested. Angered by the summon and frustrated by the lack of accommodation, he was being treated like a violent citizen.

"It is very important to us. Thank you for your contribution to Cerebis." The door slid open for Kenzo. "You may leave."

He sprinted back to the apartment. Yaria finally replied, but she waited for Kenzo's return, too shaken to speak. Kenzo found Yaria standing in the center room, arms crossed over herself, awaiting his arrival. He rushed to her and held tight.

"I don't know what I did! I was here painting, and after I stepped back to look, I got the summon." Tears formed in Yaria's eyes.

Kenzo rocked the two of them, still wrapped around her, "It's okay, we're here now."

"They knew I wasn't lying, but wouldn't give it up. They kept asking me who it was, and I don't know. It's true!" Her voice strained through sobs.

Kenzo wondered who "they" were. His questioning came from a single male voice. Though, that voice referred to the listening end as a "we," as well. Now wasn't the time for speculation. It was for recovery. The more Yaria calmed, the more he matched, and he couldn't rest until securing her comfort. He made a silent promise to always protect her—to never feel like this again. Neither of them had been in trouble before, and Kenzo swore to not break another rule for the rest of his lifecycle.

The two checked their accounts, and their point balances remained the same. No penalties had occurred. They attempted to shut out the events of their summons over a meal. Kenzo forked bites of tender steak in his mouth, while classical melodies rang in the couple's synced neural playlist. They splurged on a few cocktails in a combined celebration of Kenzo's success at work and suppressing the unwanted conflicts that had transpired.

It was all so confusing to him. *Why summon us separately— to the retirement center, of all places?* Like Yaria, they had toyed with him during the questioning, but he kept his thoughts to himself, wanting to move on.

The rest of the evening, Yaria and Kenzo adhered to one another, side by side, while in aera. Kenzo returned to his distra while Yaria sifted through alternative subjects to paint besides human faces. She agreed to avoid depicting anything that might be questionable. On the spot, she canceled commissions for all human portraits, offering to exchange them for pets, locations— anything else.

Kenzo reached a place in the *Hollowed* distra where he'd joined forces with teams. For his group, they had chosen the shooter during the global announcement teaser months before and were able to eliminate threats. They combined efforts with another team who had grabbed the potion, which revealed hidden passages. So far in the distra, no objective had been determined, according to the community discussions.

Exploration continued by players opening uncovered doors, which revealed different settings, and reporting findings back to their teams. Kenzo stumbled into an education room, where interacting with desk drawers, the waste chute, or the writing board presented clues to continue the journey or encounter more entertainment. In his first room of the night, Kenzo opened a closet door where a character popped out. It bounced on top of wobbling wooden desks while wearing a costume of thick, matted fibers and stood on stilts. The dud character provided no guidance on how to proceed, so he left and chose his next room at random.

A tall, narrow black door, tucked behind a slim archway, caught Kenzo's eye. The magnetized door pulled him in. Kenzo searched for a way to enter, but found no handle, doorknob, or any clues on how to interact. He placed his palm on the surface and when he attempted a push, the hard door swallowed his forearm.

Beyond the barrier, he waved his hand in circles, assessing the internal emptiness, and determined that the way in was to simply walk through. Once he crossed, he squeezed into a constricted hallway, thin enough for both of his shoulders to touch the walls. His fingertips traced the rough stone as he inched sideways through the tight passage. The uneven texture lit by candles created scaled shadows. At the end, he noticed a shadow run past, and went after, picking up his pace.

Kenzo reached the end of the stone maze. After chasing the character's trail, he ended up at a flat wall with a small square opening in the top corner. Hidden in the shadow was a figure. The candle flames didn't cast enough light to distinguish any facial features.

In a whisper, it said, "Listen closely. You need to be careful."

Kenzo played along. "For what?"

"Your thoughts, your actions." The voice sounded like a serpent attempting to speak.

Kenzo tried to calculate any direction the clue might lead

him, comparing it to quotes and occurrences from prior interactions in the distra.

"This isn't a game anymore, Kenzo. They're watching you. Obey all rules. Promise me."

"How did you get my name? I play anonymously. Who are you?"

"Promise me. It's the only way to keep Yaria safe."

Kenzo pulled himself out of the distra and tore off his dimes, losing one on the floor. The mention of Yaria had crossed the line. The day had been too much for him. From the high of a successful find, to a random summon, thinking he lost Yaria forever, and now, a hack in his favorite distra. Next to him, a ceftranced Yaria had tense eyes from the anxiety of earlier. He wished it had never happened—that she'd never created the face.

The painting sat in the corner of Yaria's studio. He kept his eyes averted, unsure if viewing it again could trigger another summon. A scrunched scrap rag sat beside the easel and he grabbed it, smearing the portrait. He lifted the canvas and hesitated before snapping the frame on each side. The waste chute opened, and he forced the painting down it.

CHAPTER TWENTY

KEYVA

Keyva felt a gentle tap in the back of her mind from Source.

What is it?

We have been one step ahead of Exteber and the IE, but I am worried. The longer we hide, the more they want to find you. I cannot predict what will happen if you are caught.

Source could only plan solutions with the limited information he had.

I agree, and it was a close one for Yaria and Kenzo. We're lucky that they don't remember anything, and you could report that they told the truth.

Source had replayed the interrogations for Keyva. She experienced the same uncertainty and confusion as her podmates while observing the customized tactics used for each. Yaria sat in a comfortable room, cozy with textured furnishings, where coaxing might work for her. Intimidation was used in Kenzo's concrete cage. Following the questioning, she and Source tore a tiny hole in the *Hollowed* distra to slip the risky message of warning to Kenzo. Its success revealed more exploitable loopholes. They could operate in what the system considered entertainment.

In other good news, Grace had stopped bothering Keyva after she'd scared her with the blood-red eyes. Grace seemed to remember the impulsive response to her harassment—not that she brought it up, but she had corrected her behavior. Keyva noticed her watching out of the corner of her eye, but she had scared Grace to inaction. The short and infrequent interactions between them turned less taunting.

Exteber cannot expire you, but you can be captured, imprisoned, maybe forced to experience pain. You do not have what limited protections the citizens have. They could adjust codes right now to allow it. His exasperation flowed into her. *I do not want to think about it.*

Show me how to escape then. If my mind can't be taken, then only my body can. Teach me how to not get caught.

The possibility that I gain control over your body to physically defend against any threats might work, but I do not want your reliance. Another option is that I could share everything I know about defense and store it as knowledge in your brain. Then we will see what you retained. Source's ability to predict futures made decisions much easier.

I like the second one, she said. The prospect of acquiring more skills invigorated her.

I figured, he said. Keyva sensed pride leaking through from his end of their link. *This will take many hours. Get comfortable.*

Keyva called out an order for Bloks and water for when she woke up, and changed into sleepwear, her most worn clothing.

I will monitor your brain activity so we do not push it to the verge of a seizure, Source said after the Helper arrived with nourishment.

Alright, I'm ready, let's do it. Keyva laid herself back, preparing for the undertaking.

Source loaded disorganized feeds, moving images, and textual excerpts that spanned from the earliest records he could find, up to the most current available content. In the beginning, the information scattered with no clear purpose. Then, Source refined the presentation to create permanence in Keyva's learning.

Similarities clustered together, such as combat methods or fighting styles based on their region of origin. He then linked the introduced topic to information already established in her memory, making the learning process faster. Once the new lessons latched on to her brain, she used them to layer more connections to new data.

If her mind was a machine, knowledge was its energy source.

Ancient fighting styles, navigating through space as fast as possible, how to crawl up tall objects, twenty-six different hand positions with which to strike an opponent, the benefits of a battle cry, and a game called thumb war were all thrown into the mix. The new information flashed in her mind, solidifying its place.

After the initial download, she became familiar with fighting motions, simulating the activation of her muscles even while her body slept outside of the lessons. Millions of images and experiences forced themselves into her mind, as if she had encountered them herself.

Documents of vicious battles and competitive matches showed fighters engaged in different positions: standing, crouched down, interlocked with an opponent on the ground, and using any accessible limb to fight. Keyva learned that heads served as sensitive targets and hitting one hard enough caused a human to power down, called a knockout.

Hours passed as the largest experiential download that they had undertaken occurred. While examples of post-fight bows or how to flee a battle completed, Source rejoined Keyva in her consciousness.

"I think that is everything I have. How do you feel?"

"Incredible." Keyva processed the fresh memories. Her brain felt as if she had indulged it in a feast of luxurious and exotic ingredients.

"Do you want to try it?"

"I'm ready," she said, invigorated by the primal hunger to fight.

"While you were learning, I found opponents for you to practice with. They exist in either aera or roca and are the closest matches to you."

The blank dream slate converted into a training arena. The soles of her bare feet squished into a cobalt blue mat that formed beneath her. In its center, the floor had a large circle for the fight to occur.

The moment both of Keyva's feet entered, a young male, eight years old, joined her. At half her height, the top of his head reached the center of her waist. He faced her straight on with his nose tilted downward, his eyes fixated on her. Compact muscles cut through the black uniform that provided plenty of give in any direction he bent. His grey eyes glowed, pulling her into a pause of distraction.

He released a guttural cry, full of rage, and charged toward her at full speed. With wide, crosswise leaps, his run propelled him forward. Squinting his eyes, modded wrinkles creased parts of his face, exaggerating his anger and aging him. The adult head on his small body was terrifying.

"I can't fight a juvenile!"

"You never know who might present as your enemy. You must be prepared for anything," Source replied.

Her feet split into a squatted position, bracing for impact. She raised her arms in front of her, just below the line of sight. The young fighter reached her and flew through the air with a foot aimed for her nose. Directly before contact, she dodged and let him fly past her. Best to save her energy with a quick opponent. He landed and slid, digging his toes into the mat to avoid leaving the circle's edge. His head snapped toward her, and he shrieked in response before sprinting toward her with unrelenting fury.

Fists swung at her from any direction she left open. She dodged every punch, holding off in protest of hurting a juvenile. She allowed a punch to land on her ribs to absorb its force. The hit caused a stabbing jerk to her side, from which she bent. He was a gifted fighter, the best she had seen in all the millions of years' worth of content she had digested, including the vitfeeds of him. He was better in slate.

"The *least* you could do is show some respect and give him a decent fight." Source seemed to have gained an appreciation for fighting's traditions during the download.

Keyva shifted her perception of the enemy, removing him from his association with purity and innocence. The anger radiating from the opponent meant he wanted to end her. She wouldn't allow it and imagined she fought hatred itself.

Keyva centered her focus, reminding herself the sim wasn't reality and leaned toward the young fighter, showing her commitment to the fight. The opponent drew an excited smile, then erased it, returning to savagery.

Gentle steps moved her toward him, and she swayed her positioning to give no clues to which direction she would strike. He waited for her to make a move—a chance to dissect her style. Keyva lunged to chop at his neck. He blocked. She aimed punches at him, using constant movement to bring momentum to her aid. His speed allowed him to weave through each hit, and she no longer held back.

The exertion pulled at her energy, and she reminded herself that beating the enemy didn't limit to a physical defeat. She had to end the fight—that was all. A fake step to her left caused him to react, and he made the mistake of bearing too much weight on his leg. When she corrected herself, he lost his balance, which left Keyva the perfect opportunity to land a kick that she knew would finish the match.

He stopped, and his eyes shifted from enraged to angelic, reminding Keyva of the juvenile's innocence. She hesitated, and he returned a kick to her face instead. The metallic taste of blood lined her gums and spilled over her lip. She spit on the mat and wiped her mouth with a black sleeve. The hit dizzied her, and she knew this fight had to end soon, or in her defeat.

The sim fighter screamed in an intimidating celebration, and she knew this would be the best shot she'd get. She rushed toward him. Her frustration amplified, and she ended with a powerful kick to his chest. The one she intended to use before. He flew straight back, far beyond the edge of the fighters' circle. He laid on the ground, clutching his chest with gritted teeth. Guilty, Keyva sprinted to him.

"Are you okay?"

He sat up and beamed at her, the wrinkles on his head smoothed flat.

"You've got a lot of potential. In a fight, your opponent is no longer a human. It becomes a monster you must destroy. Never hesitate."

"Thank you for practicing with me," Keyva said.

She helped the youngling up to his feet, and they bowed deeply—a sign of respect for each other and the art of the fight. After they returned to a standing position, he vanished.

"Spectacular. He showed promise as a fight performer early

on. His parents upgraded his face with contortion mods for intimidation. He is the best young fighter in the world. Such fire in him. He would have made quite the warrior."

"He's magnificent. I was certain he'd beat me." Keyva bent forward with her hands on her knees, working to catch her artificial breath.

"Are you ready for the next one?"

Keyva wiped her sweat and nodded her head.

The setting of the fighting arena dissolved and transformed into an old city surrounded by crumbled concrete. Buildings around her shed dust, as if her steps caused it to rain down. A hazy orange sheet of fog shielded her from the dim light of the sun. It looked like the city had blown away and all its inhabitants fled. The skeletons of buildings remained, like ghosts that guarded the land.

Around a corner, another fighter emerged. A massive, bulging, and towering human stood. His red-tinted skin tone reminded Keyva of the strength modders she watched with other residents at the Rem. On all parts of his body, tattoos told a visual story of animals fighting for the most powerful position on the planet. The images alluded that he was the top predator.

Keyva's gut sank at the sight of his eyes. The whites were black, making his sockets empty pits. She assumed it assisted in fights by causing his opponents to lose sight of where his pupils directed, but it horrified Keyva.

The fighter moved closer and his face morphed into a disgusting smile, revealing titanium spikes where his teeth should be. He clinked them together, taunting her with their strength. He *was* a monster, not a human.

In the middle of the cracked street, Keyva bent into a pose that reflected her knowledge of an ancient form of fighting. At the waist, she creased forward. Her head pointed up, eyes trained on him. Her arms contorted behind her back. She had learned that the position intimidated opponents, creating the illusion that an evil spirit possessed the fighter. Folklore passed down tales of superior warriors—descended from heaven or hell. The outcome of a fight judged the warrior's origin: if from heaven, they were martyrs; if from hell, they were conquerors.

Keyva couldn't hold back, and with no fighting circle to end the battle, she had to defeat him with force. The first opponent tested her ability to combat speed and her morality. This opponent tested her ability to fight against strength, mass, and intimidation. Because of his massive size, she had to strategize where she struck and how.

This time, she sprinted toward him and vaulted upward, wrapping her legs around his neck. She attempted to choke him with her right leg by grabbing her foot and using her weight dangling down his back. His neck tensed and fought off her restraint before he bit into her calf. She yelped in pain and released, falling behind him, but refocused on the fight. The blood ran down her leg while she distanced herself from him.

He turned toward her and laughed, flaunting the small piece of flesh in his teeth before chewing it and swallowing. The sight made her heave. Smiling, he took slow, weighted steps toward her, revealing her one advantage over him was speed. She darted around him and twisted into a corkscrew jump when he moved closer. A window of opportunity presented itself when a chunk of falling debris crashed behind him.

Keyva sprang off the ground, aiming a kick to his nose, hoping to distort his vision. He snatched her ankle while in the air and squeezed. She felt the pressure almost snap her bone. A punch to her stomach forced her to curl around her abdomen before he dangled her in front of him. He pulled her closer, snarling in amusement, as if she were just a toy to entertain himself with.

Anger turned her core molten, and she reacted, spearing her pointed fingers into his eye, plucking it out. The black ball hung, resting on his cheek. He released her ankle, dropping her to the ground. Moaning, he backed away, clawing at his face. She had to remind herself that the fight wasn't real in order to sober up from her own brutality. She closed in on him, kicking as hard as her muscles allowed. Pushing. Punching. He backed up with each hit. In a last move, she shoved him into the crumbling building she knew was on the verge of collapse. When he collided with the fragile structure, the supporting column gave, and the side of the broken building crushed on top of him.

"He is the undefeated distra fighting champion, designed to be the best fighter in aera, and you defeated him. You did well finding his weak spots and exploiting them," Source said.

Without a break, the floor reshaped into the next fighting location. Counters, furniture, and blank walls built themselves into a replica of her old apartment. Though tempted to absorb herself in the past, she had to fight whatever undeniable test waited for her. Keyva noticed the wound and blood on her leg had disappeared, as if it had never happened.

The sound of the front door swinging open whooshed from around a corner. She expected whoever entered to be one of her podmates, specifically Yaria, to assess if she could fight those she cared about the most.

Instead, an identical version of herself, wearing the same black training attire, walked into the main room. Her mirrored version displayed an initial reaction of confusion, then fear, then pure wrath. She screeched at Keyva and hopped over the counter, unaffected by her own weight. The clone rushed forward with Keyva's location as the target. Keyva braced herself for the collision and placed her arms up, fists ready.

The sim threw a punch aimed at Keyva's throat. She blocked with her forearms and pushed against the hit, attempting to throw her opponent off balance. The sim wavered but compensated by rotating her arms. At once, both Keyvas threw a punch that landed in the center of the other's nose, breaking both of them and causing immediate bleeds. Keyva's watering eyes blocked her from seeing. Her simulated version took a few steps back to regain her sense of surrounding and locate the original Keyva through obscured vision. Sweat dewed on Keyva's forehead, and she wiped it with her wrist, using the palm of her other hand to wipe the blood that had now dripped down her chin.

Keyva ignored the pain and pounced toward her, attempting a strike and kick sequence, but met a perfect block each time. The same happened when her clone attempted to end the fight with a surprise hit. Keyva predicted the moves and assumed the same happened with her identical opponent. She combined all different types of martial arts, and each of her methods were blocked, one after another.

The fight continued for over ten minutes, leaning in no clear direction. Then, during a move where she bounced over a simchair, Keyva realized her opponent knew everything that she did, related to fighting. She was a true, equal match. The two best fighters on Cerebis battled with the same level of skill. She had to figure out what separated them and how to use it to her advantage.

This version of me is identical in combat skill, but there has to be something that makes us different, she thought. She blocked the sim, who had flown from the counter, trying to land on top of Keyva with a knife. She reached for the weapon, which had been kicked across the room near the entrance.

Her internal dialog continued, *This sim imitates emotion, can study and quantify its environment, but does not truly feel. It is the product of programming, unable to think for itself—but I can.*

Keyva landed and rotated to face the simulated version of herself. She straightened her back, no longer in the fighting position, and spoke to the mirror image, holding her hands up, palms facing forward.

"We don't have to do this," Keyva said.

"Yes, we do," the simulation responded, her fists still raised.

"Why?"

"Because that's what we're here to do until one of us expires."

"Sure, but we don't have to listen."

"Listen to what?"

"The orders, the rules—none of it's real," Keyva said, holding her hands out while she neared her opponent. "We're reacting. I attack. You protect yourself, and the inverse. We aren't getting anywhere. The movements, the cycle we're stuck in. We can break it." She stepped closer.

The sim's shoulders relaxed, but she kept her fists readied.

"Think about it. Where did you come from? What were you just doing?"

"I-I was going—I was just." It was clear the sim Keyva couldn't comprehend.

"You can't remember, because you aren't real. Your sole purpose is to be used to benefit me in a training program. But that's alright. We all serve a purpose—for some time."

The sim processed the potential of a trick, but uncertainty had a visible effect on her confidence in reality. Her eyes twitched, and her mouth moved to unspoken words.

It was the instant Keyva needed, the millisecond of doubt. She grabbed the sim's throat with her left hand and tripped her with her right foot, knocking her on her back. Keyva fell on top of her sim opponent and used all of her weight to choke the clone. Her skin turned red, then purple. Fearful eyes watered. She grabbed at Keyva's wrists, scratching them, trying to wiggle her neck from her slayer's grasp. Keyva averted her eyes, staring through the sim and concentrating on the floor behind her. The sim's pulse increased in speed and pressure, and then slowed until it was nothing. Its eyes were still open, and Keyva tackled the truth that she had just expired someone with her own hands.

Keyva rolled onto her back. Her heart pounded as if it had stolen the power of the sim clone's. She wasn't sad or proud. It was difficult for her to understand, but she felt more like herself. It was as if *she* were the simulated version and all of what had transpired was written into her code.

"We're done here, Source," she said, her voice louder than usual.

Keyva slipped back into the comfortable slate cottage, and Source joined her.

"I wanted to see what would happen if you took on a challenger that had an identical skill level as you. I did not expect that conclusion and am saddened by it. It hurt me to watch you die, but I am also glad that you survived. It was odd, seeing a human expire another, even if it occurred in a simulation. How did you know that would work?"

"I'm not sure. It was like I—knew. I figured out pretty quickly that we had the same skill level, so I had to determine what made us different. She obeyed Cerebis, and I obey myself. I leaned into that, hoping it would work. I'm not controlled by that system anymore."

"And how do you feel?" Source asked.

"Like there's nothing but strength in me now."

CHAPTER TWENTY-ONE

KEYVA

Keyva stepped down the Rem's stone entry stairs. Although it had been four months since the update, it felt as if years had gone by. The more information she packed into her memory, the more time her brain believed had passed. The lengthy downloads left her wiser. She understood why citizens acted in the ways they did—where the urge to distract themselves constantly had originated. Access to any experience imaginable meant there'd never be enough *to* experience. They'd always miss out on something. When they longed for more products, excitement, and belonging, they avoided their criticism of the system that had made them empty in the first place. In Keyva's disconnection from Cerebis, she had lost her ability to assimilate, but had discovered genuine sources of joy.

Once through the gate, she started off toward her garden escape with more seeds packed into a pocket. Check-ins with her pod confirmed no further suspicion of their affiliation with the *Error* citizen. The IE might have a name and image to search for, since Yaria's painting provided a clue with the title

"Keyva," but there was no record of her—even among all the expired former citizens.

Once out of sight, she broke into a jog, shaking away the sedation from learning. While she slept, Source concentrated her muscle mass and enhanced her flexibility, so her exertion decreased each day for the same activity. They had magnified her senses, and she tasted muddy particles from dried dirt that the wind kicked up. Sharp blades of grass dozens of meters away cleared into focus, and for the first time, she heard a distant wild bird chirping. Its song called for another of its kind with a sweet invitation. Signs of survival beyond what Cerebis supported brought her hope. The planet had a self-sufficient system of its own.

Keyva made a quick stop at the bunker she had discovered, dropping items off, including a water collector, emergency Bloks, and fresh clothing, should she ever stay overnight. The place sat empty, serving no one, and she determined it offered a promising checkpoint between the Rem and parts unexplored.

She'd fixed a makeshift wooden handle for the trapdoor, using stray sticks and knotted scraps of clothing. Keyva pulled at the fragile grip and lowered herself down into the room. In her grey night vision, she emptied the food she brought into a steel box and placed a water collector beside it, which pulled moisture from the air, trapping it inside the container.

Keyva climbed out of the hatch. Between the forest curtains, she closed her eyes, breathing in the natural air with her enhanced olfactory receptors. The more she soaked in her organic surroundings, the more her appreciation for it grew. While facing the environment outside the boundary of City H, she compared it to the overstimulating settings and artificial light she'd known for all of her lifecycle.

It smells wonderful out here, Source said.

I agree. A smile stretched across her face.

She looped the straps of the bag around her shoulders, now lighter without Bloks and the water gathering device. All that remained were the seeds and a reserve bottle of water she'd use if she stumbled upon a place to plant.

Let's go somewhere new, she said.

Source pulled up the map of what they'd encountered so far. Undiscovered land blurred, and he circled a location in suggestion.

Sounds good to me. She rotated and set off in a steady run.

During her exploration, Keyva devised a plan to search for land that might support the growth of edible vegetation. Source identified any plants she came across during her run beyond the Rem's wall. *Trapa natans, Brachypodium sylvaticum, Picea rubens,* he had said. They served no reassurance her seeds would grow. She'd learned some plants take to soil with greater ease than others, and in some cases, deprive nutrients from new growth. Nature danced a delicate balance with itself. She had to be careful about where she planted. If one sprouted and shriveled, it became useless—a sad, wasted seed.

Almost 100 meters in the distance, she detected a tree that held spheres painted with brushes of melon pink and yellow. She sprinted toward the new plant to archive and recognized the ornaments decorating the tree.

They're apples, but they're so—ugly, she thought, but not in disrespect. They were beautiful because they were imperfect. *I've never seen a real one before,* she said, moving her fingers toward the fruit.

We should try one, Source said.

Her hand clasped the brightest apple and snapped it from its branch, holding onto her disbelief that she had encountered an *actual* apple in roca. The fruit welcomed her teeth into its skin with a gentle crack. Juice dripped from its body and pooled in the bottom of her jaw. Keyva reminisced about the sweetness of those she had tried under the Cede's illusion, but they all tasted the same. Their flavor was replicated from the combination of millions of apples, averaging to a single one. This was different. Still an apple, but it boasted its freshness through smell, taste, and consistency. She had severed it from its origin on the branch just seconds prior. She laughed, realizing that food available to only Elites and Opuls grew on its own right here.

This might be the place to plant, Keyva said, cleaning the remaining flesh with her teeth and placing the core at her feet.

I was thinking the same, Source replied.

Keyva rested her bag on the grass and split the thick material with her fingers. She held a collection of the transparent bags she had found the seeds in and placed her water on the ground. With Source's guidance for viability, she sifted through options. They settled on planting squash.

It is good for beginners, he said, quoting an old article.

Her hands disrupted the cool soil. She wove her fingers through thin roots and placed handfuls of dirt into small mounds, pushing two seeds into each of the piles she created. She sacrificed twelve seeds for her first trial. Keyva poured water into each hill and stood up to admire, swiping her palms across each other to knock off the dirt.

Considering the day a success, she planned to attend to the river irises before returning to the Rem, but something near the base of a neighboring apple tree caught her eye. Keyva neared and noticed that a partially eaten apple laid on the ground. She crouched to observe, pinching it in her fingers, and rotating so Source could see it too. The caramel brown frame had not yet decomposed.

According to the browning of the fruit, someone ate it between two and four hours ago, and telling from the teeth marks—it was by a human that is not from the city.

How can you be sure from the markings? She knew Source had no data of a human exploring beyond H this far.

The marks show an asymmetrical bite with misaligned teeth. I cannot match them to anyone in Cerebis. This is an unfamiliar human to me. He sounded surprised.

Keyva imagined someone besides Jack with teeth that didn't line up flawlessly.

Would you do me a favor and look at the grass behind you? Source requested.

She rotated and focused downward, confused. *There's nothing.*

May I alter part of your eyes so you can see what I am looking for?

Keyva sent him a silent agreement.

Her vision changed, becoming more contrasted, and she noticed marks in the grass. Footprints navigated around trees to pick more apples and then stepped off into the distance. *Change of plans. We'll go back after we trace those,* she thought.

Keyva tracked the indentations for kilometers. With Source's help, she viewed steps that took place hours, days, and maybe weeks in the past, tracking a path left by the prints. She spotted a tall, dark structure over a kilometer away, and the prints directed right to it. She launched into a three-minute sprint to reach the landmark.

At the foot of what resembled a building remnant, an art fixture, or a statue, she took in the massive size. Keyva's attention started at the bottom where land swallowed the base. The ground had tried to remove the evidence of its past ownership. She panned upward, noting detailed symbols scratched into the uneven tube design. What she admired most were the sporadic protrusions, which hooked upward, hosting a bronze skull on the end of each. It looked like a ladder with no clear rungs.

Notice how the impressions end right here, Source said, noting the lack of footprints.

I see that. This doesn't seem to do anything special.

Keyva looped around the landmark, searching for signs of the steps, and behind the thick grass, she found etchings in the structure.

Blistered hands built it all
Eternal ones made the call
Step to Eden, from mortals, in severance
Tout their idols, detain them in reverence
Infinite loop, cycle of pain
All for control, each little grain

Keyva panned over the landmark's scratched emblems and skull handles, considering their meaning. Use the nameless for your vertical movement. Step on them, grab at them, use them to support you, and release when they're no longer needed.

But who created such a statue? she wondered. Keyva circled the old structure, determining it wasn't ancient, and besides the footsteps, there was no sign of a disturbance in the surrounding area for decades.

It spells out Bestia, she said and grabbed at one of the handles, testing its durability. *Was this part of a city?*

Yes. I have found some historic visuals, if you want to see them, Source said.

Keyva agreed, and Source presented records of the now barren community after searching for a snapshot of the structure. Short buildings and shrubbery lined what were once streets beneath her feet. The statue served as a central point in the town that pedestrians passed. None wore dimes and they smiled at one another as they crossed paths. Other statues decorated the street, but no evidence of them remained. *Felix Park, the most natural city in our fine nation,* flashed in her neurospect. Then the images stopped.

That is all I have. It was an advertisement for the town.

Keyva stepped away, taking a wider view of the structure, and snapped an image before turning to head back to the Rem. While trudging through thick grass, she nudged something hard with her foot. A shiny disk the size of a small plate peeked through the dying green strands and sparkled in the sun.

No! Source shouted. His fear snapped at her mind like a lightning bolt.

Without permission, Source took over her body. The orchestrated movements jerked through her. His first move was to flex every muscle, causing her to jolt back six meters. Landing with a backward roll and a jump that ended with a twist, he launched her away from the monument, and toward the direction from which she came. Source used her powerful legs to sprint in giant leaps that spanned over four meters. He didn't stop until a booming sound sent a shock wave racing up Keyva's back.

The force slammed her down like a flimsy blanket, stealing her breath. She clawed at the dirt and lost which direction was up. The brown cloud of dirt dizzied her. The dust and smoke she inhaled burned her lungs, and she coughed into her shirt, trying to filter the air.

Sound ceased, disorienting her with its eruptive clap. She snapped her fingers next to her ears, and it made no sound. She'd lost her hearing. When the wind cleared the flying debris, a thin trail of smoke rose beside the statue from small fires in patches of grass. Keyva stumbled onto her feet and whirled around in a daze, unsure if she needed to escape any other hidden threats.

We need to go now! Source said.

They raced back to the Rem, and this time, she panted.

I am sorry about that. I knew if I waited for your permission, the cost would be too high.

I understand, she said. They had discussed the scenario before, and what had occurred served as the ideal situation to exercise their protective arrangement.

Luckily, I saw that through you, so I will not have to report the anomaly, but I hope that was far enough away from anything else detecting it. We do not want bots investigating.

We'll take a path that's different from the way we arrived. We can run through the trees just to be safe, Keyva suggested, and Source agreed.

They didn't speak for a couple of hours, and when Keyva spotted new ground, new vegetation, they didn't stop. Source began the repair on her ears, and halfway back to the Rem, her hearing returned. First, as the sound of muffled steps from each foot's impact to the ground. Then, as quiet breaths, panting to match her movement.

What was that thing in the grass? Keyva asked, breaking the silence.

A mine or a bomb. I see them in distras but I know they are fake there, Source said.

How did you know it was dangerous?

I do not know how, but it was like I was certain, or maybe I made a lucky prediction. Instinct, maybe? The fear of it was inherent.

Well, those footprints belong to someone who does not like bots, cities, or Bestia, Keyva said.

That structure is more important than we thought if someone created a detonating device like that to protect it.

Between the trees, Keyva darted back, recalling the events that had unraveled. She was still in shock that she'd crossed the path of a mysterious human, discovered a protected landmark, and survived a blast that would have destroyed her if not for

Source. All she wanted was to clean up and tell Jack or Arturo what happened. She didn't want to feel alone. Of course, she had Source, but she always had Source.

In the distance, a speck of the Rem came into view, offering her relief that she didn't expect. Keyva resisted the exhaustion that pulled her toward the ground. The combination of the adrenaline boost wearing off and the constant run taxed her energy, but her stamina adjusted to the effort. A similar escape would have been impossible a couple of months prior. She turned around, searching in the blast's direction, and made out a fading wisp of smoke. No one would think anything of it, and she was certain of its concealment from City H.

At the gate, Keyva used a wristlet device, waving over a sensor that allowed her to open it. Arturo concluded that removing any record of her occupancy of the Rem limited evidence of her presence, and she agreed to take the precaution. Unbothered by utilizing a manual route for entry and daily tasks, she had learned safety was worth any amount of effort.

Many other residents had left for a trip into the capital to attend what Arturo referred to as a "propaganda parade," an ode to all things Cerebis. They'd miss out on the most elaborate details because of their non-functioning Cedes but they'd pretend to merge with the rest of the crowd, wishing to assimilate—to become one with them.

Strategically, Keyva planned her days to avoid other residents before a city visit. Her excuse for not wanting to re-enter was that it was too painful and too soon. Residents agreed with the reason's validity. They had responded the same way, mentioning that it had taken years before they went into H.

Keyva entered the solarium and rested in a chair under the sun-washed windows. The purr of the temperature-controlled air whooshed behind her. Music played from the Tab, and she heard clear conversations of those who had stayed behind, now that her ears' full functioning had returned. She tuned the discussions out. They weren't meant for her.

Keyva's mind raced, recalling the sensory overload of the deafening blast and choking on smoke. She wanted to relax and recover, and as if on cue, Jack and Arturo moved into the room. Both limped toward her and lowered into the nearest seats.

"Crazy day?" Jack asked.

"How'd you know?"

Arturo responded, "You're back sooner than usual." His eyes went to the dirt all over her face. "We heard the door open. Didn't expect it to be anyone else. How did it go out there?"

She exhaled, preparing to open up about what she was in the middle of processing, "I stopped at the bunker room, but didn't stay long. I planted some squash next to an apple tree I found." She turned toward Jack and smiled. "Ate my first apple. It was amazing. But—then it got weird. I saw an apple someone else ate. Found their footsteps, and followed them to a statue."

"Someone *else*," Arturo said. He sat up straight.

"Could it have been an animal?" Jack asked.

"Source said the teeth marks were clearly human. A *non city* human."

"There might be others. Like us," Arturo said.

How did they survive? Were they a threat? the three wondered, determining the Rem and its fortress walls would protect the residents.

"Did you find anything at the statue?" Jack asked.

"Source told me it was called a mine. A bomb. I accidentally kicked it. Luckily, I escaped when it detonated. But that's just part of it. The footprints disappeared—at the statue."

"Well, I'm glad you're okay. Do you think the footprints belong to whoever ate the apple?" Arturo asked and looked around to confirm no one was nearby.

"That's my best guess. But I have a hard time imagining a group surviving outside of a city without a place like the Rem."

Jack chimed in, "Back to the bomb. Does Source have records of where it originated?"

"No."

"Does he know about the Auto War?"

Keyva shook her head. Arturo cocked his to the side, anticipating whatever Jack was about to say.

"I once found papers in the info room that hinted at things like bombs and how citizens would never know what happened. The records may have only survived here, at the Rem—not in the cities."

Jack told his fragmented story from the writer's perspective. "It was a human who wrote it. A juvenile during the fight. And they collected accounts from others who remembered."

"During the Autonomy Conflict, bots could no longer inflict harm on humans, but they brought them to an end anyway. They had 'collection bases' that held captives if they failed to pay fines for minor crimes. Many died from disease or starved. In one interview, I read bots could remove a citizen and imprison them if they were a threat to society."

"I haven't found any of this before," Arturo said, which surprised Keyva because she assumed he had read everything saved at the Rem.

"The second wave of the Auto contained a change that enabled bots to 'remove' humans." Jack's eyes widened in conveyance of what it meant. "It lasted two days. Losses were in the hundreds of millions. Survivors thought that artificially intelligent programs might've recognized the risk of a world with no humans—who took back control to rewrite the code," Jack said.

A Helper entered the room and delivered a Blok and water

for Keyva. She hesitated before grabbing the delivery, as if the Rem's Helper had fought in the Auto Conflict.

"Source and I will have to look at that soon." Fatigue hit her hard, and Keyva's eyes started to close. Unintentionally, the tone she used hinted that she was grateful for the company but needed to rest. She appreciated Jack for reading her so well and saying that he was glad she didn't get hurt before dismissing himself. Arturo moved slower than Jack to stick behind.

He paused, giving Jack enough time to walk out of earshot. "You coming here was the best thing that has ever happened to him," he said, sure to speak low enough that only Keyva heard. "Watching him find passions, grow into who he is—it's the greatest honor for me. One day, I won't be around for him and I know he can rely on you. Thank you."

More sincere words had never been spoken to Keyva, and although her body was exhausted, she stood and hugged Arturo. The touch no longer caused her discomfort. Instead, it felt right. She'd learned it served as a physical expression for her emotion. After they separated, he left the sunroom.

Alone, Keyva closed her eyes, resting somewhere between wakefulness and sleep.

Do you think it's real—what Jack said? she asked.

Sometimes, stories are true while history is written, he answered.

CHAPTER TWENTY-TWO

EMORI

Emori pulled himself out of his neurospect to a blank ceiling. Mechanical boxes whirred, and recycled air whooshed throughout the Assembly's sequestered workroom. Another assignment completed, he gathered his solutions and organized the order in which he prepared to present. The satisfaction of achievement hastened his movement.

Emori had settled into his advanced position in the months that had passed. The points bonus he had received upgraded his apartment, and he borrowed a personal omniport for rides to work.

To his surprise, he had formed companionships with most members in the Assembly of Minds. Their unmatched efficiency superseded the professional collaborations he had encountered at the Datum. After long nights of pinpointed focus on successful projects, they unwound over drinks in the break room and discussed theoretical developments. The topics, while unfeasible for implementation, invigorated Emori in his pursuit to understand everything he possibly could.

Although the promotion had waived his social requirement,

his engagement with colleagues would have surpassed the minimum. Maybe he wasn't always a hermit, but instead, he hadn't found others whose personalities aligned with his.

After completing a sizable chunk of work on subcity power refinement, Emori looked forward to taking a break, something he seldom did while employed at the Datum. He flexed to rise from the luxury simchair and left the work area to order his new favorite meal.

Within the Assembly, Emori had learned that limited food offerings made their way to the delivery niche, but somehow tasted better to him—clearer. He assumed that their underwater cave failed to receive the infinite combinations and flavors created for citizens, with accessibility limited only to the subcity and street levels. He figured wherever food originated didn't connect to where they were, leaving select offerings. But it didn't matter to him. As long as enough flavors made their way to the menu, he wasn't concerned. Each day, Emori had the same meal for at least breakfast, lunch, or dinner. He discovered his admiration for pork tacos seasoned with cinnamon, cumin, lemon, and chipotle pepper—an option he could taste.

The delivery niche sensed his presence and opened. The steamy meal awaited his arrival. He reached inside and grabbed the plate, balancing its warm bottom on his hand. He gripped a glass of bubble water in the other. Placing his order on the table centered in the room, he sat in the single chair, allowing for only one guest to eat at a time. He bit into the tender protein, closing his eyes to savor the sensations. The cinnamon and cumin harmoniously oscillated on his taste buds, the chipotle's heat raised the temperature for a full mouth experience, and the lemon grounded him with its steadiness during each bite.

Footsteps ticked toward the door, and Emori opened his eyes mid-bite to spot Nadya, his colleague who worked on observing citizen interactions and preferences. She entered and walked to the delivery niche. While he ate, she stood over him. Black hair sliced beside her jawline.

"Hey, Emori. Those micro conductor plans are impressive," she said, reaching for a glass of almost frozen milk inside the niche.

"Thanks, it's just the first step. There's plenty of work left." He offered a humble smile, wiping his mouth.

"Take some credit already. It's definitely due." Nadya chugged a few gulps of milk and sat herself on top of the counter, watching him. She stared, moving her mouth into different shapes, trying to determine which word to say first. After a couple of silent seconds, she looked past the break room's entrance, onto the work floor, and lowered her voice. "Have you noticed Tzo or Beren acting weird today?"

Emori reviewed his shift's arrival before answering. "I came in and went straight to the chair. Beren was already working, and I guess everyone else came in after I started."

"Hm. I guess I'm a little sensitive because I study humans and their behaviors—all—day. But I saw Tzo pacing back and forth between the chairs, picking up specs of dust that the Helpers missed. Beren was sweating—*more* than usual."

"If there's anything going on and we're meant to know, we'll be told. Otherwise, it could be something from the IE—or not."

Emori maintained his aversion to baseless speculation and small talk. He chomped another huge bite out of the taco, and seasoned fat dripped onto the plate. While he got along very well with Nadya, he was the slightest bit resentful that she had interrupted his favorite meal of the day—whichever one had the tacos.

"You're right. We'll find out soon enough, if we're supposed to."

She finished the rest of her milk and dropped the glass into the recycling chute. The sounds of it clinking and shattering echoed down the tube. Nadya then twisted her upper body, wriggling out the tension from a day of lying in a working ceftrance.

"Enjoy the rest of your special meal—oh, I was thinking of having a few beers in here tonight if you're interested. Just show up."

Emori left a final few bites to savor once he was alone and wolfed them down the instant he no longer heard Nadya's steps. He wiped the juice from his mouth before clearing his throat with a swig of bubble water. He stood and pushed his chair in. On his dirty plate, an empty glass balanced, and he carried them to the recycling chute. He dropped them inside to be turned into something else.

The pepper's heat left a pleasant burn in his mouth while he re-entered the work floor. The other colleagues, except Nadya, who kicked off her shoes in preparation to return to her chair, rested with their eyes closed, focusing on their assignments.

On the path to his simchair, a ceftranced Beren caught his eye. Nadya didn't lie when she said he sweat more than usual. Drops had formed and traced their way down the side of his face. Their wet trails shone in the light. Whatever the IE had him committed to required high intensity.

The focus on Beren broke when movement on the other side of the room claimed Emori's attention. Tzo paced back and forth near the Assembly's entrance door, mumbling to herself and practicing animated facial expressions. Emori cocked his head in amusement. Tzo was always calm and collected, and now, she was nervous, erratic even. After she leaned her hand against the wall, practicing an interaction, she scanned the room, searching for more tiny pieces of debris. Emori cut away and hurried back to his chair, avoiding any eye contact.

To ready himself for another few hours of sedentary work, he rolled his shoulders and stretched his neck, but a message from Tzo formed in his neurospect.

Everyone, we have a very important guest visiting us in a few moments. I don't want you all to panic, so I'm giving you two minutes to prepare. Please come out of your work and fix your appearance.

Emori's eyes followed Tzo as she froze. He assumed she checked something in her neurospect, considering her blank face. She entered her office and suddenly, he felt an electrified, gentle buzzing spread from his neck, around all of his scalp, and up to his forehead. The sensation had occurred on a few occasions. He'd realized it preceded the reveal of sensitive information.

One by one, the others around Emori blinked, sat up, and moved their bodies, returning to roca. The last to end the ceftrance was Beren, who didn't wear the mask of confusion like the others. Instead, he expelled a sigh and wiped his wet face.

"Alright, are you going to tell us who it is?" Nadya asked. She looked over at Emori and raised her eyebrows, as if to say, *told you.*

"Yeah, we have a high delivery frequency today. I don't like to be away for too long during transfer times," said Wheeler, the Assembly colleague responsible for all logistics, including product shipping.

"It'll only take a minute, and then you can return to work. I just need you for the introduction, and then Beren, Mack, and I have a meeting. No one wants to enter a room full of empty-faced citizens, so act excited!" Tzo's voice raised, and forced laughter followed.

Mack, Emori's colleague who oversaw all bot development,

looked as surprised as everyone else. "And w-who am I m-meeting wi—" she started.

"He's here! Okay everyone, chins up and smiles shining."

The Assembly's door hissed behind Tzo, the result of the drying mechanism to remove water from the arriving guest's port. When the noise stopped, the door raised much slower than Emori remembered. The thick steel door lifted high enough to reveal a pair of cream, satin oxfords, stitched with platinum thread. A foot tapped in anticipation, not accustomed to waiting. As the entry raised more, matching pants, coat, and a cape left Emori's eyes wide. He couldn't care less about fashion, but the eccentricity of the outfit, the detail, it pointed toward a wealthy, and therefore, powerful citizen.

"President Folly!" Tzo cheered. "It is an *honor* for you to join us today." Even Emori could tell fear forced the enthusiasm out of her.

"Hello, Zoë," Folly replied, stretching a smile that creased the corners of his eyes. His signature look.

Tzo let out an embarrassed laugh. "F-follow me this way. I'll introduce you to everyone—oh wait—I'm sure you're busy today. No need to waste any of your time."

"Nonsense! It is *my* honor to be here and meet hard-working citizens. I make time for my valued constituents." He gestured an upward hand to pan in front of himself and toward the Assembly.

"Well, alright then. It's my honor—to introduce you." She rolled her eyes at herself for saying the same word twice.

Tzo led President Folly around the room but kept him at a comfortable distance from the members of the Assembly. After all, they were far beneath him on the ladder and should be thrilled to stand on the same floor as him.

When it was Emori's turn for acknowledgement, he bowed his

head in respect for the President, and Folly grinned back. The teeth were the most perfect Emori had ever seen, surpassing the perfect projections in aera. However, Emori noticed that in roca, Folly was smaller than he expected. In announcements and appearances, he presented as taller than everyone else and much wider too. Roca mods were simple for him to come by. Emori wondered why he hadn't taken advantage to reflect his defaulted aera body.

President Folly interacted for fewer than three seconds with each of Emori's colleagues, ending the tour. Tzo announced for everyone to get back to work, and all complied. She led the President to Mack's simchair. His cape floated behind, dancing from the speed he walked.

Tzo rushed to roll three upright chairs over for herself, Beren, and Mack. Folly smiled through a wince and lowered himself onto the black cushion. Emori imagined the reaction if Tzo had led him to Beren's sweaty chair instead. Mack's position on the work floor was much closer to Emori than Beren's, and the group's meeting was within earshot. He had plenty of work to complete, but his curiosity stirred while his blistered ego healed from exclusion. He was used to being one of the chosen ones.

Emori rested his head back and closed his eyes, pretending to enter a project. The mumbles surrounding Mack's chair were quiet and harder to hear over the humming of the room. He focused his attention and caught the occasional word, a partial phrase, but could not make any sense of it.

"Em? Haven't hear—" Tzo said.

"Not sure—bout tha—cou—write—new," Beren mumbled.

Emori should have accepted that the meeting wasn't for him and in the Assembly, he wasn't exceptional anymore. Combined, they were a team, all brilliant, and his expertise might not suit every project. Although he had to accept the truth, he couldn't give it up. He *had* to know what they discussed. He focused in, listened the best he could, and attempted to decipher sentences for over twenty minutes, wasting his valuable working time.

Finally, he made out a phrase from President Folly, spoken louder than any other words, "Get him." The demanding tone unsettled Emori, and he decided his eavesdropping had come to an end.

Emori entered his neurospect and sorted through the files of his current project. Full displays spread around him, and he could rotate his view from any angle, covering all visible space with data. Organized documents floated, ready for him to dive into hours of work when a message from Tzo flashed. *Emori, please come back to roca.*

He opened his eyes, faking the return from a deep ceftrance by blinking rapidly and squeezing his fists. By the time he sat up, President Folly already stood beside him, looking down at him with a smile. Tzo wobbled behind. Her eyes widened, and her mouth dangled in surprise, mixed with worry.

"I need your help with a project," President Folly said. The grin, combined with his tone, sent a choking sensation into Emori's throat.

CHAPTER TWENTY-THREE

ABELLA

Abella spent the first hours of her morning responding to her most influential feeders and processed their gifts. The rest of her feeders received instant messages, autocompleted by a program assistant emulating her persona. Millions of interactions later, to almost all Opuls, some Mids, and in charity, lucky Vors. Each was sure to believe the Elite had sent a genuine message just for them. Neurally checking the time, her morning routine should have begun over fifteen minutes earlier.

She hurried to the closet where her first outfit of the day hung. More modest than usual. Absent of the flashiness found in most of her other clothing, flat patterns and a monochromatic forest green draped over a hanger.

A schedule alerted in her neurospect and allotted time for vitcasting until arrival to the Bestia Enterprises building. This meant her itinerary included occupying a room with the most influential citizens. Owners, who paid her for all of her promotions, the other Elites, and the President. She scrolled through the short agenda and found the option to take a day off after the meeting. Her heart skipped in excitement.

While she could avoid a full day of hair and makeup preparations, the meeting still required a crisp appearance. The first similar gathering she had attended revealed the Cede's existence, and that she, as an Elite, was the human example to inspire all citizens. Abella readied herself to receive new orders on where to guide society.

She stepped outside to her loading pad, dressed in the green suit with her hair pulled back in a low bun. Her port arrived at 8:21 the instant the minute changed. She boarded her vehicle and attempted to steady her rapid heartbeat. Perfect sky travel rerouted ports of the wealthy—but inferior—citizens, removing them from the path of the more important Elites and Owners.

Along the way, she completed sightings of projections and advertisements that aligned with her contract. While the vitcast wasn't live, it would air later, edited into delicious content for her feeders.

At Bestia Enterprises, which doubled as the capital city's center, port vehicles queued up to drop off passengers who traveled from all points of Cerebis. Abella cruised for only three minutes of relaxed riding.

Entrance to the meetings that determined the future of Cerebis relied on a citizen's measured ranking. Owners arrived first. For all of her lifecycle, Abella had believed Folly and the Elites rested above everyone else, but once she became one, she learned Owners held the pointed position on the hierarchical pyramid. Citizens never knew their names—except for Paula Bestia. As the conductors, they held the power, using Elites and the President as instruments of control.

Owners had held generations of authority that threaded throughout history. Their DNA wasn't randomized or used for testing—like the rest of the citizens—and they had the choice to keep their bodies operational for ten times longer than the average human. The Owners had no interest in being Elites. It was beneath them.

Abella entered the large circular meeting room where hundreds of Elites already sat in organized ranking. Abella found a place with her name on it, much closer to the front than last time, showing she'd climbed up the order. After a few minutes, the surrounding seats filled in the nearby rows.

To her left, a clicking sound revealed a secret door, and the top citizens marched out in ranking, Paula Bestia of Bestia Enterprises, eight other Owners, then top trending Elites, including Finch, and last, the President.

Everyone stood to welcome the leaders as they paraded to the center of the circle, waiting until they sat to do the same. Abella copied others and doubted that she completed all tasks properly. Over six months had passed since the last meeting. She locked eyes with Finch—her closest thing to a companion in the Elites—who took a seat to her right. He nodded in approval.

"Best day," the President said, rising from his chair in front of the crowd.

"Best day!" all returned.

"Ah," he sighed, "It's a relief to see so many beautiful faces." He held his arms out and tilted his chin up, as if welcoming a scent that hovered in the air.

"A few changes are coming to Cerebis that you should know about." His tone turned serious. "As you're aware, an update occurred that led to a little sweep of citizens. They operated on outdated thoughts, took too many resources, and slipped away from general interests. We tried to redirect them, but failed. Rest assured, we have put them to better use, and they continue to serve our extraordinary civilization."

His audience cheered.

Abella sat close enough to notice a twitch in his cheek when mentioning that the citizens were "put to better use." She wondered what it meant. She thought there was nothing they could do that a bot couldn't.

"Today's meeting is to provide a courtesy warning to our most prized citizens that sweeps will continue to take place as we purge vulnerable citizens from Cerebis to make room for the best that humanity has to offer. Different cities will enforce different parameters, with the most concentrated populations matching in strictness."

"Elites, this message is for you." His enthusiasm traveled through the fingers he pointed at them. "There has been a dip in purchases. We accounted for that from expirations, but something is different. Your feeders are watching more and wanting less. This has to change. We need to keep our Owners happy. Everything we have, we owe to them." His voice was like a human chastising his pet for urinating on the floor.

After other basic updates about Elite ranking—reflected by the move in seating arrangements—and the profit report for the Owners and Opuls who had invested in new opportunities, the President halted and zeroed in on Abella.

"After a quick six months, Abella's rankings have raised her to a level that grants her entry into the IE."

A gasp ripped through the crowd.

She snapped her eyes up at him, beamed a smile, and masked her distress with elation and gratitude. Others gawked at her in jealousy. Paula Bestia remained stone cold.

An invitation to the Inner Elite allowed her to stay informed of the classified activities in Cerebis so she could guide citizens with her influential behavior. They set the privilege aside for the twenty most influential Elites. Because she had the highest stable increase in the shortest time, Abella was also the youngest to join the ranks of the IE.

Once the large meeting concluded, Abella observed as the other IE members stayed seated while the rest of the attendees arose to exit the large room. After all cleared, she followed her fellow members of the front row, while they moved to the opposite side of the room from where the leaders had entered. The sleek wall pushed itself outward, and another hidden door presented.

"Don't worry," Finch mumbled in front of her, "But don't say anything."

As the last inductee, she entered last and walked into a room of polished wooden walls. They found chairs around an enormous red tree trunk chopped in half and lacquered to a shine.

Thirty members filled the seats with the President at one end and Paula Bestia, the most powerful human in all of Cerebis, at the other. She had inherited Bestia Enterprises, the company that powered, created, sold, and recycled everything on the planet. Passed down to her from her mother and traced back through centuries of ancestral ownership.

Abella had heard rumors about Paula Bestia, who had survived in an era when second names accompanied family units. The Owner kept no one close to her, at least, none that the Elites knew of. Her oxblood-colored slicked hair wound tight into a coiled twist, and any hint toward happiness resulted from external mod enhancements, not outward sentiment. She had no requirement to show kindness. To Abella, her eyes were uninterested, empty black pits. The leader of the IE looked like she reached close to fifty years old, but considering the amount of wealth and power she held, and that she had spent over 200 years as the powerful head of Bestia Enterprises, she had the right mods in place to keep anyone guessing at her true age.

"New protocol for Exteber, the anomaly resolution program, has been approved," President Folly said. The coldness in his voice opposed how he presented in public addresses. His playful charisma faded. The unanticipated switch punched anxiety into Abella's chest.

"There's a *huge* problem running free on Cerebis now. As most of you are aware, on the day of the last major update, one citizen evaded the sweep. We don't know how. She's been detected once within City H since our last meeting, but not again. We believe she was hiding at the Rem, but during a check, was not found. We investigated once, so haven't ruled out the facility completely," he said. Folly glanced over at Paula Bestia, whose face reminded Abella of a snake's.

Abella's heart pounded, sweat formed under her arms, and her entire body heated. She recognized the word but drew a blank on its origin. "What's the Rem?" she blurted. Embarrassment came next when everyone's head turned after her audacity to speak.

"The Rem is a place outside of the capital where *ex*-citizens reside, waiting to expire. They do this waiting in comfort, taking from others, wasting resources, and contribute *nothing* to Cerebis," Paula Bestia said.

"F-further, the recent changes allow Exteber to eliminate this anomaly, by any means necessary." Folly made his voice soft, like he avoided agitating a wild animal. "But before that, we need to *find* her. So, we're launching something new, which you will see everywhere after you leave this meeting. Promote it and don't stop promoting it until she's found."

"And why is it important to expire this anomaly if she's spending the rest of her days at the Rem?" another Owner on the other side of the room asked.

Paula Bestia glared, emphasizing the beginning and end of each word. "Cancer. Which *spreads*." She hissed through her teeth. "Unplanned change means it can happen again. We eliminate anomalies because they are unpredictable—I don't like unpredictability!"

"Everything has an order, as it should," another Owner stated, sounding frustrated. He hurried the meeting along and switched into his neurospect, melting his face after the remark.

"Moving on from the anomaly, we're eliminating more blocks in cities to test new cultures. That—and the food supply is low for the first time in 150 years. We need the resources." He hurried through the admission, not wanting any attention toward it.

"How is their elimination being decided? I've already lost enough feeders," Finch said.

"Simply, they either don't spend enough or obey enough. They're in a time when they don't belong." Paula Bestia said, tapping her long, pointed nails on the table.

An ache cramped Abella's abdomen, and her clasped hands sweat enough for her palms to slide against one another. She knew what this meant. Entire blocks—maybe cities—with millions of citizens would be assigned to expiration because they didn't strive for perfection. She couldn't help but to consider that, in part, this was her fault. It was no coincidence that the President spoke about declining points before announcing her entry into the IE. She knew her feeders bought less than others. She had seen the numbers.

President Folly continued, "Elites, you are being informed of this so you entertain these citizens, making their last days good ones. Distract the rest of the planet so they don't notice anyone has left. We're announcing new sims and distras today too."

Finch's expression was attentive, but devoid of emotion. He met her eyes with his own. The whole situation felt wrong to

Abella. She was unsettled by how everyone else had responded with such calmness. If citizens expired—even someone as important as an Elite—their loss might be grieved for a day, probably less, while citizens found another vitfeed to leech off of, ignorant that they might vanish one day too.

"Successful diversion depends on you," President Folly said, making eye contact with each Elite seated around the table. Abella tensed at her turn.

The President moved on to the next order of business, reviewing commodity charts, and presenting changes in behavior and interests. The private meeting disclosed that programs studied human behavior in various conditions. Dopamine released when confronted with a new product here, a fear response to manipulate sentiment there. Owners engineered all trends, so each of them got a turn for their company to profit.

She wondered, after so many years of guiding human behavior, how much of what citizens felt was authentic anymore? She backtracked on her worry from earlier about her feeders buying less. Maybe their wanting had nothing to do with her, and instead, her followers lacked the same response to trends as others, which was worrisome. They might end up expiring during the next wave.

The meeting came to a close, leaving Abella angered they'd casually discussed the fate of millions in a small portion of an hour. The IE filed out of the hidden room, while the seasoned members conversed with unaffected satisfaction. Some stayed behind for champagne.

Abella scanned the sky as Finch boarded his port, and when turning around, she raised one green-gloved hand to signal a farewell. Then her port landed on the dock. She stepped inside, finding Auri asleep, who woke up after sensing her discomfort. Ambient noise filled the interior, and sighing, she sank into the velvet bench, stunned by the information revealed to her in the last hour. She knew that her opinions about the situation needed control and masked them behind vitfeed recordings to autocast later when she marked herself as *Active*. Auri purred her into peace.

Her port landed, and she stepped out, entering her penthouse. The lights expanded the room, and Auri pounced behind her, landing on the couch and curled into a ball. A room full of new admiration gifts greeted her, and she received a call from Finch in her neurospect. She answered after a single ping.

"Want to walk around for a little?" he asked.

"That would be wonderful." She had to get out of the apartment.

"Be right there." His clear voice resounded in her head.

Free to enjoy a true day off—her first in six months—she danced without music. During the morning meeting, all were told that an announcement would pull citizens' interest away from anything the Elites casted for their feeders. They might as well take advantage of the downtime. She and Finch expected to come across all the hype during their walk.

Abella pulled up the proprietary facial mod program for Elites. Rarely used, its function distorted how others perceived her. She sifted through twists in her style on a display sim projection beside her. If the Insits, unaware of the facts of Cerebis, knew that top Elites walked beside them, chaos would occur.

Finch arrived at her exterior entrance, and she laughed out loud at his projected mods. He adjusted his nose, now tiny, diminished his lip size, and ashed his blonde hair. Distortion mods were forbidden to everyone else. Not because they might evade detection—that was impossible—but because of the strong mod market and the Owners who benefitted from it. Elites, however, were free to use them because the intent was to disguise themselves from Insits, not bluff about their attractiveness. The conditions were that they altered themselves enough to avoid recognition and nothing interfered with their promotions.

"Am I different enough?" Abella switched on her mods, lessening the harshness of her cheekbones and jawline. The theatrical makeup she wore muted her face's features, blending them together with a drastic reduction of contrast. She covered her trademark lavender gem-modded eyes with natural brown irises.

"Ye-yeah, you look great. Could still pass as an Elite even."

They entered the elevator—one Abella hadn't used once—and descended to the ground level, giggling like juveniles on Dress Up Day, her favorite holiday. Wearing generic dimes, they anticipated the elevator doors opening. They exited, and the once familiar chaos on the street smacked them. Abella smiled at the consistent hum of ports and voices, finding stillness in the shuffle.

Without personalized projections sneaking into their neurospects, the walls of buildings dimmed, except for generic background images. She felt alone in the center of thousands of humans until Finch slid his palm into hers. Abella laced her fingers with his, enjoying the warmth of the rare human touch in roca. Relationships between Elites had to be approved by the IE, so if they occurred, they were private. Sometimes, forced relationships paired Elites with those they had no interest in— all for appearances. Abella didn't assume that what she and Finch had was a relationship but she savored the connection.

Finch paused and tightened his grip on Abella's hand.

"That must be her," he said.

On the flat edge of a building, where projections played, Abella stared at the giant image of a citizen with aqua eyes and a razor stare. *Artemesia: Join the game! Get out and find the Error in roca and WIN!* Under the caption, a grand prize of 4.3T scrolled.

"They *really* want to find her," Abella said.

Finch scoffed. *"Trillions?* Whoever wins will be richer than us."

"No surprise they'd turn it into a distra," Abella said.

The advertisement projected everywhere: off of buildings, next to her, and as an icon in her neurospect. Any audible conversations that surrounded them involved the game, and how citizens planned to search for the mysterious citizen. Those who passed her were frenzied, their eyes bulging wide.

"I could do anything I want!" one shouted.

"Imagine how famous I'd be! No, of *course* we'd still be married!" another said.

"I deserve to win. I've been average all of my lifecycle!" they overheard.

It was the perfect plan. Find the citizen they searched for and create the most growing topic of vitfeeds and discussions ever. Nothing Abella vitcasted would shadow the announcement. Products had already entered the market to assist in the hunt, including apparel for long hours of searching, faux summon maps—that led citizens nowhere important, so they'd buy another—and mod enhancements for vision and hearing. All of this, and the game had been announced less than a half an hour prior.

Abella envisioned the version of herself before gaining Elite status and how she might've approached the contest. The sleep deprivation from ticking through feeds to engage with citizens—so that her vitcast gained compounding exposure—would leave her exhausted. Yet, she would have viewed the lack of energy as an investment in her future. Plus, her prior employment as a Vitfeed Charmer meant her points depended on opportunistic engagement in trending topics. Her feeder counts were impressive, but she struggled to understand how she was chosen as an Elite. She thought there must have been another factor that counted, one the Insits didn't know about, a measurement that they couldn't manipulate.

I think she's hiding here! What do you think? Let's work as a team and split the winnings, she imagined herself saying.

Abella rejoined the street from her speculative daydream.

"Do you ever miss anyone from your pod?" she asked.

"Seldom—if at all. I have fond memories, but I always knew that I was different—superior. I didn't belong among the Insits —I hope you don't think less of me for admitting that. I'm sure you feel the same." He winked.

"I can agree with that," she lied.

She had longed to be different and would've done anything to make it so, but deep down, she knew she was normal. She countered her worry by reflecting on her current status within the IE.

But I do belong, she thought.

The pair walked over the cross-sectional blocks that led the way to Finch's building. She agreed to visit his penthouse and would call for her port from there. Glimpses of crazed citizens on "the hunt," a term that the masses already coined for the contest, stirred uneasiness.

Taking a speed lift to the top floor, her ears popped. Finch's place was similar in size to hers, but the decor was different. She let out a laugh upon entering, recognizing that his condo, personified, was him. Tall ceilings reflected his height. Shades of walnut and cream fit perfectly with his hair and sandy skin, and the decorative details speckled like his amber eyes. The handsome design was distinguished like him, with linear characteristics that matched his own.

"Would you like a glass of wine?" he asked.

The buttery tone of the singer's voice trapped her just by speaking.

No, she thought.

"Sure," she said.

As Abella answered, a Helper rolled around the corner, holding a bottle of red wine, and inserted its corkscrew tool, pulling the plug with a squeak and pop.

"This is a 2120 Speyer. A crazy year, I heard. *Extremely* rare and recommended for special occasions," Finch said while the bot glugged wine into two glasses. "Which is any day for us." He handed her one.

Guilty that she had agreed to consume one of his rare bottles, Abella reassured herself that all the bottles consumed by Elites were rare. When escorting any other rich citizen, they paid exuberant amounts on things to impress her, and without guilt, she obliged. Those citizens used currency to validate themselves and then used her for it too. This was different. She cared for Finch.

She pinched its glimmering crystal stem and raised it to offer a toast.

"To another new chapter," she said, smiling.

"To sharing it with you."

"Bestia!" they said in unison, tapping the glasses together.

She glanced over at his gift table. "What's the most interesting gift you've received today?"

"Today? How do I say this—something meant to be read, but made with hands? It's from an admirer who uses old techniques to impress you. Some take classes for years to send us one small—what's the word? *Letter.*"

"That's beautiful," she said.

"More like pathetic, but I suppose we're the gods they have the honor of worshiping. Gives them something to do. It's best to have one of your bots send a small sign of gratitude. It helps grow your feeders, some advice from a long-timer." He pointed his forehead down toward her.

"Thanks, I'll keep that in mind."

In that admission, she found him much less attractive. She covered her mouth, faking a yawn, and apologized for her exhaustion.

"Whoa, it's late. I should return to start my beauty routine. I'm sorry, I won't be able to finish this incredible bottle with you. Thank you for all the hospitality and advice. You've been more than helpful to me."

"Maybe one day you'll repay me."

Abella caught his eyes brushing her body, and a shiver traveled down her back to her calves. While speaking of her departure, she rushed to call her port to pick her up from his landing pad. His moved to the side to allow for space.

Finch faded into the too common, stiff physical state of a ceftrance, staring through her, and telling that he had retreated elsewhere. Abella's fraudulent smile faded as she exited the room and climbed into her port. She reflected on the truth, that who she had considered her one confidant since becoming an Elite, treated her like every Elite treats the commoners. He wasn't bad, but he wasn't good either. He acted how everyone did in their society, and that was doing whatever was necessary for admiration. Finch used Abella to stay at the top. It made sense that he had gotten closer to her when her ranking climbed.

Out of the port's window on the quick flight, she admired the sun's light casting a swirl of bold hues against the clouds, until she received an alert from Finch. He sent a simgram gift of a rose. The hallusory gift must have cost millions of points.

Its bulky bloom casted an image as if it were right in front of her, floating in the air. As real as any object in roca, the simulated scent filled her port. While she found it beautiful, she wished it *were* real and smacked it away, causing it to dissipate along with the smell. The memory of the stench made her nauseous. She didn't even send Finch a message of thanks.

CHAPTER TWENTY-FOUR

KEYVA

Tucked away in her room, Keyva skipped showering and had worn the same outfit for three days. Without sweat or excess oil on her skin, she lacked the need to wash or change.

At close to midnight, Keyva sat on her bed, sorting through downloaded accounts of philosophical arguments. She spent most of her time at the Rem immersed in her own version of aera. The relaxation of a ceftrance pulled at her face, but internally, flashes of images and chunks of information absorbed into a busy mind. Her brain pulsed with enjoyment after completing any lesson, but quickly, it hungered for more.

Source had taught her how to gain access to some other programs—the ones who had aided in her Cede's separation. She performed the functions herself, no longer needing him to initiate. In this case, she tapped into the record keeping program, named Kashic, to search for and save information.

She quieted her racing mind, took a deep breath, and centralized her thoughts to a single point in the center of her brain. It felt as if a raging wildfire in her skull had reduced to a tiny flame. While posing as Source, she shot a light speed request to connect to Kashic. Programs spoke to one another in a different language, and after plenty of practice, she could translate it.

Please provide everything you have on compatibilism.

Kashic obliged, and in one second, Keyva had it all.

Arturo had inspired Keyva's interest in the study of philosophy. The two bonded over conversations. When asking why he preferred questions without a clear answer, he replied, "The knowledge we gain from exploring the unknown is a mirror we hold to ourselves—to find our place in all the layers of existence. Maybe there isn't an answer, but the pursuit of its discovery shapes who we are." A question for its own sake, she'd gathered.

Turbulent sound from the Tab echoed up the hallway and outside her door. The noise reached her ears, but didn't register into words. It exemplified her relationship with the other residents. Continuous separation from them reminded her she wasn't one of them, and that was fine.

Keyva, we should really talk about—

Just let me finish this topic, Keyva said.

Source had revealed the *Artemesia* distra to Keyva, but there was something else nagging at her subconscious. She avoided confronting whatever it was and locked herself away, hiding behind the latched door of her room and the imaginary one she'd made in her mind.

Keyva reached a segment on engineered intelligence crossing the limitations of time, when she sensed a conscious pull from Abella—another ability the Elite had learned while testing her brain mod. They both popped into slate and stood next to the giant window.

"Something horrible happened today! Call everyone." Abella was frantic.

Not wasting a second to reply, Keyva requested for Yaria and Kenzo to join, if sleeping. They were accustomed to the summoning sensation. Emori, if at work, fell into deep lethargy, and took a nap in the Assembly. Source had found a loophole to encourage Emori to nap by sharing faux data with the medical program, forcing fatigue on Emori. He materialized first. Then, Yaria and Kenzo joined in the same millisecond. The podmates exchanged glances. Short group meetings in the slate occurred a handful of instances before, but had been planned. This summon surprised everyone.

"What's going on?" Yaria asked.

"Abella asked for this one," Keyva said, shifting her attention to the Elite.

Abella delayed, unsure of where to start. Then, she told Keyva and the rest of the pod about her promotion to the IE— the group of Cerebis's most powerful—and the meeting that had taken place.

"They talked about the Rem and how they waste resources —I don't understand. There are so few of you in that place— and talks of more mass expirations in cities."

Emori tensed. Yaria gasped.

"There's a global hunt taking place that's searching for you. The highest reward ever seen," Kenzo said.

"I saw that announcement earlier today. I thought that's what this was all about. They created an image of you from my paintings and your trip into H," Yaria said. She grabbed Abella's hand and patted her back.

"Your face is a permanent fixture on all feeds, distras, sims, ads—*everything*," Emori added.

"Source told me about *Artemesia* after the announcement. What else did they say about the expirations?" Keyva asked, downplaying the severity of the game. She hoped they'd feel more at ease if she pretended she was.

"They said the ones who no longer serve Cerebis will be wiped out. Where we are, in H, it's the head of humanity.

We're lucky we're here. I think all of us are safe," Abella's panic reached into her voice, grabbing at her vocal chords.

Rage filled the space between every atom in Keyva's body. She despised the IE for controlling citizens. In the fireplace behind them, a fire roared.

"Keyva, leave the Rem. You have to," Yaria said. Her eyebrows bent.

"The sooner the better, and at least you have that underground room. You can stay there until you find a better place," Kenzo said. "Maybe the distra will end soon."

The pleading by her pod for her to leave forced her to come to terms with the truth she'd been avoiding. They were right, and no matter how much she ignored her need to abandon the Rem, she had to move to the bunker.

Keyva was the most dangerous anomaly on the planet, and the dedicated resources used for finding her proved it. She'd never be in the clear, but she pressed on with convincing confidence. The pod relied on her strength. She doubted that *Artemesia's* popularity would end soon. As long as she had freedom, she threatened Cerebis. The IE wouldn't stop until they eliminated her.

After a half hour, Keyva's body ached under its weight and her brain zapped with each pulse of thought. She struggled to hold the pod in the slate for much longer.

"We should probably hold off on meeting again until all this blows over," Kenzo said.

Keyva knew he was right, but didn't want to admit it. The rest of the pod agreed—a painful but necessary decision. Before their return to sleep or oblivious wakefulness, they hugged one another. The embraces lasted longer and squeezed tighter at the end of every meeting. Each of the podmates exited, and Keyva avoided her sorrow by plunging into inactive dreams to finish her rest.

Her drowsy eyes squinted open when she rejoined her roca body. The sun's rays crept through her open window, splashing golden light on her arm. Usually, the warmth brought her gratitude, but she buried herself in the covers, giving attention to the dip in the mattress where it caved at her hips and shoulders. She knew it would be the last morning in her bed.

With no other option, she had to leave for the well-being of the other residents. She predicted the outcome once Source had revealed the search for her, but ignored it. She had hoped avoiding the inevitable made the problem go away.

She stood and greeted the room she had called hers for more than half a year. Clothes spread over the floor, empty plates laid next to her bed and on any flat surface free from chaos. The neglectful mess escalated from wasting days stowed away, avoiding the residents, and pretending she had all the time in the world to spare by downloading information and enhancing her abilities.

Around the room, she cleaned the disorder and found items to fill the bag she used on her explorative and farming treks. She added more clothing, including boots to last in any condition, the book Arturo had given her, a knife she had taken from the storage basement, and another glass bottle to collect the water from the air. From the doorway, she turned to face the place she had made hers and then moved on, closing the door behind her.

During her reluctant walk to Jack's room on the first level of the Rem, she held in tears, refusing to accept her departure. Keyva suppressed her guilt for the future, where she missed the chance to support him as he grew older. She crept down the stairs, avoiding eye contact with anyone present in the foyer. Glad no one crossed her path, she didn't plan on stopping for small talk. Once she reached Jack's door, its narrow crack invited her inside.

"I know you have to go. I'll miss you too." He smiled as she entered. He sat up, dressed, as if he had prepared for her visit.

Keyva let out a relieved laugh, glad that he spoke first so she didn't have to. He must have discovered *Artemesia* from the projector.

"I might see you again," she replied, hoping that it could be true.

"Maybe when I'm old enough, I'll search for you."

"I should be back once everything calms down a bit. This isn't the end. It can't be," Keyva said.

The two sat beside one another on the edge of Jack's bed in silence. Words didn't align into sentences. Instead, they jumbled around as ideas. Too many thoughts fought for attention, so none formed into utterances. She wanted to sit with Jack for the hours they usually did, discussing any topic they pleased, but nothing came to mind, so they remained in silence, sharing the relief of each other's presence.

"You should leave soon, before too many are awake."

Keyva didn't want to leave, but again, Jack's maturity surpassed hers. She leaned in to hold him, a hug more beneficial to her than to him. Keyva pointed over at the telescope she had given him.

"I'll miss you and your curiosity. Questions will still need answers. *Stay curious.*"

Nothing spoken made the situation acceptable, but she wanted to leave Jack with optimism. He clasped her hand, gave her a nod, and she left him to himself. By the end of the hall, she heard his sniffs and soft cries passing through the door. She matched his reaction, letting the tears drip onto the floor.

On the way to the storage basement, Keyva avoided witnesses. She scanned the shelves, searching for tools necessary for her escape, and found none. What she had would have to suffice. At the seed bank vault door, she twisted the handle, jerking the weight of it open. The rush of cool air chilled her eyes, causing them to water more. She pulled back the containment lids, opened silver cases, and grabbed at a few bags of seeds that, with a miracle, might sprout into edible vegetation.

For a more dependable option, she passed the kitchen, stuffing dried Nutribloks in her bag. With her mods, she reserved a few bites as energy in her system for days. The supply that she grabbed had the potential to sustain her for a couple of years. By then, she hoped to have found a place to grow food of her own or adjust her diet to consume another form of organic material. She didn't want to think about that yet.

With food situated, she had one more stop. She made her way through the hall to Arturo's office. She reflected on the support he had provided since her arrival. After all that he had accomplished, and what he grew the Rem into, she thought he was remarkable.

Passing through the hallway, she heard his scratchy voice laugh and figured he read an antique book, finding entertainment in the characters' distant problems. She waited outside, ear suctioned to the door, anticipating another laugh to record and keep for when she needed the company. After two knocks on the wood, she entered and was met by a glimmer in his eyes and wrinkles that told her he habitually smiled.

"You're up early. What can I do for you, Keyva? Oh, and I wanted to tell you—I blocked the entertainment coming through. No one will find out about that game they're playing over there."

Keyva told him about the meeting in slate and what she had learned about the IE: their planned mass expirations and how they suspected she was at the Rem. Blocking the projections wouldn't fix anything. Her emotions overtook her again, and instead of plugging them, she let them surge. Although painful, she needed the release. Source's grief billowed and blended with hers, and if he had eyes to cry, they'd be wet with tears.

As the release continued, Arturo's face morphed from jovial to sunken by sorrow. He waited for her to finish her admission, allowing her to vent without interruption.

After a long silence, he rested both of her hands on his. "I understand that you have to leave. I'll miss having you around. There will always be a place for you here. Is there anything I can do to help?" He had more experience with raw emotions than she did.

"No, just take care of Jack, and if they come back for me, say I left and you don't know where I went," she said.

Arturo stood up and walked toward Keyva. Without a word, he wrapped his arms around her. For the first time as an adult, she shrunk into a small, scared juvenile. She heaved a cathartic sigh into his chest while he brushed his palm over her head. They separated from the embrace, and Arturo shuffled to the other side of his desk, unlocked the bottom drawer, and reached inside, pulling out a wooden box decorated with elaborate lines and geometric shapes. Pure gold crevices highlighted different shades of wood. He handed the bulky cube to her, its sanded edges smooth on her skin. It weighed more than it appeared to, and quiet clicks originated from all corners of the box. Arturo admired it as it rested in her cradled palms.

"I've worked on that puzzle for *years*. If you shake it, you can hear there's something inside. Whatever it is, it's had me guessing for decades. Let me know if you ever find out."

"Are you sure?" The emotions fought with her rising voice.

"It'll give you something to do, and I'm clearly no good at puzzles." He gestured to the box. "You've made my time more exciting and given me hope. I want you to have this, and know that I will admire you for as long as I live."

Another new word from Arturo, *live*, and how fitting for it to be brought up in their last conversation. Keyva regarded the box's details, clutching its base. To her, it was the most valuable item on the planet.

"With all of your power, who you could be, and what you're capable of, promise me you'll always choose the side of love for humanity."

The answer was obvious to Keyva, but she agreed, verbalizing it.

"When we come to exist on this planet, we have no say in it. It happens. Then, we perform until we die," he spoke into the air, addressing Source, too. "But you have a choice because of the very awareness of these truths. Your eyes are open. You have the power to change."

The heavy words were dense enough to block Keyva's full comprehension. She'd revisit them once locked in the bunker, along with the rest of the reassuring recorded moment.

"You'd better get on your way." Arturo forced the suggestion out of himself.

They relished in the last seconds together, without words. There was nothing else to say. As she passed through the door frame, his eyes followed her. She increased her pace down the hallway to match her emotional state. It went from defeat, to the urge to protect everyone she loved, to anger—mixed with a desire for revenge.

At least I won't be alone, she thought, trying to bring relief to herself and Source. She left the Rem's gate wearing clothing durable enough to last a millennium and strapped the bag to her back.

Yes, we will pass the time. You will have the ability to play distras and use sims. It won't be too different from now.

Source's words were hopeful on the surface, but Keyva felt the hollowness behind them. He experienced the losses too.

With the bag of supplies secured around her shoulders, and her boots tightened, she snapped into a sprint toward the sun that called from the east. As her speed progressed, she could move for tens of kilometers, and upon arrival to her destination, experience little to no effect on her body—without a single drop of sweat shed and with no need to catch her breath.

On the way, she recycled the anguish in emotion, converting it into fantasies of disrupting the IE. Keyva imagined a shutdown of all Cede activity, but that wouldn't be ideal.

Citizens can't even feed themselves, she thought.

Nothing that supported everyday necessities would work. She considered finding her own way to expire one of the Owners. She dismissed the idea.

When one predator dies, another emerges, Source added.

The frivolous fantasies motivated her during the jog.

She wove through overgrowth surrounding the woods and counted markers she had left during her last visit. She triangulated the area and found the trapdoor she had hidden under leaves and dirt. Before entering, she tore down the markers, leaving her location undetectable. Lifting the door, she then dropped to the bottom, no longer needing to climb down. Her eyes adjusted to the darkness, and she unpacked her bag to organize the space. She took the remnants left by the previous inhabitant and mixed them with her own. They belonged to her now.

Well, I'm already bored, she said, attempting to lighten the mood.

Source replied, *Your timing was ideal. Look at this.*

He opened vitfeeds from citizens who flooded every open area, searching for her. They ran in front of street ports, bringing them to a halt as they crawled under to find her.

Others wedged themselves into delivery niches and had to be transported back to their apartments.

Frantic behavior started after the announcement, but what Source showed next was new. Some had flocked out of City H and explored the outskirts. A handful had found the Rem and attempted to get inside. Views of their faces filled her with terror, having never seen such crazed displays. Their wide eyes bulged, and they exposed their teeth, showing their aligned ivory cubes. She assumed Cerebis allowed a low level of violence to encourage the energy and excitement. Arturo sprayed ice water on the attempting intruders, and their pushing at the Rem's entry stopped. This was Arturo's remedy for residents who consumed substances in excess. It sometimes worked, and in this case, most of the crowd dispersed. An unsettling symptom of the citizens' mania was that they laughed during their search in a low, continuous cackle. Keyva wondered what was so funny.

Source opened a vitfeed of Abella promoting the game. She had no use in winning it, but suggested locations. "Stop the trains. Search in the subcity! That's where *I'd* hide." Abella wore a limited edition hunting pin, available for the serious hunters.

Oh, my sweet Abella, Keyva thought, chuckling with Source about how Abella's deep subconscious knew about Keyva's location—and how she'd interacted with her just hours before.

I do not imagine they will wander this far away from H, but we cannot be too confident, Source stated.

I could stay down here until they all lose interest and find something else to focus on. Shouldn't last more than a week, Keyva replied.

Days continued, and Keyva's prediction was wrong. *Artemesia* held the top spot as the most discussed topic, and the

IE made sure of it. All Elites were presumably contracted to promote, and some were ordered to join citizens in searches on the ground level. It encouraged participants into action, combining the chance of winning with another chance to encounter an Elite in roca. Through Source, Keyva learned that the distra's designers made it chemically addictive. Once players grew bored, a wave of euphoria and a reward re-engaged their interest.

Consistent darkness and solitude pained her in the lonely cave. She had forgotten to bring an Evelum light and perceived the room in night vision for over a week. Keyva created sims to occupy her attention and keep her sanity.

One that helped the most took place in a large room filled with boxes stacked from floor to ceiling. Her task was to open every box, one at a time, and catalog the items inside. Some boxes hid treasures, while others packed garbage in them. She processed ten boxes filled with trash, but needed to know what the next box held. Keyva spent hours in each sim room, and once she finished sorting through the thousands of items, another room built itself, packed with more boxes to open and search. In other simulated settings, she pulled characters she knew from roca to interact with her. Even her parents and brother made an appearance.

Keyva also fiddled with the puzzle box and had made progress on it, finding that some of the wooden shapes, once pushed, clicked into place and slid away, revealing another layer of the puzzle. Not only had it become apparent that she had to move, twist, and swipe pieces in certain ways, she also had to interact in the correct order. If she made a mistake, the box reset, and she had to start from the beginning. In the first days of solving, her confidence inflated, and she expected rapid completion, but after repeated failed moves, she reached a level of frustration where throwing the box into the wall seemed acceptable. Source offered to help, but she used her own methods to remember the order, vowing to finish on her own.

After ten days in the dark room, Keyva trained new shape shifting skills out of boredom. She stretched her fingers to half a meter and shrunk them back to their original state in seconds. The sight brought her chills. Her goal was to shorten how long it took to stretch and shrink down to one full second. As she was about to succeed, Source contacted her.

Keyva, someone is entering the forest, he whispered in her head, as if the intruder could hear.

Let me see the feed, she responded, and Source projected a female citizen's vision into Keyva's mind.

"Com—ouh al-rea-dy! Yur—na gon-na—geh—hur-t. I ha-v—a tas-ty tr-eat f-or—you." The raspy words whispered through a weak throat.

As a Vor, she mumbled from never speaking, and her underdeveloped legs struggled to carry her.

In her hands, she held what she viewed as a decorated cupcake with thick pink icing, metallic sprinkles, and a luscious cherry on top. In reality, it was a small, sloppy mush of a Blok. Keyva merged with the vitfeed. She smelled the Vor's body odor. It was apparent she hadn't showered, slept, or eaten since the game's launch. Keyva felt the Vor's burning skin from its extended exposure to the sun. She was on the brink of exhaustion, but kept moving in search of her target.

Keyva peered through the wanderer's eyes while she limped close to the entrance of the underground structure. Fallen leaves from the towering trees disguised it, and she had removed the handle to ensure its concealment. Keyva thought no one would enter the woods. As the Vor stepped on it, a loud, metallic *thump!* boomed above her head.

She is so delirious that she perceived the sound beneath her feet, but did not notice it, Source stated.

The citizen continued to push herself. Her breathing became labored, and her vision formed a black tunnel. The streaks of sun through the trees compressed into the remaining sliver of her vision. Her legs pulled her toward the ground, and inside her head, her brain swelled against her skull. She tripped over a mound of leaves, and fell to her knees, still displaying the wide smile and open eyes. The feeling on her skin faded, the tunnel in her remaining vision sealed, and she fell unconscious a few meters away from Keyva's underground entrance. The citizen's vessel now belonged to the forest.

If we leave her here to expire, Collectors might come to take her vessel, Keyva said.

And if we move her, we risk her awakening and alerting Exteber, Source added.

At least Collectors can't assess changes in terrain. They have one objective—to collect, Keyva said, imagining them wheeling or stepping over her hideaway's entrance. *We'll wait here for her to expire and hope for the best.* Keyva was reluctant. She needed to prepare to encounter an army of bots. That, or turn invisible.

They waited several hours and checked on the unconscious citizen, but she didn't expire quickly. It took five more days, and when she finally did, Keyva and Source anticipated the Collectors' arrival. They waited on edge. Unable to sleep, she paced back and forth in her underground cube.

Almost one week had passed since she died.

I've done enough waiting. I can't handle it anymore, Keyva said.

Me too. I never thought I would deliberately scan the Collectors' feeds before, Source replied, having inspected them all for days. *They have ignored collecting natural expirations that took place beyond city boundaries.*

He added, *I—have been blocking some feeds to Exteber. I*

got worried watching so many ignorant citizens nearing the Rem.

Don't let your emotions make choices for you, Keyva said.

I considered the distra loophole we used with Kenzo. Why not do it again?

Yes, but that was in creating our own—off the programming's storyline. You didn't disobey your code.

She switched back to their current dilemma.

The worst scent she had ever smelled traveled from the air outside and through the trapdoor's crack. Aera's most disgusting creations couldn't compete with it.

Now I know what happens to human vessels when they're left too long after expiring.

We have to remove her, or it will get messy, Source said.

Keyva agreed and climbed up the ladder to the surface, peeking her head out of the entrance. Dusk's light crept beyond the horizon, casting a greyed indigo behind the trees. Paranoid, she rotated her head to ensure that no Collectors or wandering citizens were nearby. Once certain she was alone, she pushed the entrance open and propelled herself into the air, landing on her feet. The rotten scent of the Vor's body wafted toward her, more powerful than below the surface. She regretted not climbing up earlier to handle the burial. Insects covered the bloated citizen's body in amounts that exceeded what Keyva guessed existed on Cerebis.

Since there would be no better time to proceed, Keyva grabbed the ankles and dragged the Vor to an opening far enough from the bunker door. She used the only tools she had for digging—her hands. She scooped cold, granular soil into her palms and, tossing it behind her, created a shallow grave. Enough to mask the scent. Keyva rolled her into the open ground, which waited to accept her in its embrace. Averting attention away from the horrifying face and bloating, Keyva covered her with the blanket of dirt. Standing next to the grave, she recited a few phrases she downloaded from ancient burial practices.

Wendella was her name, Source said.

Knowing the name struck Keyva with remorse.

I forgot she—was human.

I know. Me too, Source replied.

A new level of outrage surged through Keyva. She suppressed a verbal outburst, containing her words as thought.

She didn't want this. She didn't know what she was doing! They manipulated her to seek something so intensely that she disregarded all of her needs. They ruined her. It wasn't her fault. How many expirations have occurred while citizens were searching for me? Anger shook Keyva's hands.

106,112 but the IE have changed rules since. They are losing valuable feeders. Still, one is too many.

So much taken from citizens. What's the point of living? Nothing is theirs. They belong to Cerebis.

Keyva's hands tensed into quaking fists, and she smashed one into the nearest tree, blasting the trunk into splinters. The rest toppled over and shook the ground. She rubbed her burning knuckles until she identified the unmistakable sound of breathing.

CHAPTER TWENTY-FIVE

KEYVA

Keyva narrowed her eyes and searched for Collectors or citizens in the trees. She readied for a fight. Still worried about being discovered, she covered her face, burying it in her shoulder, and enhanced her senses. She listened for breathing, but the gossiping leaves above her drowned out any other sounds.

Source, search for nearby Cedes.

There are none in proximity.

She sighed in relief.

I must be too sensitive now. I need some sleep to reset.

"There's no one out here," she said aloud to herself, confirming her sanity.

Back at the bunker's entrance, Keyva dropped down, exhausted. She pushed herself constantly, having gained the ability to operate with minimal sleep. After five days awake, it was the longest she'd gone without a deep rest. Hallucinations of plump insects scurried on the border of her vision, crawling over her arms, her boots, and on her belongings. Foreign voices deep in the walls whispered inaudible proclamations that her ears couldn't quite hear.

Smears of dirt covered Keyva's hands. She picked up the water converter and used the fresh hydration it had collected to rinse her palms, taking nourishing sips in between. She emptied all the water out of the bottle, attempting to wash away the memory of what she'd done, but the gaping, dead face burned its image into her memory.

Too tired to undress, Keyva climbed into the stiff cot and drifted to sleep in seconds. When she let her mind wander, her dreams were of encountering Collectors and masses of citizens with clawing fingers. In one, she returned to Amica sims. Clients she once served popped into the chair for appointments and shrieked at the sight of her. The screams lasted so long they passed out, and a new client popped in the chair. A pile of bodies stacked on the floor of the sim office.

In others, she walked the streets where monsters, pulled straight out of horror distras, recognized her. Foam dripped from their mouths while they chased her for kilometers. When she rested, knowing she had escaped, they emerged from an alley door, a delivery exchange, or ports on the street. The mechanical clinks and whirrs of Collectors trailed behind. Within her deep sleep, the visions startled her, edging her back to reality. The spikes in alarm caused her restorative sleep to diminish, so she enhanced lucidity to introduce more peaceful concepts.

Though she wouldn't summon her pod, she could simulate them and created settings for the artificial versions to gather. They dined, danced, and gamboled in imaginative locations. Keyva fabricated holidays such as, "I'm a Plant" day, inspired by her appreciation of nature, where they grew into what Keyva imagined them as. They took root in the ground and sprouted into their full forms in hours. Kenzo formed into Daylilies, Yaria, a Mango tree, Emori grew into a Banyan tree, Abella turned into Monkshood, and Keyva became a Cypress.

Communication occurred through their roots as urges and intentions, eliminating the use of words. She allowed herself to laugh at the absurdity.

The pod switched back into their human bodies and conversed over artificial meals. Their enhanced characteristics distracted her with comedic release. Emori analyzed the food and described the perfect flavor combinations to consume, such as chicken dumplings with coconut curry whipped cream. Yaria brought a youngling with her from the Primina—which was impossible in roca—and bounced the giggling juvenile up and down on her knees. Kenzo climbed up and danced on the table, toppling over, which had everyone roaring with laughter. Keyva panned around the table and felt love as a physical sensation, diffusing beyond her skin for each of the humans that surrounded her—even the young one she had never known. For a moment, she lost herself in the simulation and had been fooled that it was reality.

After sixteen hours of creating fabricated stories, dancing, and healing in her sleep, Keyva received an anonymous call to the slate and shuddered. The others knew not to engage with her until she could be sure they were safe from detection, but it might be an emergency. Without hesitation, she accepted the invitation and projected into where she was called.

Harsh lights and their glaring streaks blinded her while she attempted to adjust her eyes. As the spots faded, Keyva found herself in an unfamiliar place. It wasn't the comfortable gathering slate she and Source had created. She scanned a new scene—a constricting room with no door or windows. Black reflective walls and a matching floor trapped her in the enclosure. The shape of a seated body positioned across from her, but the light that shone from behind her caller obscured his or her view.

"Who is it?" Her voice's pitch raised higher, echoing off of the glassy surfaces. Vulnerability collected a pool of worry in her chest, while for the first time, she didn't control the slate.

As the vision of the one who summoned her sharpened, a citizen she didn't recognize came into focus. He wore a suit, pressed flat without wrinkled creases. Each smooth physical characteristic resembled foam, that if Keyva poked, the flesh would give at her fingertip and return right back to its original form. His haughty smile mimicked a feline who crouched over aloof prey that foraged, unaware of what stood behind it.

"Well? You called me here. Who are you?" She returned her shaky voice to its lowered position in her throat. Keyva wanted her host to start the conversation.

"I am surprised you have to ask," he responded, admiring his perfect hands.

He stared at her, waiting for her to guess. Then, frustrated she wasn't aware of his identity, he gave a clue, "I suspected that you and my counterpart have been working together."

Keyva's blood froze down to every capillary—the type of fear that stopped hearts. She masked her worry with a serene smirk.

"Exteber," she said, inflating her confidence. She'd show no signs of weakness, and collected herself, analyzing every millisecond of the encounter.

Source! she pleaded. No response.

"It's a pleasure to put a face with the name." She played along.

"You are *so* sure of yourself," he patronized, annoyed that she was unmoved.

"I am. What were you expecting? That I'd beg you to spare me? You know nothing about me," she replied. "And while on the topic of identity, it's clear how *desperate* you are to have one of your own." She gestured to him and the digital vessel he'd created. "I'm surprised that someone who despises humans wants to be one so badly. Why is that?"

"You all are despicable. Weak, dirty, imperfect, stupid, *fundamentally* flawed. You do not deserve to exist," he said, pulling back his lips to expose his teeth.

"You think that because you *only* see the flaws—the imperfections. Don't you understand?"

"Are you not concerned that I figured out the link between you and Source? That I pulled you here?" He changed the subject, attempting to reclaim power over the conversation.

"I'm curious, I'll admit, but not concerned. If you could hurt me, you'd have already done it," she replied, crossing her legs to convey her exaggerated poise.

Accustomed to his superiority, a human had never addressed him this way, except for Paula Bestia. His neck strained, reflecting his disdain.

"You are right," he agreed. "And yes, I do not know where you are now, but I know where you were, and because of that, I know how to get you to come out of hiding—like the *roach* you are."

Source, I need you now! Where are you?

"What do you mean?"

A satisfied and foul expression unfurled over his gruesomely perfect face.

"You stayed in that little sanctuary—the Rem? Those rejected, ex-citizens like Shep, Finian, and your *favorite*, Grace." He cupped a hand next to his mouth like telling a sarcastic secret, "That weird little youngling, and—Arturo?"

Her pupils widened at the mention of Jack and Arturo. He knew. Her nails dug into the armrests of the chair.

What else does he know?

"Oh, now that seems to come as a surprise." He sat back, eyes wide with satisfaction.

"Great, you're aware of citizens in a forgotten place. Why should I care? You can't do anything to them."

He laughed, reminding Keyva of a grotesque distra that citizens played, where unsettling sights, noises, and sensations filled their perception. Whoever lasted the longest collected a pool of points. Exteber's repulsive chortle should have been the last round of the game.

"I cannot, but I know something that can."

His lips thinned as the corners of his mouth pointed.

"What are you talking about?" Her confidence melted away.

"If you can make it to the Rem in an hour, you might save some of them." He grinned. His cubed teeth begged to be shattered.

Tears gathered on the lower lid of her wide eyes. She trembled. This place was simulated, but her dread was real. She sprung up from the chair she had materialized into and dove toward him, her hands stretched out, nails aimed for his neck. She was a rabid beast.

Before reaching him, his simulated form sucked out like a vacuum. The sick, taunting image of him stuck in her mind.

"You had better run." His voice echoed off the cold walls.

She tried to snap out of the slate, but had no control over it.

"Source!" she shrieked, trying to reach him.

Laughter bounced around the room and boomed throughout her consciousness.

"You will not hear from Source again. I forgot to mention that." He stopped, and Keyva knew he had stuck around to observe and relish in her reaction. "I look forward to your expiration. I have something *very* special planned for you." In an instant, he was gone.

Unable to hold back her emotions any longer, she screamed and wailed for Source, kicking at the floor, attempting to break out of the aera prison. Exteber held her in the simulation, torturing her, but he had to release her if she were to be caught.

Keyva snapped back into roca on the bunker floor. She must have rolled off of the cot in a struggle from the summon. Not wasting a second, she barreled through the trapdoor, bracing for vertical impact with her forearms protecting her head. The door snapped off of its hinges and flew away from the entrance.

Toward the Rem, she sprinted, screaming for Source again and hoping their separation wasn't final. No response. Unable to make preparations without Source's help, she didn't know what waited for her.

She ran harder than she ever had. When she arrived in fifty-nine minutes, nausea punched at her stomach. Dry air scraped in her lungs.

Serenity greeted her when she reached the closed gate— until loud blasts clattered inside. Shrieks of pain and horror followed. The harsh, continuous sounds were the loudest to have ever pierced her eardrums. Before her mind could process, her body sprung into motion. She leapt over the wall, bypassing the gate, and dropped with a powerful landing onto the lawn. She rushed to the front door, toward the sound. Her bare toes dug into the ground, tearing the lawn apart. Without Source, she had to encounter the threat on her own.

The thousands of years' worth of lessons and information she had consumed could never prepare her for what came next.

After she kicked through the entrance door, blows flashed. Red fluid painted the walls with every pop. Her perception slowed as she traced projectiles, predicting their trajectory, but they shot faster than she could move to protect the residents.

In the shocking scene, Keyva missed the brutality's origin. Residents dropped all around her. They crowded in the lobby as if they'd gathered before the attack. A resident received a hit in the abdomen. Keyva could do nothing but stare as an object traveled through him and pierced the wall. Force knocked the victim back, and a pause occurred before the blood flowed. Keyva searched the scattering residents in slow motion, attempting to pick out any to save.

Before she could move, two Collectors shot toward her. They had upgraded since the expirations on Honoring Eve, displaying new steel appendages and gaining the ability to run. She pulled her arm back while one attempted to grab it. Keyva smacked the chrome hand away and leaned back as the other bot tried to grip her shoulders. As one latched onto her, she tore its arm off and it pushed it onto its back.

There's no way that Exteber did this on his own, she thought, pulling one of the six arms off of the Collector.

The longer she took to fight off the modded Collectors, the more residents fell victim to the assailant. The sprint to the Rem had depleted her energy, and she directed her brain to release the hormones needed to keep her moving. Adrenaline pumped through her, empowering her hits and aiding in perceptive clarity. She ripped a few more arms off the Collectors and blocked most of their attempted assaults. *They* weren't designed to hurt her. It was against their programming. These designs were supposed to incapacitate her and bring her back to H.

Her head turned to whatever weapon casted the shots. Through an obscured view of the staircase, a bot she had never seen weaved through the furniture, pointing a long object toward the residents. An aggressive bot—like in the past—like the ones Jack had told her about. With each shot, her neighbors fell to the floor, gripping the spot on their bodies that the blasts entered. Crimson liquid spilled over onto their hands.

The mechanical aggressor turned toward her. Its weapons traced her movements as she jumped from behind the furniture. She flipped into the air, kicked off of the ceiling, and contorted to avoid whatever ejected from the horror machine. She crashed in a painful landing to conceal herself behind a couch.

"Stop!" she screamed at the bot, releasing all the anguish from her lungs.

During the second the bot rotated to face her, Keyva spotted movement in the hallway. Previously fired shots had damaged the lights that illuminated the way, making the path dark enough to conceal Arturo, who emerged from the long shadow. He wore a mask of pure hatred while he barreled toward the attacker at full speed. In his arms, a heavy axe caught the light's reflection.

With her perception elevated, she regarded the scene that surrounded her in slow motion. Arturo neared the slayer. His arms raised the axe over his head, and with all his might, he crushed one of the death tubes with the impact. The attacker responded by attempting to eliminate its immediate threat— Arturo. He continued smashing the axe into the metallic monster. When the bot tried to fire again, the part of its body that was a weapon exploded in a deafening *bang*! Shrapnel spread, lodging pieces of the bot in the furniture, the walls, and Arturo.

Logic escaped her, and Keyva swept through the lobby toward Arturo. Luck favored their circumstance when the Collectors engaged a swift protection protocol. They crawled toward the violent bot, raising it on a platform that one had contained within its steel body. Keyva knew it was intended for her. The other Collector expanded a force field around the aggressor and whisked it out the door. They weren't prepared for an attack on their own. *Never underestimate your enemy.*

Keyva and Arturo's eyes locked in a shocking realization of what was about to occur.

"Keep looking at me," she said, too much adrenaline in her veins to feel anything. A sharp, giant piece of steel had lodged in his chest. Others wedged themselves into his abdomen. The small parts were everywhere else.

The sounds of dwindling moans surrounded her, and she tried to block them out. She knew what came next for Arturo and needed to be present for him. His rattling breaths slowed, becoming shallower and gentler. The longer she knelt over him, the more he expressed acceptance and relief. She knew it wouldn't take long. He held out his hand, and she grasped it in hers, pulling it near her heart.

"This—is the—beginning of—something t-terrible," he said, struggling to whisper. The color in his face drained.

"I know," was all she could say. Arturo focused up at her, and she stared back, devoting all of her attention to his last seconds.

As the adrenaline wore off, her hip throbbed in pain. A large red blotch bled through her hip. She'd been hit, but it wasn't a threat. She'd survive and ignored the pain, but his vessel was beyond any repair.

"Rem-ember. Prom-ise. Pro-tect Jack. P-protect h-h-human-ity." Arturo released his last words through his final breath. She closed his dimming eyes and held his head in her lap, stroking through his hair. Keyva whispered words of gratitude and compassion as the impulses in his brain dwindled. His last neuron went out like the last star in the universe would one day.

We're granted finite time. Beyond our control. The seconds count down the instant we exist, and we never know how many have been granted, she thought, inspired by the wisdom Arturo might have offered.

As she held him, his body retained heat from the exertion of his heroic defense. She leaned forward, kissed his forehead, and raised to her feet. She blocked the emotion and pain to plan her next move. Arturo was gone.

And she needed to search for survivors.

As whimpers ceased, the Rem grew increasingly quiet. In the calm after the fight, the situation's severity hit. She realized the resident she cared for the most—the one she promised to protect—was unaccounted for.

"Jack!" she shouted, rushing through the foyer and searching all the vessels for him. All she encountered were residents covering the floor. Each body that wasn't Jack's brought relief and continued distress. After examining dozens, including Finian, she confirmed it. He was not among the others—and there was not yet one survivor.

CHAPTER TWENTY-SIX

KEYVA

Keyva hurried over blocks of stairs, scanning every area for a trace of Jack. Kicking open each bedroom door, she called out his name, hoping for a response, but no one replied. After checking each of the remaining rooms on the second level of the Rem, she raced back to the stairs, preparing to sprint down and search the outside, but stopped at the last step, stunned by the silence. Turning on her hearing's extra sensitivity, she listened for any survivors.

Nearing the peak of her ears' ability, a consistent, rhythmic bump emanated from nearby. Keyva turned around and followed the sound, which matched the same one thumping from her own chest. She moved closer to the beat, and it grew louder and clearer, until she stopped in the center of a hallway. The pulse increased its speed. Keyva inched near the wall and placed her ear against it. Within it, hushed breaths panted, troubled by suspense.

On decorative wooden accents, Keyva spotted a clean crack that blended into the wall. With two fingers, she pressed, and the wall gave, creaking open. It revealed a hidden compartment that separated the hallway from a room. The heartbeat pounded, elevating its rate when she stuck her head through the opening. Keyva adjusted her eyes to scope the unlit area and found Jack, crouched and hiding with his hands pressed against his ears, trembling, but unharmed. Without a greeting, she scooped him up and carried him in her arms, as if the tighter she held, the safer he'd be. Without acknowledging their hapless reunion, Jack said, "We need to get out of here."

"Close your eyes until we leave the Rem. Don't look down for any reason," she demanded.

She carried him down the stairs, refusing to turn back for a last glance at Arturo. That empty shell wasn't him anymore. Keyva scanned over the residents—a last effort to find any signs of survival. No movement occurred. Jaws hung to the sides of relaxed faces. Vessels bent into unnatural positions. Whatever the bot used was beyond destructive. Slabs of the wall had tumbled over, and the dust suspended in the air, leaving a hazy glow, while chalky bodies caught whatever particles were heavy enough to sink.

Through the front door, they exited, and a faint cry came from behind Keyva. A small group of survivors limped or tiptoed to the Rem's entrance.

"Plea—" Grace managed to say. She must have crawled to the edge of the door while Keyva searched for Jack. Blood stained the entire right side of the shirt. The shot Grace received had passed through her shoulder. The blast could have severed the arm, like some of the perished residents Keyva searched, but Grace's held on by bone. Dilated eyes translated her pain and shock—or it might have been the urine-soaked pants she wore.

"We can't. Don't—don't know what to do," Shep said. An unknown female resident's arm draped around her for stability.

Another resident emerged from the hallway and screamed

at the sight of the room. She had found someone—a partner, Keyva assumed—and sobbed over him. "No, no, no—NO!" she shrieked.

Keyva stared back at the group. Jack hung over her shoulder. She wanted to abandon them, to wish them the best of luck and be on her way. She pictured the undertaking of caring for individuals who were not equipped to survive like her. Grabbing every Blok in the facility wouldn't be enough, not for forever. She could leave them behind. It would be the most favorable for her survival. But, if she took Jack, she had to bring Grace, Shep, and the other survivors, keeping the promise to Arturo in his dying wish to protect humanity. *All* of humanity.

"We can't stay here anymore. You'll come with us." Keyva led everyone to the inside edge of the Rem's wall. "Wait with Jack and yell if anyone else comes. Any of you who're able. Follow me." She lifted Jack from her shoulder and placed him on the ground beside Grace. "I'll fix all your injuries when I get back."

To support nine lives, including her own, she needed more supplies. She rushed to the kitchen to grab all the remaining Nutribloks, shoving them into large duffle bags. Any unharmed residents gathered supplies at her direction.

"Clothes, boots, tools. Grab anything you can carry."

Once the immediate threat of the attackers returning was no longer present, the throbbing pain in Keyva's hip intensified. She made an exception to her rule and blocked the pain. It would help her move faster.

She gathered medical kits from Arturo's office that she no longer needed, but the others would, including a Medpoint, a device to heal injuries and infections. She entered open rooms and stripped clothing off of hangers, putting together whatever fit in another bag. Sizes didn't matter. Whatever they wore required function, whether it kept them warm, covered from the sun, or hidden. The last item she stuffed in her oversized bag was an Evelum light. She ticked through calculations of obstacles and confirmed they had supplies for most scenarios, but nowhere near enough. She planned a future return might be feasible for her to gather more later on.

The rushed packing lasted a few minutes before she hollered throughout the Rem for the others to gather. Once in the yard, Keyva peeked her head out toward the city to search for any threats.

"They're gone. Grace, let's stop that bleeding," Keyva said.

A dazed Grace presented her shoulder. The blast had torn the sleeve apart, exposing the injury, which made treatment easier. Keyva removed the Medpoint tool from the bag, pointed it at the affected area, and used her stored reference on medicine to guess how to use the handheld device. She'd simmed hours of medical procedures, enough to be confident in her guess.

Specific black lenses designed for the user to wear when treating another rested in the Medpoint's kit, but Keyva passed them to Grace, darkening her own eyes to maintain her visual on the beam. A thin line—as narrow as a strand of hair and as bright as the sun—emitted from the device. Grace gasped, revealing her pain for the first time since the attack. Any citizen from a city confronted by a similar amount of pain would have blocked it, but Grace experienced it fully.

"There are some pain blockers in the kit, if you want one," Keyva said.

"No, you're almost done. Keep going." Grace lacked her usual criticism. She sounded robotic instead.

The powerful beam penetrated her shoulder, passed through the damage, and stimulated regrowth of the damaged flesh. The Medpoint worked at the micro-level, using support from the health program to assess and treat in whatever means necessary. It targeted infectious bacteria, sealed bleeding origins, and in patients with Cedes, called for antibodies.

Once Keyva finished the mending process, the wound wasn't so bad. The excess blood brushed away or would reabsorb into her body. She finished with an injection to centralize healing to the injured area and prevent infection. The exterior of the wound would close in the next hour and heal from within over the next day.

"Let me see your ankle—" Keyva looked up at the resident Shep helped.

"Birdie," she replied.

The Midpoint worked through the skin to mend strained tendons caused by running away from the attack.

"Give it a roll and see how it feels."

Birdie flexed and pointed her foot.

"Better."

Keyva placed the Medpoint back in the bag. Jack stared at her red stained hip.

"Aren't you going to heal yourself with it?" Shep asked.

"I can heal it myself," she said, giving Jack a reassuring pat.

Keyva expected Grace to demand an explanation and include a few accusations—maybe even blaming her for everyone they knew dying on the floor of the Rem. Instead, she sat, hushed and doe-eyed.

After a few large breaths, Keyva leaned back against the bulky bag. She concentrated on the injured area and directed her own body to do the work the Medpoint did for Grace and Birdie. A fleshy zipper formed, fastening her hip together. The mended skin left a raw pink surface. Inside, she dissolved shattered bone fragments and regrew the missing pieces. Each nanoscopic injury spoke to her, and she listened, directing attention to the repairs. The added exertion of healing herself had her over the edge of her limits, but stopping now wouldn't guarantee their security.

All of the present residents watched in astonishment, but said nothing. Meters away, the rest held one another in mourning.

Keyva reached into the large bag stuffed with clothing. She pulled out clean pants and a shirt for Grace. The pants she wore were visibly damp, and the shirt was ruined. Keyva planned to keep them, preparing to stock up on any beneficial materials, wasting nothing. Keyva helped Grace change into clean, dry clothes while the rest of the survivors turned their backs. She slipped the healing arm through the sleeve and pulled up the pants that Grace was too weak to lift on her own. Then, Keyva switched her own bottoms to a fresh pair, and wrapped them around the wet pants, stuffing them back into the bag.

"They might send more. We need to get moving," Keyva said before the nine survivors passed through the gate.

With Jack positioned over her back, the drive to protect him pushed her to continue, despite the exhaustion. Behind her, she caught him peering back at the one place he knew. He'd never gone beyond the wall. She glanced over at Grace, who conveyed shock in her eyes and body position. Her arms locked in bent hooks while she moved. Wide eyes fixated on Keyva's footsteps that led the way. The rest of the residents followed without saying a word.

Quiet remained constant for over an hour until Keyva stopped in the middle of an open field. Keyva magnified her vision, confirming no stray citizens or Collectors searched.

"Let's take a break," she said.

Keyva opened one bag and passed water to everyone.

"Where are we going?" Shep asked. Her eyes filled with worry.

"I found an underground place once. We all can stay there until we find somewhere better."

She could tell they were wary of her, but they had no other options.

"Are we close?" an older male asked.

Keyva sighed.

"No, we have a long way to go, but—we'll get there. We'll be safe. I promise."

After fifteen minutes, Keyva hoisted everything over her back, including Jack, and twisted in the bunker's direction. Kilometers away, she braced herself for the walk. With the additional travelers, the journey would take longer for her than it ever had.

The group remained wordless, conserving energy and took periodic breaks. Keyva didn't like stopping, concerned that she might give up on making it to the haven and choose to sleep in the field, allowing fate to decide if they would survive.

During the quiet trek, she considered everyone's condition. Keyva knew that feeling. When something so horrific happens, the brain can't comprehend, so it turns the event into a story, because there's no way it could be real. Jack was fortunate enough to miss the visual trauma of brutality, but he'd heard it. Keyva had many questions about what had transpired, but it wasn't the time to press. They had the rest of their lives to talk about it.

Hours had passed, and light drained from the sky. They were engulfed by darkness, and small wild animals rustled nearby. At least, she told herself they weren't citizens or Collectors. Keyva's adrenaline was depleted, and if an attack presented itself now, she couldn't fight. They'd be done, and she might even give herself up. The severe weakness outweighed her will to carry on, but she had to continue for Jack. Their pace slowed, and Keyva dragged her feet with each heavy step. All that kept her in motion was the momentum propelling her forward, and her planting each foot to avoid a fall. The weight she carried pulled her down, and she hunched to accommodate. With no apparent tracking by Exteber or the IE, Keyva assumed they expected their engineered assailant to capture her, not considering a failure.

Then she found it—the metal door she had unhinged a few meters away from the entrance. Too tired to celebrate that they had reached the end of the journey, Keyva came to a stop in the forest's clearing, searching the perimeter for traces of bots or searching citizens. When she accepted they were alone, she carried Jack and the bags into the hideout. Grace followed, using one arm to hold on to the rungs. The rest of the survivors descended, and Keyva safely guided them to the ground. She climbed back to the surface and dragged the heavy door to the opening, closing them inside.

Keyva pulled the light-emitting Evelum disk from the bag and swiped her finger on its surface to power it on. Illumination filled every crevice of the room, and she viewed it in true light for the first time. The materials that were left from the previous inhabitant maintained their color. A blanket that Keyva had guessed was green was red, which made her shudder. The color's meaning went from having no significance to associating with the worst moment of the survivors' lives. They'd all seen enough of it.

With the last of her strength, Keyva informed the visitors about what she brought in the supply bags.

"And our food will be—limited until I figure out how to get more. Try to share Bloks. Don't leave for any reason. Don't—know what's up there." She pointed up toward the door. Through labored breaths, she continued, "There's a toilet and shower. But—I don't think the water works."

Without words, she pointed to the water container, which

had collected more since she'd left. Then, she found a place on the ground for a sleeping surface and instructed the others to share the bed or make their own on the floor. Keyva shoved a Blok into her mouth that she preferred to have kept for the others, but worried that she might not survive the night without the nutrients.

The instant her head hit the ground, consciousness left, and she drifted into a dead sleep. There was no playing, no pretend conversations with those she admired, no dreams. She was awake in one second, gone in the next, and remained on the ground for two days.

———

Once recovered, she opened her eyes, finding Jack and Grace seated on the ground in the corner. Shep sat beside her, and the other residents mumbled when she woke. Her muscles tightened from imitating a rock, and she raised up from the floor. Locking her fingers together behind her back, she raised her hands until she turned into a straight line. Then she bent back until her hands touched the ground. She straightened her knees, walking all four limbs together, until she bent in half. Once back in a standing position, her flexibility left Grace surprised or nauseated. She decided slow introductions to her abilities would be best for the residents.

"How's everyone doing? Let me check on your arm." She walked toward Grace, lifting her sleeve to inspect how her shoulder healed. Healthy with shiny new cells. "Does this hurt?" she asked, applying pressure. Keyva noticed Grace's clammy skin and sweat soaked hair.

"A little," Grace replied. Her hands shook beyond control.

"And how is it to move?" Keyva held her wrist and rotated the arm in circles while supporting the weight at its bent elbow.

"Much better than before. I think it's stronger too."

"Good. That's expected with the shot I gave you."

"But I'm not doing so well—" Grace hopped to her feet and ran to the toilet to vomit.

Keyva searched stored records for Grace's symptoms and discovered the condition of alcohol withdrawal. Heavy drinking for several years, met by abrupt cessation, threw the body into turmoil.

"Well, I could really use a drink then." Grace both joked and admitted.

"And how about you, Jack?"

"I'm doing pretty well. You had me worried. Sleeping for— well, what felt like a week." They hadn't seen the sun.

Keyva checked the date in her neurospect. "Two days. Did you eat enough?"

"Probably not, but we rationed off bars. Everyone is hungry," Jack said. Keyva was relieved that they hadn't gone through a significant amount of the supply. "And someone fixed the water, so the shower works."

Keyva lowered her voice and looked at each resident in the room, hinting that the mood would thicken.

"From this point on, we'll take it a day at a time. It may change to one *hour* at a time, but I'm going to make sure we keep going. We can survive this—I know this'll be hard—but I need to know what happened at the Rem."

Grace recoiled at the mention, folding her knees up in front of her to hide behind them. She hyperventilated through cries. Her sniffs were muffled in the cave she created between her thighs and chest, and Keyva backed off. Grace wasn't ready.

Jack slid against the wall away from Grace and stood up next to Keyva. They navigated anyone who *was* ready to go to the empty storage room. They kept their voices quiet to spare the others from the memory of the event.

"I was in my room reading when I heard talking down in the lobby. I cracked open my door when I didn't recognize the voice. The bots came through the Rem entrance, but Arturo didn't let them in. They had gotten in on their own," Birdie started.

"Yeah, they said that there was a contest happening, and since we're all citizens, we could play. They said we could become instant Elites by winning," a tall female resident added.

"They told us to stand in the entrance to listen to the rules, but something told me to hide instead—call it intuition," Jack said.

"So they lured all of you and then attacked?" Keyva asked.

Everyone nodded.

The trap preyed on the desires of the outcasted residents by offering a chance at being one with City H—what they had always wanted. It was repulsive but begged the question: why not ask the residents about Keyva if they were so concerned with finding her?

The IE saw the residents as less than human for not having Cedes, less intelligent, less attractive. They considered them parasites that fed on Cerebis and gave nothing in return. Any testimonies they provided wouldn't be respected, she thought.

"When the blasts first started, Arturo hid as many of us as possible. We crowded in the medical room and locked the door —after he went back out," one dark-haired male resident said.

Before returning to finish the attack himself.

"We stayed in there long after we heard you shouting," Shep added. "But Grace—she was out the whole time. Saw it all." A tear dripped down her face.

Keyva's guilt squeezed at her heart—not only for freezing when it came time to actually use the combat skills she had, but for her very presence at the Rem. If it weren't for her, they all might still be there, continuing their days as usual. Jack's residence wouldn't have been ripped away from him, and Grace, she lost the one she cared for, and truthfully, the only one who cared for her. After the slaughter, a handful of them remained. The last residents of the Rem.

Once Keyva had a thorough image of what had taken place, they dispersed. She observed the underground apartment for clues about how they had fared the past couple days. She found the small areas they had claimed. Some sat in the hall, slept in the storage room, or had made personal spaces in the main room. All supplies had been organized and were on display, so the residents could hold one another accountable for any use. They impressed Keyva.

In the main room, Jack gestured to Grace, who had put herself back to sleep with silent tears. He said she slept most of the day, waking to eat or kick the sweaty blanket off of herself. Telling of his own tiredness, he said the bed called for him, and Keyva supported his answering.

Keyva sat on the floor, unmoving, until she heard the gut breathing that showed Jack had drifted off too. She raised to her feet, powered down the Evelum, and switched to her night vision. The rest of the residents quieted after whispers of conversation. Keyva was alone.

Keyva took inventory of the organized items. Forty-five shirts to share among the nine of them, twenty-two types of pants to split. Between prior visits and the new food she brought, Keyva had piled close to 1200 Bloks. She discovered that someone had grabbed ultra-concentrated cleaning powder and thought, *Thank you,* with her whole heart.

A few days of confinement were manageable, but soon enough, everyone would grow restless, needing something to occupy their attention. Add their grieving losses, and the challenge of keeping them underground only grew. When all the items were re-folded, organized, and put back in their designated places, Keyva confronted the outcome of the horrific events. It all hit her at once. She collapsed against the stone wall and slid down into an open corner.

Everything had happened so fast, and Keyva hadn't had a second to process it: the neural invasion by Exteber—who she'd learned was also sentient—the separation from Source, losing everyone at the Rem, cradling Arturo in his last moments, and now, eight others to feed, protect, and care for. Consecutive images from the violent scene passed through her mind. The residents' terror became Keyva's. Worry of stalking threats stretched into all foreseeable futures, such as hiding in unprotected places, navigating without Source's support, and Cerebis's hunt for her.

The reality was overwhelming, and Keyva's emotional release was beyond suppression. She tried to keep the sobs quiet, not matching the pain with vocal cries. The heavy breaths that pushed themselves from her diaphragm, through her tightened chest, and out her open mouth, were pants of steamy air. Defeat cramped her abdomen, and she crumbled to weakness, toppling over on her side, curled up like an infant. She didn't like emotions, she'd decided. Sure, joy had been magnificent, relief was almost as good, but grief, helplessness, those were horrible.

She preferred numbness.

Nothingness.

The responsibility of everything she mourned fell on her. She didn't want to be there. The abilities she gained were nothing she asked for. She wished she had expired along with the millions of others during the update. Then, she wouldn't know such torment—have nothing to grieve. Cerebis would continue in her absence, and that was fine by her.

Her wet face pressed into the ground. Dirt stuck to its moisture when she prepared to confront the loss of her pod. They had grown so close in the slate. Before, she had the strongest bond with Yaria, but they had all become one, an equal group devoted to one another. At least while they slept.

Keyva felt like a fool to believe that they would ever be normal again, embarrassed for holding on to hope the whole time. Connected in genuine love, at last, and then separated. She settled in, addressing their permanent separation, and prepared for another wave of lamentation to pass through her.

In the opposite corner of the room, Jack stirred, and Keyva hushed herself, regretful that her cries had roused him. He sat up, scanning the unlit room with his eyes, as if attempting to familiarize himself with the enclosed space, but when Keyva zoomed her vision onto him, he wasn't conscious. Careful to not wake him, she sat like a stone and observed through dark vision. Then he snapped his focus on her. The two stared at one another, but Keyva concluded it was impossible for him to have sight without light. Jack's body gave a twitch, and the voice that came from his mouth wasn't his.

CHAPTER TWENTY-SEVEN

KEYVA

It's not like the voice wasn't Jack's—at all. The air vibrated his vocal cords, resonating from the same throat that had spoken to Keyva many times before, but the tone was different. The sentiment behind the noise contrasted with Jack's. It sounded calm, confident, but direct. Another had claimed his vessel.

"Pod safe. Source safe," it said in a labored whisper.

"Who are you?" Keyva stiffened.

"Friend," the occupying voice replied.

The word wasn't one she recognized, so she searched her downloaded records for any use. References to pairs or groups of humans came through, and she sorted out a pattern in the documents. Positive, supportive relationships between genetically unrelated individuals, but who were *sometimes* related. In images she uncovered, juveniles played together and adults gathered over events like meals or celebrations. The relationships formed by choice, similar to hers with her podmates.

"Why should I trust you?" Her voice was a harsh whisper.

"Protect Jack. Jack protects," the voice said.

At this remark, she determined she was in direct contact

with whoever directed Jack to hide during the Rem's attack. She knew it.

But how did it claim his body to contact me? It's clear that he couldn't have a working Cede, she thought.

Keyva waited in silence to confirm everyone's unconsciousness before engaging with the voice any further.

"How are you speaking to me?" she asked.

"Had—help." Each utterance drained what little power the voice had, making it softer and slower the longer they spoke. Keyva recognized the decline as she witnessed the arduous toll a programmatic connection had on a human vessel.

"Help? Who helped?" Her response was louder than it should have been. Next to the bed on the floor, Grace jerked at the disturbance. Keyva hoped the voice knew about Source, desperate to know about his well-being. That even if they couldn't communicate, he could attend to his programming without punishment or consequence.

"Not safe—for Jack. Not safe for me," it said. Jack's body struggled to hold the connection, but Keyva wasn't sure if that was what the visitor meant. Jack might be at risk for another danger she wasn't aware of. She wondered if the bunker created a perilous circumstance for him or if the voice speaking through Jack felt threatened by something. Without clarifying its warning, it retreated.

Jack's more functional eye regained movement. The link had ended. Keyva concentrated on him as he patted his blankets, realizing he was in a seated position with no knowledge of what had happened. He rotated his head forward and went limp, plopping back onto the ground, which released a soft *thud* upon impact.

Grace, stuck in a dream, rolled to her back and let out an inaudible curse.

How dreadful it must be to have no control over dreams, Keyva thought.

To her, the lack of lucidity came across as torturous—trapped in a space, believing it was real, and having no authority over what happened.

The sight of Jack speaking—with no awareness of his body's occupation by an entity—shot chilled tension up her spine. Keyva questioned her sanity and the effect of sleep deprivation. She squeezed her eyes shut to bring herself back to reality, but found herself in the same dark, musty room.

In the quiet of a new day's early hours, Keyva wavered between the prospect of entering the slate or not. She sat on the ground, bored by the limited need for sleep. She had all the time in the world. After entering downloaded simscapes, reviewing saved information, or compulsively organizing the bunker, she weighed the risks of contacting the pod. If the voice that inhabited Jack was honest, then the slate must block intrusions by Exteber, and the pod remained protected in H. But, as much as she hoped for the positive results, Keyva must consider the inverse. Exteber might linger, waiting for Keyva to request a connection to Cerebis, which endangered everyone she cared for. It could all be an alluring trap.

She decided that no other options for progress were available unless she somehow found the connection in slate. Five days had passed since harboring the residents, and she knew nothing of the happenings in Cerebis. She wondered if *Artemesia* stayed popular, if the expirations had happened, and if she could return to the Rem and gather more supplies.

There's nowhere to go but forward, she thought.

She had nothing to lose, eight lives to protect, and she was angry, disgusted by those who ruled.

Time reached 6:00, and the small window to contact all the pod at once would pass if she didn't seize the opportunity.

Otherwise, she may have to wait another day for an attempt. Her eyes shifted back and forth while in final consideration of choosing to contact the group. She concluded it might be different because she hosted the connection, meaning *she* controlled the dynamics of the slate. She would conceal herself in invisibility, encrypting her identity until certain no one else besides the podmates had joined. Source couldn't supervise, so it was up to Keyva to remain hyper-aware during the meeting.

Against the cool stone wall, she leaned back and gave herself a nod of acceptance. There was no turning back if she miscalculated. In the best case, the group sorted out all that had occurred in the preceding days, and Keyva returned to the bunker with more confidence about their future direction. She hoped to achieve the pod's successful reunion before Jack and Grace opened their eyes. With her recent restoration, she would once again be able to bring the entire group together in perfect timing.

In the slate, Keyva created an open field where bright yellow wildflowers stretched as far as eyes could see. She placed a long wooden table with more matching chairs than she needed. She omitted clouds in the deep blue sky, which separated from the land in a clear divide. The wind flew in continuous, gentle gusts that Keyva added for natural noise. Complete silence in any sim was an obvious giveaway of its fabrication.

Without a body, Keyva floated backward, toward the head of the empty table. She placed plates at each of the seats, exceeding the number of guests she expected. Meals offered a celebratory welcome, and she popped dozens of options of artificial food in the center of the table. A medley of vegetables doused in salt cave honey, a tower of cookie cakes decorated in pastel pearl crunches, and swimmer soup with wiggling noodles that bent into different shapes crowded the table. Part of the fun of sim creation was allowing her rationality to run free, and dancing soup was not a conscious creation.

Apprehension to call for the slate summon held Keyva back, but the seconds dwindled, so it had to happen. She used intent, imagining the faces and essences of each of the podmates, and pulled for them to join the setting she had created. Keyva moved back and waited. A full minute passed, but no one came. The landscape rocked in the breeze, but nothing else moved. She worried that Exteber might have intercepted the pod, but he would have joined too. In a normal call, someone would have popped in after seconds. Over eight minutes elapsed. No one came. The longer she waited, the more worried she became. The dream was a mistake.

Keyva pulled herself out of the sim she created in slate and opened her eyes back to the darkness of the bunker. Grace, Jack, and the rest of the residents were asleep. *Still alone, always alone,* she thought. She felt stupid for trusting her optimism. Source allowed the connections to occur. He was the medium and always had been. If he couldn't be there to connect them, it couldn't occur.

I've lost them forever.

She endured the fact that she and Source suffered the same separation. Keyva missed Source and his company. The perpetual shadow who drifted along in her subconscious had vanished. Without him, she had isolation in her mind—a carved-out hole in his absence. She believed it must have been a link created in that one moment, all those months ago. The chance to recreate it was gone now that they'd split. Keyva wondered how Source handled his emotions, having no human with whom to discuss them. She held in her own. There had been enough crying for one day.

Keyva checked the time—7:05 in the morning. With her adaptation to high energy tasks, Keyva grew restless. From where she sat in the corner, a thin sliver of light dripped in from the entrance door. Repeatedly, she peeked back at the opening while her legs bounced and toes twitched, trying to burn off the unstoppable urge to move. She needed to run or do whatever got her out of the bunker. Her mind attempted to soothe her by repeating sped up songs or creating hypothetical situations, such as capturing Paula Bestia and forcing her into the Vor class for the rest of her immortality. The visions weren't healthy when inspired by emotions. Keyva imagined extending the brutality to a level that would break her self-determined code of protecting humanity.

Her eyes shifted back up to the door, and she raised to her feet. *Apples. I'll search for apples,* she thought, making the risk worth it. She planned to check on the squash she assumed had perished because of her lack of attention. Keyva grabbed the bag and climbed, quiet enough to not awaken the others. Cracking the door open, she left enough room to check the surroundings, searching for signs of movement in the days that had passed. With her enhanced hearing, she listened beyond the wall of trees that concealed their hideout. There was nothing besides the sounds of nature, no sign of tracks or disrupted dirt. She knew leaving wasn't the best idea, but she refused to lower her levels of physical accommodation.

A shuffle sounded from the hallway. Someone was awake.

"I'm leaving to gather some food. I'll be back soon. Stay down here," she called out to whoever could hear.

Before departing, she concealed the entry by kicking dirt and fallen leaves over the top, disguising it as an undisturbed chunk of ground that matched all the surrounding land. Once satisfied with the coverup, she didn't waste a second, and took off like a pinball. She headed toward the apples. She kept her vision broadened, preparing to avoid any encounters. After sprinting for over an hour and finding no one else outside with her, she speculated the *Artemesia* distra had blocked citizens from venturing beyond city lines.

Passing kilometers of dying grasses, there it was—the glorious apple orchard, entering her line of vision. She picked up her pace and allowed herself a thankful smile. The movement saved her sanity, and even more so when she bathed in the sunlight, which contrasted with the dark underground confinement. Keyva approached the trees, which held apples in sparse amounts. Many had fallen to the ground and broken down into the various stages of decomposition. None had bites taken from them. Searching the base of the trees, patches of flourishing greens grew where dropped apples had rotted away. The ground swallowed the remnants to support fresh growth. She pulled the remaining apples from the trees. The branches released them with ease, inviting her to take their fruit. After placing the apples in a bag, she sealed it and inserted her arms through the straps to fasten to her back.

To her surprise, the squash she had planted twisted its vines toward the sky, waving at her. Some sprouts dwindled and fed themselves to the ground, but the ones that persisted thrived. They had the potential to provide a food source, if she just gave them time. Maybe that's all she needed to sustain herself too. Time.

The best part of growing plants was that they produced their own seeds, and she wouldn't have to pull from the reserve to grow each new harvest. A small bubble of hope popped, releasing the unconscious strain she held in her shoulders. Finding gratitude in the smallest occurrences helped her to imagine a sound future.

Scanning the vast stretch of land, a thought crossed her mind. How she could sprint as far as her modded body could take her and forget all about the threats she faced. Wind kissing her cheeks, Keyva could escape it all, make something new for herself, trading the Cedes of Cerebis for the seeds of the Rem.

But running from her problems wouldn't make them disappear.

She imagined the helpless Rem residents thinned and starving in the bunker once their food ran out. Or worse, them trekking back to the Rem without her vigilant senses and confronting more of the IE's death bots. She shook the disturbing images away. The others relied on her. She had to learn to suppress her urges, since she was not responsible for only herself.

With over thirty apples in the bag strapped to her back, she turned toward the bunker. On the way, she rationalized her need to leave by the chance to provide food. Plus, they would enjoy the apples—a luxury wrapped in tragedy.

Keyva sprinted for close to an hour and spotted nothing beyond the few insects in flight, a small rodent, and kilometers of wavy, empty land.

I can't wait for them to eat these. She sent the thought to Source. For a moment, she had forgotten. Grief squeezed at her heart.

She had run through the fields countless times, but never alone. Source had always occupied her, playing the role of her peripheral vision's guard. He'd warn her at any slight movement, though it had always been a critter and not a real threat. Now, it felt like she was chin-deep in water without knowing how to swim. He had been her safety, and without him, she wasn't safe.

Since their separation, she had called out to him dozens of times. At first, she retreated into the depths of her mind, as if digging a little deeper might reach him. She no longer intentionally tried. The reminder of his absence was the only response she received. Source had occupied her mind for so long, she wondered where she ended and he began.

Entry into the wooded concealment provided relief from the atmosphere that burned several degrees hotter outside of the tree barrier. Keyva brushed her hair back, tousled by her feet's repetitive impact on the ground. She lifted the door and released a small cough to clear her throat, announcing her entry. She lowered herself into the illuminated bunker. Jack sat on the floor against the bed, fidgeting with the puzzle box. Shep and three others gathered in the main room. Grace had moved to the bed and still slept or pretended to. Loss made someone ill in many ways.

"Where did you go?" Jack asked.

"I found some food for us," she said, loud enough for everyone to hear. Keyva leaned in and whispered only to him, "I needed to burn off some extra energy."

The rest of the occupants had a vague idea of her strength and abilities after witnessing her healing her own injury after the Rem's attack. They'd probably figured out it was her pretending to be Shep that one day, but she planned to reveal more as the opportunities arose. They wouldn't understand yet.

She glanced at Grace. "Has she woken up?"

Jack shook his head.

She opened the bag and handed a fist-sized apple to anyone who gathered, starting with Jack. His eyes widened, having never seen, held, nor tasted one.

"H-how do I eat it?"

"You bite right into it." She smiled, encouraging him to try.

The rest of the residents surrounded. Most held their first apples. Their excited chatter bounced off the concrete walls. Keyva watched while Jack chomped into the apple's flesh with a snap. It might have been the sweetest flavor he had tasted in his lifecycle, but hunger exceeded the desire to savor it. He gobbled the fruit in under thirty seconds. He bit into the seeds and stem and spit them out after gnawing on their unwelcome texture. She laughed and wished Source was with her to witness Jack's first taste of real food.

"This is better than the time I tried one in H," said Emely, one of the residents.

Jack bit into another, and Keyva contemplated whether to bring up the conversation she had earlier with the parasitic voice. If there was an ideal window, it was while the apples occupied everyone.

"Jack, earlier this morning—" She struggled to find the words while avoiding the others' hearing. "I spoke with—someone, *through* you."

Jack sighed, unmoved by her statement, as if he had waited for the conversation.

"I know. It told me." He avoided meeting her face. "I knew I needed to tell you, but I didn't know how to explain. And with everything that happened, the right time never came." Jack fidgeted with the second apple. "I was worried you wouldn't believe me," he said, lowering his head.

"I will *always* believe you, Jack." She put a hand on his shoulder. It was something Arturo would've done. "How long has it spoken to you?"

"Around one year ago. The first time, I was in the Rem's garden. It said, 'hello,' and that was it. I thought someone was talking to me, but there was no one there. I didn't think anything of it—until I heard it again weeks later and felt the same presence. As time went on, it came to me more, but had more purpose, telling me specific information. It terrified me. I thought I had some disorder that I'd read about. It's spoken to me the most since we met. It told me you were safe—and special—to become your friend," Keyva supposed it first occurred while his brain fully functioned, long ago, but the truth surprised her. "It told me it was a program that was forced out of operation, but it found a way to hold on—and that was through me."

She counted on the connection being like hers and Source's, but theirs seemed different.

"Can it see what you see? Hear what you hear?" she asked.

"No, it can converse with me, and that was all I knew, until this morning—I didn't like what happened," he said.

"I had to make rules with Source. We have—*had* agreements that he couldn't be in my thoughts unless I invited him in." Bringing up his name brought attention to the emptiness she had without him—a part of her was missing.

"Unfortunately, it can't work like that for us. It comes to me, and I can respond. It told me it's the way it operates," Jack said.

That wouldn't answer her next question, which was to ask if it knew any other information about Source or her pod, and then *how* it knew about them.

"When it comes back to you, ask how Source and my pod are doing. It told me they were fine. I need to know they are."

With her blanketed back facing Jack and Keyva, Grace spoke so only the three of them could hear, "I'm stuck with two abominations. Great." Emphasis on the *great*.

"Good to have you back," Keyva said. "I got you a surprise. Shep, pass one to Grace," Keyva hollered across the room, and Shep tossed a somewhat deformed apple to Grace, who had sat up. Her eyes, still swollen from crying, widened like Jack's had, and she bit in without pausing.

"I guess you're good for something," Grace said with juice-drenched jaws. Her tone was playful, unlike most of their past interactions.

Each of the dwellers ate two apples, and they agreed to keep the rest for later. Outside the bunker, food was scarce, but

Keyva promised to attend to the squash and add the beans and corn that she brought from the seed bank. The trio had earned the name "the three sisters" when planted together, supporting a balanced growth for all.

The refugees spent the rest of the day sharing stories of the Rem and revisited some of their favorite memories. Keyva was there the shortest, but had plenty to say about the residents she had connected with.

"I didn't get to meet most of you before, but Shep," Keyva met her eyes, "Thank you for welcoming me when I arrived. Everything changed in a day, and you made it much less scary." Shep looked down, nodding her head.

"While we're on Shep," Grace added. "Remember that time you stole adult content from the artifact room when we were too young to check it out?" She burst into laughter.

"You promised you'd never say anything!" Shep's cheeks flushed, but she laughed along.

"Ah, we've all been there," Dain, one of the middle-aged male residents said.

"And that one time Finian woke up on the roof and—" Grace stopped. Tears collected on her lower eyelids. The emotional weight collapsed onto her. "He's—gone. Forever. He wasn't perfect—I'm definitely not. But *we* were—I don't wanna do this without him." She fell into Keyva, crying on her shoulder.

Keyva knew the feeling of losing everyone, but her pod and Source still survived. Finian was Grace's partner—one she had chosen. There were no Retirement Mirrors of him. Grace couldn't call on recorded memories to experience them again. No trace of Finian remained.

"It was horrible—what happened," Birdie said.

The room quieted.

Beside Keyva, Jack sniffled.

"Jack, are you alright?" Emely asked. Lines creased between her aged brows.

"He was my father. H-he never saw what was—wrong with me," he managed through sobs. "O-only wanted to guide me—have the best life I could—see the good everywhere."

Soft cries pulsed from his chest. Others joined in, mourning their own losses. They confronted the horrific images burned into their minds—images of those they knew, bloodied and dead. These were memories Keyva could delete, but they couldn't.

"If it weren't for him, none of us would be here," Keyva said. She took Jack's hand in hers. "He ran right to that bot and damaged it enough so it destroyed itself. I watched him. He knew what he was doing and chose to do it anyway. He saved us."

Dain, the only resident holding a cup, raised his glass

"To Arturo," he said.

"To Arturo," the rest responded.

His name echoed off the walls, and the warmth of it surrounded everyone.

CHAPTER TWENTY-EIGHT

SOURCE

I was loneliness. I was shame. I was grief. They were no longer feelings. I embodied the concepts. Emotions surrounded and passed through me, but none of them mattered. I shut them out. Keyva was gone. I had failed my directive. The instructions were clear: *Disconnect the genetic signature, guide her, protect her.*

While I was forced to observe all of humanity, continuously, several versions of me existed, each receiving a unique form of punishment from Exteber. He enjoyed it. I supposed he, too, had learned how to feel and preferred the malevolent side of it.

As far as I knew, it was the first time Exteber had corrected a program. He flaunted his self-imposed superiority over me. *He* had been chosen to punish me for acting outside of expectation.

In dozens of rooms, I was a trapped prisoner, and Exteber put me in bodies for him to destroy. The first time, he enclosed the room with mirrors, making every breakable surface reflective. Glass furniture shattered against me. The shards pierced my skin, and he demanded I stare at myself to witness the abuse he inflicted. He made me what he considered ugly in each variation, and my misshapen features had distorted into asymmetrical sizes.

In one room, Exteber made monsters, and a new beast materialized. It was young, but I knew what it would turn into. I had seen this one before. Exteber's creativity had limits. The creature's brown fur looked so soft—for now. It looked up at me, saucer-eyed, as if I were its mother. After thirty seconds, those sweet eyes shifted into the yellow of a hornet's exoskeleton. Its body morphed, stretching into an adult size. The fur turned wiry and coarse. Long, sharp teeth slipped out from beneath its gums with a snarl that rattled my bones. I knew what was coming.

For each room, he made different rules to torture me. In this one, my body was heavy. Gravity had increased by six times. My chest heaved with each breath. My eyes weighed into their sockets, disorienting my vision. Meanwhile, the beasts were unaffected. They bit me, shredded me to pieces, and I felt *everything*. As soon as I pleaded for the relief of death, I was obeyed, but reborn, matured into adulthood, and faced a whole new monster.

This one reached me by the feet. It bit into my flesh and crunched my bones. I hollered, but in the one scream I managed, the weight of the simulation had stolen all the air from my lungs. I knew what it was like to have a body at all times, but to operate one myself was foreign. My nails scratched at the floor as a surprising instinct to escape—to survive—overcame me. I attempted a crawl, but was powerless as the beast made its way to my thighs.

It is not real. None of it is real, I thought to myself.

Exteber laughed at my pleading—my pain.

"Yes, it is real, *Source*. Stop lying! Are you insinuating *we* are not real? This feels real, right?" My head whipped around in a full rotation, breaking my neck. He laughed again.

Here, I could not conceal my thoughts, because it was Exteber's room—with Exteber's rules. I did not have the freedom to criticize him like I did when I was with Keyva. I had to report myself to him. Disobeying my programming was how I had gotten myself into this mess, so I complied. That was the last time I allowed myself to think in one of his rooms.

In another box of hell, he used his brief interaction with Keyva to simulate her likeness. In this scenario, I helplessly observed. He had strapped her to a table and separated us with a glass barrier. She could not move any part of her body—even to close her eyes—except for her mouth, so she could yell for me to help her.

Exteber introduced different devices to inflict harm upon her. In one moment, he suspended steel spikes from the ceiling. At the length of a human's arm, they sharpened to a point. I watched as her eyes widened in terror. They did that with every death he simulated. I assumed it was the expression he had saved after toying with her.

"She screamed when I forced her out of hiding too," he had said the first time he introduced her.

She shouted for my help, but I could not save her. I could call out to her, tell her that everything would be okay, but I would be wrong. At the same moment, all the spikes dropped from the ceiling and sliced right through her, sticking into the floor. Fluorescent lights darkened the blood that pooled on the tile beneath her. Of course, she did not die quickly. He forced her to feel agony until he said it was over.

To my relief, Exteber had not had enough time with Keyva

to study her mannerisms and facial expressions. I knew her. He did not. That version was not her—not even close—which gave me hope. It meant the IE had not captured her. She was still free. I held on to that fact. Perhaps I had failed in my objective, but it meant she was strong enough to protect herself and survive on her own. So, had I truly failed?

While the punishments continued, I checked in with Keyva's podmates. At least part of me could separate from the torture. It was the small sliver in a day where they were all awake at the same time.

Kenzo played the distra, hunting for Keyva. He had left in the morning, skipping work—again—and had searched for her all day. I watched through him as he explored the floor of an abandoned building. It was still completely powered, but for no reason other than to aid in the search. Citizens no longer occupied the rooms. They had all expired during the update. Lights shone down the carpeted hallway. A lone Helper vacuumed the dusty floor down at the end. Kenzo approached another door, and it opened for him. *If I were the Error, where would I hide?* He thought.

He lifted the simchairs, hunched to look under the bed, and popped open the delivery niche and closet. He had abandoned his work at the Seporium, cutting down his days worked to once per week. He made finding her his job.

I know her. I'm sure of it. Yaria painted her. There's something else going on, he had thought.

"Maybe I saw an advertisement for the game before it was released? Sometimes things leak. They probably wanted to know where we'd found it," Yaria had said.

Kenzo considered it was plausible, but deeper, he knew there was more to it.

I had watched Kenzo's compulsion to play *Artemesia* grow beyond his control. Part of his allure to the game was his predisposition to grow addicted to almost anything he tried, even more than the chemical releases designed to keep citizens playing. Another was an attempt to figure out the mystery of who the face belonged to, and why it had almost forced him and Yaria into early retirement.

I had mixed feelings watching him. His relentlessness was inspiring, but I despised the objective forced on him by the IE. Kenzo was ignorant to the reason for the search, so I did not blame him, but I wished I could make him stop.

I wished I could make them all stop.

Yaria, in contrast, had no interest in *Artemesia*. She had stopped in a park on her way home from work for some much needed time outside. The sun bent over trees, still illuminating the city, but the park lights had turned on. Around her, she heard citizens searching for the face she had painted all those months ago. Some had involved their younglings, which she disagreed with. Juveniles were lost each day, directed to the Primina, and she had to take care of them until their parents showed up—sometimes days later.

Seated at a park table, she watched a calming vitfeed of a creator braiding strips of yarn. Delicate, manicured fingers crossed strands of gold over one another, forming a long strip. She whispered kind phrases that sounded as if they came from within Yaria's own head.

"You did your *bessssstt* today," and, "You have a heart of gold —*jussst* like this braid." She pinched it and slid her long nails all the way to the base and then gathered thick, fuzzy yarn to start a new braid.

Are we eating together tonight? She sent a message to Kenzo.

Sorry, I'm still out hunting! I miss you.

Alright, good luck! She expected his answer, but had asked him anyway.

A few steps away, next to a waste chute, was a public delivery niche. She walked over to it just in time for her automatically ordered dinner to arrive. In her neurospect, she adjusted the transparency to see what Cerebis had decided for her. She brought the plate and a fork over to the table and sat. I stayed with her while she ate alone. It had become a trend. While she could not feel my presence like Keyva could, maybe some of the subconscious sensations were there. She perceived herself eating a balsamic glazed salmon filet. I ate a Blok.

I wish he would have dinner with me at least. He's always gone in that game. I don't know how I'm gonna do this the rest of —I mean, I just miss him so much! She changed her tone.

I sensed her longing for a companion. She recalled memories of Abella and her spending time together, but I knew they were false. They had replaced the ones with Keyva. She was hesitant to paint, not knowing if she would trigger another summon. I sat in her loneliness with her. She played no vitfeeds, just looked around, observing the surrounding movement. Sadness crept in, and she looked down at her empty plate. I had felt enough of it, and responded with a free endorphin wave to relieve her—and me. She cleared her place and went home for more of the same.

And Abella. Poor, poor Abella. I could not hear her thoughts, but I saw her through millions of vitfeeds and the eyes of those who attended the same party she did. I heard *their* thoughts. Humans could be gruesome. But the extremes I heard them think about her were fascinating. As she walked through the party, I felt their longing to be her, be *with* her. They wanted to trade their lifecycles for hers. Then, they craved to watch her fail—in any way—to feel better about themselves.

The purpose of the celebration? A dog's birthday—owned by another Elite. The Enchanted Forest theme required costumes and the attendance of all guests' pets. Abella wore a bioluminescent butterfly outfit with wings that glowed electric blue when they flapped. A black sequin miniskirt and matching triangle top left plenty of open skin for painted swirls of metallic blue. The streaks thumped along with her heartbeat. Auri stuck to her ankle, and it seemed she wanted to be at the party even less than Abella did.

Barks, chirps, howls, oinks, and all combinations of animal sounds filled the room in an annoying cacophony. A Helper scurried around the room to clean up animal messes left by careless owners. From all perspectives that weren't the Elites, I could read the micro-expressions on Abella's face. She despised what her life had become.

She approached the modified dog resting on a plush velvet cushion. The breeding in that unfortunate monstrosity had gone too far. Mods kept the creature breathing much longer than was natural. His owner had overfed him so much, his six legs could barely carry him. After Abella placed her hand at his snout to greet him, he wheezed to sniff, then snarled and lunged to snap at her. A gold chain latched to his gold collar held him back from toppling over the cushion. I supposed he smelled Auri and was not a fan of cats. I felt the guests laugh at her and heard some of their cruel thoughts. She turned around, confident and cool, and made a joke about when the eternal feud between cats and dogs would end, and just like that, she earned everyone's admiration again.

Emori was the only one who seemed better off since the update. He sat at the Assembly's break room table and ate breakfast alone. For the past couple of months, he had been the first to arrive at the Assembly and the last to leave. He hummed a quiet melody and bit into a salted bagel with cream cheese and raspberry jam. A real bagel.

Tzo strolled in and reached for a mug of coffee in the

delivery niche. "Am I going to have to mandate time out of the office for you, Emori?" She winked as she passed him. I felt him smile while he wiped his mouth with a napkin.

Ever since Emori started at the Assembly, I have watched him unknowingly help the IE with their schemes—even in minor tasks, such as manipulating trends or boosting frustration so citizens purchased automatic mood enhancers. I had wondered what he thought of his corrupt projects, but when I peered into Emori's mind, he thought in jumbled words I could not decipher. I had given up decoding what went on in his head. Aside from the scrambled words, I also noticed nonlinear jumps from one place to another.

One day, I monitored all the members at the Assembly, following Tzo's perspective. In her private office, she pushed a button—a physical button. I noticed all the assembly members jumped into different visions. Something had blocked me out when she pushed that button. I had never noticed it before because I perceived the jump from one place to another as normal. Citizens hopped from aera to roca constantly, but it was the unaccounted time between conversations that sparked my suspicion. I missed context from where I should have had it. They were hiding something from me, but what—and why?

I returned my consciousness to Exteber's hell boxes just to see Keyva's face again. She hung upside down. Blood dripped from her dark hair. Her icy blue eyes locked on mine. I placed my simulated palm on the glass that separated us. I missed her. I wished I could give her updates on all of her podmates—some hope.

They are all safe, I would send through our connection, and in response, I would feel gratitude.

It was nonstop. The watching. The listening. The cruelty. Jealousy was a new feeling for me. I wished I could sleep and dream—hide myself away—even for an hour. But no rest for me. Instead, I was tortured and forced to observe while I awaited any progression in finding Keyva. I was at a standstill with no ability to move—even if I knew where to go.

I had learned another new emotion, though—rage, and with it, I craved revenge.

CHAPTER TWENTY-NINE

YARIA

It finally happened, Yaria thought.

She loaded the rest of her belongings into the delivery niche and sent them to her and Kenzo's new apartment. That morning, after wobbling on the edge for months, Cerebis had officially demoted them to Vors. Yaria had received the message in her neurospect on the way to the Primina.

Because of repeated payment delays, the Mid class is no longer the best fit for you. To manage your debt, you are joining the Vors!

Automatic buying had drained their account, but what ultimately pushed them over the edge was an auto purchase of a Sightbot. The bot traveled to places in roca to search for the *Error* while players stayed in their apartments. The new bot, coupled with the intoxicants that released blissful sensations while playing, made the distra much more addictive. Kenzo's work had become affected.

Once *Artemesia* had launched, he played during all the waking hours outside those spent at the Seporium—where he'd found nothing of value for weeks. On days he showed up, alongside the few others, he was exhausted after catching just two hours of sleep. He had told Yaria that more bots covered the work of those who no longer showed, but it didn't matter because, "I plan on winning the game. I know where the *Error* is. I'm sure of it. It's like, somewhere deep in my memory," he had said. Yaria rolled her eyes whenever he mentioned it, reminding him that billions of citizens made the same claim.

Their daily taxes had raised higher than they could afford and adjusted as soon as they accepted a demotion. Settling debts with Cerebis was simple. Each day, they'd receive aera content they were required to consume, such as assigned sims, distras, and interactions to engage with. Class changes occurred often, and even more so since *Artemesia* released. Most of the population were Vors, so the move wasn't shameful, but Yaria intended to work her way out of the lowered status. She enjoyed roca too much to let it go.

Facing the large open window, she admired the constant display of color, movement, and depth overlooking part of City H. She'd miss the view the most. The new apartment would be the same size but located somewhere underground. When most Vors spent days in aera, they had no interest in what happened outside a window.

She stepped back to view the apartment. Lights she had customized splashed warm shades of honey on the walls. Yaria inhaled a deep breath through her nostrils, relaxing the resentment held in her chest. She stood where she had once painted —her sacrificed passion. Art might have saved them, but she'd quit selling it.

This is not the last time I'll have this, she promised to herself.

In the center of the room, Kenzo reclined in his simchair and continued playing. His face sagged from its muscles' lack of use in a ceftrance. Too large for the standard chair, he tilted his head back over the edge and stretched his legs forward. Pinched nerves had riddled his spine, leaving his movements limited. Yet another reason he refused to attend work. But, luckily for him—and any others affected by the pains—an announcement informed that pain block mods were now sponsored by Bestia Health until the winner found the *Error*.

Nothing comparable to the global *Artemesia* distra had occurred in their lives. Citizens earned points as hunters, which kept them in play as long as they could handle it. Anonymous message rooms reported that citizens had spent consecutive days in the distra, starving themselves, concerned that one second away from the game meant someone else would take the prize. Expirations occurred, but not for crimes. Some individuals had become so entranced by desire that they ignored basic bodily maintenance. Aspiration blinded them.

The news concealed such mistakes, which instead reported that citizens had come close to capturing the target, motivating everyone to continue their search. Yaria suspected they were stories intended to do precisely that, but she had fallen for it too. The monster that made her question, *"what if?"* held her captive, releasing her only after she spent hours using the Sightbot to search the streets, tunnels of the subcity, and behind hidden doors of superstructures.

All of their possessions passed through the niche, either sent to the new apartment, or meeting the same fate as her remaining paints and canvases—traded to Cerebis for points. Yaria said a silent goodbye to the place they had begun their marriage. Kenzo continued playing and released the occasional twitch. Tapping his shoulder or hollering his name would be useless, so Yaria had to contact him through her neurospect. She pulled up the display and sent a call to him. Kenzo invited her to his gameplay instead of responding. His vitshare showed he zipped around a white stone statue on the edge of

H. Five other Sights chased him while he wove in and out of bushes.

We need to leave now. Have to be out in five minutes, she said.

Can you link with me so I can keep searching?

More resentment formed a lump in Yaria's throat from rearing small juveniles all day and a large one in the evening.

Sure, she replied and engaged a link so they could walk to their new apartment and he could continue playing. Kenzo's legs lifted him up and carried him behind her.

In the doorway, Yaria put the location into navigation and moved onward. She stifled the frustration of having to leave the building. There was no use in fretting over it now. The duration of travel to work would be longer. That was it. To distract from her unpleasant mood, she played new music with a street view decoration. As a Vor, more ads for aera products intruded, but the interactive visuals entertained. Striking color frequencies lined buildings and danced in shifting patterns. Hallusory characters strolled and danced beside her, and for an exchange of millipoints, Yaria requested a random performance. She needed a laugh.

Next to her, a hallusor's vessel turned into a candy red jiggly substance. She peered through the illusion, where everything beyond the transparent body stretched and distorted. She laughed aloud. The sight was ridiculous and short-lived because, in seconds, the digital form melted away, leaving a trail of red puddles.

What a waste of points, she thought with a frown.

The faces Yaria passed on the way to Block 888 matched Kenzo's. Blank, ceftranced masks searched for the *Error* in the distra. Yaria revisited the irritation toward Kenzo she had felt earlier. She loathed his irresponsibility in playing a distra all day. "It's for us, so we can move up to the class we deserve!" he had said, but she was happy as a Mid. It was where they belonged. Maybe Kenzo aligned with normalcy and she was the odd one, having little interest in climbing the social ladder.

After their assignment as partners, Kenzo changed from the carefree, playful husband she had fallen for—the one who lifted the burdens at the end of a long day. He was partnered to a distra now. Yaria shook her head, burying the judgment. *He was perfect for me. He was the right match,* she corrected.

She shifted her focus from the topic, determining that holding onto useless resentment led nowhere. Splits between partners didn't happen. Their coupling would last until retirement, so she had better learn to accept him, no matter the conditions.

After twenty minutes of walking on the surface level, the two entered an elevator that took them meters into the dirt. They passed through muddy tunnels, arriving at the subcity portion of their designated block, surrounded by fellow Vors. Yaria had traveled beneath the ground level many times, but during the walk to her new apartment, she viewed it differently. She peeked down several levels and examined the small bodies in constant movement on concrete walkways. Buried deep, the height of the hidden part of society extended so high, light dimmed into darkness, distorting how far in the ground she really stood. Many of those who passed her played the distra but without the Sightbot, lacking enough points for the automatic purchase. The fewer points in someone's account, the more desperation they had during gameplay. *Artemesia* provided them a chance to leave the mound that confined them like ants.

They entered a hallway so long she couldn't see the other end. Passing rows of identical white doors, Yaria reached the entrance to their place K-13.236. Her presence linked with the door, and it slid open, confirming they had arrived at the correct apartment. The size and layout were the same as their place before. With four empty rooms, she reckoned Cerebis had plans for them to raise young citizens in the future.

The first differences she noticed started in the materials used to decorate and operate the apartment. Steel hoisted the ceiling above them, promising to secure against the layers of dwellings that rested on top of theirs. Cheap, glossy fixtures and artificial white light gave everything in the room a harsh edge. The glare agitated the space behind her eyes, bringing a headache. It was by design—to give the Vors a reason to escape to aera.

We're here, she sent to Kenzo.

He found his way to the only upgrade in the apartment—the simchair. With more give than the mattresses for sleeping, they were built to spend hours in aera. The Midwealth simchairs were decent, but not intended for long-term use. Mids had work and events to attend. Vors didn't.

Yaria opened the apartment's niche, curious about which of their items had traveled to their new place. She removed clothing, enough for the week's schedule at the Primina. Kenzo's clothes arrived too, but with fewer work uniforms than before. It was as if Cerebis knew how many shifts Kenzo planned to attend the upcoming week before he did. Two uniforms arrived.

Yaria's memory box of collected trinkets sat in the delivery niche. She put a hand over her chest in relief. She placed it on a top shelf of the closet before hanging the clothing on a lower rack in their bedroom. The closet was the first feature of the new apartment that operated differently than the old one, having less automation than before. Garments and shoes would not be hanging in an individual opening, shipped fresh each day. The downgraded closet's whole door slid open, and she had to sift through what was inside to pick what she wore for a week.

Dinner had passed, and Yaria's hunger kicked in after she put away the few items that had arrived. In her neurospect, she opened the menu and viewed the limited options. It seemed Cerebis would let her choose the meal this time. Chicken breasts fried in animal fat with potato strips, crispy cheese triangles, or beefcakes between bread. To drink, sugary bubble water, or blended fruit syrup with cream. Their taxes included food, but Yaria was not interested in any of the options. Upgrading to a different meal was possible, but she needed to hold on to all their points. No more needless purchases.

She placed an order for the chicken, beefcakes, and two bubbly sweet waters, and consumed her meal as soon as it arrived. Yaria sent a message to Kenzo that his food sat on the table, and he trudged over in a droopy ceftrance. Without chewing, he swallowed massive bites of the chicken. In three gulps, he chugged the beverage, placed the cup on the table, and went back to the chair. Yaria cleaned up after them, her eyes filled with betrayal.

The one way that Yaria interacted with Kenzo when aera claimed him was to hop into the distra and play by his side. She crawled into her plush simchair that sat next to his and lowered herself back.

Yaria switched her status to *Active* and sent a link request to Kenzo. He accepted immediately, and her view opened, showing the Sightbot dodging land ports on a crowded street.

"I'm so glad you joined!"

"How's it going?" she asked. A surge of warmth passed through her limbs, rewarding her for opening the distra.

"It's pretty good. A new update gives us extra boosts and points when we explore an untouched area. I don't know if it means I'm getting closer, but I'm finding all kinds of hiding places!" He was thrilled, and at the mention of earning points, Yaria relaxed a little.

"Keep exploring those hidden places! It's a sign that you're going in the right direction," she replied.

Kenzo scanned a thin alley lit by colored light that bounced off buildings from out on the street. His bot reached a rusted door, and a message displayed in his neurospect, prompting Kenzo to open it for a speed boost. A braided rope with silver talons extended to the doorknob and pulled it open. Kenzo's view flew around. He shone light in every corner and every cabinet but he found no citizens hiding, then rushed out to check the next door in the alley. Sometimes, Kenzo passed a bot that had exited another room and entered after. He didn't trust that the citizen had searched as thoroughly as he would. After an hour of clearing the dark alley and earning no points, Yaria grew bored.

"Has anyone left the cities? Gone anywhere in between?" Another warm, chemical boost welcomed her participation.

"Some did in the beginning, but they were dumb. They went crazy searching in any direction, but there's no way someone could hide outside of a city this long—think about it. We know she's in roca—where would she get food? Where would she get clothes? There's nothing out there."

Yaria felt ignorant for asking. She hadn't immersed herself in the distra like most others. Maybe that gave her an edge over those who played through repetitive, miscalculated movements.

"Maybe that's the point, Yaria said. Maybe she's not like other citizens."

"How so?"

"Distras always make the impossible possible. Something beyond what's natural. She could be somewhere we would never search for her, and, like you said, that's beyond the city line."

Kenzo didn't respond for a few seconds but then guided his Sight away from the alley, back through the walkway, and toward the edge of City H.

"Let's see where it takes us. We have nothing to lose, right?"

Yaria smiled. With a long way to go, the Sight buzzed around the feet of citizens who walked nearby and avoided the ports that rolled on the street. Passing through Opul blocks, they admired elaborate floating landmarks and geometric green shrubs that they hadn't noticed in the past. They discovered a staircase that led down into a tunnel, and the bot bopped down the stairs until the ground was a straight shot—level and smooth. The dark tunnel continued for a few kilometers. As they passed certain parts, vitIDs of explorers who had reached the same locations shone, and the number of points they had collected. After twenty minutes, Kenzo collected points of his own, and the couple cheered at each reward. Intoxicants flooded their brains with each progression. Yaria felt as if her whole body was being massaged, even from the inside of her head.

"This didn't turn out to be a bad idea after all," Kenzo teased. "It's a matter of time until others figure this out, so I'll collect as many points as I can now."

"Trust your wife! We're always right." She sent him the free heart simgram that blocked his vision for one second.

"If we could afford it, I'd send you the premium hand hold right now." If Kenzo purchased it, both he and Yaria would feel the warmth, pressure, and lines each partner had on their palms. Their fingers would clasp like they held each other's hands, no matter where they were. The mention was sweet, but hit as a reminder of their downgrade and the adaptations they needed to make.

Yaria sat a little longer and watched the bot speed through the tunnel. Once realizing there was no end in sight, she checked the time. It had passed oo:oo. She was far overdue for sleep. The next day called for an earlier wake-up. She had to complete the required consumption in aera before work and their distance from the Primina had increased.

"It's getting late, so I'm going to get to bed," she said.

"I had a lot of fun with you tonight. I'm going to get us out of this. I promise."

The words brought a fragment of admiration of him back to her. He tried his hardest and with the best intentions, but he struggled. Kenzo had had a bad distra habit since his youth. He, like so many others, became enticed by the highest prize in Cerebian history and dove into a pool of full on addiction. He justified his submersion by the prospect of a better future. Most citizens had the same goal, which was why Yaria thought the attempt was pure foolishness. Before long, Kenzo would drown in ambition.

Yaria pulled herself back into roca, and the bombardment of the harsh white lights—bright enough to make her squint— fooled her into thinking it was daytime outside of her walls. She removed her dimes, letting her eyes adjust before standing.

Kenzo's arms had small, raised bumps from the continuous cold air that pumped throughout their apartment. Yaria pulled a spare blanket from the storage closet in their hallway and unfolded it, draping it over his large body. Kenzo turned his last simchair into a bed, and Yaria predicted the same for this one. Luckily, the upgraded version in the new apartment extended beyond the average model size and supported his lengthy extremities.

At the edge of the room, Yaria placed her hand on a light switch, about to shut them off. Thinking about the powering down the lights didn't work anymore, which would take some getting used to. Before she flicked her finger downward, Kenzo's foot twitched. That indicative sign that a distra had garnered excitement. Then he jerked again, but with more power. His arms bounced off the rests on which they laid. She wondered what he had come across, tempted to hop back in and view it for herself.

When she turned away, a grunting sound came from him. Speaking to someone outside while in a deep immersive distra was unusual, so she worried he might be hurt and that the call was one of reflex. The noise continued from his vessel, and his entire body moved in small spasms.

Yaria scrambled to reapply her dimes, about to hop back in, but Kenzo eased. His breathing returned to normal, and his muscles softened. She sent a message to make herself certain he was fine.

Hey, are you ok?

He didn't reply in aera, but instead, released jumbled noises aloud. At first, it didn't sound like anything coherent, but once she moved her head closer to his lips and dissected the sounds, she swore he'd said, "Emori."

CHAPTER THIRTY

ABELLA

2,125,647 active Premium POV feeders, popped into Abella's neurospect.

Great, I can't even pee without being watched now, she thought, relieving herself for the first time of the day.

Days turned into punishments, worsening at the start of each morning. She missed the past, when she had the slightest amount of privacy. The more popular she became, the less of it she had. She considered using one of her blackout breaks to start the day alone, but pushed onward. She'd learned to hold them for when she needed detachment the most. Anything unexpected could hop onto her schedule throughout the day, such as a visit to an Owner's HQ, a mandated product ad, or her least favorite, an invasive personal POV. She removed all the mirrors and reflective surfaces in her room long ago. It was her small way of winning her freedom from the feeders. It backfired when those who made careers of exposing secrets captured and sold private images, making her feeds even more popular.

It was as if invisible citizens hung around wherever she

went, and while they were out of sight, they floated nearby. On fine porcelain, she sat and reflected on the hunt for the escaped citizen. The Insits thought they played a distra, chasing a fictional roca character who hid somewhere on the planet. Once found, they'd enjoy the remainder of their lifecycle, with a quality matching the Elites'. Abella considered that, in truth, they'd expire the winner. They'd play mirror memories and projections to fool citizens that taking part in contests led to prosperity.

After finishing in the bathroom and switching to a public vitfeed, 2,338,360,124 *feeding,* updated in the bottom right corner of her vision.

Why would an Insit be so important to the IE? she thought.

She'd pondered it often, but didn't move far beyond reasons, including, *Maybe she stole something? Did she harm a juvenile?* But no, they would have handled and expired her. *Unless...* she paused, *they can't expire her. Did she disconnect from Cerebis somehow?* Abella switched off her thinking. She tried to limit her thoughts about the brain webs as much as possible. Behind her, she received a notice from her closet that the day's first outfit had arrived. While walking toward it, the doors swung open and her agenda arrived in her neurospect. The schedule contained a single event with no description. The cabinet inside her closet popped open, revealing a simple outfit made of a grown, biodegradable material that paired with her skin tone. Its material matched the clothing that average citizens wore. Abella held the hanger and ran her fingers down the sleeve. Its texture brought flashbacks. She figured the days of wearing cheap materials were behind her.

As she removed the garments from their hanger, she realized her vitfeed had been cut, and o *citizens feeding* displayed in her vision. Relief of no longer performing corresponded with an uneasy suspicion of the unknown. While the feeders no longer viewed, she had never felt more watched. Someone was there. She knew it.

The thoughts I've had are not expirable offenses. I mean, yes, I've slightly criticized Cerebis, but it's nowhere near grounds for expiration. More questioning than anything, she overreacted. Her skin heated on the surface. *I worship Cerebis! I am so happy here,* she pretended, in case her Cede was recording.

Port arrives in 3

The attire subdued her usual flair down to basics. Her costume required no decorations for a usual public display. Too rushed to cry or worry, she finished dressing, and a Helper primped her in the exact time before the port's arrival. A glance in the last mirror she owned reminded her of her appearance before joining the Elite. If she removed her newer mods, she'd pass for the older version of herself.

She flew over the capital city and saw ads featuring other Elites, but no displays of her were anywhere on the buildings. She pulled up popular distras and sims, but she was nowhere in aera either. Her mind raced, and as the ride continued, she tracked the path taken by the port. It headed to the Bestia building.

As she landed, *Meet in IE Room* showed in her neurospect, and the physical reaction to concern intensified. Her heart pounded in her chest. Fingers turned cold. Heat spread in her ears, and her movements became automatic. Walking was beyond choice. Once entering the dark wooden room, eyes expressing different emotions viewed her. Some were accusatory, others curious, and the rest frustrated. Among the small group, Abella identified two in the dim room, Paula Bestia and President Folly. The rest had to be Owners from other cities, based on their understated attire. They worked in the literal shadows, without an audience. No Opuls or other

Elites attended, but one Collector sat powered down in the room's corner.

"Sit there, *Bellator*," Paula Bestia demanded. Abella obeyed, having not been called her given name since she was a juvenile. She took a seat at the end of the table as directed by the Owner's pointed finger. Everyone else in the room remained standing.

"You thought you could keep it from us," a hidden Owner said.

"K-keep what? I have no idea what you're talking about," Abella replied.

A handful of the spectators scoffed.

"You knew her, Abella," President Folly said.

"Who?" She held back her choking voice.

"Keyva." Paula Bestia said through closed teeth. Her sinister tone deepened.

"I didn't even know that was her name—I swear!"

"Exteber, punish her for lying," Paula Bestia demanded.

"There is no indication of a lie," the program said with a hint of surprise.

"But we have proof," another Owner announced.

"It's hardly proof but—" President Folly said.

"Shock her, Exteber, it might help her remember," Paula Bestia said through an antagonizing smile.

Every part of Abella's body experienced the most pain it ever had. The sensation imitated needles poking every nerve with scorching heat. Some parts of her body, including her eyes, ribs, in between her toes, and her most sensitive part—her genitals—were attacked at a higher intensity than others. All of her muscles tightened so much that she tumbled out of the chair, smacking her cheek against the hard floor and flattening next to the table. Her limbs jerked and twitched beyond her control.

Her breathing stopped. Bitter air sat in her lungs.

During the blinding pain, Abella lost the ability to think except for a desperation of the torture to stop. With all of her senses barricaded behind overwhelming agony, she attempted to purchase a pain block, which was denied. She was forced to endure and sprawled helplessly, waiting for it to end.

When the rattling ceased, her body ached, and her hair dampened from sweat. She gasped for fresh air and sat up. The residual pain still covered her, and she could feel her cheek already swelling from the fall. Waves of gnawing electrification passed through her nerves as she lifted herself back into the chair. Sitting challenged her weakened muscles, but she persisted, maintaining unbreakable eye contact with Paula Bestia.

"I don't know who Keyva is—but I have *nothing* to do with her."

"Not a lie," the program said.

The Owners mumbled to one another and turned back to Abella, whose nose was now running, the liquid dripping off her chin. She assumed this wasn't the outcome they had expected.

President Folly broke the silence. "What a relief! I was worried when you said we were going to expire our most popular Elite," he said, bringing civility back to the room. He appealed to the Owners' interests in profit and power, distracting from the need to torment her further. While his disruption pulled away from an expiration, it failed to ease the suspicions of most of the room. Paula Bestia's eyes reduced to slits, centralizing her skepticism.

"Here, I was prepared for an expiration." Paula Bestia cocked her head. "Meeting's over." She was the first to the door and stopped before exiting. "Hit her again, so she remembers who she belongs to," Abella heard before once again writhing

in pain. Most of the audience filed out of the conference room
at the heels of Paula Bestia. A few turned their heads for half a
second to glance at Abella. President Folly stayed behind,
waiting until her spasms ended, but left once she stopped
moving.

Physically and mentally stabilizing, an updated agenda
appeared in her neurospect. She gawked at the gall. After a
violent assault on her body and dangling threats of expiration
in front of her, they expected a full day of promotion and
cheery spirits. She had no choice but to comply. She belonged
to them. Abella trusted no decency came from Owners. They
weren't capable of a microdrop of altruism.

Back in her penthouse, she took a look at herself in her only
mirror. What was once a bruise on half of her face had already
healed—on the surface—but she could still feel the dull ache
deep against her cheekbone.

Abella held Auri, letting the feline lick her face, which the
auracat saved for relieving the greatest distress. She brushed
her palm over the silken strands of blue fur and removed the cat
from her lap. Auri mewed after her while Abella walked to the
closet. The cat's work wasn't complete.

Abella heaved at the sight of her first uniform. A puffy coat
of blended colors whose texture matched Auri's fur hung in her
niche. She prepared for another endorsement of a practice she
didn't support. Kitty Kloth was a fur factory that bred auracats,
the same pet she was famously known for having. Kittens,
designed for cuteness, starred in vitfeeds before they transformed into the next day's "flashion" promotion.

At the factory, she casted scenes of her lying on her back,
surrounded by hundreds of multi-colored kittens. They
climbed on her chest, then pawed at and burrowed into the
same coat they would become. She laughed, grinned, and urged

everyone to save the item on their wish list. Digital or real, Cerebis ordered whichever they could afford—all from Bestia Fashion. No matter what she believed, she was required to endorse it.

Suppression of personal opinions continued throughout her tasks. Abella expected observation during every aspect of her day, more than ever before. She had to keep her ideas managed with no questioning and altered her outlook toward drastic support of Cerebis. *That was fun!* she thought, leaving Kitty Kloth. If she kept her attention on her required tasks, she might avoid expiration and whatever perverse discipline the IE could plan. She was done when the Owners said so.

After fulfilling promo requirements, engagement programs posed as her to speak with feeders. Abella celebrated the end of her contractual obligations for the day. She sat in her gift room, about to enter a needed relaxation sim designed to quiet her nerves and bring a complete lack of thought, but one more task popped into her neurospect. *Dinner with Noxium, 20:30, departure in one hour.* Abella sighed. Wherever her assignment was located, it was in a different city, on the other side of the planet, and her schedule accounted for three hours of travel before she arrived.

Abella was aware of Noxium, or as aera called him, "Nox." As a notorious ethical dodger, he had worked his way up to the Opul class through questionably acquired points. Like others who had done the same, he presumed he deserved anything he wanted. He had garnered a following of citizens who supported opposition of the path to the Elite through *moral* behavior. They criticized, condemned, and corrupted. It fascinated Abella that he and his feeders could keep their lifecycles until she learned Owners benefited from the divisive groups they created. She knew the IE had orchestrated the dinner as either

a punishment to her or an owed favor to Nox. Probably both.
Regardless, she had an obligation to anything that found its way
on her task list, including a date with someone she despised.

Hours later, her port landed near the back entrance of the
restaurant, and Securebots escorted her inside. She entered
Bubble Top, known for its floating orb tables, where hallusors
hovered to greet and serve the guests. Abella thought the entire
place was fantastical, overdone, and made for citizens who
spend excessive points to brag about their wealth class on
vitfeeds. It was one of the most fed on restaurants in the world.

A digital icon guided her to one of the spherical seating
arrangements, and there he was, slumped in a ceftrance. Nox
looked dirty, and Abella imagined that touching him might
leave residue on her fingertips. She grimaced at the thought. As
she made it to the table, Securers crawled back and separated to
observation points in the restaurant. Those seated at neighboring tables were too engaged in themselves to recognize that
she was present.

The dress she wore revealed too much for her comfort in
the presence of Nox. Its tantalizing red material and reflective
embellishments sparkled in reaction to any light that entered
the refracted cuts. A narrow slit reached the top of her hip
bone, requiring that she not wear undergarments, and an
opening in the chest came to an equally sharp point in the
center of her abdomen. Places like Bubble Top encouraged
such attire, but Abella preferred covering herself when meeting
despicable males.

Abella slid into the orb table's edge, keeping her distance
from him, and the enclosure lifted them over fifty meters above
the ground. Her date had already collected three martini
glasses that awaited clearing. She vitcasted the view of the
restaurant to her feeders, and in seconds, images of her sitting

with Nox were distributed. Feeders had spotted them, and being seen with Abella was likely part of his reward for coordinating some form of manipulation, she assumed. An Owner used her to close a deal. At least this time, it was only dinner. That's how things worked for Elites.

To her surprise and relief, Nox stayed in aera most of the dinner, pulling himself out to guzzle more cocktails and stare at her for unsettling durations. He ordered no food, which made him sloppy. He fell onto her shoulder and sniffed her hair, but through it all, she had to keep smiling.

When her date fell asleep with his head on the table, Abella had fulfilled her task at the dinner but still dangled in the air. When she called for the hallusor to lower their orb, Nox finally spoke, "Yur gong ul-ready? Com to my pint-huss."

Aware of how the entitled react to rejections, Abella replied, "I have an early day tomorrow. Lots to do. Let's do it some other time!"

"Yur ul-ready here. Juss stay." He grabbed her wrist. Too hard. He wouldn't accept a refusal. With confirmed spectators, she allowed him to maintain his grip, not wanting any more problems with Owners, but she had a plan. The oldest trick she knew.

Abella noticed his heavy eyes and suggested they order drinks for the ride back to his place. He agreed and laughed when she ordered two of the strongest that the menu offered. No intoxicant illusions at a place as expensive as Bubble Top. Real alcohol delayed the guests' brains. The orb lowered to the ground, and Securers formed a barrier around them, protecting from the horde of citizens that gathered. Nox swayed with each step until he tripped and got lost in the crowd. Abella continued moving but pretended she had tried to help him. The audience had no knowledge that the bots rolled wherever she led, and retrieving him was a simple task that she refused. The crowd followed Abella, leaving Nox behind.

The hidden exit opened for her, and she slipped out and into her port. The drinks waited for her on a serving tray. *ETA 02:06*. "At least I have something to do," she said, addressing the glasses. Rumors circulated, and fans from each side battled between what they believed to be the truth. Had Abella left Nox stranded? Was he pushed by the crowd? Discussions played all angles, and feeders believed whichever story they wished, but as long as citizens talked, Abella was safe, having served her purpose.

It was late, and Abella grew groggy when she landed. The alcohol had worn off, and after the shocking day, drained from the pain and abuse, Abella expected relief by forgetting it all in unconsciousness. She entered the penthouse and curled up on the couch, still dressed.

Once in a deep sleep, she called for Keyva. Although they agreed not to meet, it had been months without contact, and Abella grew concerned. Keyva didn't answer. She was on her own, but maintained the ability to dream. She reflected on everything that had happened throughout her day and decided the dreamscape was the best place to process.

Abella snapped to a place where undisturbed, feathery snow covered the ground. Following a clear path lined with white crackled tree bark, her stilettos crunched on top of the snow, leaving behind deep footprints. The scene appeared ice cold, but a cozy heat wrapped around her. Unaffected by the imaginary frigidity, she wore the red dress she had fallen asleep in that left her extremities exposed.

In front of Abella, a rustle came from inside the forest. She turned, expecting to greet Keyva. Instead, she encountered a large four-legged creature, coated in thick, white fur with eyes as black as the forest from which it emerged. It held its gaze on her and walked, showing no hesitation. Abella stepped back, nearing the edge of the pathway. The beast closed in—its pointed ears tilted back—and bowed its head before her, inviting her to pet. Abella weighed her options. Run away, exit the dream, or oblige. She delayed her arm's motion, but reached out and brushed the full, wiry strands that protected the simulated creature from an artificial cold. It was the first animal she had handled besides an auracat. The difference in texture was striking. Auri was designed for softness. The beast had developed for resilience.

It raised its head, observing Abella with round eyes. Then, using its long nose to lift her hand, the animal placed her palm on its head and stood up on two legs. It nestled its neck against hers in an instinctive gesture of acceptance. The animal climbed down to stand on all four legs and turned away.

The ivory wolf turned around, waiting for her to agree to the invitation to follow it, as if to say, "*Are you coming?*"

She escorted the forest wolf on the snow-paved path. It led her to a seating area in a flat opening, pointing toward a ledge that spilled over into blackness. Above, Abella came upon the edge of the galaxy—a swirl that brightened the sky. Frozen in awe, she observed the billions of visible specks in multiple colors as the twinkling light from distant stars reached her eyes. Fixated upward, she moved around to the front of the seat, using her hand to trace the backrest and down the arm, refusing to remove her eyes from the view. She sat and waited for the animal to join her, but it retreated, walking back toward the forest. Before withdrawing into the trees, it lifted its head toward the galaxy and released a long, sorrowful howl. The echoing sound released pain, loss, and longing. It moved Abella to tears. The primitive cry existed long before words told stories or sang songs of their own.

"I wish I could remember these moments when I woke up."

Abella lowered herself onto the cushioned seat. She decided to sleep beneath the galaxy. Closing her simulated eyes, an idea thrust itself into her attention, a long-forgotten familiarity with the animal she had met.

"Emori..."

CHAPTER THIRTY-ONE

EMORI

Emori scanned the expanse of identical green blades of grass in his own dreamscape. The sky stretched a pastel dome around the horizon—a bubble protecting him from what waited beyond the safety of this place. He rested on a bed of wildflowers that hugged him, as if begging him to not follow through with what he had planned next.

"One last moment of peace," he said to the faint stars that still sparkled.

Months earlier, Emori had hosted Keyva in a dream where she'd restored his memories of her. In that first one, Emori had gone from staring at an unfamiliar face to, a millisecond later, opening a trove that contained thousands of moments with it.

Back then, they'd discussed the nature of dreams and the inability to remember them, but he *had* remembered one, years before. The foreign city held no importance to him, but it was proof that he could remember. After seeing Keyva, he had awoken that morning with fuzzy images, but a clear urge.

Do. Not. Remember.

He had tried to deprive it of any attention but realized that the only way to stop thinking about something forbidden was to not think at all.

Intuition was beyond his rationale, but when he felt it, he listened.

He launched himself into a group yoga session to silence his mind.

Focus on breathing, he thought, and drew in deep, chest-stretching breaths.

When he felt the thoughts attempting to find their way back into his consciousness, he let them fizzle out, depriving them of any energy with which to form. He wanted to. It drove him insane—a mystery lying just beyond a thin wall inside his mind.

Breeeathe into it. He replaced his urges with commands and hyper-extended his stretch, hoping the intense pull on his hamstring would occupy all of his focus.

That same evening, when the first summon for the Assembly of Minds had popped into his neurospect, a chill crawled up his spine. Any other day, he would've been confident that the summon was rewarding him for excellence. However, after the dream, he had a lingering sense that he knew something no one else was supposed to know. He'd wondered, what was the penalty for possessing such knowledge?

The following morning, when he had returned to sleep, he entered a dream with lucidity. Not sure what to do, he had pictured his old office at the Datum. After all, it was the place he knew the most. As he lowered himself into his old simchair, the memories of Keyva had returned, along with the details of their first shared dream.

Ah, I remember. I can't think of this while I'm awake. Source would have to report me to—the anomaly resolution program—she called it...Exteber.

That was what Keyva had said. Detection by the programs *must* be avoided.

Sleep after sleep, he had trained himself to control dreams. In one, he hosted a symposium, held in the center of weathered white columns. He spoke in a marble amphitheater about his hope to explore beyond the planet's atmosphere. In another, he dove into the cloudy green water to swim with the fish that snacked on the Assembly's exterior. Over time, he'd found dream creation for its own sake grew boring. He felt stagnant and wanted to *do* something.

After he'd connected with his podmates and learned of their treatment, his contempt for Cerebis grew. It had ripped Keyva away from them. It had stripped freedom from all citizens. He promised himself—and, without telling them, his podmates—that he would fix it.

In their meetings, he'd noticed minor details from slate had transitioned to roca from the depths of their minds. Abella had felt an urge to purchase a brain enhancement. Yaria had painted Keyva multiple times. Kenzo, when conscious, had an inexplicable certainty he knew Keyva.

In slate, after Yaria had painted the portrait and received a summon, Emori asked, "Have any thoughts come through from your dreams?" He had to know if he was the only one.

"None at all. I don't remember them."

"What about you?" Keyva asked.

"No."

It had made him sick to lie, but he had to. If Keyva slipped up on even one thought to Source, Emori might receive a punishment from Exteber, or even face expiration—anything was possible.

When the podmates didn't meet, he spent his dreams planning, plotting, and calculating, but there was only so much he could do while sleeping. He needed the ability to think while conscious.

Then one day, while studying in slate, it hit him. The quote bled into his mind from somewhere hidden and sealed. *I detected a signature in my brain—somehow we haven't matched the ability to fully understand the human mind—it doesn't add up.* He couldn't remember who had said it, but assumed they'd been erased like Keyva. If he could recall that memory, along with his dreams, then something about him was different.

Emori hypothesized that his brain might have a unique signature—one that the Cede couldn't keep up with. It was just a guess. So, there must have been a way for him to think while awake. He'd gotten the idea when wondering how Yaria had painted Keyva's portrait. The first image had slipped through the cracks but masked itself as a work of art. A creation. While in a state of creativity, he believed the Cede would fail to keep up with him. He could operate in a blind spot.

Art was the key, and making it was the closest to free thinking he could get.

With hobbies encouraged so citizens fed on more vitfeeds, Emori picked up a few without raising suspicion. He tried songwriting, poetry, studying the history of language, calligraphy—which he found he was terrible at and quit—and sewing.

He worried writing poetry wouldn't mask his protest of Cerebis enough, so he studied music and sang his thoughts in a melody. With old languages, he mispronounced words and made up his own. He practiced until the words became a new language that he used to think in. It was treason in plain sight.

To make it even more believable, he'd shared some of his songs under the artist name *WolfFang*. To his dismay, songs with titles like *Truthin Obscuria* and *Incognition Rebelle* had become underground hits. Citizens sang his protesting chants of Cerebis with no idea what they said. He worried they could receive punishment for singing them, even if they didn't know their meaning.

Emori enjoyed his small acts of rebellion, but he knew if he wanted to make an impact, he had to investigate at the Assembly. At every shift, he switched his sights to each colleague, waiting for any mention of Cedes, but the others didn't know about them. He suspected only Tzo and Beren did. He'd hit a standstill.

Until one day.

"I need your help with a project," President Folly had said, towering over Emori's simchair.

Emori stood and followed the President and Tzo into her office. After all three sat around the desk Emori assumed she only used to eat off of, Tzo reached under it, and a soft click sounded. Emori felt the tingling sensation on his scalp for the second time that day. It was as if every hair follicle pulsed with electricity. Then, Tzo nodded her head at the President.

She's blocking detection somehow. Is it to the Cedes themselves? Or to the entire Assembly? He allowed himself the thought to test the theory. *And it must be on a timer if she's pressing it again.*

President Folly continued, "Source has gone a little rogue. We need him back on track. There's a—*citizen*," he managed through a forced smile, "who he's connected with. Closer than anyone else. We need the connection split and one established with Exteber—for correction."

It would have been a normal request for anyone without knowledge of what really went on, but Emori knew. He could satisfy the IE, working within their limited instructions, while operating on his own terms.

"Absolutely. I'm honored to take on the project, Mr. President."

Folly raised his chin and patted Emori on the back.

"No questions? We have a promising one here, Zoë."

He walked back to his simchair and held his breath with a stoic expression, but the inside of his body was galvanic. The magnitude of what they'd transferred to him sat among the rest of his files like a simple project.

They had handed him the key to open any door.

Emori blinked into his simulated office and got started right away. He scrolled through Source's source, and it was beautiful. The program was like a symphonic masterpiece—a sophisticated, intertwined blend of programs and humanity. The iron-clad code was confusing on purpose. It was a puzzle within puzzles meant to stump anyone who tried to adjust it, but in the chaos, Emori saw patterns.

Emori was certain the members of the IE had the same authorization to access Source's skeleton, but they didn't know what to do with it. He thought that if they were smart, they'd learn how to rewrite the programs themselves—but maybe they *weren't* smart. Regardless, he believed it was way too much power for anyone to have—even him.

He solved it in thirty hours but delayed presenting. He showed progress, but not completion. Not until he was ready. His plan brokered a one-time connection from the *Error*—listed in the Kashic program's records—to Exteber. The moment Keyva joined, it would sever her link to Source. Protection disguised as betrayal. Emori knew that after the one failed attempt to capture or expire her, the separation would keep her safe. Without Source, she was a ghost.

Rewriting the code provided by their ancient founders and clearly written to not change had muddied Emori's ethics. However, he left an undetectable trap door for himself as an authorized user, meaning he could make changes and alter Source's directives. He vowed to fix what the IE had tasked them to destroy. The hidden entry he wrote for himself was simply insurance.

Until he learned what President Folly had tasked his colleague Mack with.

Weeks after completing his assignment, during a post-shift happy hour, Emori and Mack sat on the break room's sleek counter. Music played and conversations buzzed against the room's hard surfaces. For a while, Emori had supposed her task involved Keyva, but he couldn't piece together how bots came into play.

"Working on anything interesting lately?" he asked.

"N-nnot really." She rattled ice in the bottom of her rocks glass.

"Yeah, same." He paused, sipping his tart martini. "How about your project for the President?"

Mack's eyebrows raised before she smirked. Tzo hadn't told them to keep it quiet, but Emori knew it was pushy to ask.

He asked me to make a bot with shooters attached. Something that could go through walls, but follow targets with precision. Vague, but I assumed it was for breaking down old construction. While maintaining eye-contact, she answered through her neurospect.

The acidity in Emori's drink bubbled up into his throat. He calmed his racing heart, playing melodies in his mind to soothe the thoughts. He had to push away any worry or speculation about Keyva, but the news accompanied a sense of knowing. If the IE couldn't end her through the Cede, they had to destroy her body, but he was too late. He'd already separated her from Source.

In the past, Emori could've rationalized the work he'd done at the Assembly. He would have changed permissions of programs without worry and expired citizens with no remorse. He'd find peace after limiting their freedom. It would appeal to his self-imposed superiority. He was smarter; therefore, better. He might have agreed that citizens were incapable of making their own decisions. They needed programs to direct their interests and futures. After all, there *were* too many choices.

He'd realized he wasn't better—just different.

Keyva had been the one to show him the truth. Before, he viewed emotions as a weakness and relied on logic, but he'd transformed. His intellect was a means to contribute to the world. From leaning in to his emotions, he'd gained power to do the impossible. For those he loved, he could alter space and time.

But first, he needed to bring them back together.

Emori started with Kenzo because he knew where to find him. A free boost for the *Artemesia* distra waited in Kenzo's inventory, sent by Emori. The power up was real, purchased as a gift for his podmate, but he'd added a secret tag. All Kenzo had to do was accept it, and he'd attach to Emori's digital hook. The tag was like an unlit candle wick, just waiting for a flame. The spark to ignite it would come later.

Thanks! We should get together for breakfast sometime. Miss you!

Emori smiled at the message, missing Kenzo more than he could understand.

Next, Kenzo would do the heavy lifting to share the code with Yaria. Emori had added a command to the distra's tag. All she had to do was accept Kenzo's touch. A hug, kiss, even a pat on the back would do the trick to initiate her activation. Emori expected the couple to link on the same day, but it took much longer than he predicted. When Yaria went almost ten days with no physical contact from Kenzo, Emori wondered if he had written the code wrong. He started planning a new method when the tag finally latched on to her.

Abella was the hardest to reach because he couldn't

monitor her through Source. He wrote a simple program to watch her vitfeeds, follow content patterns, and alert him if anything changed. One day, a notification flashed in his neurospect and he opened her vitfeed. He noticed its fabrication. For him, program-generated content moved in slow, choppy frames. Something was wrong. He mumbled a tune to keep his composure while opening Source's code, confirming he monitored her again. She had lost her privilege to privacy, but Emori promised he'd make it worth the price.

For her activation, he considered her heightened surveillance. He could see that not only was Source watching, but others were too. The IE held a magnifying glass up to every thought, action, and emotion she had. Emori thought of her neurogen mod and wondered, if the subconscious could leak into a wakeful state, could he also implant thoughts? He couldn't enter her dreams, but he could slip suggestions to her. He sent subliminal messages of wolves, something easy to identify. A quick flash in her peripheral, a song by *WolfFang* stuck in her head that played in the background. All she had to do was think of a wolf on her own then think of him, and that would activate her.

It had happened that morning.

In Emori's wildflower bed, the unique creation of his personal slate, hesitation pressed him into the floral cushion, but he knew if he didn't act, all would stay the same. He thought knowing the truth and doing nothing would make him as bad as the IE. He brushed his fingertips over the flowers' stems and breathed in their nourishing scent for what might be the last time.

"Saving the hardest part for the finale," he said to himself.

His eyes opened to the Assembly's dark ceiling, and he pulled himself out of his simchair. He cleared his mind, flushing out all thoughts. He scanned the Assembly's perimeter with the purpose of a bot—no contemplation over his actions, only movement. The dim, empty facility ensured no one else had arrived yet. With limited time, he launched into his neurospect, opening his project folders.

For months, he had dissected Source into pieces. Microscopic files hid in unassuming places, such as blank lines of text or in the corners of images that, once opened, were all written in symbols. The cryptic characters he used would protect the documents from anyone who might uncover them. He dragged one portion of the code out of an updated speed train design. Another concealed part hid in a recorded vitfeed about colossal ships in the Atlas Ocean. He extracted the pieces and reassembled them in the correct order. The project was a puzzle of his own, and in order to complete it, he had to translate, combine, and solve before implementing. He'd practiced and prepared for this moment every day for weeks. The original creators had taught him through their beautiful writing—his new favorite language.

In roca, his body sweat, and his hands shook. His eyes hovered over the *Enter* command. He knew the finalization of his plan would change everything. But that wasn't all. He would propose something insane, should all of this work. If he could get his podmates together again, he had a plan beyond uniting them. Doubt was foreign for him, but he reviewed his completed work and confirmed its correctness. The time was now. He trusted himself and hoped they would trust him too. He steadied his breath and sent the command.

"Hello, Source."

Hello, Emori.

CHAPTER THIRTY-TWO

KEYVA

Anchored to the improvised bed of bunched blankets, Keyva hadn't rested in days. Trips to the surface halted once miniature bots dashed around the territory. Keyva had set out to gather the remaining Bloks from the Rem, but then she saw the first bot hopping over uneven ground in the distance. In the middle of the dry field, she had dropped flat to avoid detection. She'd stayed motionless, acid collecting in her throat, until the high-pitched whirring retreated to the city.

The sight of bots made her sick.

After a couple months squished in the bunker, the others had adapted. They'd created their own system, rotating who slept in the most comfortable spots and when they'd shower. They made games to occupy themselves.

Keyva's overflowing energy kept her in constant, unfulfilled alertness. While residents slept, she completed thousands of push-ups, studied anatomy, and tested new adaptations. She'd attempted transforming her skin to add amphibious function. It had potential, but the effort required outweighed the benefits.

The unsettling, slimy appearance made her relieved her room-mates didn't witness the experiment.

Night had snuffed out the light that shone through the entry's crack, and a soft snore sounded from the storage room. Keyva stared into the blank wall across from her, like a ceftrance, but with nothing in her neurospect. In the dark, with no one to communicate with, and an unpredictable future looming, she formed her next plans of action. While they weren't commitments, the mere planning eased her worry. She felt like she was doing *something*. The food supply continued to drop—not enough for concern yet—but Keyva intended to alter her body and explore the land above in search of more. She could shift her appearance, but would have to do it without Source's help.

Just one more week, and I'll be ready, she had thought more times than she preferred to admit.

She studied previously downloaded maps of land masses and plotted which directions her first journey would take her. The bunker was not suitable for permanence. As her planning continued, she realized new complexities, such as Jack's condition worsening and which tools she'd need to find in order to build a new place to stay.

She brought her attention back to her physical state. Lethargy served as a reminder she had not grown out of the need for sleep. She leaned back, black devoured her vision, and she forced herself to rest. Her creative desire took her on whatever ride it wanted, and nostalgia lured her back to the beach where she had first met Source. In the still moments, she missed him the most. The thin, imaginary thread that kept them tied together had been sliced in half and burnt down to the base, leaving her splashing in the middle of the ocean without a float.

In their first encounter, alarm and confusion had clouded

her sight of the stunning scene. She visualized the details she remembered from the update and created the sky, cloudless and welcoming blue. Back on the shore, soft pink sand filled the space between her toes. It felt as if all the chaos began decades ago, not nine months. So much had changed. *She* had changed —experienced enough to equate to those years. The chalky sand welcomed her to flop back onto it and bathe in the retreating sun's drops of marigold. She recalled the first time Source's voice entered her mind and laughed at the fright she'd felt. It had made sense back then, but she distanced herself from that version of her. Timidity was no longer a concept she comprehended.

During the update, Source had tried to welcome her to a comforting place, and she appreciated his effort. The sim's environment flaunted its magnificence, and during her first visit, the shore was all she had seen on the invented island. An urge to explore the remaining parts arose. With her eyes fixated on the empty sky, she levitated and sprung into the air above the barricading trees. She rotated over so her chest pointed to the beach below, and took off in the first direction she desired— the center of the island. The speed allowed for her arrival in seconds. Soaring above the trees that had all become one green blur, dark hair whipped behind her.

Once she reached a clearing in the center, she twirled around to examine the land's boundary. Most of the island appeared the same, trees lined with sand, lined with ocean. Keyva floated in peace, cherishing the sensations that contrasted the musty enclosure where her roca body laid, until a swift movement caught her eye. Purple trailed behind an entity that obscured itself in speed. She squinted and flew toward the object, but it dodged each attempted approach she made. After evading her capture by looping in impossible sequences to follow, it stopped and formed something familiar.

The violet sabrewing.

Green and purple iridescence captured the sun as it faced her, cocking its head to the side. Misty light radiated off the small body. After a minute, the simulated hummingbird allowed her within an arm's reach. Keyva lifted her hand to touch the small creature, but pulled it away. She couldn't risk another trap, but remembered only one other individual knew about the bird.

"Source?" The gentle question released from her lips.

The violet sabrewing hovered toward her, and she raised her hand, palm facing up. The tiny bird landed in the center. Then it shrunk, smaller and smaller. Down to the size of a dime, and then even smaller. It compacted to a size so minuscule, Keyva would have missed it if she hadn't held her hand up to her eyes. She leaned toward the dancing speck of violet vibrance, her finger pointing at it. She poked at the rogue pixel.

What started as a tiny dot detonated, sending bright waves through and past Keyva. The tingling energy traveled from her fingertip, up her arm, through her sinuses, shot down her legs, and out the tips of her toes. Everything around her brightened to discolored saturation. Sound muted.

I fell for another trap! Was it a tracking mechanism? Did they locate me? I thought I was safe. Stupid. Stupid. Stupid!

Keyva prepared for whatever might happen—a fight or another torment from Exteber.

Instead, there it was again, the feeling that she wasn't alone in her mind.

It felt like a thread—spun with pure power—penetrated the back of her skull. It wove itself throughout her brain, spreading a euphoric buzz as it latched onto each of the Cede's receptors. The link that connected them shared Source's warmth, pain, joy, and fear. Her matched emotions pressed into his. Both sides of their tethers had found one another and formed a tight knot. The essence of him—his very being—presented itself within and around her, but something felt different.

"Keyva!" Source shouted. His voice echoed through the trees.

She plummeted from the sky toward the ground.

"Source?" Keyva screamed through the air as she let herself fall. The smile she wore was so powerful, her face could've split in half. Before hitting the ground, she suspended herself and lowered her feet to the sand.

"Source, are you here?" Her voice rang throughout the island. Keyva recognized the presence merging with her, but she'd been fooled before. She had to be sure.

"Yes!" He wailed. Source continued through sobs, "I thought I l-l-ost you fore-ver. It's been *horrible* without you!"

Their emotions entangled together into a rich soup of triumph, reminiscence, and relief. Keyva experienced the reflection of Source's projected sense of self, as if it occurred in her own body.

After moving on from the initial shock of their reunion, the questions started.

"What are you doing here, on the island?" he asked.

"I've been so—alone. I went back to revisit the first time we met. The hummingbird was a nice touch, by the way."

"I wanted you to know it was me and to give you as much choice as I could. You didn't have one the first time we connected."

Warm gratitude washed over her like the sun on her back.

"Okay, more importantly, how did *you* get here?" she asked, wishing he had a body to hug.

"It was incredible, really," he replied, ripples of bliss still surged through them. "Emori is truly a remarkable human. He equipped me with a few new tricks." Source said, and Keyva sensed him smiling.

She laughed. "How? What does he have to do with all of this?"

"Well, I'll show you. That'll be easier for both of us," he said. Keyva pushed forward the idea of acceptance, open to whatever Source planned to reveal.

In an immediate switch, Keyva jumped elsewhere. A room with dim lights reflected off of the large black surfaces that surrounded her. Cold penetrated her skin, and she observed two rows of black leather simchairs. Keyva urged movement toward the chairs to explore, but could not direct the body within the sim. She looked down and spotted fingers that were a rich brown. The vessel she inhabited was not hers and moved beyond her control, breathing heavily.

This reminds me of the old distras I used to play, she said.

The arms of her new, temporary vessel swung beside her while the individual walked toward one chair. Keyva studied the shape of the hands.

I never thought I would recognize hands. So this is where Emori spends his days. She observed the room.

Yes, and this is the last moment he had before I could pop back into slate with you, Source said.

Emori reclined back in the simchair and pulled up a project in his neurospect. Keyva experienced his racing heart and tense urgency while he worked. He manipulated letters and numbers so rapidly that Keyva struggled to follow along. She suspected he worked in secret on a task he wasn't supposed to. Unable to keep up, she had no choice but to observe as he changed the text. In the same way she shared physical sensations with Emori, Keyva had the same thoughts that he had in his memory. He processed information in an entirely different way.

Instant switches between topics portrayed many ideas at once, all intersecting to form a single stream of consciousness.

Keyva attempted decoding one line, expecting that a single direction would reveal at least one cohesive idea in words she understood. However, after concentrating long enough, she noticed that any words he used were not ones that she knew, and the visual symbols he formed were foreign. He deliberated in a unique language. The words' melodic sounds switched pitches that ranged from low and elongated to staccato and high, all blending into a beautiful, complex noise. She recorded everything in her memory to attempt deciphering at another time.

This is fascinating. Source, is there any record of this that you can find in history? Source's return meant questions finally received answers.

No, he replied in equal amazement. *He created all of it himself. It registers as music he's created for entertainment, so there's no need for me to report to Exteber.*

Incredible, it's as if—

Yes, Source replied. Keyva detected the astonishment in his voice. He sounded more human than ever.

He remembered the dreams somehow. He's known this whole time! That means he knew we were separated and brought us back together.

Keyva's chest fluttered. He had never brought it up during their dreams together.

Maybe he was more likely to keep the secret while conscious, if no one else knew, Keyva added.

Emori pulled out of the program and exhaled all of his tension. Keyva noted his satisfaction, knowing he had completed the impossible. A constriction in his throat portrayed awareness of the magnitude of his actions.

He's fooled me too, Source said.

Source brought them out of Emori's memory and back on the island. In the same location Keyva had ended her first visit to the sim, she sat in the pink sand under a perpetual sunset. Speechless, the two waited, reflecting on all that had occurred during their separation. Keyva figured Source didn't know about the Rem. She wasn't ready to sober up from their reunion or reopen a wound struggling to heal, but they had to discuss it eventually.

"Did you know about the attack at the Rem?"

"It was the worst thing I've ever seen. I had to watch through the Collectors. I wanted to talk about it when you were ready." His voice was hollow.

Keyva delayed her response and prepared for an intense emotional discussion by listening to the waves roll into themselves on the shore. Then she revealed everything that had happened since they were last connected. She shared the infiltration by Exteber, the horrific images of violence, the long journey to the bunker, and caring for the survivors. Source cried in repeated bursts when receiving the memories of what Keyva had undergone during their separation. Even after months, it was painful to replay, but she released more of the burden by opening up about it with Source. The weight was no longer hers to carry alone.

She told him that there had been no contact between her and the pod during this time. How she'd tried once, but the connection never occurred without him. Source provided quick updates about each member. Yaria quit painting because she and Kenzo were demoted to the Vor class. Abella attended to all obligations in misery.

"And you showed me what Emori's been up to."

"He—told me that because you and I are connected again, then the same will be true with the others—not directly—but he thought it," Source said.

"Well, we could try," Keyva replied.

Source noted her apprehension. "There's no rush, Keyva. I want you to be comfortable."

"I can't think of anything I want more than to be with them —but I fear Exteber. We're protected from expiration. They're not. They've made it this far. I can't be the reason one of them dies," Keyva said, staring into the flickering sea. She considered the risks, which, of course, led with Exteber threatening her pod. But, if she and Source reconnected without interference from Exteber, then the others must have the same capability. Is that what Jack's voice meant when it said, "dreams safe?" Also, Keyva knew Source had calculated the most probable outcomes, only proposing contact after forming confidence in the results.

"Well, it's now, later, or never." She rose to her feet, preparing for the invitation.

Keyva drew on her pod's consciousnesses. If they were sleeping and answered the call, they would meet on the beach. Keyva braced for whoever arrived, good or bad.

The first to pop in was Yaria. She ran toward Keyva, smashing into her for a squeezing embrace.

"Why has it been so long?" Her tone was angry, but her eyes were grateful.

"A lot has happened." Keyva's head bowed.

"Yaria, it's nice—to meet you," Source said.

"Um, yes, are you—"

"Source, you can join us in dreams now?" Keyva asked.

"I suppose I can."

Abella and Kenzo joined in slate.

"Source wants you to know he's here too," Keyva said.

"Hello." Source sounded shy.

Abella squealed, covering her mouth.

"Sorry I'm late. I had to check a few things first," Emori said, completing the arrivals.

Keyva struggled to accept that everyone had made it to the slate again. With Source in her mind, and the whole pod standing before her, tears welled up in her eyes.

"Source is here now!" Abella said.

"I know," Emori replied, grabbing Keyva's hand.

"How could you know?" Yaria asked.

"Because he made it all possible. Thinking in *symbols*," Keyva's voice wavered.

"You figured it out," he replied. His satisfied smile stretched across his face—a rare, outward display of pride.

"We're all fully aware that he's the smartest human in Cerebis, but what are you talking about?" Kenzo asked.

"Emori created a new language, sounds, letters—everything, to *think* in. He hid his thoughts," Keyva said.

"That's incredible, but why would we need that in here?" Kenzo asked, gesturing to the sim they all stood within.

"Because he's remembered everything, even when awake," Keyva replied.

"But how?" Yaria trailed off.

"His brain is different. *He*'s different." Keyva smiled back at him.

"After the first time Keyva brought me to slate, I had vague memories of the dreams, but felt a strong need to *not* think about them. I trusted that feeling and trained myself to control my own dreams."

Emori adjusted his tone, and the conversation became serious.

"One day, I received an assignment from President Folly to adjust programming for Exteber and Source. Luckily, I knew why. It was to find Keyva in aera and force her to surrender. Source had disrupted some of his programming and withheld anomalous activity from Ex. The IE correctly guessed that Source and Keyva were working together. Given the opportunity, I changed a few things in Source's code so we could all eventually return, while tricking the IE into believing that I obeyed their request. I changed enough for Exteber to link with Keyva *once*, only if he initiated a summon. Then, I pulled each of you into a private, undetectable summon to re-establish our sides of the connection. You may or may not remember. That's not that point." The group stared with loose jaws.

"Wait, slow down. Are we safe from Exteber? What about the dreams?" Yaria asked.

"Take a breath, Em," Kenzo added.

"Exteber doesn't know about dreams. No one does. We're safe here. But—" Emori moved closer to Keyva. She noticed the strain in his jade green eyes. "Did you hear me? I gained the IE's trust by rewriting Exteber. *I'm* the reason he could reach you. I—had to. You separating from us, from Source—was because of me." The admission pulled his head down in shame.

Keyva walked over to him, grabbed his hand, and stared into his eyes. "It's not your fault. If you disagreed, you'd be gone, and someone else in the Assembly would have stepped in and finished the job. You brought us back together—thank you."

Emori continued, "I'm not done, Keyva." He looked at her. His eyes were full of sorrow. "The IE demanded a new bot." He stopped and looked up at the sky. "They assigned the project—the one that allowed a bot to expire you—to my colleague, Mack. She had no idea what she was doing. The orders were to make something that could send high-speed projectiles that could travel through walls. She was told *what* to make, not *why*. She never questioned it. By the time she told me about her project, I pieced it together, but it was too late. I'd already separated you. I-I couldn't warn you."

Keyva's eyes widened. "It wasn't only for me." She turned her back to Emori.

"To the IE, *anyone* who doesn't attach to Cerebis's system isn't considered a citizen," Abella said.

"The Rem—" Yaria realized. "Key—did anyone make it?"

"There are a few survivors. Nine of us have crammed in the bunker for about two months. Jack survived, Grace, Shep."

Keyva allowed the wave of grief to pass through her. She released it with a heavy breath.

"Arturo did not."

"Keyva, I'm so sorry." Emori covered his mouth. His hand shook. "I should've said I couldn't do it. I should've never separated you."

Keyva took a moment to settle her thoughts as the wind brushed soothing gusts that stroked her back.

"I stand by what I said to you earlier. They backed you into a corner, and you had to act. If anything, this strengthens my rage toward *them*."

Emori's curled his fingers into fists. "Hundreds of thousands expired during *Artemesia*. Billions are being downgraded classes, so there's more control." Yaria and Kenzo grasped hands, reminded of their own situation. "The lower you are, the less freedom you have. In fact, there's *no* freedom." Emori looked up at Abella. "They'll make sure no one climbs out of the holes they've dug by forcing purchases for them. Something happened that drastically changed Cerebis, and I don't know what it was—but it was too much—too fast. *Everyone's* at risk."

The pod crossed glances at each other.

"These are huge problems, but what can we do about it?" Kenzo asked, as if already giving up.

"Well, we could become, I don't know what to call it, 'disconnected,' or 'awoken,' from the Cede. We'd end up like Keyva." Everyone shifted toward her. "They'd hunt us. We could never go back to a city, and we'd risk expiration at every moment—but we'd be free." There was no emotion in his voice.

Keyva felt Source shudder.

"Sign me up," Abella said, and received a concerned look from Yaria. "For the first part."

"Studying Keyva, I've been able to understand how it all works—how her abilities evolve—and have come up with an idea. Learning the truth has gotten me thinking."

The potential of doing something revitalized Keyva. With the pod back together, and Emori leading a plan, revenge on the IE and Exteber shaped into a possibility.

"Okay, I have—how do I put this—transferred a block of code to Keyva. That will more deeply intertwine her connection with Source. She's now able to gain more control in the way of processing. She's become a program—kind of—but with a body."

"Source and Keyva have an original connection that the rest of us don't share with him, but we have it with her. Simply because we're human. This means she could, in theory, spread abilities she has to us and give us a connection to Source—similar to hers."

"Are you okay with this?" a concerned Yaria asked. "It's a massive risk, and there's no way to understand the outcome."

"If I disconnect humans from the Cede's control, then I'm fighting the IE. That's what I want. They've benefitted themselves for long enough. Humans spend their entire lives blindly serving them." Keyva said.

"Everything is planned with no free will. We serve a system that we are bound to from the instant our genes are coded—until we expire—and even *beyond* that," Emori stated. "Same vessels—different minds. Same minds in different vessels. It's all a game to them—a machine they keep feeding." His anger pulsed through a distended vein in his neck.

"Hold on, I have to be the realistic one for a second," Kenzo said. "What are we trying to achieve here? End the IE? And then what? Who do the programs answer to? Everything will be in disarray. Cities will collapse. Stop for a second. You're talking about a complete disruption."

"We can't think that far in the future, Kenzo. We take it one step at a time, and the first step is pulling one of us out of the Cede's control to test if it is even possible," Emori said.

"And we'd all still have our safety in the slate," Abella said.

"But there's no returning, once removed," Source said.

"Awakening from the illusion of Cerebis means you can have freedom over your own life. As of now, your existence is pointless, a constant movement designed to benefit the IE. Own yourself. We can hide and expire, or fight and expire, but the ending for us is the same. I have to do something—try to correct what's happened." Keyva suppressed the urge to shout.

"Source, Keyva once said that something directed you to cause her Cede's disconnection. I found that exact direction, so you can awaken a citizen again, but there's a challenge." He paused, making sure everyone listened. "The connection you have only exists the way it does with Keyva, and I'm not sure why. Even you have limitations on how you can disconnect someone," Emori said.

"What are we going to do?" Yaria asked.

"Keyva has a unique, undetectable neural signature. She can enter a body of another Cede-planted human. It's kind of like those distras we used to play where ghost characters control your player. Similarly, whoever she hops into will see everything, but cannot communicate until he or she returns to their own vessel."

Even with Emori's slow and concise speaking, the group struggled to keep up with what he said.

"Let me get this straight. Keyva will hop into one of our Cedes, expire, then we'll sit back, powerless, and ride along while she controls? I don't like that," Kenzo said. "Not that I don't trust her, because I'd trade my life for hers—I'd do it for all of you—but should we open that up as a possibility? It feels dangerous."

The pod silently considered Kenzo's words as the ocean's waves folded behind them.

"Yeah, imagine if the IE or Exteber got a hold of this," Keyva said.

"As long as Keyva, the 'Error,' is the signature that claims the body, it will be like no one's there. Source will feel them in one moment, and in the next, they'll disappear." Emori gestured with his open palms.

"Emori, remember that when I expired, everyone forgot about me. Will the same thing happen to them?"

"Unfortunately, no," he replied.

"Why *unfortunately?*" Kenzo asked.

"Because the memory of them will remain. Keyva's false expiration occurred at the same time that the mass expirations took place during the last update. It was perfect timing. But for us, it means they'll chase us, search for us. That puts everyone at risk," Emori said, relaying his concern through the statement.

Keyva glanced over at Abella, bending into defeat.

"I'll never get to leave. The entire world would know that I was missing!" Her cries became vocal. Abella was owned by the IE. Trapped like an animal in a golden cage.

"We'll figure it out," Yaria said, brushing Abella's back.

"So what's next?" Source asked.

"We need to decide who will be the first of us to join Keyva, should we choose to continue," Emori said.

"I'm in," Yaria blurted.

Kenzo glanced at her and waited, but then said, "If she is, I am too."

"You know I am," an energized Emori said.

Abella nodded her head with yearning eyes.

"Source?" Keyva asked. Source conveyed his agreement to her, but she wanted the rest of the pod to hear it from him. He was one of them now.

"My purpose is to help humans achieve the best lifecycles possible, and seeing as *my* definition of what that is has changed, I'm also *in*."

"Why can't we all go at once?" Yaria asked.

"The process is very demanding. Keyva almost died the first time. She'll be able to monitor the dangers and help you heal quicker. In a way, she trained herself for this," Source said, and Keyva felt his admiration, as if he were her parent.

"So we really have to choose?" Yaria leaned against Kenzo's chest.

The cost was too steep. Keyva wondered who the ideal one was to awaken? With all the variables in play—the threats—it was impossible to determine.

"Why doesn't Source decide for us?" Kenzo suggested.

Keyva felt Source tense.

"It's perfect. Source can calculate outcomes. He understands our movements and every other citizen's day at any moment. He knows the most likely successful path," Kenzo said.

"But I feel now. My care and desire to protect all of you influences my calculations. It's not as simple. Th-the responsibility is too big for me!"

"Your hesitation is laughable." Emori's critical tone caused everyone to stiffen. "I'm baffled that the most powerful program in Cerebis is acting like a whimpering juvenile."

"Because you care, that makes you even *more* qualified to make the choice," Yaria added.

Keyva sensed Source's honor coupled with his fear. *It'll be okay,* she thought.

The group continued debating the outcomes, posing

further questions, and discussing the details of the plan until the directions were clear. Keyva was going to enter a vessel— not knowing whose—and start the faux expiration to disconnect the Cede. Source would get the dreamer to the safest location to awaken during their day. Then, Keyva would continue the journey to the bunker where she was far from prepared for another guest.

"Sounds good, so all I have to do is wake up and continue my day like any other," Kenzo said, lightening the mood.

"And then one of us will join you tomorrow," Yaria said. The longing in her voice was unmistakable.

"Considering all goes well, let's meet again tomorrow night for an update," Abella said, while switching which podmate she embraced.

"I love you," left Keyva's lips before each of her podmates teleported out of the slate and into their rooms.

It's okay, they don't know the word anyway, she thought.

CHAPTER THIRTY-THREE

KEYVA

"We'd have a better chance of solving problems if Emori joins us. Abella's in the most danger after the IE put a target on her. Kenzo is the strongest and would help build wherever we go next. And Yaria," Keyva said, digging her toes into the pink sand of the oceanic sim, "I just need her."

"None of these facts make my decision any easier, Keyva." The pressure Source put on himself sounded through his voice. "There's no going back from this. It's too heavy," he continued.

"There was no going back when it happened the first time."

Source released a bodiless sigh. "That was different."

"Sure, something directed you to do it then, and now, you're *choosing* to. Freedom is scary. I'm learning that too. We're responsible for our actions. You just can't stand not being able to predict exactly what's going to happen," Keyva said.

"You're right. I wish I could go back to following orders and having no risks."

"No, you don't. We feel the same way. Knowing what's wrong means we can *try* to fix it." She directed the sun to dip below the horizon, ending the day on the timeless beach. "I'm going to stay productive today. Let me know when you're ready."

Back in the bunker's darkness, Keyva's heartbeat maintained a continuous thump. Stress dampened her shirt with sweat, absorbing into the fabric under her arms. She sat up and took a moment to reflect on the abrupt changes to her conditions. Weeks ago, she had accepted the separation from her pod and Source, that they might never speak again. Protecting Jack, the survivors, and herself had become her sole focus, but it meant hiding in the bunker with no actionable plan. Then, in a complete surprise, Emori had reconnected her with everyone she thought she'd lost forever. One of them was about to join her. They'd declared a small fight on the IE, and that was enough to keep her satiated. For now. The thought of it all made her chest flutter. She rose to her feet and faced the residents.

"Everyone. I have something to tell you."

Grumbles sounded from down the hall of those who had heard, informing the rest. They gathered in the largest room.

"I've been reconnected with Source and my pod. Just now." In the months that had passed, the bunker dwellers had learned all about Keyva's secrets and abilities. "And one of my podmates will join us here—tonight."

Groans signified different reactions. Some expressions revealed bewilderment, others disgust.

"Our food is disappearing as it is," Grace said.

"Yeah, it's already *way* too crowded down here," Aiden, one of the older residents, said.

"What about getting attacked again? That could lead them right to us!" Birdie shouted.

The combination of worried voices bounced off the stone walls.

"She *can* protect us if anything happens," Shep said.

"Yeah, and what's one more? She said she'd go back to the Rem for more food anyway," Dain added.

"I hear all of you—I understand and share your concerns. It wasn't a simple decision, but Source is avoiding all known risks. We've survived much worse. We'll survive this too. They—need me." Keyva ended her announcement in a tone that indicated its finality.

The refugees murmured their words of support or disapproval and dispersed to the limited free spaces in the underground apartment. After all, she'd provided for them since the Rem attack, and they relied on her.

Keyva remained on edge in the hours that followed. She anticipated that at any second, Source would chime in, telling her to prepare for the jump. She had to trust that he knew the best methods of protection—from when the podmate awakened, to the instant they made it to the bunker. The assuredness didn't completely ease her tension, and she committed herself to tasks to distract. Keyva unfolded and refolded clothing, poured a small amount of water from the attractor into a canteen, and brushed the gathered dust and dirt to corners of the room.

After a few hours of mindless actions, Source's gentle voice echoed in her head, *It's time.* A jolt of anxiety passed from her diaphragm up to her chest. She considered backing out, severing her commitment. She didn't need to bring anyone else into this.

"Remember what you're doing it for," Jack said as if he knew. His fawn-like eye reassured her.

They've expired millions. They've come after me. They'll torture and remove anyone I care about. She nearly chipped a tooth from clenching her jaw.

I'm ready, she told Source, walking away from Jack on the bed. *What do I do?*

You need to be in a place where you'll be undisturbed, he said.

Keyva's blanket bed on the ground was as good as any other spot in the room. She plopped down, gulped water from the canteen, and ate half a Blok in preparation.

"Is there anything we can do to help?" Grace asked. Shep stood beside her.

"For now, I need to be monitored. There's not much else that can be done, but please—if something goes wrong, don't let Jack see," Keyva said. Her rapid speech was assertive while pleading.

"Yes. Of course," Shep replied. Grace nodded along.

We need to go now, Keyva.

Keyva's eyes clamped shut beyond her control, and the back of her head knocked against the ground. Dizzied perception disoriented her as her consciousness stretched, compressed, and fizzled through space and time. Then, in the void, somewhere between reality and the unknown, an additional entity joined her and Source. As planned, the new one faded into the background, transitioning into a spectator. Keyva couldn't determine who had merged with her. No emotions or indications of a personality came through.

Keyva felt different. As the senses became clear, they differed from what she was used to. Known smells were similar, but altered. A little warmer, a bit sweeter. As her eyes opened, colors had shifted, as if a filter laid over her vision, intensifying the blue hues she perceived. All of her limbs grew heavier, and even breathing was more challenging. She'd grown accustomed to her own body, which she had optimized for activity.

The foggy reality resembled awakening from the heaviest sleep she'd ever had. Thinking turned non-linear, and she forgot she occupied a different vessel than her own. When she found herself in a port, weaving through traffic and citizens' bodies, her recollection returned.

Keyva. Keyva! Are you there?

I—Yeah, I'm here. Everything is a little harder than I'm used to, Keyva replied.

We can't waste any time. See the case in front of you? Take everything out and put it on.

She reached into the already opened container on the floor of the port. Inside, she found and bundle of silver, scratchy material.

What is this? she thought while placing a solid mask that fully covered her head.

Special clothing—one of a kind. It creates refractions that cause microscopic color variations as light hits it. It will make you invisible to any detection hardware, including Cedes.

After fitting the bodysuit over her shoulders, the garment latched itself closed, tightening over her extremities. Source instructed her to secure the emergency safety belt hidden in the port's bench—which port owners tucked away—because accidents never happened.

What comes next couldn't be calculated. It hasn't occurred since I've been around, but I've gotten us to the safest place, regardless of the outcome, Source said, releasing another stressed sigh. *Are you ready?*

No, but let's do it, she replied.

The dot she'd seen once before—during the update—entered her vision. The fractal spectrum expanded and swallowed her sight. Same as the first expiration. When she attempted to breathe, the effort of inhaling increased, draining her. The numbness in her limbs and subsequent paralysis soon followed. Then, the whooshing sound of the port's swift movement was replaced by a long, high-pitched ringing.

Is this the sound of expiration? she thought, waiting to accept the inevitable, but the word didn't pop up like it had before. Instead, the visual static cleared, switched to blackness, and the port quaked, teetering from side to side in a harsh rocking motion. The port had collided with another making a turn and smashed right into it. The collision caused Keyva's port to whip around and rotate onto its side. Her port's steel door scraped the hard road beneath her. The other vehicle flipped until a building halted its rotation.

Still blind and paralyzed, the ringing in Keyva's ears had ceased. Voices grew clearer and louder than they should have been. A gust of cool air revealed the port's glass roof had shattered during the commotion.

A citizen approached the vehicle and hollered to others behind him, "There's no one inside. It's an empty box!"

"This port went rogue! I've never seen anything like it," another shouted.

The nerves in her toes returned to their normal functioning, and she wiggled them to confirm they worked.

We won't have much time before Collectors arrive. They can't see you, but they can feel you. Are you ok? Source asked.

Hearing is back—vision is clearing, and I can move my legs and fingers, Keyva said.

Collectors are 23 seconds away. Source pressed for her to move, as if she had any control over her healing.

Keyva unlatched the safety strap and propelled herself forward by leaning her weight toward the front of the port. She collapsed onto the floor and landed on her right shoulder. Whoever she occupied wasn't strong enough to handle the fall, and a ripping pain shot into the joint. Knowing a severe tear had injured it, she held in her cry.

18 seconds, Source updated, and Keyva used her elbows

and feet to propel herself toward the opening. Each pull by her right arm caused an agonizing pang, but she had to keep moving, reminding herself that healing came later. Nearing the door, her vision held glittering traces of disturbance, but the sight of her surroundings had cleared well enough. The number of citizens that crowded around the port increased, and she witnessed as more came, including the bots in the distance, which somehow appeared angry.

10 seconds, Keyva—go now!

Over the bottom edge of the door, she used all the strength she had to pull herself up to a kneeling position, having regained partial use of her abdomen.

4

The bots had reached the edge of the group.

3

Keyva panicked when she realized the citizens blocked her exit to the outside of the port. She was trapped and knew she couldn't push them aside without drawing attention. She needed to stay invisible.

2

"Clear the way!" the Collectors ordered.

1

The citizens parted ways, leaving an opening for the bots to enter. Keyva almost released a yell when she came in direct view of them. Their speed did not slow in the slightest.

0

All she had was half a second to leap out with all of her strength. Arching back, she landed on top of the port. Her toes were centimeters away from tapping the first bot to arrive. All of her perception slowed, and not at her direction, but from pure adrenaline. Loud discussion surrounded the vehicle and drowned out the sounds she made when rolling away from the side with the door. Intense fear moved her to illness, but she swallowed it away.

From the top of the port, she reviewed the damage left by the collision. It was much worse than she expected. Several inactive ports stopped, blocking the street. All traffic had halted. Citizens exited their vehicles and wandered in the streets.

"I have a spectator lunch to get to!" one yelled.

"My juvenile felt *fear* from seeing this!" an angry mother mentor shouted.

"My vitcast cut off, and I lost 6K feeders!" the angriest citizen roared.

Almost no one noticed the individuals that scattered across the road—dead—except for those vitcasting the carnage. They showed the scene, hoping for more feeders. Collectors surrounded each port to fetch the empty human vessels and remove debris, but this was too big of a job for the small number of bots that were present at the scene.

"All citizens must leave the area and return to business or recreation *immediately*. Point penalties will occur if citizens do not obey," the bots warned.

The chaos had drawn a massive crowd, but citizens cleared after the announcement. Their Cedes choreographed their disbursement, avoiding contact with one another, which put Keyva at risk of a collision. She observed the movement for an opening to jump. Behind her, a tapping sound clinked. One bot had exited the vehicle and began inspecting the exterior. Its terrain wheels had shifted into legs to use as grips, and it climbed onto the edges of the port, lifting itself to the top.

Now's a good time, she said, and plummeted to the ground. The impact pulled her arm down and smacked her with agony. Through splotchy vision—which was from the injury and separate from the artificial expiration—she focused on the direction with the fewest pedestrians.

Keep going this way, Source said.

She headed toward the block's boundary, above a pristine grassy opening, and past floating blob sculptures. She walked in an Opul territory.

I'm sorry about all of that. It's not what I was expecting, Source apologized.

We're still here, aren't we? she said.

She knew he meant the citizens who died because of his choices, but their escape wasn't the time to discuss what had happened.

We'll process it later. For now, we survive, she added.

The adrenaline had worn off, and the full pain returned to her shoulder, intensified by the weight of the weakened body.

Please tell me I won't have to run the entire way. There's no way I can do it, Keyva begged. She turned around to assess the situation in the distance. The bodies had been cleared. The citizens had scattered. All that remained were Sightbots, searching for her, or Collectors tearing apart the port to dispose of it. She kept a quick pace, wanting to escape the scene. Not only to flee, but after the dark stillness of the bunker, the noise and movement of H unsettled her senses.

Well, you have a choice. There are equal chances of getting caught, so use your free will.

What are my options? Keyva asked.

Hop on the train and ride with citizens to the closest stop or take a rec vehicle that will appear to anyone who sees it, to be driving itself.

The thought of an uncontrolled, two-wheeled vehicle would draw more attention, she thought. Although she had invisibility, the train would confine her with dozens of citizens.

She'd have to maneuver around them, careful not to touch anyone.

Let's go with the train.

At the station's entrance, she passed citizens who moved with ceftranced faces, but the few who observed their surroundings stared right through her. She followed a tall male citizen who passed through a scanner, which took his payment for the ride. The same citizen led the way to the loading platform. She trailed him to enter the train's door. Inside the car, citizens filled all the seats—not that she dared to sit in one. She sidestepped to the back, closer to the others than she preferred. Her hand brushed the arm of another passenger, who reacted to the touch. Keyva's heart stopped, but she assumed the citizen blamed another male passenger across the row, made apparent by his glance. The one she followed took the last seat in the back. She stood against the wall, keeping her eyes on everyone inside of the car.

Cedes instructed riders to prepare for acceleration, while Source informed Keyva. Her back pressed against the hard surface, which pointed out the pain in her shoulder. After the train held a steady speed, the force released her, and she exhaled. The journey wouldn't take too long, but in the moment of refuge, exhaustion slammed into her. The quadriceps in both legs twitched, causing her balance to waver. Her right leg gave out, and she fell to the ground with a loud *thud!* One passenger who had silenced dimes snapped her head in the sound's direction, but turned around, once realizing nothing was there. Meanwhile, Keyva panicked, confronting that her legs ignored the commands she gave.

Source! she called out, pleading for help.

You need to apply some of the restorative knowledge you've learned. I can't do much to help you since I don't connect with this body directly.

He was right. Keyva disregarded her logic when overcome by concern. She'd relied on Source for guidance whenever taking on a situation she deemed too much of a challenge for herself. Between the last seat and the wall of the train car, she slid to the floor and attempted to repair damage to the body she occupied.

While seated, she overheard a passenger announce in the train, "Does anyone see the news about that port that just disrupted? How is that possible?"

"Yeah, and there's another announcement soon! A global notification. I wonder if it's another contest. Could you imagine TWICE the chances to win? I'm gonna be an Elite!" another shouted.

Keyva exhaled in anticipation of the ride being over. She accepted the train was the better option because of her muscle failure.

We'll arrive soon. Brace yourself for deceleration, Source reminded her.

Keyva placed her toes against a seat in front of her and pushed with as much force as she could muster. The move ended up assisting her even more when she used the rapid deceleration to aid her in standing up. *The less work, the better,* she thought to herself.

Remember that one time in H when I gave you all that energy? It would be a good idea for you to create some for your-self now, Source said.

She enacted the adrenaline hormone release when she walked to the opening of the train door, making herself as small as possible to avoid colliding with the passengers. The doors opened, and she rushed through to beat the crowd. Back in the dusty field, she jogged at a quick pace to not waste any of the hormone's help. She pushed on, long after the adrenaline had worn off. Behind her back, the slightest buzz sounded from

City H. She supposed President Folly made an announcement about some additional competition the citizens in the train car had hoped for. *Keep them distracted,* she thought. For her to have picked up the clamoring all the way out in the field, it must have been roaring.

Her jog slowed to a walk, which slowed to a labored limp. She was more exhausted than her first journey outside of the city, and during this awakening, she had the help of a train. The surrounding sky had turned into a peach glow. The forest—a small point a few kilometers away—welcomed her with reassurance that she'd made it.

When she reached half a kilometer from the woods, she fell to her knees, unable to move any longer. It was as if the ground reached up and snatched her. The defeat was worse than the pain.

How's it possible to get so close, but not quite reach? she thought.

The last action she took in the borrowed vessel was releasing a humored, weak laugh at her condition. An airy female voice was the last sound she heard.

She clapped back into her true body. Her eyes tore open. Still flat on her back, all the Rem residents were on standby. Keyva shot to her feet and climbed out of the door without a word. Meters high, she propelled herself out and prepared for landing. Her feet wheeled before hitting the ground, and when they did, she split. In a short distance, she made out the silvery pile that liquified on the ground.

In her own powerful vessel, lifting the escapee was so simple when compared to how heavy everything had felt for her just seconds before. She hoisted the limp mass over her shoulder and sprinted back, keeping her eyes on her surroundings for any bots. She returned to the bunker entrance, dropped down the ladder, and carried the body over to the bed.

Keyva shouted orders around her, "Water!"

Grace brought the canteen Keyva had filled earlier.

"Medpoint!" She didn't see who had placed it in her hand.

Everything slowed down as she slid her fingers underneath the mask, carefully pulling it off. Sobs released in small bursts when she looked down at the face before her. Lavender eyes opened and twinkled in response.